The Ghosts of Red Sands

A Memoir of Surviving the Bureau of Indian Affairs Residential Dormitory

By ~ C. F. Brown

~ Where memory lingers, even ghosts have a voice~

For all who endured and survived the B.I.A.

We are still here....

I0634099

Dedicated to

My Sons –

Tommy, Kyle, Todd, and Nathan –

Acknowledgments:

This book would not exist in its current form without the care, insight, and generosity of those who walked this journey with me. For those who gave me the courage to complete "The Ghosts of Red Sands".

To Auntie Vivian Arviso and Uncle Sam Deloria—thank you for reading, editing, and encouraging me through every version of this story. Your wisdom, cultural insight, and deep belief in these pages gave them strength and direction. I am forever grateful for your time, your honesty, and your heart.

To Sean Cridland, thank you for generously allowing your powerful image to grace the cover. Your photograph captured the spirit of *The Ghosts of Red Sands*—the memory, the landscape, and the silence of Tohatchi Flats.

To Ralphaelita Arviso, thank you for the beautiful photograph featured on the back cover of my beloved *Stone Castle*, once vibrant, now a distant memory. Your artistry adds warmth and dignity to this book, and I'm honored to include your work.

To my daughter-in-law Marlana—thank you for designing the book cover with such vision and care. Much love!

To my son Todd—your creativity brought everything together in a way that honors the heart of this story. I'm proud and grateful to have your talent woven into this project.

For Gramps and Gramma.

Author's Note and Fiction Disclaimer

The Ghosts of Red Sands is a work of fiction. Although inspired by the author's lived experiences, cultural history, and personal reflections, the characters, institutions, events, and dialogues have been fictionalized. Any resemblance to actual persons, living or deceased, or to real organizations or events is purely coincidental. This narrative is intended to honor Indigenous resilience and identity, but it does not represent any specific individual, community, or experience.

Copyright:

Cover design by Marlana Laughter & Todd Begay
Front cover photo inspired by © Sean Cridland, used with permission
Back cover photo © Ralphaelita Arviso, used with permission

Picture inside is of me when I was in 2nd grade and after my long hair was chopped off while a ward of the BIA Residential Dormitory.

ISBN: 979-8-9992728-0-5
First Edition: June 2025
Printed in the United States of America

Chapter 1 - Beginnings

I left Red Sands Residential Dormitory 16 years ago, in 1974. It seems like a lifetime now, yet the memories come flashing to the front of my mind from time to time. In the stillness of the early morning, those long years still wear on my soul. For sure, if it weren't for my three best friends, the loneliness, nightmares, and hunger for sustenance and love would have broken me. I'm sure of that, now. My life did not start at Red Sands Residential Dormitory though. I was named Florence Ann Arviso, after my mother's mother. I was also born on the same day as my mother's father, Edward. These things I didn't know until I was 5 years old, when my world changed. As I look back, change became a stable friend and I learned to rely on it, just in case.

My dad was stationed at Ft. Campbell Army Base in Kentucky, but I was born in Clarksville, Tennessee. We lived in a Vagabond mobile home in the older part of the military housing, which was surrounded by rusted green military equipment that stood still in time behind 7-foot chain linked fencing. This part of the Base was where all the military families who were not white lived. It was a lively place, as I can barely remember. I relied on my mother's memory of how the Black ladies taught her how to cook neckbone, collard greens, corn bread, and buttery grits. In turn, my mom made them fry bread and tortillas in exchange for their soul food. These are things I craved when I was waiting in line for our endless mystery meals at Red Sands Residential Dormitory. The one thing I remember the most is the music. There was always some type of music playing as I developed my taste for soul food and watched mom make frybread to a golden crisp. Music drifted down our side of the Base. I remember everyone gathered at the family park, bringing a delicious dish to share. My dad and his Black comrades would lounge under the tall Ash trees, waiting for the frybread to come flying out of the frying pan. The whole neighborhood smelled delicious when golden frybread and chili beans were on the menu. My dad was an expert at the harmonica, while the others played their guitars or drums. They would play the blues, jazz, or try to play whatever was popular.

During those times, I was called "Stone". I remember hiding when my dad came home and he would say, "Where's my little Stone?" He always found me because I hid in the same place each time. I remember my parents' smiling faces and the feeling of their loving hugs when I listen to oldies. My nickname came about when I would light up and start bouncing my head whenever *The Rolling Stones* music came on the transistor radio. Even though that time of my life lived in a distant past, the sound of jazz music and smell of soul food brought back faded memories. I remember how my mother and dad expressed their love and affection for each other and me. I learned the power of prayer sitting by her when she prayed with the Black ladies for their husbands' safe return from somewhere across the ocean. I had no idea what dad had endured jumping off planes in enemy territory during his time in WWII's European Theatre. I had no idea that he decided to retire from the military after serving 17 years. I have faint memories of how depressed he used to be when he returned from the battlefield, and how mom had to cheer him up. He would say, "You don't know what I had to do and see." His eyes would have that faraway look, as mom made his favorite home cooked meals. My dad polished two rows of medals and replaced them one by one on the uniform he proudly wore. As I look back and knowing our cultural ways, I came to understand the mental anguish he must've endured. The kind that could only be washed away with sacred ceremonies. I also had to come to the fact that mom and I would be the ultimate sacrifice of war.

I remember it was right after Christmas that they started talking about packing up and moving. Even in the winter snow, by January everything was put in boxes and shipped to our new home. All I knew was that mom, me, a few of our belongings, and a one-way ticket boarded a Greyhound bus, headed to a place mom called - home. I tried to ask my mom where my dad was and why he wasn't with us, but she just told me not to worry about him. "He's busy," was her only response. I felt scared the entire trip. During the trip, I remember stretching our legs and getting some food at the different stops along the way. People left the bus and new people came in. We slept on the bus as best as we could. People talking loudly would come in waves. There were crying babies that wanted to walk up and down the aisle. I do remember it smelling like diapers, sweat, stale cigarettes, and leftover food. We changed buses twice once we passed over the vast Mississippi River. It took 4 days to get to the place where we finally got off the bus, for good.

I didn't know where *home* was, but as the bus went from town to town, the landscape changed from big cities with people to thick forests to flat hills and finally, the giant red rocks and a desert with very few trees. There were very few people and just about everyone looked like us. It was weird because I did not see one Black person or any guys in uniform. When we got off the bus, dad was waiting for us in his brand new 1960 green Chevy C10 truck. I never found out why he didn't take the bus with us. I was so happy to see him, but mom was acting mad. I felt like something wasn't right, maybe it was the move and all this driving. After getting some delicious A&W burgers and root beer, we went to the store for food to take *home*. We drove endlessly into a barren land where the afternoon sun melted patches of snow across the red sand and sagebrush. Short, twisted trees dotted the horizon, a stark contrast to the towering pines of Tennessee. Horses, cows, and sheep roamed, while an old man on a donkey, flanked by two dogs, herded his flock along the dusty roadside. The rugged washboard dirt road made the truck jump up and down. I thought the truck was going to jump off the road a couple of times, but Dad managed to keep the pick-up truck on the narrow road. After what seemed like hours, we crested a steep hill lined with juniper and cedar trees and there was a small community nestled below. There were a lot of round wooden homes and some square homes that had gray smoke billowing out of the rooftops. Across the bridge was St. Anne's Catholic Church with bright red and yellow plastic flowers planted outside, and a brown lawn that seemed out of place in the red desert landscape. A statue of a man stood at the top of the step, as if guarding the entrance. I was almost 5 years old when we started our new life there, but as it turned out it didn't last very long. The safe life of the military base and playmates soon became a distant memory. The memory of the trip across the country flew through the wide eyes of a child with wonder. I found myself stepping into this world with heavy shoulders and a world of problems that didn't exist before. I noticed right away my parents were not getting along and were arguing in a language they used from time to time, and I didn't quite understand. I had heard this language when Mom prayed and when Dad sang his songs, but I was never taught what they were saying. I was old enough to know anger and could see it in both of their eyes for the first time in my life. When they weren't arguing, it was so quiet all I could hear was buzzing in my ears. I wondered what would change next.

Our *new home* was a round, one-room Hogan with a dirt floor and a musty smell that hinted at long abandonment. The potbelly stove in the center, with its pipe extending to a smoke hole above, promised warmth during frigid nights. My eyes scanned the room as Mom inspected it in silence. I clung to her side, uncertain of this strange place, while spiders scurried to evade eviction. A wobbly wooden table and chairs, their cushions softened by Mom's carefully sewn towels, completed our sparse new world. For the first time in my life, I slept on a ragged couch next to my snoring parents. The rusted metal coils creaked with every move. I took naps from time to time and could feel the springs poking into my back. I didn't know how two people could sleep on that narrow bed, but they made it work. Mom cooked our meals on the same stove that warmed our Hogan, humming 'El Paso' by Marty Robbins as she cleaned. She sprinkled water on the dirt floor, packing it smoothly, while I marveled at her practiced efficiency. The cold drink from the windmill tasted sharp and raw, unlike anything I've known before. Canned food and powdered milk replaced fresh dishes I missed, and the outhouse's chill became another adjustment to this new life. Dad spent his time chopping wood or next door with his mother, my grandmother. I had learned that my dad's family called this round house a Hogan, and that we lived in the community of Klagetoh. I could sense my mom's dissatisfaction while she spent hours trying to get the place clean. The routine wheelbarrow trips loaded with water tanks took the better part of the mornings. There was no place to keep our food cold, and the canned food was stored on the weathered wood shelves. While mom still made her frybread and tortillas, she never cooked my favorite neckbone, collard green, grits, or cornbread ever again. There was no running water or electricity. I took my baths in a large basin Mom used to wash our laundry. At night, the dim kerosene lamp lit my three treasured books. Mornings meant hauling water and chopping wood, while frigid winds seeped through the cracks of our Hogan. Thin blankets and layered clothes couldn't fully ward off the cold, despite my parents' efforts to keep the stove alive through the night. After a couple of weeks, I noticed dad would leave the house and come back early in the morning. There were times when he did not return for days. When he finally came home, he would be drunk, and an argument became the normal routine. I had never experienced this kind of anger until we moved to this new place. I became frightened when I noticed dad was gone and learned to hide when I thought he was home. He quit saying, "Where's my little Stone?" when he came home. Life turned upside down when my little eyes had to watch him hit mom repeatedly. From then on, the only music that could be heard came every Sunday morning from St. Anne's church. The organ music filled the valley, seemingly giving its parishioners marching orders once a week.

Three Hogans in which stood near ours, home to my father's mother and brothers. Dad's mother greeted us with a hard stare, her beady eyes and furrowed brow radiating disapproval. From the moment we met, Dad's mother, Gramma Bah, made her disdain clear. Her sharp-eyed glare passed over me before settling coldly on Mom. When Mom offered her hand, she ignored it, muttered something to Dad, and slammed the door behind her. Whatever she said made mom look sharply at Dad, who hung his head down in shame. Disappointed, he took a deep breath and told us to go back to our *home*. I asked them why she acted that way that was followed by unsettled silence from both. My mom wasn't one to talk negative about others, and she would bite her lip and sigh. Over time, I understood her reaction was to harbor dislike. From then on, he would go to her house by himself because we were not welcomed there. I never knew why Dad's mother didn't like us, but mom made sure I stood behind her anytime we encountered her outside. In a short time, I found out that she only spoke the language Mom and Dad spoke when they were mad at each other. I started thinking that the language they spoke was made for angry words, but I was wrong…they did not want me to know what they were saying. Afterall, even Gramma Bah spoke with anger. Dad tried to explain her actions with, "That's just how she is." I remember how kind and loving my friend, Patty's grandmother, was and wished I had a grandmother like her, not this mean one. My heart ached for the years before we came to Klagetoh.

When we were all settled, Mom started teaching me why she and Dad spoke a different language. "Florence, we are Navajos. We call ourselves, Dine' – The People. This is where your dad was raised. Don't worry about Gramma Bah. She's mad because your dad didn't tell her he was bringing us here. It was a surprise she wasn't ready for or even wanted. We'll just have to stick together and find a school for you in August." She said that as she bit the inside of her lip. When the cold was too unbearable, Mom had no choice but to go to Gramma Bah and ask for some rugs or blankets we could use to keep us warm. She returned with a few tattered rugs and old blankets. "Well, anything is better than nothing", she sighed. That was the only kind thing she did for us during those cold days. I decided we might be able to find some happiness, after her kind gesture.

Each time I went outside to play, Gramma Bah would shout, "You leave me 'lone!!" with a hateful stare and clinched teeth. Those were the only words she ever spoke to me during the five months I lived in Klagetoh. I decided that those were probably the only English words she knew. This whole place felt cold-hearted. Dad became cold-hearted, first towards mom and then towards me. His family was cold-hearted. The weather made me so cold that my heart hurt not knowing what was really going on. I wished for the days there was music outside and people laughing, having fun. Since we got here, I realized I didn't smile much and there wasn't much laughter. My Dad's brothers' kids were not allowed to play with me, so I played in my imaginary world. I thought of the friends Patty and Maria I left behind and wondered what they were doing. Did they miss me, like I missed them? The only laughter came when dad started drinking and dancing around with Hank Williams blasting from his new transistor radio. I noticed mom started to join in the drinking too.

The nearest town was 75 miles away and all the roads were dirt. Hardly anyone had a vehicle and most rode horseback or walked to get to the nearest Trading Post, which sold only canned goods, and supplies needed for a pastoral life. The Trading Post also served as a post office and the community gathering place. Nights were filled with barking dogs and the familiar cries and smells of sheep. If the wind shifted from north to south the cold canyon winds would chill our bones. The country sounds and smells replaced the hustle and noise of the city.

When it started to warm up, dad started taking Mom to town without me. Each time, I cried and begged them not to go or to take me with them. I hugged Dad's legs and held Mom's arm tightly, but they left me behind each time. As soon as they were out of sight, Gramma Bah, shouted mean Navajo words that always started with "Ch'įįdii'!", as she whipped me with her straw broom. She locked me in my Hogan without any heat or food. For the first time in my life, I met hunger..endless hunger..always hungry. I found a way to sneak out the window, so I could run to the outhouse. I was so hungry that I started to eat the tops of the little dandelions that grew wild. They were tasteless but crunchy and helped settle my stomach on those days. I learned to hide food in a secret place for those times I was left alone with that hateful person. It seemed like endless hours before I heard the noise of the Ford pick-up truck and saw two drunk people staggering through the creaky door, feeling their way to their creaky bed. It was during those five months; I learned to hate the smell of whiskey.

One day, I watched an old Ford F100 turquoise truck driven by a lady stop in front of Gramma Bah's Hogan. The truck bed was filled with 5 children. The older ones looked to be teenagers, while the youngest one could be the same age as I. The lady stepped out and was greeted by Dad who was chopping wood for his mother. Soon, the sounds of an argument between the two of them filled the once quiet air. I watched their argument move right outside of our Hogan and that's when Mom got involved. She shushed me and told me to stay inside. I felt frightened and hid like I had learned to do. I had never heard Mom raise her voice until that day. Then, an unimaginable thing happened. I put a chair below the window in time enough to see the lady attack Mom. The two struggled while pulling hair and swinging fists. I looked to see where Dad had gone, and wouldn't you know; he was just standing there letting them duke it out! I felt a tinge of betrayal from the person whom I adored but found myself not recognizing. The person who once made sure we had a safe, warm home, love, and plenty of food, began to act like his own mother. My innocent eyes became terrified to witness my father's increasing alcoholic rage as it showed its ugly terrifying self, especially at the beginning of the month, when his hefty pension check came in the mail. Dad had bought a mailbox in Gallup and that is why he traveled there so often, not returning for days at a time. Like clockwork, he hoarded his money, and his drinking buddies soon became casual guests outside our Hogan. Dad would pull out his harmonica and play some of the familiar tunes that made me drift into the past. Soon, Navajo songs filled the drunken air, while the open flames of fire splashed their gross shadows across the dark night. I cannot forget the few months we spent in Klagetoh. Mom seemed to forget she had a child and followed Dad into alcoholic oblivion.

It wasn't until I turned 7 that I found out that the lady who Mom fought with was Dad's first wife, and that those were his children, too. Dad never told Mom he had another family. Mom was devastated and felt betrayed. Much of his pension check soon filtered out of his hands and into his first wife, Susan, and her kids. The rest was blown on alcohol. I learned Dad and Susan were high school sweethearts and that she patiently waited for him to return from his military service. Promises that were not kept seemed to be a habit. As I look back on that day, I guess I can't blame Susan for being so angry.

The tension between them grew and I just knew my life was about to change again. The anger between them had built up so much that the tension was bound to blow up at any moment. That moment came on a Friday night when Dad showed up drowning in alcohol. The fight was an awful sight. The guy who always came home with a handful of goodies and something special from his faraway travels only showed up for himself now. It was a relief when the weather started to warm up and spring meant that the flowers, birds, and rain showers would blanket the Earth. As spring brightened our surroundings, I remember Mom started hitch hiking into Gallup to look for Dad at the American Bar or Eddie's Club. One time she took me on an adventure. I never walked so far in my life. It took us 3 rides and 4 hours to make it to Gallup. No wonder it took them so long to get back home. I figured that's why Dad chose to stay there instead of traveling the long distance to our little shack. He was used to the good life. The town where the bus dropped us off also had a train running through it. I wished the three of us could hop on that train and return to our happy life in Tennessee, but that was never going to happen. Those happy days became a distant memory. American Bar and Eddie's Club were filled with drunk people, mostly Navajo men and even women. The smell was putrid, but they didn't seem to mind. Laughter and country music drowned the traffic noise outside. A few couples danced and twirled around the wooden floor. Compared to this, Klagetoh left little to be desired. I wondered why we didn't just move to Gallup, so we would not be hated, and I wouldn't be left behind to wander around alone.

The last straw came at the end of June, when we returned from Gallup. We discovered all of our belongings had been stolen from the storage shed. All those priceless treasures my father bought me from his trips abroad, gone. Looking back, at that moment in time, it seems like all of life was stolen from me. At the time, I didn't realize that that would be just the first time. The regular drunken fights turned violent, and it wasn't until Mom was beaten so badly that she reached out to Father Cormac at St. Anne's. He helped patch her up and made the call that would change both of our lives one more time.

Over the years that followed, I learned that Father Cormac spoke fluent Navajo and translated his Bible into our language. My little mind was amazed to meet him and to hear his voice on the transistor radio. Father Cormac would become a staple in my life and would serve as a turning point in our lives…for good and for bad and by five-years-old, I understood the word change.

I never met my mother's family until that Saturday in June. We had endured so much hardship, heated days and cold nights, endless hunger, hateful stares, brutal beatings, and unwarranted broom spankings. It seemed like the Sunday church songs that filled the valley were prayers for the heavens to open and that the Angels knew it was time to swoop down and take us from this horrible nightmare. Like magic, after Sunday church, the dogs began barking as two trucks came barreling towards our *home*. I heard the first truck come to a stop, the metal truck door slammed, and I saw a tall man with green eyes and a shorter muscular man jumped out and approach the door. Mom took a look at herself in the broken mirror and tried to cover the bruises on her face with make-up. When she instructed me to stay inside, I felt frightened, like I had become used to feeling. But when I saw them embrace, I immediately felt relieved as Mom talked to them. I could tell it took all of her strength not to break down and cry as they surrounded her with the hugs she had missed. I soon learned they were Uncle Ed and Uncle Benny, Mom's younger brothers. Their eyes sparkled as they took my little hand and gave me the kind of hug that I hadn't had in months. "You're the little one we heard about! It's good to finally meet you, Shimá yázhi *(my little mother)* With eyes raised, they looked around with exasperated disgust. The other truck held Mom's cousin brothers. It had been many years since they had seen my mom. I later found out that my parents met when mom was going to Albuquerque Indian School and dad was on furlough from the Army. They fell in love, eloped, and ran off to the East Coast where dad was stationed with the 81st Airborne Division at Ft. Bragg, North Carolina. I could tell my uncles were not happy to see their sister all bruised. They asked the whereabouts of my dad. I'm sure they had a few things they wanted to tell him. Stern words from mom's parents were on the top of the list. I heard Uncle Ed say, "Mom and Dad didn't raise you to be anybody's punching bag." I watched mom shed tears and held her head down in embarrassment. It was a good thing dad was in Gallup because I'm sure there would've been another fight that I did not want to see. It was much later that I learned how hurt and worried my mother's parents were all those years of not knowing where their first born had disappeared to, with a man they never gave their approve of. I had no idea dad was 10 years older than mom when they met. He had already served 12 years in the military by the time they met.

We set about packing up what was left of our belongings, tying them down in the back of the flatbed of the truck. Gramma Bah for once said nothing, staying locked in her hogan peeking out every now and then. When we finally had everything packed, I looked back at the room I called home for five months, knowing I would not miss any of it. I rode in Uncle Leonard's truck while Mom went with her brothers. I took one last look back as we slowly drove to the main dirt road. My uncle assured glance said, "Don't worry. You are in good hands now, Shimá yázhi."

As I look back, the familiar smell of Garden Deluxe whiskey and Lucky Strike cigarettes were my final memories of dad. It would be 20 years before I saw him again. For sure, I never wanted to see Gramma Bah again. Later that night, he returned to find us gone, and a note telling him we would never be coming back. The Angels took us to safety and a new life and like magic we were headed to a place called Tohatchi. The radio was tuned to the Sunday Hour always ended with "Amazing Grace" sung by Father Cormac.

I remember seeing little towns like Klagetoh between my short naps along the way. Their wool plaid shirts that I used as a pillow were nice and soft. I noticed that all four of them smelled like oil or car grease. We passed a bigger town that Uncle Albert called Window Rock. "This is the capital of the Great Navajo Nation." The two of them looked at each other and chuckled. It took four hours to get to Tohatchi Flats. The washboard dirt road that led to Tohatchi Flats was even further from any store and pretty much anyone else. I had gone from one isolated desert to another. Only this one felt different in a good way. We drove what seemed like forever. The winding bumpy dirt road into oblivion. Finally, the truck went around a 100-foot sandstone hill that revealed three rectangular stone homes, a corral filled with sheep and goats, and another filled with horses! There were a few chickens and a couple of ducks that wandered around the front yard, as if they owned the place. I knew they would become my friends, because I didn't see any kids. Any place was better than that hateful place called Klagetoh. Dogs barked, alerting two people who were peering out the window. Soon after that, a tall man wearing a blue plaid shirt and denim pants and a short woman dressed in a matching blouse and skirt, came out of the stone house. I just knew my mom's heart was beating fast as her eyes hugged the ground. I watched mom's parents grab and hug her so hard that, at the time, I thought it shook all the tears and hate she experienced those five months into one moment. I took a deep breath of relief as Uncle Anson helped me out of the truck. Being five years old, I started to make sense of my new life and the new people who came and went. I will be forever grateful for those who stayed.

I quickly clung behind my mother's pant leg. My grandparents looked down to see my little eyes looking up at theirs. "Shimá' this is your granddaughter, Florence." My Grandfather had the greenest eyes that sparkled behind his glasses, and he stole my heart. I just knew that Mom and I were going to be ok. "Yá'áh'tééh Shí sóóké *(Hello my grandchild)*. You have your grandmother's name." He spoke English!! Thank God!!! His smile went from Gramma Florence and back at me. He took my hand and the six of us went inside the shade house where the smells were so delicious! There, Gramma Florence's brother Juan and sister Anita was enjoying fresh brewed coffee. The stew was boiling over the open fire, and soon frybread was being made to a golden crisp – just like I liked it! Everyone greeted each other with respect and love. I learned that mom's sisters and other brothers wrote letters the many years she was gone, so the family knew we were doing ok. I hadn't felt this happy or smiled so much in so many months, that I was afraid that it might not last. My new favorite meal was mutton stew with corn and squash, and while I thought my mom made the best frybread, I was wrong. Gramma Florence made the absolute best and fluffiest frybread in the world. It was so yummy that I embarrassed my mom by licking the bowl. Everyone looked at me and then burst into laughter. I sat there satisfied, with a face full of grease. It had been months since I saw my mom relaxed and happy. It didn't seem like mom missed dad, or she was good at hiding it. I missed him, but it wouldn't be long before I forgot how he looked or how his voice sounded. The smell of whiskey and cigarettes is something that I would always hate. For sure, I did not miss Gramma Bah or how she yelled, "You leave me 'lone!!" In the time I spent at Tohatchi Flats, I never saw the violence or drunken anger we left behind.

This place was one room but became my castle that I would love and long for, as I grew older. My Stone Castle. There was a potbelly stove in the middle of the room, a couple of twin sized beds, and three roll away beds covered with a blanket and tucked in the corner. The white metal cupboard held all of Gramma's coffee cups and pots. She put the plates and bowls in the drawers below so that she could reach them. There was a massive loom where Gramma sat weaving her gray, white, and black rug. I sat next to her, watching her move her fingers in and out of the strings and pounding down each new row with precision. I was amazed! Gramma and Gramps had the biggest hands I had ever seen. I decided that they grew huge with all the ranch work they had to do from sunup to sunset. It didn't take long to get used to the day-to-day routines of life at Tohatchi Flats. They were hard-working people and were up early with the chickens. Each morning, Gramps would brew Gramma a pot of Folgers coffee while she made tortilla dough. They talked to each other in the Navajo language about the day's chores. I began learning Navajo words for coffee, horses, truck, and others important words. In no time, I knew they were talking about everyday ranch life and things that needed to be done. It seemed like I was always hungry. My eyes were peeled as the tortillas bubbled and puffed when turned on each side, then Gramma would stack one on the top of the other one until she was finished. Finally, she poured me a cup of dumpling soup, and I gobbled it all down so fast that Gramps had to slow me down. "Grandchild, slow down! You will get a stomachache," he chuckled. His hazel eyes gave an uncomfortable stare at mom, as if to scold her for not feeding me, but little did he know what we went through. Or maybe the bruises fading on mom's face and hands said it all.

As time went on, I grew to feel comfortable around my Grandparents when my mom was away at work. They lovingly took care of me and even took me on a different route to Gallup. The first time I went with them, I was scared dad would see me and take me away with him. I never did catch sight of him. Gramps always bought me a bag of jellybeans. He would take out all the black ones for himself, and hand me the rest. I noticed Gramma had her own candy stash. If she wasn't weaving or tending to the cattle, Gramma would make her own blouses and skirts. Her father, my Great Grandfather Charlie adorned her with the best turquoise necklaces and bracelets. Gifts given to her by Gramps and her parents were carefully stored in a small blue suitcase that she hid under her bed. I learned that Gramma was her dad's favorite. I also learned that she was a tough woman and could do all the things a rancher had to do. Over the years that followed, I watched her rope, brand the cattle, break a young horse, and all the things horse owners must do to keep things in order. These were just some of the skills my Gramma could do!

My daily routine started by following Gramps out to the corral as he let the sheep out early in the morning and then tagged along to help herd them after breakfast. Gramps' pubby dog, Lucky, was always nearby. Gramps would whistle the familiar song that stuck in my mind forever. While waiting for breakfast, Gramps would read the local newspaper, the Navajo Times, and translate the news to Navajo for Gramma to understand. I don't remember

Gramma speaking any English and seemed to remain faithful to her Dine' language. The love between them didn't have to be announced, they just lived it. As I look back on my early years, and the times I spent with my grandparents out on Tohatchi Flats, I would learn to thank the Holy People, God, and the Pope for keeping mom and me safe those five months of hell.

There was always work to do out on Tohatchi Flats. Every weekend, one by one my uncles and aunties and their kids would make the long journey to spend time with Gramma and Gramps. In the early evening, I climbed the sandstone hill behind the house to watch the sunset, but also because I could watch the dust rise and the faint headlights slowly make their way closer and closer to the ranch. The quietness of Tohatchi Flats came alive for three days a week. I couldn't wait for Friday night to arrive! One by one, their vehicles made the 15-mile trek across the desert and finally made their final turn around the sandstone hill. My cousins rushed up the hill to greet me and there we waited until everyone showed up. There were 10 grandkids, including me when I arrived at the age of five. Over time that number grew to 31, altogether. We played outside, herded sheep, rode horses, and just went for long walks during our visits that first summer, and so many summers after that.

In the first weeks at Tohatchi Flats, my mother caught a ride with her brother Levi to look for a job. It wasn't long before she found a job in Shiprock, New Mexico....100 miles from Tohatchi Flats. It was also then that my mother and grandparents began talking about enrolling me in school. It was also when my new life at Tohatchi Flats would turn upside down. "Red Sands? Where is that?" My eyes filled with tears as I wondered if I would ever really find a home that didn't change. "Shi'yázhi, it's a boarding school that everyone is sending their kids to so kids can get an education while us parents' work. You will live there and go to school while I work", she explained. "Don't worry, I will visit you often and we can write letters to each other. I need to get on my feet and soon I will come and get you for good." She assured me, but for some reason I didn't believe it would turn out that way. My life had taken too many turns at that moment; I just became a walking question mark. I thought of questions like; "what if dad finds me and takes me away?" "What if they're mean like Gramma Bah?" "What if you forget me?" "Is there a school in Tohatchi Flats I can go to?" All these questions came bursting out of my mouth and I was only five years old. My mother tried to assure me, but her eyes told another story. Once again, I felt that familiar uncertainty I had felt came rushing to the forefront of my mind. My grandparents sensed it. While we let the sheep out Gramps said, "This Red Sands school will be for your own good, Grandchild..you need to learn to read, write, and do math in order to get ahead in this world... You still have some time before we take you." I watched him take a deep sigh as my eyes hugged the rising sun that had peeked over the horizon, ushering another day. Deep breath, sigh.

Over the summers, I learned my Grandparents had two different homesteads, as Gramps called them. While mom was away at work, we spent time traveling up the mountain to Asaayi. My cousins Chuckie, Ben, Jr., Burton, and Shreeve rode in the bed of the truck. There was a lot of work to do, and Gramps always needed help mending fences, rounding up the cattle, or gathering wood for the winter months. The mountain air was refreshing, and the cool breeze made the trees sing! It was a big relief from the Tohatchi desert heat. There is a big lake just down the mountain from my grandparents' place. The boys walked with me over there to go fishing while our grandparents went to Gallup for supplies. My cousins wrapped fishing wire around an empty aluminum can and tied a bomber lure with corn as bait to each of their lines. Cousins Chuckie and Benny Jr. whipped their fishing line over their heads like a roper would trying to catch a steer. They flung the line into the lake, then carefully placed the cans on a Y-shaped stick to hold it in place. The rest of us gathered wood for a fire. It wasn't long before they caught eight trout fish in all. They gutted the catch and threw the head and insides into the lake. "This is thanks for feeding us on this fine and glorious day," Cousin Chuckie snickered. I watched as Shreeve bring out the bowl of sliced potatoes and bacon slices along with a roll of aluminum foil. The potatoes were placed inside each fish, then bacon strips were carefully wrapped around each fish and then sealed in an aluminum pocket. The fire was nice and hot with charcoals glowing underneath. Chuckie carefully placed each fish packet under the charcoal and added a little fire on top. In a matter of minutes, we all had a nice meal of fish, potatoes, and bacon, that became my second favorite food! I would wish for this kind of food when I had to try to like the mystery meal at Red Sands Residential Dormitory.

As the end of summer crept upon us, there was also a cool breeze that took the place of the sweltering desert heat. It wasn't long before I noticed that I hadn't heard any angry words, and no one ever drank alcohol. In the early mornings, like clockwork, Grampa and Gramma rose before the sun and prayed using corn pollen. I found myself standing next to them as the sun peeked over the horizon. Gramps offered the pollen. I learned to put a little at the tip of my tongue to help me watch my words and thoughts. A little bit was sprinkled on the top of my head, and the rest I sprinkled before me to let Mother Earth know I was giving thanks for a new day, for good health, and a productive day. They used the Navajo language in a soft and gentle way. Gramps explained to me that it is good to give thanks to the Holy People for the rising sun, good health, plenty of food, and enough work to make the days go by. I noticed there was a hogan next to the stone castle at Tohatchi Flats and a hogan next to the mobile home up at Asaayi. Their hogans were a place for prayers and singing. Gramps spent his evenings practicing his favorite Peyote Songs with the comfort of a warm fire. If we were quiet, we could sit and listen. The smoke flowed up the chimney pipe and exited out to the sky that sparkled with millions of stars. They seemed so close it was like I could reach out and touch them. Gramps pointed to the Milky Way and called it The Corn Pollen Path and the road on which the Holy People traveled each day. Over the years, I learned that Gramps and Gramma were very spiritual people. They truly cared for each other just by the way they thought of each other, each putting in their own helping hand to get things done.

We spent most of July and part of August at Asaayi to keep cool. Gramps herded his sheep in the valley between two tall mountains that were lined with cedar, oak, and pine trees. Gramma continued weaving her rugs. My uncles and cousins went deep in the mountain to chop wood for the winter months. Like a lot of weekends over the years, my mom, aunties and uncles and other relatives showed up for a Native American Church Meeting to prepare for everyone's returned to school. In the early evening, once everyone was fed, including the Roadman, there were prayers and the passing of peyote medicine. It was really bitter, and I didn't like it. My Mom suggested I put a little on my tongue, but even that was too much. My cousins also put a little on their tongue and passed it on to those who sat on the south side of the hogan and then onto the north side. On the South side were male members of the Roadman's family, my uncles, extended family members, and any helpers. Uncle Benny, who kept the fire going, had the role of Fire Chief at each of our family prayer meetings. My mom and aunties sat next to us on the north side. Each took the bitter medicine, passing it until it got back to the Roadman. The praying and chanting went on all night, with a few breaks for fresh air. It was the first of many all-night ceremonies attended in my youth. I remember falling asleep to the beat of the drum. The Roadman would purposely sing and shake the rattle extra loud in order to wake us up, because we were not supposed to go to sleep at all. The lack of sleep was to raise our endurance to face all that life was going to offer – good or bad. We went outside right before dawn to stretch and get some fresh air. The crisp cool night air was very quiet, except for Yazzie Tsosie's dogs barking in the distance. In the morning, my Auntie Teri brought a pail of water and one cup. She knelt facing west and prayed for the water. She carried the pail of water to each of us from south to north and one by one we drank the power of all the prayers from the same cup. Right after that, Aunties Mary and Sarah brought in bowls of fruit, meat, and bread. The delicious food was blessed by the Roadman. After a bit of a break, the rest of the day was filled with the regular ranch work that needed to be done.

Those two months flew by so fast, and, before I knew it, it was time for me to get ready to leave Tohatchi Flats and another change in my young life. Once again, my world would turn towards loneliness. It became the theme of my life – waiting and being alone.

Even now, at 30 years old, I can still feel the isolation of my time at Red Sands Residential Dormitory, and the happiest memories were the times I spent at Tohatchi Flats. Gramps taught me that a book could be a companion, and that it was ok to re-read a great story. For the longest time, I didn't know that his favorite companion was his trusty Bible, which he fondly referred to as "another great story." My love for reading came from his example. During the 9 years library books and my own writings became my favorite companion. I kept all the letters I received, my secret thoughts in a diary, my poems, and pressed flowers in separate notebooks. Sixteen years later, as I prepared for my last trip to Red Sands Residential Dormitory, I unlocked the familiar blue footlocker that was filled with some of those writings. I smiled as I flipped through the faded notebooks that held the scribblings of an elementary girl. The calendars Gramps gave me at the beginning of each school year were carefully stacked to remember the past. My finger traced Gramps' words that were meant to assure me that I was not really alone. I found this writing dated November 26. 1972 when I was in 6th grade. This is one of my favorite stories.

"Tohatchi Flats – A Special Notebook"

There is a sacred place called Tohatchi Flats. It lies in the Checkerboard area of the Navajo Nation, near the community of Crownpoint, New Mexico. The Arviso family called it Muddy Clay Flat. Gramps called it Tohatchi Flats because he is originally from the mountain community of Sawmill, Arizona, which is 50 miles west. When we drove down the Chuska Mountains, it descended into the flat white sand San Juan basin. It was a beautiful sight as the beam of bright yellow sunlight cast rays across the land, we called home. It is a place where survival means you must carry your own water from the windmill, maintain a supply of canned goods, and above all be willing to work from the crack of dawn into the darkness.

The nights are pitch dark and the stars twinkled across the vast black-blue sky, telling all on Mother Earth, "You are not alone." The Milky Way that spanned majestically across the purple sky from north to south is known as the Corn Pollen Path and a constant reminder that the Holy People expected a life of balance – Hozho. The desert-ridden basin ripped of its natural vegetation in the 1930 Dust Bowl used to be known for its fresh springs, watering holes, and farms that dotted the Flats. Gramma spoke of the most beautiful tall sunflower fields that grew year after year. The orange-yellow green fields filled the Flats with butterflies, bluebirds, and other critters. Gramma fondly remembered those days as she gazed into her childhood. She loved Tohatchi Flats, and while there weren't any more fields of sunflowers, she had kitchen towels with sunflower prints to remind her of days gone by.

From the mesa that overlooked the stone castle, the faint headlights of distant vehicles traveling North or South on U.S. Highway 666 fifteen miles away, was a source of entertainment. Thinking back this was a weird kind of entertainment, but I sure missed it. The rancher's life and the heat of the summer sun was grueling and not for the faint of heart. Patience was a virtue for sheepherders watching their sheep graze on sparce vegetation that somehow survived on very little water across the vast desert of Tohatchi Flats. Gramps and all his grandkids filled countless hours reading books and eating raw onions with a lot of salt. His faithful sheep dog mutt, Lucky, was really the sheepherder. Gramps once reported, 'Lucky is a good sheep dog. He teaches all other sheep dogs." Lucky was a long-haired white dog that had brown tipped ears and a few spots of black here and there. From a distance he looked like he was a wolf in sheep's clothing as he roamed the ridges in the back of the stone castle. He was the leader of dogs and had been for many years. Gramps was always bringing home strays but Lucky, well, Gramps was the lucky one to have found such a good companion.

One year, Gramps attended a Native American Church meeting at his brother Anson's home, where he met visitors from Oklahoma. Lucky had traveled with them from Oklahoma to New Mexico in the back of an old Ford F100 pick-up truck. There was no room for Lucky to travel back, so they gave Gramps Lucky. From then on, Lucky was a faithful friend and soon learned how to herd sheep and enjoy onions with salt, of course. "Sometimes life brings you a bit of help just when you need it,".. Gramps said about Lucky. In turn, Lucky loved to hear Gramps sing his Peyote songs and listened to a good story or two when they were alone. Every now and then when he would begin to howl as if to sing along, Gramps gave him that over the eyeglasses look and Lucky would slowly crouch down, eyes lowered, and a little whimper of apology. Gramps always gave a little chuckle and a loving pat on the head for those times.

A few tears rolled down my cheeks, as I tightly held those precious notebooks and the life, I left on endless pages all those years ago.

Chapter 2 – Journey To Red Sands – A Remembrance

My early years became a memory not to be spoken of or to be forgotten. By the third year as a ward of Red Sands Residential Dormitory, I became wise to the empty promises of tomorrow. I became silently determined to do what I could to "get ahead" and it was at Red Sands Public School that I did learn to read and do math, just like Gramps said I would. My red wooden pencil became my friend because I could make it say what I was thinking. Writing became a part of my routine, while wondering how this all was "for my own good." Gramps' words that bounced around in my eyes while I was at Red Sands Residential Dormitory. Words that I often tied to the different experiences either I or others went through as we spent our tender years in a cinder block building with a tall fence to keep us imprisoned.

Memories of those nine years flashed before my mind with an odd sense of anguish and uncertainty. Each year, I wasn't sure of what I would find when I returned to this place, I will never ever call home. From Kindergarten to eighth grade, I kept my memories encapsulated in notebooks of all kinds, as time ticked, ticked, ticked, year upon year. The hardest were the first four years.

After spending my first summer with Gramps and Gramma, it was the beginning of the time I had to leave my beloved Tohatchi Flats. I remember the weekend before the next change in life; my Grandparents returned from Gallup with a few school supplies. My little hands sorted through notebooks, pencils, crayons, a box of envelopes, and a light blue footlocker to keep my clothes and things while I was away from home. Mom took me clothes shopping in Gallup during the 4th of July holiday. I didn't get to see her before I left home that day. I discovered that she had written her address on 12 envelopes and my Grandparents on the other 12 with my name on the top left corner – with no address. I guess I should've noticed that I didn't have an address, but being that I was five years old, I just saw my name. Each of the envelopes had a United States Flag stamp for delivery. Gramps took extra special time to write down all the things he knew would be going on at Tohatchi Flats throughout the calendar year that he bought for me to count the time. I decided this was so I would know that the work did not stop even though I was not there to help.

I recall the morning was just like all the others. The early morning air lay in silence and reverent stillness as the sun's rays began to cast light across the land. It was as if even the animals and birds knew something was different. A few sheep let out the usual baaa', as the bells on their neck jingled to signal, they were ready to be set free. Gramps was up early making our coffee and mixing the slop for the sheep dogs. Gramma mixes the dough for her delicious tortillas, while cooking eggs and bacon. Other than that, it was just like any other day. For me, it was a day of sadness and wonder. At five years old, I was being shipped off to a world where the everyday life of Tohatchi Flats would soon seem to fade and drift into wonder. As we loaded up Gramps' GMC truck that he named Red Robin, I watched him use his red bandana to wipe a few tears rolling down his eyes. He was careful not to let me see him, but by then, I was a very good observer. We ate breakfast in virtual silence. Each bite was so hard to swallow. I decided to remember every taste of Gramma's fluffy tortilla, scrambled eggs with green chili, bacon, and coffee with lots of goat milk.

As each day drifted into another, I began to wonder if she cared about me as much as she seemed to care about her job. For many years, I wondered if she ever spent her time looking for my dad at the bars in Gallup. Even though I started to forget what he looked or sounded like, I also wondered if my dad ever thought about me – his rolling stone.

Yet, there I was watching my belongings loaded onto the truck, not knowing it would be the beginning of a nine-year journey – a destiny my innocent mind would struggle to understand. Gramps checked the oil and filled the windshield wiper fluid just in case there was rain and a muddy return. Gramma tidied up the place and packed lunch. In silent contemplation, I helped her put away the breakfast dishes I had washed earlier. I sat on Gramma's soft bed and looked around, hoping I would remember every detail of the castle I loved. I studied her newest rug design and looked forward to seeing it finished. I laid down to get one last whiff of Gramma's scent of cinnamon and vanilla. I went outside to the sheep corral. My hands glided over the wood planks that kept the sheep corralled and safe. I went to the horse barn and brushed Big Mac, just in case Gramps didn't have any time when they returned home. I crawled up to the barn loft and smelled the fresh hay and thought of the fun my cousins and I had playing hide-n-seek or playing cards to keep us cool in the summer heat. These are the memories that kept me going.

"Well, Grandchild it's time to get on the road. We have a long way to go." Gramps said as he peered into the barn. He walked slowly back to the stone house as I followed behind, trying to make the time slow down. Gramps gave his final orders to Johnson Bowman, our neighbor, whom Gramps relied on to tend the sheep on the days he would be gone. There was a cool breeze that whipped up the dust around the sandstone hill, as if to point the way out of Tohatchi Flats. He looked up at the dark clouds growing on the horizon for a few seconds, wondering if it would yield a late afternoon shower. That would mean muddy roads. As usual, Gramps opened the notebook stored next to the door, wrote the date, time, destination, and time of return. It was a

way of communicating with each other. In case one of our relatives came to visit, they would know where my Grandparents were and when they would be returning. If they were up in the mountains, most likely the visitors would drive up the mountain to meet them. There was a notebook stored at the mobile home in Asaayi that also served the same purpose. What a tale these notes would tell, tracing everyone's whereabouts over time.

With heavy hearts, we took a collective breath and a moment of silence. Gramps eased his truck onto the 15 miles of dirt road that led west to Hwy 666. The three of us sat in silence as Red Robin jumped up and down and side to side; behind us, dust chased us down the path. I made myself memorize every inch of those 15 miles as I watched the sandstone hill fade into the distance from the back window. At the gas station, Gramps filled up the tank, washed the windshield, and checked my luggage that had bounced around as we made our way down the washboard road. Gramma and I sat there taking deep breaths trying not to cry. She stroked my braided hair and spoke some words of comfort. Her gentle voice and soft eyes told me that she was concerned and sad that I was going far away from Tohatchi Flats. Gramps opened the truck door and handed me a small brown paper bag. Inside, it held a bag of jellybeans, green apple gum, and some other candy. "Don't cry, Grandchild. You will be ok. The goodies are for later," he said as he handed it to me. "The bullet pop is for now." There were three orange and cherry bullet pops for us to enjoy. Gramma and Gramps talked about different things along the road. Every now and then, I caught a few familiar words and put the story together. Gramma was talking about how hard it was going to be to leave me at Red Sands Residential Dormitory. She was also worried that they would be back so late, as the dark clouds spoke of incoming rain.

I cried myself to sleep on Gramma's lap and jolted up just as we drove into the Red Sands city limits. Gramps found a clearing on the roadside to pull off so that we could eat the lunch Gramma had packed. He unfolded the tail gate, and Gramma placed a blanket so we could sit. She carefully untied the Blue Bird flour sack and handed us the tortilla and mutton sandwich she had made from last night's dinner. I savored each bite as if it was my last meal. I wanted to remember the taste of Gramma's tortillas because I didn't know if they made tortillas at Red Sands Residential Dormitory. I studied both of their faces. The lines on their faces told of the hard life they lived out on Tohatchi Flats. From what I could tell, they wouldn't have it any other way. I could see the veins bulging on their large hands. I would find out later that Navajo people viewed those veins as a sign of someone who knows how to use their hands to work. I would say that is true of my grandparents. During the two and a half months I lived with them, they rarely sat around to rest. Something always needed mending or cattle needed tending to, day in and day out. Gramps started to tell me about the calendar he had bought for me. "Grandchild, I want you to know that even if we don't visit all the time, we are thinking and praying for you. The Holy People know who you are, have faith in your prayers too. Don't worry about what your mother is up to. She'll get on her feet and before you know it, you will be with her again. Make sure you write to us with the envelopes she made for you to use. Remember, your studies are the most important thing right now. It will all be for your own good. You will see, Grandchild." Gramma held my hand and gave a nod in agreement. She said a few words in Navajo that meant, "be strong. You come from a good family, good blood. Make us proud, Grandchild." There was an awkward silence that was broken by the shriek of a hawk circling high in the air. We all looked up together, while Gramps made the comment, "That is a good sign – everything will be like it should be." I wanted our last meal to last forever, so I ate as slowly as I could, but my Grandparents kept looking at the time and at the impending storm in the east. After thirty minutes, we packed up and got back on the road.

There were fancy cars packed with families passing in both directions. Gramps' dusty pick-up truck with the metal stock rack and the ball of bailing wire fastened near the back, was out of place. I noticed a line of pick-up trucks turning onto the highway which I would learn later led to places like Chinle, Ganado, or Tuba City. We passed wooden teepees that were used as a motel for tourists who wanted to live like a Native American, if only for one night. There were the usual stores, like Walt's Hardware and the 5 & Dime store that sold just about anything you could want. Gramps drove down 11th Avenue and turned left at Erie Street…yes, eerie for sure! About half a mile away, we saw the beginnings of the 6-foot chain link fence that surrounded Red Sands Residential Dormitory. I noticed there was a roll of wire that was draped down along the top of the fence. I took a closer look and saw spikes every few feet. There were silent stares, as we all took a deep breath. My wide eyes and curled eyebrows showed how big and scary the place looked! I reached for

Gramma's hands and squeezed them real hard. I felt myself start to shake, tears welling in my eyes as I finally had a visual of the fourth place I never wanted to call, "*home.*"

When we got to the end of the fence, there was a large open gate that held a sign that read, "Welcome to Red Sands Residential Dormitory". In the smaller words below, it read "No Trespassing". Gramps drove between the gates of the fenced compound. There was a slight drop and then the cattle guard rumbled beneath the tires, straining to hold up the heavy truck. The stock rack loudly shook everything from side to side. The dirt parking lot was packed with trucks, cars, and even a horse with a wagon. There were signs to tell us where we had to go. Gramps pulled out my footlocker and carried it to the back of the line. There were so many people, Gramma decided to stay in the truck. We slowly made our way to the first window where Gramps was given a clipboard with papers for him to fill out. Then we made our way down the hallway lined with chairs where other parents and their kids filled out the same paperwork. I think I was the only one being dropped off by a grandparent. There were girls of all ages. Little girls were silently crying as they waited. I felt like crying too, but I had to stay strong. I'll cry after Gramps and Gramma leave; I bravely told myself. Deep breath, sigh. The next line led us to another window where I was issued a rough gray blanket, sheets, and a pillow. Gramps took the papers to a window; there a lady inspected them while she looked at me from the top of her glasses. She was a short, chubby Navajo lady, I learned was Mrs. Yazzie. She spoke in Navajo to Gramps, who used his hands while explaining something to her. I could feel the tears start to well up and my stomach started to turn. I swallowed hard and took a deep breath as my wide eyes looked around the room that was filled with people and crying girls. As soon as Gramps was done with the paperwork, another lady took us down another hallway to a long room that was lined with rows of metal bunkbeds from one end to the other, like the Army barracks I remember seeing when I lived in Tennessee. She took me to the third bunk and said, "This is where you will stay. Your clothes will go in the closet, and your footlocker can go under the bed.

You need to keep your area clean." Then, she said something in Navajo to Gramps' as he nodded. The lady quickly left and came back with another girl and her parents stopped at the next bunkbed saying the same thing to them.

As Gramps helped fix my bed and he explained that if I don't keep my area clean, I would be punished. Our eyes met and my bottom lip quivered. My eyes told Gramps I didn't know what punishment meant so he made me promise to keep my area clean. By the time my bed was made, my clothes hung, and my school supplies tucked into the little cubby above my clothes; there were about 15 girls of different ages making their beds. Gramps tucked my footlocker under my bunk next to the wall. He handed me the key as we walked back into the large room that was not as full as before and out to the parking lot where a lot of vehicles were gone. Gramma, who had patiently waited for us, was asleep. Gramps gently touched her shoulder to awaken her from her nap. "It's time for us to go back to Tohatchi Flats, Grandchild. Now that we know where you will be and where you will sleep, I feel everything will be ok." My chin quivered. I bit my lip and held in tears as long as I could, but they came gushing out like a river. Gramma and Gramps surrounded me with hugs and together we shed our last tears. I held on tight knowing I wouldn't see them for a long time. The smell of car oil and Vicks emanated from Gramps' blue plaid shirt. Vanilla and cinnamon drifted off Gramma's velveteen blouse. Even after twenty-five years, a whiff of these special smells brought back memories of this departure and the beginning of my journey alone – the one that was supposed to be for my own good. I knew it took us hours to get to Red Sands Residential Dormitory, and that it would be dark when they returned to Tohatchi Flats. They walked me to the entrance outside of the multi-purpose room, gave me one last hug. As I stood at the top of the landing, I watched them slowly walk to Red Robin. "Study hard, be good, and always remember your prayers," Gramps departing words meant to assure me only made me feel abandoned. Slowly, they drove out of Red Sands Residential Dormitory parking lot. The rattling of the stock rack as the truck glided over the cattle guard and the bump to the paved road was so loud. As they turned left on Erie Street, I waited until I could not hear the rattling of the stock rack anymore before I sat on the concrete step and wailed for what seemed like an hour. One of the ladies that checked me into prison touched my shoulder and together we went to enter the building. I stayed for another hour looking out the huge window just in case they changed their minds and decided to turn around. "Please turn around! Please take me home." I begged the Holy People, God, and the Pope to hear my prayers, but that never happened. I took a deep breath, dried my tears, and decided I had no choice but to go to my bunkbed home. I had felt scared before that day, but the terror of being left to face life left a scar so deep I spent years trying to heal from the loneliness that it became a companion.

I sat on my bed hugging the blanket my mom had bought me. It still held the scent of cedar smoke Gramps had used to bless me the night before and a faint odor of vanilla and cinnamon. The little girls on either side of me and on the other side of the hall were doing the same thing. Our innocent souls were left there without any instructions. I could hear whimpering all the way down the barrack like hall. I decided it was ok to join in. I dozed off and jolted awake to hunger pains and the smell of something delicious emanating from somewhere in the distance. We must've been there for three hours when a tall chubby Navajo lady laden with a ring of keys and a starched pressed blue grey uniform dress came marching to the middle of the hallway. Her long black hair was held in a big bun behind her thick neck. She had a round face and brown eyes that were covered with large-framed rectangular glasses. With a loud voice she shouted, "My name is Mrs. Becenti. I am the boss here! Welcome to Dorm A. You kids need to keep your places clean! The restroom and showers are down the hall. The kids in this Wing will be taking showers on Sundays, Tuesdays, and Thursdays. You kids need to keep the reshroom clean! Don't throw toilet paper on the ground! By now, your stuffs should be unpacked! Make your bed and keep your places clean! You will eat in the cafeteria, but fursh you line up in the middle of this hallway and walk ober der in one line." Her round nose flared with each command as her large belly jiggled. Thick brown socks covered her fat legs, and her fat feet were squeezed into black leather lace-up shoes that squeaked with every step. I noticed she talked with a weird accent.

It was 4:00 p.m. by the time she finished inspecting each of our "places". I could hear her getting mad at some of the girls who were still crying. "Dry up doz tears! You are here, now! Get used to it!" Her loud voice echoed down Dorm A, shook the thin windows, and rattled our innocent souls. Her keys made a rhythmic jingle with every move. I wondered what all those keys would open or lock. I decided to learn the noises she made, as I watched her every move and learned to stay invisible when she was around. She left Dorm A and walked down to Dorm B, where the older girls lived. Her fat, round feet pounded the tile floors as her wide hips shook the keys back and forth. I could hear her shouting the same commands that faded as she made her way down the bunkbeds in Dorm B. Rattled, I looked in the bag of goodies Gramps bought me. At the bottom were two packs of sunflower seeds. I ate a few of those to calm my stomach, making sure I didn't make a mess. The bag still held Gramps' scent gave me comfort. There was an uneasy quietness that I learned to understand after Mrs. Becenti's rants.

The girl who had the upper bunk climbed down and together we sat on my bunk, exchanging names and making small talk. "My name is Garnet." She was shy. Her dusty brown braided hair hung down her back. She pushed her black footlocker next to mine. "My name is Florence, and my mom said I was going to be in kindergarten, how about you?" I asked. "Me, too!" We smiled at each other in silence. The girls from the next bunk joined us.

"Where did you come from, Florence?"

"We drove a long way from Tohatchi Flats."

"How about you?" I thought, if she says, Klagetoh, I'm in real trouble because my dad might find out where I was and take me back to that awful place!

"I'm from Tuba City," Garnet chimed in. It's a long way to the north too. Are you scared? I am."

~ 30 ~

"Yes, it's a long way to Tohatchi Flats to the east. It took us all day to get here. I'm supposed to be here for my own good, how about you?"

"Yeah, it's for my own good to be here too, I guess" Garnett glanced up and quickly hugged the ground.

"Hi. I'm Clarice. I'm from Ganado. I know where Tohatchi and Tuba City are because my parent drive all over the place selling jewelry." Clarice looked at the fourth girl and ask, "What's your name?"

"I'm Ruby. I'm from Window Rock. It took a long time to get here too."

That is where our friendship began. We were four scared five-year-olds left there to survive and thrive somehow, alone together. Our curiosity made us decide to look down the hall to the end where there were double doors that led outside. I tried to open it, but it was locked. "I'll bet one of those keys that mean lady has will unlock this door." Ruby chimed in. As we walked back to our bunkbeds, I noticed the girls at the end of the hall were a couple of years older than those at my end of the hall. I guessed they assigned our bunkbeds by our age. With heavy hearts and a few more tears shed, we huddled together and talked about what we liked or where we were from. We sat on the bottom bunks enjoying the green apple Jolly Rancher sucker Clarice had given us. She showed us how to crack the sucker in half so we could enjoy the other half later. I decided I was going to be ok, and Clarice was going to be my best friend.

My mind wandered as I looked at the off-white walls, ceiling tiles with tiny holes, and square tiles that covered the floor. The floor tiles were shining so much that I could almost see my reflection. I also wondered where Gramps and Gramma were by now. I wondered if my mom was going to visit me soon. At exactly 5:00p.m. there was a loud bell, and then Mrs. Becenti, in all her glory and power, marched into Dorm A shouting, "LINE UP GIRLS!! LINE UP!!" One by one we learned to quietly line up and walk to the cafeteria. Mrs. Becenti's keys jingled as she marched down the line. Her beady eyes and curled eyebrows glared over her frames at the girls who weren't standing exactly like she wanted. Our little eyes witnessed one girl pulled off her bed by her ear and ordering her to get in line. She screamed out in pain, but Mrs. Becenti just said, "You were here last year! You should know how to get in line! You should know how to stand up straight, too! Do you want manual labor?" The girl quietly said, "No." Our eyes hugged the ground with hearts thumping, learning to fear Mrs. Becenti on our first day away from our families. Mrs. Becenti pounded her feet to the beginning of the line, while her keys made a steady jingle tune. We quickly learned that tune and the heavy rhythmic gait of her feet alerted us whenever she was on her way.

Finally, it was time to eat…sigh!! Like mice, we learned to line up from youngest to oldest and marched into the cafeteria for breakfast, lunch, and dinner. I could smell something yummy but couldn't figure out what it was. We got our plastic trays and silverware and scooted them down the long metal counter. The smiling Cafeteria Ladies were plump Navajos who wore white dress uniforms and hairnets that held the same large bun on the back of their necks. Each of them scooped whatever was in their pan into one of the five compartments of our plastic trays. Ruby whispered from the back of me, "Do you know what this is? Have you eaten this before?" I shrugged my shoulders. I asked Clarice and she shrugged her shoulders. Garnet took a guess and said, "I think it's goulash. My mom makes it when she doesn't have anything else to make. It's like mixing up all the leftovers in one pot." "Look at that girl. She spit out what she just ate," Ruby chimed in while we looked at the girl and then at the food on our plate.

Mr. Begay the Dorm Aide pointed to the place we were supposed to sit. "This is where you sit from here on," he instructed the kids as they got their goulash. His voice conveyed his warmth, and he didn't wear a uniform or carry a ball of keys. Next thing we knew, loud noises were coming from the other side of the cafeteria. I hadn't noticed there was another hallway there until then. In marched the boys – youngest to oldest, in a line. That must be where the boys stayed. I was beginning to think all the Navajo parents were too busy working to keep their kids at home. I took one scoop of the mushy goulash and immediately understood why that girl spit her scoop out. The first taste was like a mystery. Each of us looked at each other with curled eyebrows. We managed to finish most of our food as Mr. Begay instructed us to do. The fluffy tortillas saved the day. I would learn to look forward to the times when the Cafeteria Ladies made fresh tortillas, like mom and Gramma did. I learned that other times my hunger was too powerful, and I had no choice but to eat the multitude of mystery meals they fed us. My memory of the first day at Red Sands Residential Dormitory is etched in my mind.

One by one, we dumped any uneaten food off our trays and thew milk cartons in a different garbage can and in a line, we exited down the same hallways back to our dorm. Clarice noticed some kids were walking out the double doors that were now unlocked, so we followed them outside. There was a large playground with swings, three merry-go-rounds, six teeter totters, four tables, and benches where kids had already begun to play or hang out. We spent two hours playing when another mean Navajo woman who wore the same outfit and carried the same ball of keys started yelling at us from the double doors. Mrs. Hagga blew her whistle and ordered us to line up and get inside. Watching Mrs. Hagga act like Mrs. Becenti, I began to think that Red Sands Residential Dormitory had an endless supply of mean women who locked and unlocked the doors to fresh air. We spent another hour in the Multipurpose Room watching *Swiss Family Robinson*. Garnet, Clarice, Ruby, and I enjoyed the Jiffy-pop buttered popcorn and root beer they served us. Although we dared not let anything fall on the sparkling floor, I decided this place wasn't going to be so bad after all. Looking back, I decided the movies and snacks were a feeble effort to make us feel safe and comfortable…for our own good. I tried to remember those happy days from Tennessee, but like almost everything in my life by then, I had no choice but to let them fade into a distant memory.

At bedtime, my mind wandered about my Grandparents and if they had made it home before the storm that was looming over the horizon when we left. I was sure the tears cried that the first night would stain the floor and never wash away our sorrow, but before long, Dorm A fell into an uncertain silence with a few squeaky springs, now and then. The scent of vanilla, cinnamon, and cedar smoke, and my blanket gave me comfort and helped me drift into unsettled sleep. The next morning, we repeated the same thing: lining up for breakfast, going outside to play, coming back in to watch T.V., or reading books. Dinner was beef stew, but it didn't really taste right. The fluffy, golden, buttered yeast roll saved the meal, though. I decided that the Cafeteria Ladies opened cans and heated up our food, then took special care to make the bread. After dinner, we finished watching Swiss Family Robinson. This was the very first movie I had ever seen, being that before I came to this place, everyone in my life either read books, newspapers, or listened to the radio. I used to think there were little people inside the radio speaking to us, but when I saw the reel-to-reel spinning around showing us the movie, I still had a lot of questions. It was a good movie, but I remember I didn't quite understand what I had watched.

I had been at Red Sands Residential Dormitory for one week, according to my calendar. Then on day eight, after breakfast, we heard the clinking keys before Mrs. Becenti entered Dorm A with her orders. My heart jumped every time I heard the noise of keys and the sound of squeaky shoes. She ordered us to line up and the next thing I knew, we were marched from the Red Sands Residential Dormitory compound, down a long sidewalk to Red Sands Elementary School. There, a tall white man greeted us in the gym. The girls and boys of Red Sands Residential Dormitory were divided up by grade level. Two blonde, white ladies took turns calling out names, forming two lines.

They took us to two different classrooms. Miss Lilly was me and Clarice's teacher and Miss Hannah was Ruby and Garnet's Teacher. We walked into the classroom where kids who didn't stay at Red Sands Residential Dormitory were seated in the desks at the front of the classroom. They all turned around to gawk at us. I looked around and saw a bookcase full of books. I was surprised because my name was taped to the top of my desk like everyone. Miss Lilly spent the days teaching us the alphabet, color words, and how to use a pencil the correct way. For many weeks, she routinely gave these instructions: "I start at 2 o'clock, pass 10, pass 8, touch the baseline, and back up to 2 o'clock. Ok. This is how we learn to write our letters perfectly." Miss Lilly instructed us in a soft voice, and I learned to find comfort. "Your clock letters are letters /a/, /c/, /d/, /f, /g/, /s/, /q/, and /o/." And, when we write letters /b/, /h/, /i/, /j/, /k/, and /l/. We always start at 12 o'clock and go straight down to 6 o'clock at the baseline. This helps our letters to stand tall and not lean." When she said lean, she would lean her body to the right. As she gave instructions, she walked around the room checking to make sure our letters were perfect. An occasional, "Good job," or "Nicely done, young lady," or "Uh, oh. We don't go below the baseline." Her voice was calm and gentle. Not like Mrs. Becenti's harsh tone. Miss Lilly even looked at us like she liked us. Her long blonde hair was tied into one ponytail that hung down her back. She wore a pretty dress every day. Wouldn't you know, she smelled like vanilla and cinnamon sugar! It was easy to find comfort in her presence. We looked forward to her reading a couple of books after lunch. Right away, I noticed lunch at school was a different story! It was actually yummy! Two things to look forward to!

Before we knew it, Friday came. I saw kids being checked out for the weekend, by their parents. Ruby and Garnet said goodbyes and were checked out right after school. That left Clarice and me to huddle together in an almost empty Dorm A. The first weekend dragged by with the same mundane routine and before I knew it, Mondays turned to Fridays, and weeks turned to the winter months as I crossed off the days on my calendar. I was not checked out, but Gramps made sure he wrote letters that told of the goings on out at Tohatchi Flats. Letters from mom came far and few between and always ended with a promise of a visit I learned not to expect. I drew pictures and wrote a few lines about what I was doing on the backs of each. I practiced my letters so they would be perfect, and Gramps, Gramma, and mom would know that I was learning to read and write. These were tucked into the envelopes mom had prepared for me and sent off to my Grandparents and mother. I savored every word they wrote with an ink pen and imagined what and where Gramps was talking about. I taped each postcard in my "Letters from Home" notebook. When I was lonely, I took the notebook out of my footlocker and read them over and over again. I ran my fingers along the lines to feel his gentle hands and knew his heart was right there. He always remembered to put in a dollar bill so that I could have some snacks every now and then. I remember the first couple of weekends were unbearable. I did remember to rise early and pray for safety and believed that the Holy People, God, and the Pope heard my words. It wasn't until the 6th weekend that my mom finally came to visit.

She had borrowed Uncle Leonard's truck, but only for the day. I was finally one of those kids who was checked out, even if it wasn't overnight. I found comfort and happiness to smell that familiar grease, oil, and Gramps' smells. We spent our day at a place I learned later was called Heward Park where we had a picnic of Kentucky Fried Chicken, mashed potatoes, and biscuit with honey! Mom told me about her factory job assembling components for the government. All the workers there are Navajo, she explained. I found out she was renting a room from her cousin Roberta, who was also working at a place called Fairchild. She asked me how I liked school and what I was learning. I gave her the picture of our family, that Miss Lilly had us draw during Art time. There was mom, dad, Gramps and Gramma in front of the stone castle and the golden sunrise. In the distance were the sheep waiting in the corral and horses eating hay near the barn. I made sure I drew the sandstone hill, too. I tried to draw a horse and cow, but they looked like dogs. I felt awkward when Mom took one look at the picture, folded it in four and put it in her purse and say, "You did a good job, Shí yázhi." I could tell she didn't like that I included dad. Next time, I won't include him. By then, I had forgotten what he looked like and how his voice sounded, anyway. I guess Mom didn't forget what he did to her, because she was quiet and turned her eyes to the tall pine trees that moved with the slightest breeze and to the kids' playing baseball across the park. She quickly changed the subject, telling me about the snacks she had brought me from Babbitt's grocery store. It was a two-hour visit and before long it was time to return to my *home,* so we packed up and drove to the gas station. She filled up the gas tank before checking me back into Red Sands Residential Dormitory. She tried to give me the leftover chicken, but I insisted she might need it on her long trip back to wherever she lived. I proudly showed her where I slept and kept my belongings, hoping she would notice that I straightened everything up for her visit. She frowned as she looked around and peered down the hallway. I felt another bit of awkwardness, so I decided to show her where we went to play. She looked left and right as we walked down the long hallway towards the double doors. With a look of disgust she said, "This looks like an Army barracks and smells like feet," she said under her breath. The sounds made by a few kids, who were hanging around in their bunk area, drifted down the "barracks". I took a deep breath and let go of her hand to open the heavy door. I showed her the playground where we spent our time when we weren't at school. I pointed to the gate and explained that we walked through the gate down the sidewalk that led to Red Sands Elementary School. I told her my Teacher Miss Lilly was nice and smelled like vanilla and cinnamon sugar. I told her everything about my daily life, but she didn't seem to be listening and kept looking at her watch. I didn't dare mention Mrs. Becenti though. I wished that time would stand still, or that mom would take me home with her, but before I knew it, it was time for her to make the long trip back to Shiprock. I walked her to the door and onto the concrete porch that held a row of six steps that led to the dirt parking lot. We gave each other the longest, tightest hug. Mom was wearing perfume that smelled like roses, and I noticed that she had lost weight. The tears I had stored in my heart rushed out of me and onto the green polyester pantsuit she had made for herself. I felt my mother's tears land on the top of my head and my hair wet.

"Shí yázhi, study hard and remember to write to me. I will do my best to visit you again soon. Gramma and Grandpa will pick you up for Thanksgiving break. I will meet you at Tohatchi Flats and we will celebrate your birthday with Grampa!!"

"I love you Momma. I miss you every day! I am lonely but I have friends here. Don't worry about me, I will be strong and remember this is for my own good. Right Momma?" I felt like I was talking to myself, and over time I was right.

"Yes, Shí'yázhi – for your own good." I noticed she looked at her watch and let go of my grip.

I watched her climb into Uncle Leonard's truck, named Bluebird. I remember standing at the top of the porch and waiting for Bluebird to rumble over the cattle guard, roll over the bump and ease left onto Eerie Street. I watched until I could no longer see the Bluebird, took a deep breath, wiped my tears, and wandered back into Dorm A. My innocent almost six-year-old mind remembered thinking that I would not be seeing her at Red Sands Residential Dormitory again for weeks or even months. I was right.

Chapter 3 – Time Ticks By

I learned that if I kept myself busy, time would go by fast, and Thanksgiving would arrive soon. I check off the days on the calendar Gramps bought me. Weekends came and went. The usual sounds of kids getting checked out and then long lonely weekends alone became routine. My penmanship was getting better, and I learned to love reading. I had to get special permission to check out more than 2 books from Mrs. Haney, the school Librarian. She made me sign a paper that said I would have to pay for any damages or God-forbid if I lost a book. The characters in the books soon became my imaginary friends on those long nights, especially if all three of my friends got checked out. I found myself looking forward to the movies they showed on the weekends. I had no choice but to think of Red Sands Residential Dormitory as my *home*.

It was probably after the third weekend that Clarice started bringing me something special from home. Homemade tortillas with grilled mutton, chocolate cake, and frybread were my favorites. One Sunday, she even brought me a pair of pants and a blouse with tiny flowers on it. She found it at a place she called Monkey Wards and begged her mother to buy it for me. I later learned that the store was called Montgomery Wards. I was so excited and yet felt secretly embarrassed. My four sets of clothes could only be switched around in so many ways. Now, I have five sets. I used the few dollars my Gramps and mom sent me to buy bobby socks at the little store tucked in the corner of the Multipurpose Room. There they sold candy, pencils, notebooks, socks, underwear, t-shirts that had Red Sands Residential – Home of the Roadrunners printed on the front. I wore my new outfit for Picture Day.

It was only a couple of weeks after we had been dumped off at Red Sands Residential Dormitory that I started to observe everything. It helped me feel safe for some odd reason. I noticed Garnet's parents began to pick her up every other weekend. I was happier the weekends she didn't go home. We took turns reading the books I had checked out. She taught me how to play string games. We competed to see who could swing the highest, until Mrs. Hagga put a stop to that sort of fun. It didn't take long for us to begin hating Mrs. Hagga, especially if she had the night shift. Garnet was an observer, too. She didn't say much, but when she did, I could tell she was paying more attention than I thought. I remember the time she alerted me about Mrs. Hagga. "That lady smells like whiskey! Look at her eyes. They're all watery. When we were on the playground, I overheard some of the older girls say she makes them do her duty work at night! Watch out for her, she's evil!" My eyes grew wide, and I suddenly felt scared knowing that whiskey made my dad angry, every time! I decided not to get in Mrs. Hagga's way.

I turned the pages of my notebook from August to October, remembering what it was like to be five years old and alone in a place where they put us kids to live on our own - together. With a deep sigh, my memories drifted to the anxious feeling I had knowing it was almost Thanksgiving, and that my Grandparents would soon arrive to take me home – to Tohatchi Flats. I also noticed the leaves on the trees were turning yellow and the sun was coming up a little later than usual. Lately, there have been black clouds growing in the distant horizon at different times of the day, but mostly during the early evening. I wondered if they were filled with rain or heavy with snow.

For Halloween, the Dorm Aides put together a costume party. They put boxes of costumes, for us to choose from, on the tables in the Multipurpose Room. I chose Snow White. It was a plastic costume with strings at the collar to tie behind my neck. I wore it over my clothes. The plastic mask had Snow White's face painted on it with black hair and a red bow. I remember it made my face sweat when I breathed in and out. The plastic costume made noises when I walked. They decorated the room with orange and black streamers everywhere. They had games like Pin-the-Tail on the Donkey, cake walk, and music for dancing. Clarice wore the Wonder Woman costume, Garnett wore the Cowgirl costume, and Ruby chose the clown costume. The shuffling noise our costumes made filled the hallway and the Multipurpose Room, but the music soon drowned it out. Before we knew it, we were sweating and having fun. By the end of the night, the snow had started to fall. We piled on our extra blankets to keep warm from then on. The morning snow had piled to 2 feet and was enough for us to make snowmen. We had a snowman contest. The girls that dressed their snowman like a witch won! Our snowmen stood outside until they melted into the ground and turned to ice.

I didn't know that one of the papers Gramps had filled out was for Tribal Clothing. It was a Navajo program that provided clothing, jackets, underwear, socks, and shoes once a year. It's a good thing our Tribal Clothing came in because I didn't have a warm jacket. The one I got was brown and had white fur around the hood. The mittens were also brown. With the clothing they gave me, I now had 7 sets of clothes and a pair of track shoes. These are things I wrote about to my mom and Grandparents. Gramps letters told me of how he and my uncles herded the cattle and horses down from the mountain to Tohatchi Flats. But the sheep were loaded into the long, Army green, horse trailer hitched on the back of Uncle Benny's truck, named Bronze Bullet. Gramma had finished weaving her black, grey, and white diamond patterned rug, and sold it for $10,000 at Richardson's Trading Post. The money would be used to buy hay, grain, and everything else they needed. Gramma had already started another rug that would be brown and gray. To my delight, the letter Gramps sent also had five one-dollar bills tucked in the middle and best of all he folded a teaspoon of corn pollen in a small paper he marked "open carefully." Ten more days until Thanksgiving break! Letters from mom were farther apart and fewer in between. I remember wondering what kept her so busy. Who knew? I remember writing to tell her how much I missed her and asked why she didn't write to me. I was too young to understand why she became so distant or why she never answered my endless questions.

The one constant was the activities at school that kept me busy. Miss Lilly took down the Halloween art and put up the turkeys that we made with our handprint and construction paper. Both

Miss Lilly and Miss Hannah displayed these turkeys outside their classrooms. Miss Lilly got some pinecones that we decorated with pipe cleaners and construction paper to make turkey centerpieces. We had fun trying to make the turkey stand on the pipe cleaners. The fun times at school helped balance out the bad moments and bad food at Red Sands Residential Dormitory. Clarice, Garnet, Ruby, and I carefully stored our pinecone turkeys in our footlockers. Each day the four of us walked to school, played with each other at lunch recess, and walked back to the dorm after school. This became our routine, day in and day out. We learned to depend on each other in the short amount of time we had been left at Red Sands Residential Dormitory. I remember thinking that we had no choice.

After school, we practiced our handwriting, addition and subtraction with Mrs. Montano, the nice Dorm Matron. She had black curly hair and spoke with an accent. She told us she was Mexican and grew up in Red Sands. Her father worked on the Pacific Railroad that ran East and West through town, and her mother stayed at home to take care of her and her two sisters. She brought her transistor radio and let us listen to music while we did our homework. Her perfume smelled like the honeysuckles that grew along the fence at school. She had thin fingers, wore paint on her nails, and red lipstick. Her smile held the most perfect teeth I had ever seen. Mrs. Montano always wore a dress. She would bring us the popcorn she cooked at home until Mrs. Becenti put a stop to her kindness. It wasn't long before we all began to really hate Mrs. Becenti. Unexpectedly, I found a chalk board in the corner hall with dormitory workers' names showing if they were on duty or off. We would take turns sneaking over there to see who was on duty. We learned to check the On-Duty board to warn each other who would be on duty. Mrs. Montano didn't have a ring of keys, nor did she wear a starched stiff blue uniform like the others. She asked me if I was Mexican, and claimed I had a twin in one of her nieces. As I look back on those early years, my prayers were answered by the Holy People, God, and the Pope, because Mrs. Montano was a kind, gentle, and caring person. Unlike Mrs. Becenti or Mrs. Hagga, we looked forward to seeing

Mrs. Montoya after school and having her nearby until the night shift ended. At times we found ourselves calling her mom by mistake.

Like clockwork, the day shift checked out, while the night shift checked in, always hovering over us and keeping track of every second of our time. My nine-year prison sentence had its ups and its downs, for sure. I always give thanks to the Holy People, God, and the Pope for sending me Mrs. Montano and my three friends I learned to call sisters. These are the seven people I counted on, as I learned why Red Sands Residential Dormitory was for my own good.

Chapter 4 - Home for the Holiday

I wrote or drew pictures in my notebook at least once a week. This entry was the week before Thanksgiving Break.

November 14, 1965. I can't wait for five days to go by fast! Gramps wrote they would be here to pick me up at noon on Friday! ☺

One by one, I crossed off these days on my calendar. I remember the excitement I felt Thursday evening. I couldn't wait to find out how many lambs and colts were born, and who would show up first. I COULD NOT WAIT!

Miss Lilly took down the turkey hands we made, while Mrs. Barber gave us the spelling test. "The first word is /the/. It has 3 letters." Students looked at the ceiling, trying to remember each word as they spelled and wrote each word. There were thirty-five words including the number words to twenty and ten color words. I studied hard over the weekend because I wanted 100%. I could see some of the boys, including Terry Yazzie and Cory Bennett, tapping their pencils on their head, struggling to write the words. When the torture was finished, Miss Lilly had finished taking down the turkey hands and asked for volunteers to pass them out. Catherine and Margaret were picked to do the job, even though there were a couple of brown hands that went up. Clarice and I learned not to raise our hand to volunteer, because most likely we would not be chosen to do one of Miss Lilly's many chores. Catherine and Margaret were rewarded with a butterscotch drop. We carefully put our turkey hands in our tote bags and walked down to the library. I loved Library Days! We went to the library two times a week. Mrs. Haney a skinny short. white woman wore her black and white hair pulled in a bun behind her neck, like Mrs. Becenti did. She knew where all the library books were and always had a suggestion for those who didn't know what to check out. We could check out one book. I picked the book *Madeline*. Clarice picked *We Like Kindergarten*. I remember wondering if I would ever see a river like the one in Tennessee. I guess this is why I liked *Madeline* so much. We used to go on picnics near the water. There was no water, only the red dirt and red sandstone hills here at Red Sands. I felt sad because I was starting to forget what Tennessee looked like, and what it was like to have music all around, two parents at home – or even one parent nearby. The first ninety-eight days at Red Sands Residential Dormitory taught me to keep my eyes open, follow the rules, and time was a constant companion.

The Cafeteria Ladies were busy cooking turkey, mashed potatoes, and the fluffy, buttery yeast rolls we loved on the day before I would be finally check out for the Thanksgiving break. By dinner time the cranberry jelly was chilled, and the spice cake frosted, and like mice we lined up as soon as we heard the jingle of keys, the shuffling of the starched stiff uniforms, and the sound of squeaky shoes getting louder as the noise went from Dorm B to Dorm A. In ninety-eight days, this was the first one Mrs. Becenti did not pull anyone by the ear, and she actually looked a little happy, probably because she would have the dorm to herself.

Everyone had a smile on their faces as we marched one by one down the hall and into the cafeteria. The delicious smell of our special dinner was scooped onto the plastic trays. There weren't any noises in the cafeteria as the kids gobbled down the food that we could recognize. The smell even matched the taste – for once. Clarice, Garnet, Ruby, and I took our time eating. We knew that the next meal would be mystery meal or one of their **B**eans for **I**ndian **A**lways on the Menu-day.

As usual, Ruby and Clarice were the first to get picked up on Friday. Through the huge window, Garnet and I watched them slowly ease over the cattle guard and disappear. We shed a few tears. Garnet's mother and her new stepdad showed up around an hour later.

Garnet whispered, "Great, he looks mean. I already don't like him. Pray for me, Flo."

"I will. Pray for me, too."

The new stepdad picked up her footlocker and loaded it in the back of his light blue Monte Carlo. It had a huge window in the back curved like an upside-down bowl. Garnet peered out the window, waving to me, as I stood at the huge window in the Multipurpose Room. I took a deep breath and hoped that Gramps would be there soon. I laid down on my bunk for what seemed like an hour, when Mrs. Hagga's ugly, wrinkled hands roughly woke me from my sleep. "Hey! Get up! Your Grandfather is here! Get your stuffs."

I didn't mean to fall asleep, but the excitement was too much. The sadness of watching my friends leave became a routine over time. Finally, Gramps arrived to take me to the Promised Land. I dragged my footlocker to the Multipurpose Room, where Gramps stood in a line before checking me out. I sat waiting on my footlocker and ran to hug his leg as soon as he turned to greet me. He grabbed my hands into his and gave me a big hug!

"It is so good to see you, Grandchild!" He picked up my footlocker and together we walked down the steps to where his faithful steed, Red Robin with all its stock-rack glory waited to carry us home. With the tailgate down, he pushed it right under the back window and tied it down with a bailing wire. I was walking on clouds! I didn't see Gramma in the truck. Gramps explained she had to stay with the sheep and wait for the rest of the family to arrive. Gramps lifted me onto the seat, locked and closed my door. He took a deep breath, looked up in the sky then his watch and said, "We have a long way to go."

He fired up Red Robin and soon we were rumbling over the cattle guard, over the bump, and easing onto Erie Street. I made a mental note of every step of the way so I would know what mom, or my grandparents were seeing when they dropped me off next time. We merged onto the main highway, that was packed with vehicles traveling both ways. The wind picked up and the dark winter clouds meant it would begin to snow soon. We ate the tortilla and mutton sandwich Gramma had made us, while Gramps drove. There was no time to stop. It wasn't long before I fell asleep. I woke up to Gramps, whistling the familiar Peyote Song

I learned to love. "You must have been tired, Grandchild. You slept for two hours. Who is Mrs. Hagga?" He chuckled. "I was tired, Gramps. You do not want to know Mrs. Hagga." He turned his head to look at me, but I kept my eyes straight and took a deep breath. I recognized the vast desert landscape and knew I was almost home. We stopped at Ya-ta-hey for gas. Gramps handed me a paper bag with the usual goodies for us to savor. Even though it was snowing, we enjoyed the orange and cherry bullet pop while Red Robin bumped up and down as the stock rack rattled to the tune of the freshly plowed snow-covered dirt road.

The road that leads to Halgaii was covered with a light dusting of snow that started falling earlier. The black clouds billowed overhead as the sun slowly set behind Chuska Mountain. I pulled the brown jacket with the furry hood around me as I scooted next to Gramps. He reached behind him and pulled out the Pendleton blanket they kept in Red Robin for those cold days. The familiar vehicle oil and Vicks comforted me, and I knew I was home. The winter sun was slowly drifting to sunset, by the time we reached the end of the 15-miles it took to round the sandstone hill and reach the stone castle. There, yellow orange light emanated from the lanterns as shadows danced from inside the window. Gramps parked, unloaded my footlocker, placing it in the shed. I opened the door and burst in to see Gramma had started another beautiful rug. Gramma waited by the potbelly stove with a happy smile. "Yá'áh'tééh, Shí'yázhi'!" I rushed to hug her, while Gramps' stayed outside to check on the livestock before joining us.

It looked like she was about halfway through and would most likely be finished by spring when they would take it to Richardson's Pawn Shop in Gallup or to the Crownpoint Rug Auction. I hooked my jacket on the wooden coat rack next to the door. I sat by her side and felt like I had just left yesterday when her soft hands gently squeezed mine and her loving eyes smiled at me. I will always remember that moment. I quietly sat by Gramma trying not to disturb her rhythmic pounding with the wood comb. White wool thread made from wool sheared from the summer before was woven in and out across the warp of the loom. I would learn later that Gramma had the Tó'dí'ch'ii'ni'

(Bitterwater) Ladies from Two Greyhills card the wool for her into balls of thread. Gramma stored her wool thread in a tall wicker basket that had a lid. When she got down to the end of the line, she stopped and lovingly looked down at me. She said some words to me that I recognized as, how good it was to have me home and if I was hungry.

I had memorized her face so I could remember her while I was gone. I had forgotten she had light brown eyes that looked like root beer bottles when light shines through them. Her reddish-brown hair was held in a Navajo bun with a white yarn holding it together in a knot. This is the traditional way Navajo men and women wear their hair. She stood up, gave me a side hug, and expressed her emotions through the loving words rolling off her tongue. "Shí'yázhí', you look so good to see after a long day of work. We missed you very much!" Gramps translated her words to me as she stirred the stew on the potbelly which roared with a fire that heated up my castle in the desert. I remember smiling seeing the pictures I had sent posted here and there on the wall. I could see Gramma had unfolded my bed and placed it in the corner. Gramps went back outside to check on the sheep, when the first of our relatives started arriving. Some would sleep in the Stone Castle and the others would sleep next door at Gramma's brother Charlie's home. My younger cousins Ernessa and Cheryl slept in my bed, while the boys slept in another fold out bed. Every corner was occupied and served as a place to sleep. Gramma took her special cup, filled it with tea, sprinkling sugar over the top to give it some flavor. She pushed it across the plastic tablecloth with the sunflower print to me and began to flap out some tortillas for our dinner. Soon, the smell of stew, fresh tortillas, and Navajo Tea filled the air. Bowls and spoons were set out. I blew my tea until it was cool enough to take a drink. It was heaven!

I remembered gathering Navajo Tea during the summer before I had to leave for Red Sand Residential Dormitory. It seemed like a long time ago when we went up the mountain to the place where they grew wild. Five months ago, seemed like a long time ago in the mind of an almost six-year-old. I helped Gramma and my cousins bend the stems into small bunches that were tied with thin white thread. They were hung from the ceiling to dry, like the chili ristras at Genaro's Mexican Restaurant. I noticed that in this one-room living space, much could be stored. So much was done in that calm warm place; weave, cook, eat, sleep, and gather. The wooden, shade house that Gramps called a Chaha'oh' stood silent weathering countless winter storms. It was used for outdoor cooking and living during the spring and summer. Aside from the weather, not much had changed on Tohatchi Flats. That was o.k. by me! My dream has come true and now I'm going to enjoy every moment I have, being away from Red Sands Residential Dormitory.

There is a calm, cool, winter freeze as the nearby Chuska Mountain exhales a sign of relief. Bright umber sunlight slowly drifted beyond the western horizon and the clear skies dimmed with the twinkling lights against a deep purple sky. I remember all of this, along with the pitch-dark nights that settled across Tohatchi Flats like a safe blanket.

As I look back at the intrusive and destructive Bureau of Indian Affairs Dormitory life was meant to "kill the Indian and save the man," my Dine' teachings and memories are what kept me sane all those years ago.

While spending year after year in a sterile world, the stories my Gramps told us echoed across the miles comforted and kept me sane. I remember the smell of cedar wood drifting from the old wood stove, simmering, crackling, and popping like a symphony. Firelight seeped and danced through the cracks of the steel pipe lifting the smoke out into the night. Every note created a dramatic backdrop to Gramps' stories. The one I loved the most is the Navajo Creation Story, the foundation of our existence. Gramps was already 60 years old when I met him. His long stride, hazel eyes, and steel stare were humbled by the sacred words gifted by the Holy People – Diyin Dine'é'. His large shadow grew along the wall that was the home he built for his 10 children. He taught all of us to have a good work ethic, as well as to enjoy the simple things in life. Storytelling was one of those simple and important things. Certain stories were told in the summer and certain stories were told in the winter.

By the second night of my Thanksgiving break, most of my cousins had arrived and settled in, it was time for Gramps to tell the Creation Story of the Dine. "Grandchildren, the Creation Story is one of the most important stories you will learn about where we came from and can only told during the winter months." We gathered on the floor or wherever we could find a place to sit. My uncles and aunties were next door playing a card game called Navajo 10. They put two decks of cards together for the game. It is a complicated game to learn.

His shadow danced, swaying back and forth, and like clockwork his long arms flayed here and there. His massive hands helped to tell the story passed down to us, The People – Dine'. Even though, Navajo is a label given to us by the Mexicans, we refer to ourselves as Dine' which means "The People". The Creation Story is only retold during the winter. This was the one story we waited all year long to hear.

"My Grandchildren, our Dine' culture begins in Nihodilhil – the First World. It is surrounded by four clouds columns. There was White Dawn in the East, Blue Daylight in the South, Yellow Twilight to the West, and Black Clouds to the north. This is where Diyin' Dine'é lived with the insects. The place where the Black Clouds in the North meets the White Cloud in the East is the very place First Man was formed. Along with him was formed the most beautiful and perfect ear of white corn with twelve rows of kernel covering the whole ear. Gramps took a deep breath, cleared his throat, and took a drink of water.

Next, the place where Yellow Cloud in the West meets with Blue Cloud in the South, is where First Woman was formed. With her came a beautiful perfect ear of yellow corn." Our little eyes were wide with curiosity as Gramps' voice became loud. "The Holy People did not like it when First Man and First Woman went against their teachings – so they destroyed the First World with fire. First Man took a Big Reed and planted it in the east, where it grew very tall. This is the path all the creatures used to escape through to the Second World." My cousins and I looked at each other not knowing if First Man, First Woman, or the creatures would make it…all sat quietly as we were taught to do, whenever Gramps or Gramma speaking or talking. Gramps shifted his body, and his shadow swayed with him. "First Man, First Woman and the creatures made their way up to the Second World – Ni'hodoot'izh – the Blue World. It is here they found birds, insects, and animals. First Man used his medicine bundle that carried the four clouds he had brought from the First World, and like magic the clouds rose again at the edges of the Second World." We silently clapped; glad they made their way out of the First World safe while imagining a world that was blue. Gramps peered at us over his eyeglasses and cleared his throat. "In the Second World there was suffering and sorrow, because we know that the Holy People will punish those who violate or do not follow their teachings. The Holy People once again became angry and destroyed the Second World with wind. First Woman and the creatures looked to First Man to find an escape. He sent Zigzag Lightning, Straight Lightning, Rainbow, and Sunray into the four directions, but they were unable to find a way out!" We scooted together, scared because it sounded hopeless. Finally, First Man decided to make a prayer stick of Whiteshell, Turquoise, Abalone, and Jet. He drew four footprints on it. They all stood on the footprints and rose up through the reed plant in the south and escaped the Third World." We took a collective deep breath of relief, as Gramma stirred the fire and added another log. The flame in the kerosene lamp swayed and danced from light to dim and Gramps' shadow grew to the ceiling of our castle. Gramps took a swig of his water and cleared his throat. "As they escaped from the Second World, First Man carried with him the inner forms of earth, plants and clouds. "The Third World was Yellow – Ni'haltsoh." The little ones thought of the Black World, the Blue World and imagined a world that was Yellow. "When they emerged to the Yellow World, they found two rivers, a female river running east to west and a male river running north to south. First Man put a Whiteshell in the east, a Turquoise to the south, an Abalone to the west and Jet to the north. He blew on them four times and they grew and expanded and met overhead. This is where they made a Hogan that became the world. First Man took soil he brought from the Second World and made the sacred mountains. Dawn Mountain to the east, Turquoise Mountain to the south, Abalone Shell Mountain in the west, and Jet Mountain to the north." I was amazed because I knew about the Sacred Mountains and now, I know how they were formed. "The Yellow World is where First Man, First Woman, the creatures and all who came from the Blue World would meet Coyote – Maii. Maii is important to the Dine' culture – he can be smart, and he can be sneaky.. In the Yellow World, Maii stole the Water Monster's baby. The Water Monster began to flood the Yellow World and everyone had to escape. Once again, they escaped through the tall red reed. It was turkey who was the last to leave as the flooded waters rose to cover the Yellow World. Grandchildren, turkey's tail feathers touched the foam of the rising waters, and this is why his tail feathers are white." I remembered the turkey hand and pinecone turkey we had made in Miss Lilly's class. My turkey didn't have a white tail, and Miss Lilly didn't tell us to make the tail white. I reminded myself to bring out my pinecone turkey centerpiece for our meals.

Gramps continued, "The next world is called the Glittering World – Nihalgai. This is the world we live in today. It was locust that reached the Glittering World first. Glittering World was covered with water. They tried everything to drain the flood, but every time the water came back up. It was First Man that discovered that Maii stole the Water Monster's baby. Being the Leader of everyone, First Man had to force Maii to throw the baby back down the red reed and that is when the floods receded. First Man once again placed the Sacred Mountains where they belonged, he began to take out the stars, the sun, and the moon, and place them in the sky. He placed them carefully one by one. Maii, being sneaky, became impatient. That means he couldn't wait. Maii snatched up the corner of the blanket the held the stars and flipped them randomly across the sky. Those are the stars you see in the sky at night. It is in the Glittering World that Changing Woman was born. When she became a woman, she gave birth to the Hero Twins – Monster Slayer and Child Born of Water. Their father was the Sun. They wanted to meet him, so they took a dangerous journey to the Sun. It was the Hero Twins that killed the monsters of the Glittering World. They made the Glittering World a safe place to live." Gramps drew a deep breath, a sip of his water and cleared his throat. The little ones drew a deep breath too.

"I'll tell you some more when you come back from school. Grandchildren, never forget where you come from. You come from courageous people and good blood."

The little ones moaned, "Aww Gramps, we're not tired! We want to hear more!" "Grandchildren, it is late, and tomorrow is another day."

Gramps looked at his Grandchildren with loving, hazel eyes over his wire framed glasses and said, "Grandchildren, your Gramma is asleep in her chair. She needs to go to bed too."

We looked back to see Gramma's holding her head with her hand and sound asleep.

"Okay, Gramps."

A lonely column of cedar smoke drifted from the embers that Gramps took to the fire in the potbelly stove, and we stood in line. This offering to bless ourselves. One by one, we blessed ourselves with cedar smoke. I learned to start with my feet, go up both legs and finally to my head with the cedar smoke. We gave Gramps a hug and tucked ourselves into the warm bedrolls.

Dreams of the Black World, the Blue World, the Yellow World and their Glittering World danced in their dreams….fitful dreams ensued. Yawning, I thought, "We live in the Glittering World"…smile sigh..deep breath… sleep.

Meanwhile, Gramps gently nudged Gramma awake long enough to take her to her bed. Gramps looked lovingly at his Grandchildren, knowing they would be gone in a few hours – he didn't look forward to the long quiet months, quiet days, quiet minutes, endless seconds, out on Tohatchi Flats. Deep breath, sigh, fitful dreams. My mom, who arrived late at night, stayed at Grandpa Juan's house with her siblings.

Early the following morning Mom came to join us for a small breakfast. It was so nice to be next to her again that I didn't want to leave her side. She told me about how her job kept her busy, how people in Shiprock were farmers, and how she was saving money for a home for the two of us. What I didn't know was she was working twelve-hour shifts that sometimes landed on the weekends or lasted into the evenings. This is what kept her from visiting me or checking me out for the weekend. I tried to believe her, but for some reason my instincts told me something else. I wanted to ask her about dad, but now wasn't the time. I gave her my turkey hand and some pictures I drew that didn't fit in the small envelope. This time she carefully placed them in her new blue suitcase. It was then that I noticed mom didn't have the ring dad gave her, she gained a few pounds and didn't really act the way she used to. She seemed to be more relaxed. It was so nice to be with her and smell her rose perfume. I also noticed she was wearing a cowgirl style, polyester pantsuits, and boots. She kind of looked like the ladies I saw dancing at the bars. As I sat next to her, I prayed to the Holy People, God, and the Pope to make this time go by slow.

The next day we went to Grandpa Juan's house to set up his long table for Thanksgiving dinner. My mom, aunties, and Gramma were busy cooking. Gramps and my uncles did their routine ranch chores, tending to the horses, cattle, and sheep. Finally, it was time to eat!

I placed the turkey pinecone centerpiece next to the candles Auntie Teri had lit. Auntie Margaret placed a beautiful bouquet of flowers next to our items. There were sunflowers, white chrysanthemums, and a few white carnations that smelled so nice! I knew the sunflowers were for Gramma, but the chrysanthemums and carnations were a mystery.

We all stood up for Gramma to give a blessing for the food. The men took their hats off, and we all bowed our heads to the prayer I learned to bless our meals.

As the Bluebird sings at dawn.
I breathe in the cool air to nourish my spirit.
As I sing words East to offer my Corn Pollen,
I ask Mother Earth and Father Sky to rejuvenate my
spiritual, physical, mental, and emotional health.
Through the blessing from the Holy People.
I shall Walk In Beauty of love and happiness.
The blessings shall always restore unity of my family and
community.
Hózhó Nahasdlii'
Hózhó Nahasdlii'
Hózhó Nahasdlii'
Hózhó Nahasdlii'
It is finished in Beauty.

.

She took some corn pollen from the tá'di'díín bag, placed some
on the tip of her tongue, the top of her head and sprinkled the rest
towards the East. She passed her tá'di'díín bag to her left and each
of us did the same thing. After the corn pollen, water was passed
around by Auntie Sarah. It was finally time to sit down and dig
into a real meal! The kind where the look of turkey tasted like
turkey and not the mystery food that came out of a can. There
were jokes, laughter, and everyone getting seconds of their
favorite dish. I loved the green Jello, marshmallow, pineapple,
walnuts, cottage cheese, whipped cream salad. I found out it was
called Grasshopper Salad. I leaned over and asked Uncle Ed if
there were real grasshoppers in the salad. He laughed and said,
"No, Shí'yázhi' it's just a name." In Navajo he told everyone what
I had asked. Everyone busted up laughing! I turned beet red! One
thing for sure was Auntie Teri's pumpkin pie was to die for! I
remember looking forward to these two desserts at our family
dinners from then on.

Just when I thought our meal was over, my mom placed a large
box on the table. There was a large rectangular birthday cake with
these words written on it, "Happy Birthday, Grampa and
Florence!" I took one look at Gramps and right then, I knew why

we had such a special bond. We shared the same birthdate – November 22nd

"On 3 – 1, 2, 3, Happy Birthday to you!" The sound of everyone singing for Gramps and me was the topping of my Thanksgiving Break! We blew out the candles together and everyone clapped. My mom cut the cake and as the Birthday Girl it was my job to serve everyone a slice. Auntie Sarah scooped out the ice cream. The chocolate marble cake with the white frosting and Neapolitan ice cream melted in my mouth! Gramps and Gramma gave me a silver bracelet with a round turquoise stone that fit perfectly. My mom got me a red View Master with Pinocchio and Snow-White pictures. There were color pencils, crayons, pencils, a pick-up sticks game, two balls and a set of jacks, two sketch books, and two lined notebooks. My eyes lit up after Cousin Chuckie showed me how to use the View Master. We spent the afternoon taking turns looking through the pictures. I also got a new jacket and some clothes from my aunties and uncle. Gramps got a Wrangler Jacket that had a thick lining for those winter days, and a turquoise and coral bolo tie. His eyes twinkled and he smiled as he tried on his new jacket. "Nizhóni'yeé' (*beautiful*) It feels just right!"

After the meal was cleaned up, my cousins helped dry the dishes while mom and her sisters washed them. Gramps, Gramma, my uncles, and other relatives drank fresh-made coffee. Later, they set out to finish tending to the horses, cattle, and sheep for the day. Gramps took the sheep out for a bit. My cousins and I walked around where he was herding sheep, enjoying the cold weather. There wasn't enough snow to make a snowman, though.

Memories of my first Thanksgiving at Tohatchi Flats will hold an indelible place in my heart and soul.

Chapter 5 – Movie Night

I remember being in fourth grade and having spent over one thousand days at Red Sands Residential Dormitory. I reminisced about the good days and the bad days along this nine-year journey. The good times included movie night. The powers that be allowed a treat-night that included a reel-to-reel movie. Over the years, we watched movies like "The King and I"," Mary Poppins", "The Song of The South", and "The Wizard of Oz.". These were all good movies and all of us were thankful for having the "opportunity" to watch these movies. First, and every time, we had to watch, "Mr. Bungle Goes to Lunch" to learn lunchroom manners. It would've been funny to see one of us throw our tray off the table, like Mr. Bungle warned us not to do. To this day, we made sure our hands were washed with a lot of soap before we ate, and we checked our hair to make sure it was neat. Too bad, our food didn't look like what Mr. Bungle was going to eat. The endless list of dos and don'ts a child of the Bureau of Indian Affairs had to abide by, came in many forms.

After each movie, and for a few minutes, everyone left the Multipurpose Room happy and uplifted. This was probably because there were stories of people with impossible troubles and impossible adventures, and the lessons were miraculously learned at the end of each story. The "Everyone lived happily ever after" theme among Disney films was a topic in Miss Clayberg's English class. Most students bought into that hopeful image yet watched as their parents were truly unhappy in their desperate lives.

By now, we knew NOTHING ever ends, "Happily Ever After." It was this year, in particular, I found myself thinking about how my life would turn out after all. That didn't stop me from dreaming about flying to Neverland with Peter Pan or following the Yellow Brick Road. Film night was a night where there was utter silence during sleep. The dorm was completely quiet as we all dreamed of happy-ever-after's.

For the next month, in true Navajo fashion, the girls referred to the boys as, "The Tin Man" or "Oz" or "Peter Pan". In turn, the boys referred the girls as "Dorothy" or "Wendy..." and the Matron on Duty was always, "The Wicked Witch of the West." "Triple W" if she was nearby. Hahaha!! We made up code names for the Matrons so they wouldn't know what we were saying.

Rumor had it "The Good, The Bad and The Ugly" with the tall drink of water, Clint Eastwood, was up next! Ooh! The show was to be on Thursday after dinner at 6:30pm sharp. Plans were set as soon as the announcement was made. After school, we rushed to Safeway for our goodies. During dinner, we pretended to wolf down our food, but quietly pushed it aside. Clarice was picked to bring her tote bag to hold the goulash we hated. Outside she dumped her tote bag, and we rushed to grab pillows and claim a good spot on the floor of the Multipurpose Room. For sure, we didn't want to be like Mr. Bungle, or else!!! Ha! Ha! Pillows marked our spot...that was an unspoken rule.

The movie started out at an old ranch that looked like the place at Tohatchi Flats but, with a Mexican flair. The way Cowboys hunted each other and just went about killing each other was a scary thought for the us. Watching Clint Eastwood finesse his way around the movie captured our undivided attention from start to end. Tuco was forced to be his gullible companion, we all were for sure Blondie would kill...but he needed him. Angel Eyes was so good looking, but he had to die. We never thought Blondie would give Tuco his share; but then again, Blondie saved Tuco throughout the movie so...there you are...no wonder Blondie was "The Good."

The music was something else in and of itself. The way it moaned and whistled and knocked hard made it come to life. As always, The Good always got the prize at the end and was even nice enough to share the ill-gotten booty. That was a movie we could see over and over and over again. All agreed. One by one, the lights were switched on and the students scurried around to sweep up the popcorn and pick up any trash, so as not to cross the

Matrons on Duty. For sure, we didn't want either of them to pull a "Mr. Bungle", and start telling us all about good manners, as if!

Watching Western movies like "The Good, The Bad and The Ugly" brought a rush of memories, like I was born a hundred years too late. I think we are all old souls, my sister-friends, and I. I wondered if the people in the old West read at all, because I never saw any books in those kinds of movies...just guns and whiskey. I wondered what kept them going in all that heat and uncertainty.

I thought about writing a poem about Clint Eastwood before going to bed. Meanwhile, Garnet and Ruby were busy reading the latest "Hit Parade," and Clarice was busy stringing a silver beaded necklace for her next "show." That movie was pretty good, Clarice mused. "Yeah, Clint Eastwood is so handsome and tall! OOOH Weee! I wonder what he looks like in color," Clarice said, making us roll over with laughter.

I felt blessed to see the desert, to be in the midst of the scenery that almost mirrored Tohatchi Flats, if only for a couple of hours.

Blondie
Tall drink of water
Riding rugged lands for gold
Ill-gotten booty.

Clint Eastwood
Chiseled jaw, green eyes
Tall stature, smoking rifles
Cowboy rides solo.

Movie night was a taste of the *good life*. There was some dreaming of gun fights and that ominous music that drifted up and down the hallways! For sure, it didn't take long for Dorm A & B to settle into silent slumber. It was going to be a good sleep...dreaming of the Old West and Blondie....oooooohhhhh weeee!!!! Smile...sleep...sigh...

Chapter 6 – The Making of Our Friendship

By the end of fourth grade, I had spent 1,044 days as a ward of Red Sands Residential Dormitory. The early years became a black and white memory not to be spoken of but carefully recorded in several notebooks so my roots would not be forgotten. I continued my silent determination to do what I could to "get ahead" and it was at Red Sands Elementary School I learned to be a poet. I found a love for writing. My repeated words read, "For your own good…" were written many times and in many notebooks. These words would echo in my memory, and over the years my wondering what it meant became a source of sarcasm. Year after year, I was brought back to Red Sands Residential Dormitory …and gladly returned every summer to my beloved Tohatchi Flats. The summers were filled with work, traveling from one ranch to the other, or to town for laundry and supplies. No harsh rules to remember and lots of freedom roaming around. It was even more exciting when my cousins stayed for the summer! Days were filled with horse racing, herding sheep for endless sweltering hours, enjoying cool nights looking at the vast starry nights from the top of the hill. No worries. The visits my mother promised, whether to Red Sands or the Stone Castle turned out to be once in a great while and nowhere near "often." Over the years, we grew apart and I hardly knew who she was anymore. In the meantime, my uncles along with a lot of Navajos, were drafted by the Army to fight the Vietnam War. Time stood still out on Tohatchi Flats, and I realized the people who did not change were my three friends and my grandparents. The wooden barn held countless letters from Gramps, carefully placed in empty shoe boxes and stored in the blue footlocker I used at the beginning of this journey.

Over the years, I relied on Garnet's math skills, and she relied on my writing and reading skills. I noticed Garnet reading a book that looked a lot like the one Gramps read when we herded sheep. I remember him looking in the air and saying, "Grandchild, here is another interesting story." He called it the word of the Lord. I learned Garnet's mother mixed her Navajo tradition with any number of churches established across the Navajo reservation. In fact, she bounced from church to church, searching for her soul. Like Clarice and I, Garnet found time to pray in her own way. From the same chalk board, we learned the schedule of the Matron on Duty and what time we could sneak outside. Sneaking out in the morning was easier than the evening. Both of us had our own corn pollen pouch, blessed before we started the school year. Prayer-time helped a lot, especially those nights when the nightmares spooked me out of my sleep. I remember being awakened at midnight by noises of someone moving around in the bathroom or turning on the faucet at the end of the hall. There were many nights I was so scared I couldn't move.

Clarice and I had learned to practice traditional ways, which required self-discipline and the need for spirituality. The thought of being lazy or eating too many sweets was a "no-no". Instead of spending our free time at the playground, we ran the length of Red Sands Residential Dormitory. We did not have siblings, so we decided to call each other sister. Clarice's parents were self-employed and took her to many places I could only wonder about as she described their travels.

Clarice, who was from Ganado, but lived wherever the business was good; was one of my favorite and best friends. Every weekend she walked in with her newest beaded creation. She was one of the lucky ones, because her parents came to take her home every weekend and she always came back with something new. I grew close to her because soft-spoken Clarice knew about the Navajo ways, and she was good company during morning prayers.

One thing we did to start our day, the right way, was to run. I remember it was just another Monday morning, at the usual 5: 00 A.M, when Clarice and I got ready for our run. We tried our best to leave before the sun came out and hoped the gate was not locked. Carefully climbing over could take five minutes and a risk of getting caught meant manual labor as a punishment. There were a couple of times when either one of us ripped our shorts or sweatpants, which was not a pretty sight.

"Ready?"

"Yeah, just a sec." I quickly braided my hair and off we went.

As we walked out towards the darkened eastern sky, we reached into our pockets and pulled out our *tádidíín* pouches, gave an offering of sacred corn pollen to the Holy People and for another day. Prayers for our family, prayers for a good day, prayers for time to go fast, prayers for guts to take the treatment dished out to us, prayers for good grades, proceeding with more prayers, every day, year after year. At times, I wondered if praying for something unknown was even worth it. Yet, faith and courage were what all children of Red Sands Residential Dormitory had to count on each day.

I recall, Clarice and I were the only ones outside saying morning prayers, joined from time to time by others who dared to practice our ways. That is how our friendship became more of a sisterhood. At first, we just said a simple prayer, but as time went on, we began to sing the songs we learned. If it wasn't for Clarice, Red Sands Residential Dormitory would have been unbearable. We learned to time our escape so that the Matron on Duty did not find us A.W.O.L. each time. The prayer song was simple, eloquent, and spiritual, passed down from generation to generation and then to us.

By this song I walk.

By this song I walk.

By this song I walk.

By this song I walk.

I am walking by it.

By this song I walk.

I am Talking God.

By this song I walk.

I travel with Dawn.

By this song I walk.

I travel with White Corn.

By this song I walk.

I travel by Hard Goods.

By this song I walk.

I travel by Hard Rain

By this song I walk

I travel by Corn Pollen.

By this song, I walk....

In Beauty I pray before me

In Beauty I pray behind me

In Beauty I pray all around me

In Beauty it is said.

Breathing in the spring air seemed to bring a sense of freedom like nothing else. Our muscles burned as we ran until the white beams of sunlight filtered over the eastern horizon and began our run back towards Dorm "A," silently thinking of days gone by and times to come. The thought of the end of the year dance was on our mind as it neared.

We smiled because we knew we had begun the day properly. What my mother did not provide, the universe gifted me through the kindness of others. Clarice showed me how to be creative and generous.

"Flo, I bought you something from Gallup," Clarice said as she twisted the buckskin tie around her pouch.

"What? I hope it's mutton samwich..aay" I asked, while we started for the dorm.

"Well, let's just say you're gonna love them." Clarice was always so giving.

When we snuck back into Dorm A, Clarice presented a shoebox! I was shocked, as I hurried to open it with anticipation. "Yep, I thought we could use a new pair of track shoes, so I begged my mom to buy them. I figured you're about the same size as me, so I hope they fit." Clarice, smiling from ear to ear, watched me inspect them with excited approval.

"Perfect! Thanks! Now we can go for a longer run after our morning prayers in style, groovy! Of course, that'll mean we'll have to get up at least thirty minutes before "Mrs. Hagga, Bagga, Sagga" starts her yelling!" I saw on the Matron on Duty Board she is substituting for Mrs. Yazzie.

I gave her a tight hug, smiled, hugged my new shoes, then leaned back on the steel bunk and smelled the new rubber soles. "Oh! Thanks, Clarice, you're the coolest, you know." "Yeah, I know, besides, these track shoes will help us beat our mark before we leave this place. We better get to breakfast before we're late for school."

It was 6:00 am and there goes Mrs. Hagga standing at her usual place at the end of the hall yelling, "Line up girls! Line up!!! Mrs. Hagga yanked Garnet by the ear and forced her to quickly get in the line. That was standard practice for this place and many other **B**ullying **I**ndians **A**round residential dormitories. We all lined up in silence. Ruby stood in front while I stood behind Garnet trying to get her to stop crying. "Shhh, stop crying or she'll give it to you worse!"

All morning long that image faded in and out and made me wish for the comforts of my home on the reservation... Times like this made me wish that Mrs. Hagga would be yanked by the ear so she would know how painful it could be...but wishing only took up time and there was nothing I could do but comfort Garnet, who was already feeling bad about her weekend. I knew that at Tohatchi Flats I would never be treated like they treated kids at

Red Sands Residential Dormitory.   "For my own good, yeah right!"

<u>Feel Like Running!</u>

Sprint! Sprint into the twilight—
Where sunrise shimmers, wild with light.
Challenge me, if you dare,
Across the blazing cardinal terrain!
Dare to chase me through the flare
Before I vanish past the far-off plain.

Chapter 7 – The Haggster

As the minute hand clicked to twelve and precisely at 5:30 A.M. Like clockwork, "Get up Girls!! Get up!" Mrs. Hagga yelled, alarming everyone in Dorm A. She would proceed to Dorm B and the girls in Dorm A could hear her manly voice overpower the hallway.

Mrs. Hagga didn't take leave today, and the substitute we wished for would not miraculously appear – which would mean that we would have to deal with the Hagster twice that day…she always did double duty. Eyes-rolling..

Mrs. Hagga was a city Navajo who seemed to hate reservation Navajos. She spent the better part of thirty years living in border towns, making a living serving as a Bureau of Indian Affairs matron in several dormitories. She claimed to be a devout Christian but had an insatiable taste for alcohol. At an early age, I had seen what alcohol did to dad, knew the smell, and learned to avoid the Haggster as much as I could. Mrs. Hagga was quick to admonish any mention of traditional ways. Oh, that's just heebee jeebees and hocus pocus she would claim. None of that Navajo stuff is real. The only one that is going to come down and save you from the heavens, someday, in the near future, was her Lord Christ and Savior, she often warned. The funny part of it was, she claimed we *had* to go to *her* church each Sunday, otherwise we would never be saved from our heathen ways. Eyes rolling...

By 8:30 pm in her drunken stupor, she would try to lecture students about God often reading from the Bible, but no one ever believed her describing that the end would be coming any time soon, especially at Red Sands, Arizona. Give me a break! I rolled my eyes avoiding the whole scene. Mrs. Hagga must have thought we didn't know that she drank alcohol while working, because she always had a cup of coffee or orange juice close at hand.

Geez, Mrs. Hagga scared the life out of us when we were little. Her big-boned, big nosed, big face overpowered and petrified us

0in our tracks. Mrs. Hagga was blessed with double-wide hips and a long ass butt that looked like the back end of a cow. Her labored breathing could be heard over the cling clang of her keys and the scratchy sound of the starched matron dress she wore with pride. Mrs. Hagga did her best to fix her hair in one of those 1940s hairdos! It was one of those hair styles where she rolled her hair in half circles on either side of her head. Other times, her hair was rolled in a ball held in place by a black hairnet. The kids made fun of the brown arthritis stockings she wore to cover up the fat legs that sagged over her black loafers. Her fashion sense left a lot to be desired to be sure.

As we got older, Mrs. Hagga wasn't as scary, but we soon found out she easily flew off the handle and into an alcoholic rage, even when she was sober. It was easy to predict those times because her nostrils would flare, and she would start to stutter and sweat. We learned to find the nearest exit when she was ready to explode.

Even the older girls dread Mrs. Hagga's presence on these days. She was not as harsh to the older kids, because one time, one of the girls pushed her down and beat her up for being mean. Mrs. Hagga quickly kicked her out of Red Sands, exiled to the Promise Land, never to be seen again. After that, the girls in Dorm B didn't suffer the wrath of the Haggster, as much.

Every morning at 5:30 A.M., *THAT PHRASE*, echoed throughout the dorm halls, gnawing at my last nerve, making me want to yell, "Shut up, Mrs. Hagga, Shut UP!!" "Gosh, these dorm matrons must go to boot camp then to matron school in order to be so military!" I thought, but did not dare to voice my opinions, because I have gotten my own share of punishment from the D.M.'s, as Ruby called them. Ruby was always reading up on the Vietnam War and found that the Demilitarized Zone was something that we had at Red Sand Residential Dormitory; so naturally, the dorm matrons were Charlie, and we were on either side of the D.M. on any given day and at any given moment. In other words, there were no holds barred in their treatment of girls and boys who acted too much like Navajos, and those who stayed

0here so long that they too learned to be very militant in their thinking.

Once, one of the high school boys who we called Strawberry Freckled Face because of all the pimples he had on his face…well anyway, he was caught with Schlitz beer in his dorm room and was punished severely. Instead of making him do manual labor, he had to run up and down the football field 100 times! The boys were talking about how his feet were so blistered; he could not even walk and had to stay out of school for a week. Some of the boys sent out a note asking for money to pay for his bandages and ointment. Everyone pitched in whatever way they could. The matrons never figured out how the kids got together to save one of their own. The bottoms of his feet toughened, and he eventually ran away, returning home, like the rest of us contemplated, planned, but never had the guts to do. We guessed his parents kept him home because we never saw Strawberry Freckled Face again. Another soul exiled to the Promised Land.

After that, we all felt bad that we called him that, in the first place. A place like this makes a person do weird, out of the ordinary, things like making life hard for those that are not good looking or don't speak perfect English. "At least we gave money to heal his feet." Garnet always had something good to say.

Bureau of Indian Affairs residential dormitory life was a place where kids could learn to be sneaky and learn to retaliate… The trouble was not getting caught, or learning to look innocent when the crime scene was discovered… "We must get back at the Haggster, Clarice demanded during lunch recess! She is just getting on my last nerve! Let's think of something to make her really mad, without getting caught. What is one thing that we can't stand that she does? "

"Oh, when she yells at us to wake up! That gets on my nerves! Ruby added.

"I know!", Clarice agreed. After school, let's go to our good old friend and uncle, Harry Billy. He can help us!!

I thought, what is she going to do now, but I was right there ready for this scheme. Harry Billy was not only the butcher, but also the radio announcer for KDJI. He announced all the news in English and in Navajo. He was like a friendly messenger from home, every blasted day we spent at Red Sands Residential Dormitory. He always kept us informed of the latest reservation news. He was a comforting voice in times of loneliness and was one of those people who made an impression on the lives of many Red Sands Residential Dormitory prisoners. There was a light at the end of the tunnel when you heard Harry Billy's voice speaking Navajo, about Navajo life, to Navajo people across Navajoland, and Red Sands. How awesome was that…now let's use him to make the Haggster pay!

"This is Crazy Injun Number 9 wishing you all a great day, today on this beautiful sunny and glorious Monday morning......!" Then Harry Billy faded into speaking Navajo telling the audience about what's going on in the surrounding area. He was the number one advertiser of the Powwow Trading Post where you could find anything you needed and things you didn't know you needed! Harry Billy provided us with information about Navajoland. He told us what was going on, who was having ceremonies, where there was a great sale on mutton…that for a long time was torture for those of us who loved mutton. Of course, that would be every student at Red Sands Residential Dormitory. Yes, Harry Billy was a great big, gigantic part of our Navajo life here at Red Sands Residential Dormitory. It was almost as if Harry Billy was our uncle; advising us of who we were as Navajos, and what we should and should not do while we were held like prisoners at Red Sands Dormitory. The thing Harry Billy did was tell us what was going on in the Promise Land – Navajoland, the place we keep at the tip of our tongues and the top of our minds.

The time ticked away, but when the bell finally rang FREEDOM! We were out the door like a light!

"Okay, what's the plan", Ruby demanded.

"Wait a minute!" Clarice chided.

We practically ran full force down Elm Street to Babbitt's Market where Harry Billy had his head down, concentrating on a side of beef. He looked up, curled his eyebrows, and smiled with a twinkle in his eyes.

"I know that lady. She's not very nice. is she?" was Harry's only comment after he agreed to be our sneaky coyote!

The next morning, the girls who had radios strategically turned the volume to high, and placed them up and down Dorm A & B. At precisely 5:30 A.M. the Haggster opened her mouth we were quick to turn KDJI on with the sounds of Harry Billy. Usually, Harry would start with the news or by announcing the next song...but this time, he came on the air without any announcements! Instead, the song "Bad Moon on the Rise" by Credence Clearwater Revival blasted the air waves down the halls of Red Sands Residential Dormitory! The radios were set on the highest volume so for once in many years, the Haggster's voice was never heard! She was so mad and red with anger as she marched up and down Dorm A demanding us to turn off our radios, that the girls in Dorm B snuck across the hallway to find out how the Haggster reacted. The commotion was our saving grace as the Haggster turned her attention to rushing them back to Dorm B in their night gowns. The Haggster was silenced! That stunt made history, and we were all happy about getting back at her, without being sent to Eugene, the Manual Labor Guy.

After that, different girls made their requests for Harry Billy to play a different rock-n-roll song every morning when Mrs. Hagga was on duty. As the music filtered its way down the hall and back again, those of us who knew the words sang while we got ready for another week of school. "Hey, the Hagster's on the rise!!" Literally! On most days, Mrs. Hagga would just go up and down the hall, yelling at the girls for every little thing, even when the music was turned down. It was one of those great feelings that dormitory life provided; hearing the whole hall full of music and the sound of our revenge anthem... it was wonderful!

On that spring day, at precisely 5:30 A.M. the students in Dorm A & B finally got their revenge on the Haggster. There was nothing she could do. How could she send a hundred and fifty students to The Manual Labor Guy or worse yet, The Room….the Head Matron and Superintendent would be aghast at her incompetence. She didn't say a word, spending most of her duty in the Matron on Duty office, head down, eyebrows wrinkled, "secretly" sipping the vodka and orange juice drink she loved.

Everyone in Dorm A & B remembered that incident for the rest of their lives, and "Bad Moon on the Rise" would live on, as a song of freedom. Laughter and smiles at the thought were shared for many weeks….

"The Haggster was up again tonight, hanging low and mean over the hills, just like last time."

"Looks like the Haggster's on the prowl again," she said, squinting at the clouds. "That never ends well."

When the Haggster's high, the dead don't lie.

We loved to make up our own words to the tune! As the guitar bridge echoed loudly and the four of us stood proud with sneaky coyote smiles! The music fades…one eye is taken for an eye….so her Bible reads….reality hits!

Life was good that day for everyone in Dorm A & B. We all had a reason to smile. That day will go down in infamy and will be remembered by all who lived at Red Sands Residential Dormitory in 1973.

The Haggster

Mean Starchy Matron

Roams the halls with angry scowl

Hagga Bagga Witch!

Harry Billy
A comforting, gentle voice—
Whispers of home, of songs with hidden truths.
"Crazy Ingin Number 9" by choice,
Harry Billy, our long-lost uncle.

His voice alone
A thread that pulls us home.
Harry Billy—
Saving our lives
With every word he sez.

In a time when we were feeling like we had no control of our lives there was a way to express our oppression, our rage, Harry Billy was our voice. He made the Haggster bow down to the almighty gentleness of a humble butcher who made our day and our lives, with one song at 5:30 A.M. That was so cool! Honestly, I don't know why we didn't think of doing that before!

Life was good, if only for that moment in time.

Chapter 8 - My Friend Garnet

As I look back at our times, it wasn't until fifth grade that Garnet began to share what happened when she was checked out for the weekends. I found myself being jealous of Garnet, Clarice, and Ruby for being checked out. Little did I know what was really going on with Garnet because she was very reserved and held her comments close to her chest. As I learned the reality Garnet lived, I quickly felt guilty for thinking her life was something to envy. Reality bites when it is revealed.

Five-year-old Garnet Chee stepped into Red Sands Dormitory the same day as Clarice, Ruby and me. As we grew older, I teased her because she was the shortest of us four girls, standing five-foot four inches and weighing less than 100 pounds. Over the years, she became the eldest child of four and the only daughter, which meant she became sort of a slave to them. By Navajo standards, the daughters are expected to do more than their brothers do, so living at Red Sands Residential Dormitory was like a reprieve to her usual duties. Her thin dusty brown hair was always tied in a ponytail; otherwise, a slight breeze would blow her hair into a tangled mess. At Red Sands, a slight breeze was usually followed by a big gust of silt-like winds which, during the summer, could rise at least a mile and sweep across the whole town for several hours. It was during that time of the year that Garnet had to take extra care to cover her hair and her fair complexion; otherwise, she'd spend hours untangling the bushy mess. Her large brown eyes shaped like olives matched her high cheek bones. Her skin and cheeks were always red, and the sun made her eyes water, so she squinted most of the time leaving tiny lines on her temples. The desert sun shone on Red Sands most of the year and that meant she was a shade of brownish red most of the year. Garnet was always a sweet girl and come to think of it, she hardly ever or practically never complained!

Garnet remembered getting to know the "Giirs", as we referred to ourselves while learning to cope with the scary unknown world she walked into each weekend. Back then, everything at Red Sands Residential Dormitory was huge; now everything looked old and huge. Like myself, with time, Garnet considered us to be her long-lost sisters.

Daisy, her mother, had been married three times and always managed to pick a loser. Probably because she went shopping for her men at the American Bar or Eddie's Club... This time he was Frank Yazzie from Steamboat, Arizona. The last one, was Gary Begay, who came from Teec Nos Pos, Arizona, in the northern part of the Navajo Nation. He was really into Holy Rollers, and it irritated Garnet that she had to sit outside the tent and listen to their hoop and hollering and his incessant mumbo jumbo about Jesus and the Bible and other Christian things that Garnet already knew but vowed never to believe. Her mother had become a real fanatic, and Garnet knew it wouldn't last long because of their appetite for liquor. Revival then drinks – didn't make any sense at all... Don't they know about Saddam and Gomorra? Church abuse...everlasting rolling eyes. Her life was a deep breath followed by a defiant sigh.

Garnet's dad was a guy by the name of Raymond Chee, whom she never met but was always curious about. Her mother never spoke of him, and Garnet learned not to ask.

Her mother's favorite drink was whiskey, any kind, any flavor – the cheaper, the better, and the more the merrier. Over time, the smell sickened Garnet, but she learned to see it as a signal of her need to protect her mother, her little brothers and whoever her mother happened to call her "husband".

Garnet learned how to drive at the age of nine. It was a summer to forget but one that taught her to survive. After the Girrs said their goodbyes, Garnet sat in the back seat of her mother's gray Chevy Impala thinking how long she and Frank had already been drinking. The odor was familiar and disgusting. She vowed never to drink a drop of alcohol. The odor was so saturated in their bodies that their sweat poured out and smelled like Garden Deluxe, sometimes Twister.

The odor brought disturbing memories of whether she would die on the way home or on the way back to school. So, it was by fourth grade, she learned how to drive by watching. The 150 miles that it took to reach her home in Tuba City, Arizona stretched between vast grassy, now-fenced lands, that either bordered Navajo County, the Hopi Tribe, or the Navajo Nation. All that territorial fencing was thanks to the Bennett Freeze controversy she heard her aunt and uncle talking about during her weekend visits.

It wasn't long before I noticed that Garnet was picked up almost every weekend, whether she likes it or not. I never knew what happened to her when she left Red Sands Residential Dormitory, but I secretly envied her mother's devotion to not forget Garnet; drunk of not.

Every Friday, as they drove, Garnet counted some fifty signs warning people *not* to trespass and that either the State of Arizona, Hopi Tribe, or the Navajo Nation would "prosecute you to the fullest extent of the law", and impound your horses, sheep, or cattle. "Whatever that meant," Garnet often thought as she learned to recognize the signs as mile markers and served to let her know how many miles it would take to get to Tuba City, weekend after weekend, year after year. It was confusing because the white people told the Indians to stay on the reservation. Then, they tell them to send their kids off the reservation to go to school. Hmmm. It wasn't like she wanted to stay home, but as she got older, she often wondered about the legal part of those signs. She sarcastically wondered why the Whites let their horses and cows roam outside of the fence causing accidents, especially at night, which was pitched dark and dangerous during the winter months when she could barely see the road, let alone the faded lines. It was a guess, but she learned to look at the mileage on the odometer to know where she was and how far she still had to go to get home. Garnet also observed the different police that regularly patrolled the road in the different areas. She spent time reading the Owner's Manual while cleaning, and doing laundry, while passing the time for her weekend to end.

As the Chevy Impala coughed its way to Interstate 40, Garnet just knew that she would need to figure out a way to get them to stop at the nearest gas station so she could take over the driving.

Frank Yazzie was a mean alcoholic who worked odd jobs for a living. He made just enough to cover his habit with little to spare, so her mother had to do laundry for the Trader who ran Tuba City Trading Post. It was a meaningless job; she had lost the dreams alcohol squelched and eventually didn't remember who she wanted to be when she was young. Garnet was too scared to ask her those kinds of questions for fear of getting whipped when her mother had enough alcohol in her to make her go crazy with anger, apologizing when she sobered up. It was an endless cycle. Garnet learned when to pick her battles or ask personal questions, so she learned to exist by keeping her eyes on the future, knowing the light would become brighter with knowledge.

Daisy pushed Garnet as a child, wanting her to be successful, even if it meant sending her off to live in a dorm and go to a public school where she knew the white kids could and would be mean and get away with it. At times, when Garnet's mother did not show up, she knew that Frank was hiding out in Gallup or Page with all those drunks who sleep in old cars that white people did not know where to put and had dumped them in the nearest ditch. Daisy would spend the whole weekend walking the streets of border towns until finally someone would give her news of his sighting.

Usually, he was at American Bar or Eddie's Club. Gallup, New Mexico the so-called, "Heart of Indian Country" was notorious for ridiculing drunken Indians. Many business owners eagerly took silver and turquoise jewelry from Navajos, Utes, Zunis, Hopis, and Apache's only to trade for peanuts with ridiculously high pawn interest rates. The bar owners were equally willing to serve all the alcohol a person could stand or more. The store owners were no better.

It was a known fact that border town police officers could be ruthless when picking up public vagrants. Some of the drunks Frank knew were badly beaten before arriving at the jail as if that would solve the problem. They should have told those bar owners not to serve Navajos alcohol, or they would be thrown in jail! I mean why serve Navajo's alcohol when they know very well it's against Navajo laws, or some prohibition law that Garnet sort of knew about. For as long as Garnet could remember alcohol was a way of life for her mother.

What the white merchants failed to see in Garnet's view was that the Native Americans in the surrounding area, were the ones paying their bills and helping them build the biggest houses any Native American could never imagine owning, let alone getting a glimpse at the inside. Garnet's interest in learning the legal system silently grew as she read countless books about how the United States Government was founded and how the Founding Fathers made laws never meant to pertain to us, Native Americans. They even called us "merciless Indian savages", in the United States Constitution! Who were really the "merciless" ones or "savage" thieves, they wrote about hundreds of years ago? Garnet's secret passion to become a lawyer grew over the years. She wanted to right the wrongs she saw and only spoke about this to me, her best friend. She made it her mission to spend as much time at the Red Sands Public Library when she wasn't chumming around with us.

As time went on, after reading the letters her mother had received from the Social Services Department, she discovered the fact that her mother could very well lose all her children to foster care. Garnet was not going to foster care and set out to save her family, because it sure didn't look like her mother was in any hurry to change.

Garnet tried to find the perfect moment in time to express her concern to her mother, but her mother was always busy with everything and yet nothing at the same time. So, she told her brother, Turquoise, who was two years younger and had a different father from the Ute Tribe, she would protect them. She also made sure she taught him how to find a safe place for him and their little brothers whenever the drinking turned violent.

Like a lot of Native Americans, her mother named all her children after something in nature. Her brothers were born from another relationship were White Shell Boy who was 4 years younger, and then there was Frank Yazzie's son Cedar who was the baby and 7 years younger than Garnet. They stayed at home with her mother and went to school at Tuba City Day School. Garnet was constantly worried about them but had no choice but to leave them behind.

Garnet taught her brother Turquoise how to cook and care for his younger brothers. She taught him when to find safety from the alcoholic rage Frank Yazzie was known to go into – mostly at the first of the month and as a means to escape the house, so he could spend his whole disability check on his drinking buddies at the Gray Hills Tavern ten miles south of Tuba City, Arizona. It was the nearest watering hole to Tuba City, serving Navajos and other community members, as there were whites and Mexicans that worked in the area. Anyway, it was just another place for people to drink themselves into oblivion.

On those days, Turquoise would keep his brothers at his friend Michael's house until way past 10:00 p.m. Michael's mother didn't seem to mind and soon found herself including them in her dinner plans and sort of adopted them while they were in elementary school. She too knew the consequences of notifying the "authorities" at social services or the police department. They would make a big mess of it and then all the kids would end up separated and the family would no longer be a family. Having different fathers meant their mother was the only thing they had in common. Garnet heard of a family whose kids ended up in Flagstaff, Phoenix, and Utah. They never heard from each other again. She was determined to keep her family safe from the "authorities." They were NOT going to break her family up! The library kept her informed of different ways to cook, raise and teach kids. These things she could teach Turquoise. The one valuable thing that she happened upon was books about law. These books would change her life forever. During the quick weekends and long summer, she spent her time teaching her brothers how to read and do math, and how to take care of themselves during the week. Garnet was notorious for collecting scraps of paper, newspapers, straws, cans, everything! She was like a little pack rat. One time she was embarrassed when I made a comment that Garnet saved everything just like my Gramps!

"No, she claimed! All Navajos are collectors...just in case"...they laughed.

"Yeah, just in case. Gramps always said that...he had "just in case" stuff all over the place."

On any given weekend, Frank Yazzie was busy trying to instruct Garnet to turn around so they could get more liquor, but that meant another hour or two before they could even begin driving home.

He sang loudly to her mother, "Com on, Ruuuuu-bbbbby, Don't let me take your love to da town...Jus go 'hed and turn 'round, aay." his favorite line from a Waylon Jennings album that Garnet grew to hate. "Gorn, please turned around to Lucky's. It's the closest."

She also hated it when he called her Gorn. "It's Garnet! And my mother's name is Daisy! Shí'yá'dí!!" *(exasperation!)*

Garnet knew he would talk her mother into making Garnet turn around. Over time, she gave in to the fact that she would drive them home, even if they drank all night. Garnet knew the way and exactly where the police officers waited for speeders and especially people who were drinking and driving. And she knew if she kept the car at a speed of 55 miles per hour, negotiating the middle between the yellow line and the white line, she would make it home while her mother and Frank drank themselves into oblivion in the back seat. After a couple of these "drives" home she began asking her mother to bring her brother, White Shell Boy, so he could keep her company on the long drive home, but Frank didn't like him.

It wasn't hard for Frank to persuade Daisy to go into the bar, any bar. The Border Towns had a bar on just about every corner, which Garnet thought should be against the law...ugh!! Daisy faked her protest, ended up agreeing as usual. Daisy knew what a real fight meant, and she calculated her every word, every move so that her man wouldn't explode into a violent rage. This went on for five years. She had met Frank at one of those Holy Roller revivals in Kayenta. Like fate would have it, that also was also the time she would find out that her then husband Gary Begay had a wife in Kayenta, never mind the one in Ft. Defiance. To make things worse, each wife had kids who were about the same age as Garnet's little brothers. So, there Frank was to rescue her from one dysfunctional relationship to the next. Garnet never figured out how this worked but it did.

When Garnet was younger, she wished that her mother would just write to her and send her money, so she wouldn't have to deal with another "stepfather," as her mother wanted her to refer to them. That was awkward for her because none of them ever treated her like a daughter. What she wanted to do was spend time with me, Clarice, and Ruby or whomever didn't get picked up for the weekend – but mostly me. But now, she had her little brothers to think about and so being picked up meant that she takes care of them at least for the weekend.

Garnet sat outside in the car slowly eating the greasy Kentucky Fried Chicken her mother had bought for the drive home. The can of Pepsi was nice and cold and burned her throat as she gulped it down. She knew it was about 7:00 p.m. because when the sun set, the neon blue and red lights on Red Sands Saloon lit up and always seemed to startle Garnet. Trucks and cars pulled up and Garnet watched as the ones that stayed got out of their vehicles and walked towards the doors. A couple of hours later, the same people would stagger out, tumble into their vehicle, then spin out of the parking lot with drunken laughter coming from every window. Sometimes they would leave happy and sometimes they would be fighting. Twice, Garnet saw a couple leaving with different people. At different times of course. Many times, her mother and Frank Yazzie took two and a half hours to get enough to drink and finally came out of the door that Garnet kept a close eye on.

With time inching its way towards midnight, Red Sand's finest were patrolling the parking lot looking for someone to take out their hatred on and then later threw them righteously in jail. Garnet had secretly witnessed such violence on occasions when she had to hide and wait..and wait..and wait…

This time the parking lot was packed and had waves of giggling children who were also hiding in their vehicles. There was a point in time when the children fell asleep, and Garnet startled by the sound of the police officer walking on patrol. She slowly inched under the dashboard, pulling an old blanket from the front seat to cover her. As the sound of the police officer's voices came nearer, Garnet could hear her breathing get louder and louder. "Oh, please don't find me," she thought, knowing the car doors were unlocked and wishing she had locked them like she said she would. She thought about the little children also trying to be quiet. As their voices got nearer, her heart was beating louder than her breathing.

"See any of them?" One officer said to the other, as they played with their wooden baton. Their flashlights flashed across and into the car before they moved to the next car and on down the row.

"Nope. No little prairie niggers hidin' out here tonight. Let's go check Hal's." The other officer's voice faded in the other direction.

"God damned dirty drunkin' Injuns, keeping us busy....voice fading across the parking lot. Door's slam, tires peel out, and a sigh of relief.

The ten minutes it took for them to look through all the cars seemed like an eternity and by then Garnet needed to go to the restroom. Peeking out the passenger window, she saw the taillight of the patrol car leaving the parking lot and heading towards the other liquor store in Red Sands.

"Whew!" Garnet pulled herself onto the front seat and slowly opened the door and ran to the nearest sagebrush next to the gate that surrounded Red Sands Saloon. She could hear the music blaring from the bar and wondered when they would get drunk enough. "Better get some sleep," she thought as she crept back into the car.

The sound of the car door opening and the flashlight shining in her face startled Garnet, enough to jump up and wonder where she was, quickly remembering. She shuffled to the driver's seat as she threw the blanket and pillow to her side.

"Scoot over, Shí yázhí." Her mother commanded as Frank's glossy red eyes peered over her shoulder.

"No. I'm going to drive. I can do it Mom. You guys are too drunk to drive, and we have a long way to go." Garnet convincing her mother while glaring at Frank. "Mom, Please!!!"

Daisy sighed and looked back at Frank who was already taking a swig of his whiskey bottle that was carefully wrapped in a brown paper bag, as if people didn't know that it was a bottle of whiskey...duuh!

"Okay. Well get in the back. Are you sure you know how to get out of here?" Garnet rolled her eyes biting her tongue at the sarcasm that could have caused a fight.

"Frank, get in the back," Daisy commanded. It was odd that he agreed without protesting or creating a scene.

"Gimme som dat chiggen, ShiHeart. Oh, Ruuuubbbby, why did you take your love to da town – now look at me.."...he crooned as the smell of alcohol made its way to Garnet's nose. "Gornet, are you reeely gon driv? You bedder watching for doz cops." *Chi'íídii Siláo'* níjooshłaah! *(The police are devils that I don't like!)* He managed to spit this out as his eyes squinted and his body moved uncontrollably, already showing signs of passing out.

He better not piss on himself, Garnet thought. "Dear Holy People, Jesus, and the Pope, please help me!" Garnet glared at her mother and pulled out of the parking lot.

"Geez, Louise! God, please make him pass out in five minutes!" Her mother always granted all her "husbands" need for more whiskey – the Devil's piss! Garnet eased the car out of the parking lot and thought about turning on the radio. On second thought, silence would make them pass out faster! Daisy sat up against the back seat, as long as she could, acting as if she needed to guide her only daughter, Garnet, who sat on two pillows with the seat pulled as far forward as it could go, to the turn off that took then to Tuba City. It was pitched dark with a few stars sparkling here and there. It seemed like the only car on the road in the universe was that Chevy Impala. The only thing she recognized were the few sagebrush that grew next to the highway. Otherwise, the rest of the scene was a blank picture, left to a person's imagination to think of devils, demons, witch crafters and other unholy things that creep in the dark. With the lines that were supposed to keep her on the road, faded here and there it was hard to know if she was on the right side of the road or near the edge. Her mother taught her that the police watch to see if the driver is "negotiating the center line," as she explained. "If someone isn't negotiating the center line, then the police would stop them and check to see if the driver and passenger were drinking. So, you need to remember that, especially at night." "Look at the big picture, negotiate the center line and most of all DON'T PANIC and slam on the brakes!" Things that Garnet learned to keep in mind as she eventually made her way from any number of bars from Gallup to Farmington to Red Sands...all roads leading to Tuba City, eventually.

Another Friday late night, and true to form, she passed the Navajo County Sheriff at his usual waiting spot. Garnet thought it was Mile Post 147, and it would take another five miles until she reached the Navajo Nation boundaries.

Thoughts of the school year and her friends and their funny adventures filled her mind. The road stretched with a few hills to break the monotony, so Garnet decided her mother and Frank were in a deep sleep. She turned on KDJI oldies hour and in her own words sang along to The Momma's and the Pappa's, "All the leaves are gone, and the mood is gray, and the mood is gray.....I've been for a run on a summer day....I'd be free to roam, if I was on my own. Arizona dreamin', on such a summer day." She sang along remembering the times at the old ranch house where we loved to sing to the songs on the radio -with out own words, that is.

Suddenly, a Navajo Police vehicle appeared over the hill and soon was behind her flashing red and blue lights. She knew it Navajo Police because of the round headlights...Sheriff had square lights, and the State boys had big rectangular lights. Within seconds, her heart jumped out of her chest as she remembered to slow down and pull to the side of the road or as much as she could. There ain't much of a shoulder to stop on, so it was dangerous to stop on Navajo roads as her mother explained one day. The Bureau of Indian Affairs Roads throughout Navajoland were notorious for not having much of a shoulder. Breathing hard, she reached back to wake her mother who was out of it. "Mom! It's the Police!" She would not wake up in the seconds Garnet tried to wake her, but before she knew it, the Navajo Police passed by her at a high rate of speed, assuring her that an accident or incident would take their attention away from a little girl driving her drunk passengers to safety in the middle of the night. Her mother not waking, Garnet pulled back onto the road still shaken. Whew! Close call! Thank you, Holy People, Jesus, and the Pope. Crossing her heart... Deep breath...keep driving...almost home.

"This is Harry Billy, Crazy Injun Number 9 coming to you from KDJI" and the music of Merle Haggard began to take the vibe to an awkward place, and Garnet wasn't about to listen to country music. She was a rock-n-roll girl and wasn't about to listen to Merle stinkin' Haggard. Frank might come to and start singing the words all wrong. The silence was deafening and with nerves frazzled, she switched the radio in time to hear, "Stairway to Heaven" by Led Zepplin. "All right, now that's more like it., Uncle Harry needs to get up to speed!" she thought. "There's a lady who's.... and the melody filled the dark drive."

In the heart of Hopi Land, Daisy finally woke up. Garnet didn't know it at first, but when she peered into the rearview mirror, her mother's glassy eyes startled her. Daisy was looking around with wide eyes wondering where they were and getting her bearings. She seemed to be going right back to sleep. Yep, probably a fitful dream – if you can dream drunk. Garnet would never find out. When Garnet's looked back on the road, she saw what looked like a witch crafter standing in the middle of the road ahead. Stammering to find the brakes, she slowed the car down without startling her mother and Frank.

At first, she was ready to yell or scream or really freak out, but she remembered that it was that time of year when the

Hopi Kachina's were out at night. Letting out her breath, Garnet slowly began to accelerate past the Kachina as it watched her pass, never moving. When she looked in the rearview mirror, it had already disappeared into the darkness.

"We're almost home Mom." Garnet announced.

"Gosh, how long have I been asleep?" Daisy whispered, not wanting to wake Frank.

"About one hour, Mom. How come you didn't bring White Shell Boy? This time he could have helped me stay awake and face the police and the Hopi Kachina?" Garnet demanded.

"He had to stay with your brothers because the new neighbors called the Social Services on us, and we have to watch what we do and where we go."

Daisy's announcement was Garnet's worst fear.

By the age of eleven, she knew that she would not have a family if her mother messed up one more time. She would not have a family if her mother didn't quit drinking or marrying guys who were drunk, like Frank. "Mom, you have to leave Frank. Take him back to his house. He probably has a family somewhere just like Gary. I'll help you. This summer we are going to make some changes to help us to be a family. Please Mom: *you* have to quit drinking too."

Silence.

Garnet was shaking, but had to calm herself down, trying to stop the tears streaming down her face. Daisy silently listened to her daughter draw in deep breaths now and then and knew what she was doing was not good, but quitting was the hardest thing to do.

By this time, she had driven deep into Hopiland, with only 30 miles left to get to Tuba City, but Garnet knew she could do it. Frank who was still passed out had greasy lips, a greasy face, his favorite Kentucky Fried Chicken crispy crust bits stained his worn-out button-down cowboy shirt, yet he sleeps into oblivion. Garnet was glad there were no violent incidents so far. She never passed any police or came across an accident. As she reached the top of Third Mesa, the lights of Tuba City could be seen against the clouded sky. "I did it!" Garnet whispered, shaking, sweaty hands. Garnet couldn't wait to get over with this weekend so she could go back to her reality at Red Sands Residential Dormitory. Thank you, Holy People, Jesus, and the Pope, for getting us home safely, sigh, deep breath. She spent the whole trip wondering about Chuska Boarding School, and if her mother really was going to enroll them there next year. Garnet wasn't sure she could survive life without her sister-friends.

As time went on, Garnet found herself facing a lot of weekends and summers where she had to drive her drunken mother and another one of her drunken boyfriends to safety. A month later, instead of dealing with problems, the nosy neighbor and social services breathing down her neck, Daisy chose instead to move to Frank's home in Steamboat.

Turns out, he did have a house there like he claimed. No secret wife to speak of much to Daisy's relief. Daisy spent the rest of Frank's last days raising their sons, while watching Garnet become ever distant. The house was nestled at the base of a giant red rock cliff that used to house a river in ancient times. The stream now extinct, housed all of Frank's clan – which were the 'Áshiihii or Salt Clan. It was a good place for her brothers to live because there were plenty of horses and sheep to tend. While Daisy envied her only daughter, she knew that she had made many wrong choices in her own life and the consequences were too hard to swallow.

It didn't take long for Frank to drink himself to death. He and Daisy didn't have the constraints of nosy neighbors to keep a close eye on them. The thing was now that Frank was gone, what would Daisy do? Her parents had long since passed away and most of her siblings were scattered here and there and didn't keep in contact with each other. She truly felt alone.

After years of abuse, Daisy had no choice but to get sober in order to return home. Daisy spent much of the time thinking about Frank and when they were together, fighting him, trying to find him when he took off, or keeping her sons from being frightened by his rage. His death was as hard to endure as was their life together. Frank's family let her stay, but with her older brother's approval, she was allowed to move back to her native home of Hunter's Point, Arizona.

As for Garnet, that was one of the turning points of her life. Her goal was eventually to go to law school. The problems at home she knew were not escapable but fixable. Meanwhile, the reality was that others, too, waited for a new and different prison sentence to begin once they returned home for the summer. I realized Garnet was one of those who didn't quite like living at Red Sands Residential Dormitory and didn't quite want to go back to where she called home. She learned to be patient while her mother went through her trials and tribulations. Being the eldest child was about being tough and patient. She had no choice but to learn to be the caregiver and leader of her siblings at an early age.

Deep breath..new reality... and no more midnight drives to Tuba Chizzy... eyes rolling..

Garnet, Who Drove Through the Dark

She was five with red cheeks
and ten with a steering wheel.
Dusty brown hair,
secrets in her throat,
and whiskey sweat in the air.

No one knew
how many fences she passed,
how many signs warned her to stay out,
when all she wanted
was to belong somewhere.

She drove through black nights
on faith and fumes,
memorizing the hum of broken lines,
learning the law of silence:
Don't cry. Don't ask. Just drive.

Short as a whisper,
but stronger than most storms,
she folded sorrow into stillness
and wrapped it in ponytail bands.
She never complained.
She just got home.

Chapter 9 - Ruby Quite Contrary

Ruby Reynolds, on the other hand, had everything handed to her on that Tribal Government worker's platter. She entered Red Sands Residential Dormitory, sad and afraid...just like the rest of us. She went through life trying to be a part of something and nothing at the same time. Standing 5-foot 6 Ruby grew to be the tallest of the four of us. Ruby's high cheekbones and wide white teeth made her cheeks cave into two long dimples when she smiled. She thought she inherited her looks from her mother and suspected her height came from the father she never met. Although Ruby secretly wished to cut her hair, she had no choice but to wear her hair long black waist length hair three different ways; two braids on either side of her head, or one thick braid down her back, or a ponytail. She was spoiled but like the rest of us, came to live at Red Sands Residential Dormitory for reasons out of our control. We took her in as a friend and tolerated her negativity because she was our sister, and sisters stick together. Over time, we came to be interested about the dealings and welfare of the great people of the Navajo Nation...as Ruby always declared. She also kept a lot of secrets we would not know about until much later.

She wa s born and raised in Window Rock, primarily because her mother Carol was an executive secretary for the Council Delegates of the Great Navajo Nation, as she put it. Ruby's grandfather was a former Council Delegate from Lupton, Arizona. At that time, the Great Navajo Nation was in the midst of political turmoil with the outside world and our neighbors the Hopi Nation. What we learned over the years, was that the many needs of the people of both nations and the monies to fund them always coming from the white fathers in Washington, or Washingdon as Navajos referred to the United States Government. Monies for hospitals and quality health care were debated endlessly while the tribal coffers were meager at best. Ruby's grandparents came to visit them in Window Rock, which meant a slew of Council Delegates past and present, would take their lovely time eating dinner while discussing what the Navajo Nation should do or not do… Ruby was surrounded by people but from her perspective, she spent her time watching and listening and never participating. It is no wonder she got into trouble trying to be heard or noticed at school.

Once her mother hosted one of those, "bring your kid to the party" parties in which ten-year-old Ruby was quickly bored, because all the kids were at least four and five years younger. After several attempts to resist, Ruby ended up babysitting the kids in her bedroom, while their parents and her mother danced to Country Western music and got plastered. Ruby was so mad when she returned to Red Sands Residential Dormitory that she just had to tell us how "those brats ate all her cereal and made a mess before their parents rose from the dead, red eyes and all." After similar weekend visits, she wished her mother would leave her at Red Sands Residential Dormitory, but she knew better than to not keep up appearances. Ruby was so good at babysitting that the group started asking her mother to all kinds of parties and to make sure to bring Ruby. The only good part about babysitting was the money! By the time she was thirteen, she had earned $1,432.00, which she kept in a shoebox under her bed at home. She often spoke of buying her own car so she could travel to Hollywood, California and see all the movie stars we read about in *Teen* magazine or *Tiger Beat*.

The last two years she was picked up by her grandparents every weekend. When she returned from her weekend adventure, she often complained her mother was never home, and that she was always in meetings, going to conferences, or spending her nights at one of those gatherings the legal gurus held to discuss serious decisions on "tribal politics and what the Navajo Nation Council should do or not do" regarding the many issues, Ruby was always ready to report about. Most of her reports were confusing but when she talked about water, mineral rights, and the endless talk about coal, that's when my ears perked up. Those were the things my grandparents talked about in a serious way.

At first, Ruby's mom came to pick her up every weekend, until one day she stopped showing up. She later told us that her mother had found another man Ruby would have to call, dad. Not knowing who her father was, Ruby's mother introduced her to any number of "friends" who managed to disappear before the sun came up. Ruby had everything she wanted to an excess, but what she secretly yearned for was a real family with a father and siblings - not the endless list of boyfriends she would never get used to or speak about!

It was then that we also noticed Ruby began to be called to the office at school a lot. I began to think it was because she was so used to getting her way and that's what got her in trouble. Ruby did have a big mouth and wasn't afraid to use it, mostly at the wrong time. On our way back to the dorm, she told us that once again, she got into trouble for talking back to the teacher. She had to clean the tables in the cafeteria after lunch for two days. It would be a repeated pattern for Ruby to be sent to the office for saying this or that. Ruby didn't care to keep her bunk area tidy even though Mrs. Becenti or the Matron on Duty would pull her by the ear and yell at her for not following orders. Her mother or grandparents were quick to arrive at Red Sands Residential Dormitory just in time for Ruby not to get sent to Eugene the buck-toothed Manual Labor Guy. They never knew that she did get the punishment of being sent to "The Room" a couple of times by Mrs. Becenti. It was worse when Mr. Levinstein made his beady-eyed appearance. Ruby called him Frankenstein. We called him Ichabod Crane because of his pointed nose and tall skinny stature. No one liked him. No one.

Ruby drew the coolest fashion outfits she claimed she would make some day. It was amazing what she could do with her 12-piece colored pencil set. Her fashion designs were taped all over her bunk area. She didn't seem to mind that her hair was bushy either. Ruby, Ruby. Time after time my eyes had to witness my friend being abused and I could not do anything but help her pull herself together after each time. I felt sorry for Ruby. We all felt sorry for Ruby. As the years turned into another, we tried our best to keep Ruby out of trouble. We did not want her to be sent to "The Room" as a punishment. Mrs. Becenti marched up and down Dorm A and then Dorm B warning us if we had too many manual labor write-ups, the next step would be punishment in "The Room". From kindergarten it was pounded into our innocent minds about manual labor, punishment, and the mysterious room – which was supposedly the end all of punishments.

Ruby always gave us an inside view of what was going on in Window Rock, although I learned to take her reports with a grain of salt. She began by telling us that Chairman McDonald and the Navajo Tribal Council were protesting the death of Larry Casuse, a Navajo activist. By Ruby's account, Larry took matters into his own hands by taking the Mayor of Gallup hostage, demanding the City of Gallup to close the bar they named, Navajo Inn which was right outside of Window Rock city limits and was notorious for serving Navajos alcohol beyond the legal limits and often led to hit and run deaths, lethal beatings by white police, and white teenagers robbing Navajos of what little money they possessed. Navajo Inn bar brought in the most money in the entire state of New Mexico. Larry stood up for the Navajo people and was murdered by the Gallup Police, who claimed he was a terrorist. It was also at this time that Native American men and women joined the American Indian Movement (A.I.M.) and were planning something big.

It was true that Navajos were getting ripped off by Gallup store owners. This went on at other border towns and Chairman McDonald was determined to get a handle on the problem. We never knew if Ruby was telling it like it was or exaggerating, but that didn't stop us from listening. Ruby's mother worked for the Navajo Council Delegates which meant she heard or had to type everything that was going on with the great Navajo Nation – "down to the detail," as Ruby always ended her sentences.

"There were all kinds of Navajos being killed by the whites in Farmington, too", she elaborated. "The whites just rob them after they leave the bars. A lot of Navajos were missing and feared dead at the hands of the Farmington whites, their bodies found near the oil fields north of Farmington. Those white teenagers even cut a finger off their victim for a trophy. The Navajos in Shiprock are in an uproar, too. The Council is worried because the Navajos working at Fairchild were claiming unfair pay and wanted to protest. A.I.M. was a part of this protest, too!"

I remember wondering if this meant my mom was in some kind of danger or maybe she decided to join the protest. What Ruby was saying left an unsettling feeling in my stomach.

"Chairman McDonald was dealing with Water Rights issues every day. Water that already belonged to the Navajo People was being claimed by everybody and anybody who lived near it, and those greedy White people who wanted to use it for mining coal or uranium. Imagine the Navajo Nation paying for water that already belonged to them. Precious water wasted to get that black rock that made coal companies rich off the backs of Navajos who were paid very little, and those who didn't have a choice being pushed off their own land by the state governments. All the Councilmen were trying to figure out what to do. My mom and her friends are so mad about the water rights problem! All these problems!" Ruby arms were up in the air and were always out of breath by the end of every one of her reports of the Great Navajo Nation.

We let out a collective sigh of relief that Ruby was finished with her update. Chairman McDonald this, Chairman McDonald that…at times the news put a fear in the girls; other times it was just about enough to make us want to cover our ears. Ruby had spent so much time listening to the people her mother worked with, she began repeating them.

I believed what my Gramps always said about McDonald. "He tells you one thing in English and then turns around and says it in a whole different way in Navajo – like us old Navajos don't understand." Gramps warned us that a person who points his finger at another, thinks only of himself and that they might be a crook. Gramps was always right. The truth was that the Navajo Nation Council was lied to by the white lawyers and the Coal Company, because that's what always happens. The white lawyer's salary was paid by the Navajo Nation while they quietly took a cut from the coal and oil companies. In the end, the Navajo people were the ones who lost out, but the people kept voting in the same people, year after year. Gramps always had these kinds of conversations during a few family dinners in the summer. My uncles were miners at Peabody Coal Company, so it was Catch-20-20 for them and their pocketbook. I couldn't imagine hearing about all this stuff every time I visited home.

"Geez, good thing we're held captive by choice here at R.S.R.D." Clarice sarcastically announced. "Sounds like all those people are just giving up all the Treaty Rights." Clarice was an activist deep down, but it was only when Ruby gave her report that we saw that side. Finally, Ruby always concluded her report with, "You never know what's going to happen in Window Rock next"…shrug her shoulders and then she sighed, as if. Ruby Ruby, quite contrary, oh, how your stories grow?......the Great Navajo Nation…hmmm…

"That's what you think…" Gramps always had the last word, even if he was a hundred miles away.

Ruby, Ruby. She was a strange character. Ruby started out being thin and gained weight over the years. She spent a lot of time eating the candy and junk food her mother and grandparents showered her with before taking her back to Red Sands Residential Dormitory. It was as if Ruby's mother enrolled her to keep her out of the way so she could live *her* life. You know, "out of sight out of mind." I caught my thoughts and decided, "for my own good, probably also meant for my mom's own good." You never know. Ruby was somewhat naive, and I overheard her teachers talk about how she had a backwards way of thinking. This was because Ruby was always trying to start an argument defending the Navajo People, and the Great Navajo Nation.

Ruby was always causing trouble with her harsh words and mean spirit. The only friends she ever had were Clarice, Garnet, and me. Sometimes we took turns being mad at her, or so she thought. Ruby secretly envied Clarice and me because we ran every morning. She had tried to join us but being chubby caused her to get out of breath right away and she soon gave up. Besides, she was used to getting as much sleep as she could squeeze out of our strict schedule. Her footlocker was always locked so that no one would steal her treasured snacks or her secret notes. She knew that she ate too much but couldn't control her hunger. Even if we tried to help her. It would only last until the weekend. When we were in first grade, her front teeth were all capped with silver because they had rotted from too much sugar. We tried to get her to quit eating so much candy, but Ruby was a lazy girl, used to having everything. Her favorite words were, "I want…. I gotta have… I need." Ruby was an average student, barely getting C's and an occasional B, but in all her days at Red Sands Public School, she never earned an A that we knew of. Poor Ruby.

Ruby learned about our Dine' way of life from her Grandmother Ruby, for whom she is named. Her grandmother took care of her while her mother worked all those long hours. Ruby grew up hearing her mother and grandmother arguing about her mother's decisions that took her time for overnight meetings and sometimes the entire weekend. Ruby cherished the times they had running down the road and learning how to pray with corn pollen. Her grandmother always sang the prayer, "With This Song I Run," during those times. She explained to Ruby that it was a song for traveling, and prayers for safety. When Ruby was five years old, her grandfather stepped down from the Navajo Council, and they decided to move back to Lupton. That was when her mother had to figure out what to do with Ruby. Red Sands Residential Dormitory was one of many options but became the place where Ruby would live while her mother lived her life… "for her own good."

Ruby once confessed that she never had a Kinaaldá, because her mother was at a conference in Chicago. Her grandmother was very upset that Ruby's coming of age came and went, without any prayers or songs to guide her into womanhood. No wonder Ruby was overweight, I thought. The *Kinaaldá* is a coming-of-age ceremony that is celebrated by all members of the girls' maternal clan, and she becomes the embodiment of Changing Woman.

I remember when I was the *Kinaaldá* (*Changing Woman*), all the *Tsenjikini* (*Honeycomb Cliff Dweller Clan*) women, men, girls, and boys in the area came to pray, sit in reverence, participate and to run with me in the early morning, noon, and before the sun set. Singing, praying hour after hour, minute after minute. Repeating songs and prayers as they are spoken by the Medicine Man is a hard thing to do. It was easy to watch my cousin-sisters go through this passage, but when it was my turn, well, that was a different story. It seemed like torture, but a newfound self was the result. Like Clarice, Garnet and I became Changing Woman and entered our new life as a young woman at the age of twelve.

When I became the *Kinaaldá*, I felt that I had begun to understand the mystery of knowing. Early in the morning, I ran as far as I could into the Tohatchi desert. Everyone who came to the ceremony ran with me, being careful not to run ahead. Those who could not keep up had to wait until I turned around and passed them on the way back to the Hogan. Anyone who turned, before the Kinaaldá, would age fast. Sitting up all night and running three times, each day was more than I thought I could endure. I had participated in other *Kinaalda's* before but until I experienced it myself – well, I just didn't know how tough I would have to be.

I remember Auntie Teresa telling me that I would experience a certain amount of understanding about life once I started to really live my life. I began to wake up to the things that were happening around me after my ceremony. Things don't just come to you; you must work for them. When you go to school, you must be tough enough to experience whatever it takes to get an education…good or bad.

Auntie Teresa was the one who brushed my hair with the straw brush, put it in a bun and tied it to make me a good thinker. All the while giving me advice about the things that I would need to know as a woman. You need to be patient now that you are a woman. Wait. Don't be too quick to speak. Watch your words! Words can harm others! Words are sacred! Talk is sacred!

For sure, had I heeded those words, I would've saved myself from punishment, BUT, right before summer, I had a lapse of judgement and should have remembered those words of advice.

My need to rush to speak caused me to have to stay for summer school, which was somewhat of an embarrassment when I tried to explain things to Gramps, Gramma, and mom why I wouldn't be coming home for the month of June. I couldn't blame my behavior on Julia James, the City Navajo, who had provoked me into an argument at her usual insulting post outside of Red Sands Elementary. She was a year ahead of us, and thought she was all that, and a cup of tea! That summer I had to be patient for one more month before being set free for the month of July. I learned my lesson.

Being patient is something that takes a lot of toughness. Everyone that stayed at Red Sands Residential Dormitory pretty much experienced the same pain, loneliness, and memories of families that patiently awaited their return in a distant somewhere. Navajos are not resilient; they are also tough enough to be patient and survive through the prayers of our ancestors. The Navajos who endured The Long Walk and four years of subjugation by an imposing force had to be tougher and more patient than I would ever know. The Navajo's who endured four years of starvation and watched each other helplessly wither away prayed for hope at the end of the ordeal, patiently surviving. Staying at Red Sands Residential Dormitory was nothing like what Navajos endured one hundred years ago. I felt embarrassed to think my time here was so awful or that Ruby had it easy.

Hearing some of the things that Ruby's mother had to deal with at her job, helped me know that, at least, the Navajo Tribal Government held firm on requiring the United States Government to uphold its Treaty obligations, as Gramps once put it. It sounded like things were looking up for Navajos in 1973.

While Ruby tried her best to remember what her grandmother taught her, she also had to block out the bad parts of being at Red Sands Residential Dormitory. Her reports of the Great Navajo Nation overshadowed why Ruby never told anyone what really happened to her in "The Room". If she told her secret, the news would hit the headlines of the Navajo Times – Former Council Delegate Granddaughter Molested by BIA Dorm Superintendent.

The consequence of telling this secret would be bad for everyone. Not only to her grandfather's reputation but to her mother's job. Superintendent Levinstein scared her down to the core and she knew he would keep his threats. Ruby feared disappearing into thin air like a high school girl named Dorothy. So, she endured the hated abuse of Frankenstein, who stalked and stole her innocence whenever and forever. Being the head white ass in charge, he managed to get her called to his office at any moment. Ruby hated white people more than anything on God's Green Earth. She made it a point not to even listen to the white kids who tried to talk to her in class. She just ignored them, and eventually they quit trying. Even though her visits to Window Rock had their ups and downs, she relished the weekends with her family. Besides, Window Rock was close enough to Gallup that Ruby could go to a movie or buy something with her hard-earned brat-sitting money.

On those weekends when she didn't have any brats around the house, her cousin Merwin would come over. They tried on make-up and fixed their hair in different ways. They always had great fun and Ruby always had money to burn. Merwin was girly and he acted like a girl; always waving his hands when he talked or wanting to try on Ruby's dresses and shoes. It was fun, and she enjoyed her time with Merwin. Ruby was Merwin's only friend and he longed to see her for the weekends. The boys at school would make fun of him and beat him up in the bathroom a couple of times. He always bounced back by the time she pulled up to the driveway. Merwin was always waiting for Ruby, rain, or shine.

Ruby talked Merwin into helping her brat-sitting to earn money for the summer break. They were planning on traveling to Disneyland in California. They heard they had to have lots of money, or they wouldn't have any fun. There were about 20 weekends until the end of May, so they made a goal of earning $500 each. Merwin squealed. Ruby rolled her eyes when he squealed. When they were younger, Merwin wanted Ruby to call him Sash because that was his pen name, and he was going to be a writer of romance poetry, as if! Ruby played along with him but only in private. On one of their long drives home from Red Sands, Ruby asked her mother why Merwin acted like a girl. "Ruby, there are what Navajos call, "twin spirits", and Merwin is one of them. In our Dine' Creation Story, the Twin Spirits are holy. Merwin is holy. Just let him be who he wants to be. He's family." That was the end of that discussion.

On a regular weekend visit with Merwin, Ruby announced she had decided to go to school at Window Rock High School. No matter what my mom says, I am NOT returning to Red Sands Residential Dormitory! I think I'm old enough to take care of myself

Merwin waved his hands ecstatically! He could not wait, finally a friend to hang around with at school! He would be entering the ninth grade, too, so that was just perfect for him. "Okay, so first we gotta get the same schedules". His mind was already ticking.

Ruby rolled her eyes, because deep down she was really going to miss her friends. Leaving Red Sands Residential Dormitory was going to be easy. It was a place she grew to hate ever since she turned 10, when she found herself in trouble for the first time. She didn't even know what she did, but she was marched into the Matron On Duty's office to face Mrs. Becenti, the most horrible person alive!

Ruby was always being blamed for one thing or another. Her snide remarks somehow ended in the punishment of "the Room", while other girls got away with similar misbehavior. Ruby never spoke of the trauma and abuse that she had to endure while in the infamous room, although I always wondered what it was like to be put in solitary confinement overnight in the small dark, dirty cubby hole she described it to be. I tried to tell her not to say anything by giving her *the eye* when she started speaking out. Garnet tried to stop her by nudging her whenever Julia James began her insults. But Ruby was determined to be Ruby.

It wasn't more than a 5 foot by 5-foot room that was located in the back room of the Matron's office. Many stories came from that experience and many girls shuddered at hearing them thinking of ways they could avoid "The Room" all together. Garnet, Clarice, and I had never had the bad fortune to visit the room, but we heard plenty. Ruby on the other hand, would rather not speak of it at all, especially since her life was threatened. What most kids didn't know was that the **B**ureau of **I**ndecent **A**ffairs Superintendent kept an eye on "The Room," because he always seemed to show up right before someone was punished.

The girls were not sure what Ruby had done this time, but she was summoned to Mrs. Becenti's office, which usually meant – "The Room." The third time Ruby was escorted to that despicable place was when she mouthed off to Mrs. Hagga. As she entered the dark encasement, she could smell the stench and filth. She could see the marks that other girls had left behind, including foul language about the dorm employees. One thing Ruby remembered was that little U-shaped metal object by the front of the door. Legend had it, as early as ten years ago, girls were shackled if they dared speak the Navajo language or be naughty in the slightest way. But in Ruby', it was just an excuse to abuse kids.

At precisely 12:00 midnight, Frankenstein unlocked the door to "The Room" and winced at the stench that emanated. His greedy mind didn't care about such things because he had to act quickly before the night ladies arrived to check on the girl. He slowly took her to the floor and caressed her juvenile breasts as she gasped in horror, knowing what he was going to do. "Mr. Levinstein, No!!" Her screams of protest were never heard, and all she could do each time his hideous face came close to hers; she spit at him and try to kick him in the groin. She never knew that in his twenty years with the B.I.A. he had his way with all the girls he wanted, and no one was going to keep him from Ruby's innocence, for he knew she was likely to end up getting in trouble again and again, destroying her innocence.

He found ways to create trouble for her, just so she would end up in that room of horror. She knew he made trouble for the little boys, too, because they had a place called "The Room" too. All she knew was that if she told a soul, she would be dead, just like Dorothy – the girl Levinstein threatened Ruby with when she didn't come out of the corner of that small room. "You don't want to end up like Dorothy, do you?" he would chide. Ruby never found out what actually happened to Dorothy, although he made it sound like he killed her. Perhaps, she is the ghost that hangs around Red Sands Residential Dormitory. None of Ruby's friends ever found out about this part of her life at Red Sands Residential Dormitory, although she came very close to telling them from time to time. The thought of death clouded the thoughts engrained the mind of a ten-year-old, as if the veil covered her mouth and mind. Ruby, instead, unloaded her hate onto the pages of the notebook she kept at the bottom of her locked footlocker.

Ruby was a loner all right. She was a loud-mouthed loner by choice and for her own survival. No one was going to break her stride or the brick shield that she built around her tumultuous life. Her mother would not believe her if she tried to tell her. She was so busy trying to please this Council Delegate or that tribal official, to notice that something was *really* wrong with her only child- cast to the wolves of the B.I. fuckin' A! she wrote cursing in her angry pencil. As long as they picked her up on the weekends, she was doing well in school and she was alive, there was no reason for them to worry. After a year of abuse, she had thoughts of running away. Sick ass white devil, she thought hating them all! The hate sent chills down her back, and she needed to take a very hot shower…the kind of hot that kills germs.

Each time she was finally released from the room, Ruby was like a zombie, and we would sit in solemn silence as we tried to bring her back to reality.

"Come on Ruby, you gotta bring yourself out of the darkness," Clarice would whisper trying to offer candy. "Get her in the shower.

"Maybe that'll wake her up – we need to get to class…the test!" I insisted, as I offered some bitter root medicine and corn pollen.

Clarice said a prayer for Ruby while we walked her towards the bathroom and into the shower. As we helped her undress, we noticed a smell that was unbearable. We gasped and thought that smell isn't urine…what could it be?

"Gosh, what happened to you in that room? What could be in there to make you smell so bad?" Garnet thought innocently.

Like many times before, we helped our friend back to life and it wasn't until we ate breakfast that Ruby finally started to respond.

She thought, "Okay, get yourself together. No one is to know. No one is to suspect anything happened," she instructed herself for what seemed like the millionth time. "Well, I guess I just had to make one last trip to "The Room" before the end of the year," she managed to say as she drank the last of her milk. All the while, she thought of ways to kill her perpetrator – that fiend! Staring at the wall, that ugly, white colored wall she grew to hate. He will get his just dues someday. All Ruby wanted to do was to get the hell out of this place, and as far away from *him* as possible. Ruby spent a lot of time vomiting and taking showers as though it would wash away the stinky smell of rotten teeth and whiskey. Ruby was not alone, and countless children were threatened with silence, or banished to the Promise Land.

I wondered what Ruby angrily wrote in her notebook. She spent a lot of time looking at fashion magazines. She would sit at Vance's Barber Shop and look at all the latest hair styles and the clothing they put on the models… She spent a lot of money on magazines only to cut them to shreds matching this half with that or liking what she saw, but not the color. She wanted to be a fashion designer for famous people. She wanted her name on all the tags. Designed especially for You, by Ruby or something cool like that…or maybe she would make up a catchy name. She wanted to take Navajo fashion into the future. She started learning how to sew from her grandmother when she was eight. Her grandmother had boxes of fabric scraps she used to make quilts or pillows. Grandma Ruby's house was filled with hand-sewn items.

Grandma Ruby gave most of her scraps to Ruby and Merwin for their summer fashion show. Merwin, I mean Sash, was a good model with his skinny model hips and all. On the weekends she found herself hand stitching her latest redo. Some of them were just ridiculous. Some came out pretty good, but Sash always managed to rip the hell out of the piece trying to take it off... "We gotta get that stitched right so you won't be ripping the hell out of my designs Sash!"

"Uhh! His hand on hip, back of hand on forehead, he exasperated, "Sorry dear, but you know I'm still learning to perfect my model undress style...you know. AND, Girl, you need to watch your words! All that cussing?" He smacked lips and kissed the air. My back turned - eyes rolling.

"Ruby, I found this silver material! Surprise!" To her delight there sat four yards of silver polyester material! "What shall we make? Let's make matching Go-Go outfits," Sash gleamed with delight. "No, let's do a theme. Let's see.."

"I know, how about Egypt. We can paint our faces, make those headdresses our of cardboard and use this to make some of our garments!" Sash exhaled...pouted...I thought we could do a 60's something or another"....sigh...back of hand on hip...as if... My back turned, eyes rolling.

"Sash, you're so extra!"

"Okay maybe we can have a competition to see which we will do. What do you think?"

"Okay, depends."

"Depends on what?!..."

Sash was so unpredictable! He had absolutely no guts! Geez! Let me think... Sash walks back and forth hand on chin thinking Ruby thought and thought....no, too hard for him....no, too hard for him... she had to think of something easy enough for Sash to do......Then it came, "How about a hairdo contest. You can do grandma's hair, and I'll do moms." Holding hands, jumping around, scream, how groovy that's gonna be!"

"Let's go ask." Sash covered his mouth with both of his hands and turned his eyes from side to side..as if.

The results were hilarious. There was Grandma Ruby with her hair all braided around and around her head with pink and purple satin flowers stuck here and there. Sash made sure she had on some gaudy white plastic circle earrings and the reddest lipstick he could find in his mother's Avon samples. She sold Avon for a living. Sash had a little suitcase full of make-up samples.

Ruby used so much hairspray that her mother had a six-inch 1960's bouffant hairstyle that flipped up in the back like a fish tail. Ruby made sure her makeup was just right, eyebrows defined with black liner, lips emphasized with pink lipstick and brown eyeliner around the edges. Ruby used a lighter foundation than her mother normally uses, so she looked a bit white. It was hilarious. When they were done, they just burst out laughing…knowing it might be a tie for the ugliest hairdo on Earth!

"Mom, Gramma, you can't look until the judging is done! Okay, Grandpa…you decide. Who won the contest for the best hairdo?"

When Grandpa walked into the living room, he was speechless. He was halfway between laughing out loud and seeing his lovely wife look so young with that hairdo and all those flowers. His shoulders shook. He blushed…stammered trying not to laugh out loud Well….let's see walking around both hairdo's; hand on whiskers.

"I think it's a tie. They're both, uum, interesting hairdos for this day and age. Anything you thought of today can be found in those magazines at the barbershop. So, yeah, it's a tie." Ruby and Sash hugged but there was still no decision.

"Well, are we going to get to see our hairdo?" Gramma asked. They both walked to the bathroom and looked in the mirror. There was so much laughter coming from there that Ruby and Sash felt like rookie hairdressers. The first time is always the worst. Just like when you make frybread, the first one is always the worst…Sash hugged Ruby assuredly. Silence. Laughter…back to the drawing board.

Grandpa and Grandma talked about that day for a long time, bringing some innocent laughter to their old age. "You should put flowers in your hair more often," he kidded. Smile.

"Shall we flip a coin?" Sash offered a quarter and the opportunity to have first dibs. "Heads." "Okay I'll be tails…" Flip….reveal….heads!!! "Egypt, it is!" "Alright, but my turn after that, deal?" "Deal." The race was on. They had to get gold, dark purple, dark green and….they planned on Saturday night some ideas for the fashion show. Sash was so excited she could hardly sleep. She spent her time doodling and looking for the right pattern while Ruby was exiled to Red Sands Residential Dormitory. Sash always wanted everything to be grand… There had to be a stage with dark purple curtains…it needs to be painted black with lights. Her mind was tick tick ticking..always…

It took three washings for Carol to get all that hairspray out of her hair, but it was fun and the most fun she had spent with her daughter in a long time. Fleeting guilt…but only for a moment. Sigh. Deep breathe…

After that, Grandma asked Sash to do her hair the same over and over again because Grandpa like it so much… sweet.

Ruby had such a great feeling at the beginning of 1974. She knew that there would be a life after Red Sands Residential Dormitory because the time was finally ticking down to zero... Her fashion ideas were a secret she kept from her friends. Like Florence and Clarice, she had notebooks of magazine cut outs glued with her own interpretation next to each, and a piece of fabric or two. Mrs. Heap had a ten-cent bargain scrap bin Ruby loved to rummage. Mrs. Heap always greeted Ruby with a "Whatcha looking for today, Ruby? Got some new fabric in the back." "Thanks Mrs. Heap." Ruby only bought fabric at Mrs. Heap's Thrift Shop. Never would she ever think of buying, much less wear, anything from a used clothing store. She secretly smirked at Florence, Garnet, and Clarice for wearing used white people's clothes. Ruby always had brand-new clothes and brand-new shoes, but she never wore any of her creations.

Ruby was a bit of a snob. She thought she didn't belong at Red Sands Residential Dormitory, but there was really no one to watch her while she was growing up. So, she ended up being watched by the infamous Bureau of Indian Affairs, AKA Hitler, AKA Big Brother. Sometimes, she thought about how her mother was so gung-ho about tribal issues, yet she fed her own daughter to the wolves... Her mother would never know how much her need to be free of motherly responsibilities for this so-called education had cost Ruby...never.

Ruby secretly envied Florence and Clarice's close friendship but never butted in on them. Clarice was just too calm for Ruby and sometimes she wished she could be just as reserved...but she was afraid that would make her soften and then she would spill the beans. She knew that Garnet had it the worst out of all of them. Ruby never told anyone she saw Garnet in the parking lot of the Red Sands Saloon...probably because she didn't want to admit her mother Carol was inside getting alcohol for her groupies waiting in Window Rock. Better to be loud and obnoxious. Window Rock Fighting Scouts, here I come, maybe!! Deep breath, sigh...

Of the four of us, Ruby was the one who would leave, not only her spirit, but the innocence of her childhood at Red Sands Residential Dormitory. It would be ten years before Ruby shared her tormented childhood with me. One day, a package arrived in the mail. Inside were the notebooks Ruby kept in her locked footlocker. I was always curious about what she was writing so fiercely. Never did I think it held what I read. She promised me never to compromise her freedom – I never did.

Ruby, Ruby the true survivor of Red Sands Residential Dormitory horror. I finallgt understood Ruby's past behavior and decided though we didn't know, we protected her by sticking by her side. I couldn't get myself to write a poem for Ruby...all I had was silence, silent tears, and anger ensued....ANGER!!

Chapter 10 - Julia James, the City Navajo

While Ruby expressed her hatred towards white people, there were Navajos who didn't like Navajos at school. Julia James and her sidekicks were those kinds of Navajos. Meaning they ridiculed those of us who lived at Red Sands Residential Dormitory. Her torment started when she showed up at Red Sands Public School in 5th grade. We did what we could to avoid her, but I had to feel the results of her wrath by spending June at Red Sands, instead of enjoying my summer out on Tohatchi Flats. Like Ruby, Julia got in trouble with her smart-alecky mouth and often ended up wiping tables in the cafeteria on the same day. It was a relief this year because she went on to high school. Red Sands Junior School was about one fourth of a mile from the dormitory, so it wasn't that far to walk. The only thing was we had to pass by the high school to get there and that meant dealing with *"stinkin"* Julia James. She was about the meanest Navajo girl we ever met. Her parents *lived* in Red Sands, so she did not live at Red Sands Residential Dormitory. In her mind, that made her better than us. "Joe-babes", is what she called everyone who stayed at the dorms. I did my best not to have any reason to be near Julia James. We still cannot figure out how she passed eighth grade and went on to ninth grade. We were just glad she went to high school and could not torture us "reservation Navajos" with name calling.

Last year, I was just about ready to punch Julia in the face, but, just then, Mr. Thomas the Principal, happened to walk by and put a stop to Julie James' latest argument, and me trying to defend myself. We were both caught red handed. Our punishment was to spend the four weeks stuck here in summer school, as we were suspended for "fighting" even though there was no fight. At the dorm, I tried to plea my case, but there was no way out. Eugene, the Manual Labor Guy, took ten long minutes to figure out a punishment for me and came up with the lame task of picking up rocks and trash for an hour each day. I turned this into a search for nice rocks to keep for my collection. When he finished deliberating, he summoned me to the window. His black hair was sleek back with Alberto V-O5, and his face was riddled with pimple scars. His teeth were so crooked it looked like someone just threw them in there, but he smiled anyway.

"Here, you start as soon as da summer school gets here." He walked away, without seeing the scowl on my face followed by my look of deep sadness. How was I going to explain this to my grandparents and mother?

"Well, I see you both are picking up speed on your wardrobe... about a year too late!" Julia and her groupies laughed. "Those shoes have been out of style for *ages*! Your reservation Navajos are so Johned-out!"

The girls laughed, and all Clarice and I could do was glare at the group and keep on walking. Just when I thought we were at a safe distance, Ruby *had* to open her mouth!

"Why don't you pick on someone who has a mouth as big as yours, Julia the City-J-o-h-n!" Ruby said. The way she said it you could hear her voice go through her throat and out her nose. "If anyone's not up to speed, it's you! You think you and your white friends can...."

"Miss Reynolds, Miss Arviso, move on and get to class," said a voice from the window. It was Mr. Lopez, the high school art teacher. "Miss James, I want to see you in my classroom right now."

Without a thought, we swiftly ran toward the junior high, and to our classes, just as the first bell rang. "I'll see you at lunch." I said, "These shoes you got helped me run fast."

"Florence, running will be our story when we leave this place," Clarice replied as she stepped into Mrs. Rainer's noisy classroom.

I stared into the lockers and took a deep breath, understanding what she meant by leaving this place. Deep breath, realities change with time..sigh…

Meanwhile, Julia sat at her stiff desk and waited for the Substitute to arrive. Her heart always skipped a beat when she was near Raymond, a quiet guy who looks like he's half Navajo and half white or Mexican, she couldn't tell. She referred to him as a half-breed, so her white friends wouldn't find out she had eyes for him. She thought about Clarice and her geeky friend, Florence, and winced at her own summer of pain. Not only did she have to go to summer school, but after that she had to go home, and chop up the wood her dad was going to take to his relatives on the reservation, a place she hated to visit. Then, she had to make bread and cook for her dad and two little brothers. The only punishment was chopping wood. She had been cooking for her family since her mother ditched them for a better life in California. How does a 10-year-old child learn to cook without burning down the house or making everyone sick? Well, once a month, the Librarian sets up a "Free Books" table. Julia, luckily, found a recipe book with easy recipes. Her aunt helped her perfect her dough to make frybread and fluffy tortillas. The kind that melts in your mouth, her little brothers would say every time she made them. Now, she could cook just about anything. Her arms ached for days after her punishment was over. Knowing her relatives would have firewood for the winter made the pain worth the punishment. Florence Arviso would never know how much she loathed her bold rezzy attitude, or that she secretly admired her for being so smart. For sure, she wasn't going to get hooked up with a half-breed and stuck on the rez! I am *not* a Rezzy Girl!! I am a California Girl! Yet, Raymond was so good to look at, and it was hard to keep him out of her mind. She forced herself to look away. to focus…yes focus on getting out of Red Sands.

What we didn't know was that Julia James was the daughter of Tina and Reginald James and grew up in Riverside, California – part of the relocation Navajos. She didn't know anything about being a Navajo. She only knew a few Navajo words. She secretly watched Florence and Clarice go through their ritual runs some mornings, pretending to understand what they were doing. Her white friends thought the dormitory Navajos were low class or no class and encouraged her to ridicule them, whenever possible.

Julia was stuck in two worlds with no roots in either world. Her parents were so far removed from their own parents that Julia didn't even know her Nali or Chei', except for blurred memories of short visits to deliver food or wood for the winter. Her mother's siblings were still living in California, and wondered why their sister, Tina, had moved to Red Sands in the first place. Reginald's elderly father was now living in a nursing home in Chinle. His mother died of diabetes while he was in high school. Tina and Reginald had many fights about returning to California and Reginald's wishes to teach his children about their Navajo culture. They compromised and moved to the outskirts of the reservation. His great plan to teach his children ended in long hours at work and endless bills. Eventually, Tina and Reginald split up, and Tina returned to California without her children. Julia grew up without her mother, didn't know her culture, or who she was, and her whole world was shattering around her. She was a lost child, with a determination not to let anyone know, especially the rezzy dormitory kids.

Her bold in your face demeanor was a cover up for the loss she was feeling in her family life. Julia peddled candy and gum to the kids at school for extra money. She was determined to save money, move to California, and go to cooking school. There was no way her mother was going to return to Red Sands, so Julia had no choice but to make California her goal. She felt cheated that mom was not there teach her how to be a woman. Julia lived her life waiting for a letter from her mom but when they began to trickle in, she knew that something or worse, someone was taking up her time.

"My future is not going to be living in this dump forever!" Julia told herself every day so as time went on and her nest egg grew, she knew it was a possibility her dream would come true. Meanwhile, Julia had to teach her little brothers how to cook simple things, in case she had to stay late at school or go to a game that would end late. For the past year, her father was gone for two to three weeks at a time for work, traveling the railroad. Julia thought of how she had to prepare her little brothers to care for themselves when the time came for her to leave Red Sands for good. She set her sights on her senior year to leave.

She thought of leaving like the Beverly Hillbilly's…. "so she loaded up her bags and moved to Beverly…Hills that is..black gold, Texas tea…" A better life is always one that begins in Californ-i-a.. Smile, deep breath…. got to leave those middle schoolers alone…

Julia felt like some kind of impending change was about to happen in her life. She could not put her finger on it. She had saved $1,000 secretly selling snacks to the white kids at school, who always had money. By the end of high school, her goal was to add another $1,000. She noticed one of the girls selling beaded jewelry, and thought of learning to make money like that, but she had no idea how to bead. There weren't any free books on how to do native bead work at the library. She thought of asking that chick but, Naah. Maybe she'll ask the Librarian if she could look out for some free books that teach beadwork. Or maybe I'll raise my prices by a nickel….good plan. Smile, sigh…California here I come!!

Until the summer of punishment, I wondered why Julia James didn't like us because we were all the same. If it wasn't for her best friend Denise, a half white and half Mexican girl who had to go to summer school because her family was too poor to feed her at home, I would never have known the sadness Julia covered up with her aggressive behavior. I decided it was best to avoid Julia at all costs. Nobody liked summer school, but the food was way better than what they forced us to eat at Red Sands Residential Dormitory. AND I learned that everybody has their own story. I decided a long time ago that I would put my story on paper…and I might even include Julie James, the City Navajo.

Julia James, the City Navajo

City girl with frybread hands,
rage tucked beneath a perfect braid.
She laughs the loudest so no one hears
the silence waiting at home.

She calls us "Joe-babes"
to forget she once forgot her own clan songs—
born of concrete and strip malls,
shaped by absence and railroad ties.

Julia, who sells Skittles like secrets,
dreams in California colors,
her pockets lined with gum and grit.
She can cook a storm and swallow sorrow whole.

We saw a bully.
She saw a road.
And all the while,
her heart packed its bags for Beverly Hills.

Chapter 11 – Gaining Wisdom

After years as a ward of the Bureau of Indian Affairs (B.I.A.), some things are worth holding true to… For me, it was my circle of friends that I lived with since kindergarten for my own good. We grew up to be sisters and talked about life experiences in the dorm and at school. We experienced and witnessed verbal, mental, spiritual, and physical abuse at the hands of the B.I.A. and, in the midst of the public school's watchful eyes. All those emotions of being away from home…from our mothers and fathers and grandparents; uncles and aunties and cousins. Abuse, we were forced to swallow and learned never to speak out loud for fear of more impending retaliation. Our time was regimented as if we were prisoners. There was no freedom unless we stole it. We had no choice but to endure life away from our natural environment. Events like Movie Nights helped us dream of a life in Never, Neverland, even for just a minute. Stealing freedom through our runs, times roaming around, always mindful of time. Those events shaped us.

Reality bites when the sun rises, and everyday routines continue. The captives of Red Sands Residential Dormitory were coming of age in a time of Women's Rights, The Vietnam War, Segregation, Black Panthers, Second Class Citizenship, Whites who hated Black people enough to kill them in broad daylight. Martin Luther King, Jr. led the Civil Rights Movement, but the Matrons would not allow us to watch any of this on T.V. so we had to find out what was going on by sneaking The Red Sands Tribune into the dorm. We found ways to sneak out of the dorm when the guards were not watching, and we learned to not feel guilty about it.

An unspoken thought was that Indians experienced segregation, out-right murder, hatred, and Second-Class Citizenship for hundreds of years, yet we remain invisible targets. Our stories are worthless. Even in the 1970's, the White Man still got away with atrocities.

"We survived through the prayers of our elders and the belief that we are the Children of Holy People," Gramps would assure us, with that far-away look.

I knew that without Gramps and Gramma, I would be wondering where I belonged – especially if we had stayed in Klagetoh. I hadn't thought about that place in a long time.

Wandering, I Ponder
Do you ponder, or do you roam?
Is it meaning that you seek—
or simply space to be alone?

I wonder what truly holds weight,
what matters beneath the noise,
as I wander this winding path
called life.

…endlessly isolated,
yet never without thought

The Navajo people live in diverse worlds depending on their choice. Some choose to live in a border town, existing between two worlds: mainstream America and the Navajo Nation. Those Navajos must compete with the whites, Mexicans, and Blacks. Many of them find themselves living on the brink of survival and poverty. On the other hand, very few can survive living on sheep herding and the ranch life alone. Long ago, the only competition was a horse race, or a poker game called Navajo 10. Many Navajos incorporated K'e' (traditional ways) with the ways of Christianity, Holy Rollers, Gáamalií (Mormons) and other churches. Uncle Ed would say, "When you replace your traditional life it is easy to see it as less than, and time will steal sacred songs and prayers. Just look around, across the Navajo Nation there were at least five different churches in any small community…all trying to meet their conversion quota…to save our souls from our "heathenish" selves." I noticed that I too, chose to be Catholic and Traditional. For sure, I NEVER chose to be locked up at Red Sands Residential

Dormitory. Being observant is not a choice, it is a must I learned from my family. The clouds, where the sun rose and set, the way the wind blew, and the movements of the stars. Living at Tohatchi Flats a person must be observant or else you might find yourself stuck in the mud. In these long years, I counted 22,660 tiles that made up the floor in Dorm A.

When I read teen magazines, the surveys always reported whites, Blacks, and those they considered "Others," like Asians. There was never any consideration to how Natives or Mexicans felt about anything.

For that matter, I noticed that Native Americans were never identified as people on any of the magazine polls I read. The only statistics they keep on us were how many of us die of diabetes, cirrhosis, or alcohol related deaths. Flipping through different magazines at Safeway, I noticed the charts that have people, but I never saw where the Navajos fit in. Never minding where I might fit in... To be sure, the magazines I enjoy and faithfully read helped me believe that it was possible to be both adventurous and at the same time grounded in my Navajo traditions. This was a good thing for me because I am high spirited and understand the dos and don'ts of *being* a Navajo. Those are things I live by and will always be a part of daily life.

With Mrs. Becenti's strict "White Man's Ways", we stood a chance of figuring out how to live in both worlds. Eventually and inevitably, we learned to become aware of and awake to our non-Navajo environment as we grew up at Red Sands Residential Dormitory, longing for our home and fiercely missing each other in our absence. The feeling was always on our minds- all of us living under the roof of the Bureau...the idea of being oppressed by people, like how Mick Jagger sings of being under someone's thumb. Even the language we had to speak in secret or not at all. For sure, I, too, would experience a certain amount of knowing. A knowing that is so deep that it emanates from the very fabric of the Navajo culture and embedded in the language.

Yes, we are different, but to me, it was a good difference. What I didn't realize was that the standard for "good" in the White

Man's world was practically the opposite of what I thought, or so I thought, by my own personal observations in my thirteen years. They live from the outside in... I knew very well I was supposed to be living from the inside out. Reality is reality... My reality was patience...

Mrs. Montano was the angel that watched over us, even though we didn't see her every day or every week. We soon learned to review the Matron on Duty schedule, to see when Mrs. Montoya would be on duty. Those were the days we learned to love and remember as the good ole' days of life at Red Sands Residential Dormitory as six- and seven-year-olds. Now, we could rush to the Safeway store to get goodies because we knew Mrs. Montano allowed it and wouldn't be breathing down our neck like some of the other Matrons. Clarice found out that Mrs. Montano was on duty that night for Mrs. Hagga. That was something of a mysterious because Mrs. Hagga was *always* on duty – drunk or not. The good part was that Mrs. Montano always meant *popcorn* and the *privilege* of staying up to watch late night T.V. One time, there was a movie on called, *Hush, Hush Sweet Charlotte* with our all-time favorite actress, Betty Davis. The story about a poor cousin who wanted to take over millions of dollars by making Charlotte, played by Betty Davis, think she was going crazy. *Picture Mommy Dead* was another film forever burned in my memories, especially when I got up in the early morning hours and peeked around to see if any of those ghosts would suddenly appear and scare the living daylights out of me. Of course, they never did.

Praying and running were always a choice for Clarice and me. At times, I wondered why more kids did not get up in the early morning and prayed with us. The two of us have been praying for as long as I can remember, and it was as natural as it should be and would be if we were at home. Living in at Red Sands Residential Dormitory too long can bring children to a point of not remembering their Navajo teachings... maybe because we were scared into submission and dare not practice the Beauty Way and walk the Corn Pollen Path. Some are too brainwashed to think that being a Navajo is any good. Either way, we made our way outside each morning – rain or shine. Choices…

We were finishing the eighth grade, and in one of hundreds of the Bureau of Indian Affairs Residential Dormitories built across the United States meant to acculturate and assimilate us by washing away our culture through their harsh system. Meanwhile, we attended public school at Red Sands like hundreds of Navajo students. Like everyone else, I learned to both love and hate my life at Red Sands Residential Dormitory. I prayed for the days to go by fast so that I could return to Tohatchi Flats, where I was free; to be able to go outside of the house and explore all day long and no one would think anything of it.

Meanwhile, I had to correctly manage the mundane life the "**B**laming **I**ndians **A**gain" dictated without being sent to "The Room," the place of punishment. We had fun making up different sayings for the acronym B.I.A. – we probably had a thousand of them by now. The B.I.A. was and is the "State" to which the phrase; "Wards of the State" refers. It was like big brother or a hovering nemesis, one that takes its duty to us Navajos, as serious as a coyote spying on the flock, or worse yet, one that makes tremendously questionable decisions in the name of the almighty White Father. I would find out in the future that it would be a long hard battle to remove Tribal Politics, Government and Federal Monies from the clutches of the almighty Bureau of Indian Affairs, and the battle seemed to be a losing one at that…that is, according to Ruby. I took her reports of the Great Navajo Nation with a grain of salt, but I looked around and must agree.

I made the choice not to let the Bureau of Indian Affairs to be my only reality. I liked to float to these memories because it made living under the clutches of the B.I.A. bearable. If my mother had not made the choice to leave my father, I would never know the warmth from Gramp's' hazel green eyes as he would pull out his spectacles, as he called them, and begin reading under an old cedar tree or a salt brush or whatever kind of refuge the land provided out on Tohatchi Flats. "Grandchild, this is another great story…" as he began. Gramps taught me to have a large vocabulary. In the background, I imagined hearing sounds of Gramma's wooden comb pounding the strands of wool into another beautiful rug. The smell of firewood and fresh coffee filled the air, and you just know you are home and safe.

Even Mrs. Gardner would be impressed with Gramps' English vocabulary. He knew how to use many long words that I had to look up later when he was not looking. Although Gramps made it to the seventh grade, he had to quit so he could herd his mother's thousand sheep and care for the cattle and horses. He lived a rancher's life and that was that - to be self-sufficient was the goal in a Navajo life he always advised. All of us knew Gramps and Gramma had a special bond of love and patience shared between all their grandkids, but I spent most of the time with them. The *Life Magazine* with President Kennedy on the cover was always lying around ready to be read and re-read. Nineteen-sixty-three was an awful 60th birthday year for Gramps and Gramma. A picture of President Kennedy remained on the walls of the Castle House for all time and eternity, as Gramps would put it. I found myself flipping through that magazine year after year.

One thing that was particularly funny about Gramps was the way he collected things, anything, and everything! You name it, he probably had it in his treasure trove of *junk*. "No, that could be useful someday," he would demand as Gramma tried to throw away some of the clutter. He had jars of nuts, bolts, nails, screws, buttons, and bundles upon bundles of bailing wire. Sometimes the neighbors would stop by to see if Gramps had this part or that; and lo and behold, he usually did! From time to time, the muffler on Red Robin would be tied up with bailing wire; usually in the spring after winter thawed into mud.

I grew up learning that Gramps was very intelligent and didn't need to go to college to know how to take things apart and put them back together. He also knew how to improvise. Cousin Chuckie once asked about how the moon and stars changed places all year long and Gramps knew the answer exactly. I used to check to see if he was right by looking in the Encyclopedias in the Multipurpose Room, but after a few times of finding Gramps correct, I quit doing that. It was all because he would read and read and read while he was herding sheep. It could be boring all alone out there at the Flats, I reminisced the times when I had to do it alone. That was the reason I sent Gramps books that I had read making sure there was enough postage to send it back before it became overdue. Gramps always sent a brief message about the book, a few dollars, and the latest news about Tohatchi Flats…and always a reminder to say my prayers.

The funny part of all of this reading was that Gramps told those around him, no matter who it was - human, horse, cat, dog, even insects - he would tell his story loud enough so that even the land knew what he was reading.... Gramps, being a quarter French German, was raised to be a humble sheepherder and cattle rancher – self-made, self-sufficient. He could compete with John Wayne and win. Honestly, I think Gramma would beat both hands down!! Yes, it was a good choice to leave Klagetoh and that hateful life. That's one good choice my mother made for me. Not sure about the choice of Red Sands Residential Dormitory/Public School life. I thought. "It's for your own good, Grandchild, your own good."

Reality beckons and another year comes to an end. For English, I had to write a final paper about an event, or a person that made an impression on her life. I had to think about the theme or lesson learned from my life experiences thus far. I thought about many things that made an impression on my life, and the other things from the assignment. There were so many things that I could think of, so, I began to write about how it was to leave the comforts of home and my loved ones every fall.

LEAVING TOHATCHI FLATS – A YEARLY EVENT

By Florence Arviso

On an early fall Monday morning, the smell of a delicious mixture of leftovers and yellow corn meal shifted through the crisp cool air as I stirred. The strong smell of sheepherder's coffee made its way to my senses, and I could stand it no more. Gramps was up before everyone milling around in the kitchen – living up to his "Early to bed, early to rise, makes a man, healthy, wealthy and wise" motto. I was startled awake by a noise on the roof, or I thought it sounded like it was coming from the roof. As I opened one eye and then the other, a squirrel made its way on the round wooden beams, finding a hole, jumping in, and then disappeared into the darkness. I turned to face the hair of the goatskin I always slept on. I knew that smell would always comfort me, and that it would not be there tonight. The thought of the rough dorm bed sheets and hard mattress and ooh the awful detergent smells! "Well, I better get up and make use of as much of this day." This was how my dreaded trip back to Red Sands Residential Dormitory began from the time I stepped into kindergarten until this my ninth year. I remember wishing each year, I could go to school closer to my Gramps and Gramma. Each of those nine years came and went. The most painful ones were from kindergarten to third grade. By nine years old, I had become programmed to relish the times out at Tohatchi Flats, wishing each day to slow down.

I remember the first year like it was yesterday. Quietly, I stretched and made my way into the kitchen. "Gramps," what smells so good, is it breakfast?" Gramps smiled as he continued his early morning routine. "No, it's slop for the sheep dogs," He smiled then laughed as he stirred with the long wooden ladle, he made himself." You want some coffee, Grandchild? It should be ready by now. Then you can get ready to take the sheep out for Hosteen T0dach'77'n77." "H1gosh99, Sh7' Cheii," (*Okay, Granmps*) I replied slurping my last cup of the best coffee in the world.

The only thing that helped me survive the B.I.A. ordeal was thinking about how much more comfortable and fun while enjoying the thought of going home would be during school breaks. Each year since I was five, I had to make the same journey away from the people I loved and longed for, all those 260 days. I marked the calendar day by day, month by month. Marking time as if it would help making time go by faster.

My mind sees every detail, every smell, every sound, everything! I remember that day as if it was yesterday. What was pitiful was that every year was exactly the same; the long drive, the sadness, the empty feeling and then the joy of seeing friends – yep, the memories of the beginning of the year have been the same for nine years. Impressions of home are stamped in the mind of a child, while living the regimented life at the Bureau of Indian Affairs Dormitory.

The day was like any other day at The Ranch because someone still had to do the everyday work; no matter what else might be in the plans. My Mother was always busy working at Fairchild, which was 100 miles from Tohatchi Flats. Fairchild was a company that made electronic parts for the military, so she could never take me back to school. When I look back, I know my mother was working to make things better for me. Sacrifice is not a stranger in our lives. My Mother, Uncles, and Aunts worked so much, Gramps and Gramma's home was a haven for us during the summer. That's what you call the Navajo tradition.

Each year, the last minutes before leaving my home were filled with sadness. Gramma cooked her specialty and my favorite breakfast: *n1neeskaadi* (tortillas), scrambled eggs, bacon, fried potatoes, fresh green chili, and the green steel thermos filled with freshly brewed strong sheepherder coffee. My coffee, which was usually half coffee and half goat's milk. Gramma smiled as I cooled the coffee in my favorite stoneware cup. Gramma told me that it belonged to her dad, Charlie Arviso. It was a special cup, very old and favorite for the both of us. I taught Gramma to play paper, scissors, rocks to get to see which one of us would win the use of her special cup. The comforts of homemade food left an impression on the taste buds when eating the bland canned food, the Bureau of Indian Affairs feeds the students year after year. Grandma's tortillas were so good they melted in your mouth!

Gramma had the longest hair I had ever seen. When Gramma combed her hair, it took two strokes to get to the end! My hair is only down to my waist, but I knew that I would have long hair like Gramma too one day. Navajos are not supposed to cut their hair because it is like cutting away your family. Tradition is a way of life. There is no compromise on traditional ways. They are what they are.

Tradition also means work. Every summer, everyone would help shear the sheep. The wool would be washed with yucca root in boiling pots on an open fire. During the summer we would travel up to the mountain and collect different flowers and plants that would be used to dye the wool. We helped card the wool while Gramma spun it into yarn balls. She could weave the most beautiful rugs. Gramma's rugs are double woven -- a style that is very hard to do. Her rugs had one design on one side and the colors and design are reversed on the other side creating the illusion of depth. Her famous diamond double weave can be found all over the ranch house, and in many of our relatives' homes. I inherited the soft voice her grandma had and sometimes it is hard for people to hear us speak. Most of my Arviso family members are soft-spoken, hardworking, ranching people by nature. My Gramps would say, don't let that soft voice fools you. She also carries a heavy stick. It didn't dawn on me what he meant until I learned about metaphors this year.

The usual breakfast conversation was hushed to almost silence – a silence that leaves an impression on the mind of a Bureau of Indian Affairs child that I would be living in a certain kind of silence when I woke up the next day. I looked at Gramma and then at Gramps and knew that there was so much said in that silence. I took a BIG gulp and tried very hard to fight back the tears.

"Gosh Gramps, can't I stay here and go to school at Tohatchi Day School?" I begged, as the tears eventually began to flood down my cheeks.

Year after year, Gramps would say, "Well, Grandchild, your mother, your grandmother and me -- We want you to get a good education and when you're at Red Sands you get to go to public school. We all think that's going to help you get ahead in life."

"But Gramps, I can learn from you. You can teach me while we herd the sheep on the weekends and the teachers at Tohatchi Boarding School can teach me the rest and well... I can always teach myself." I had to learn the hard way not to ask but we all knew that there was not anything they could do about my schooling. Sacrifice can be a sad waiting game, especially not knowing the outcome or "reward".

I had no choice. I was going and there were no two ways about that! I knew that if Gramma had it her way, she would keep me there to help, to keep them company, and to give them someone to look after beside each other. Separation leaves an impression on the life of a Bureau of Indian Affairs child. It was an impression marked by yearly sadness and eventual heartbreak.

Harry T0d7ch'77nii, our sheep herder, would always join us for supper and at a certain point, I knew the conversations would turn to the upcoming schedule --the do's and don'ts to flock control, any reports of bears, bob cats or wild dogs...including coyotes. Harry also helped Gramps around the ranch. He was one of Gramps' staunchest supporters when it came to the Vietnam Conflict. Everybody had something to say, and they switched from one subject to another. I knew that they were as worried as Gramma was, about Uncle Benny and Uncle Leonard, being in Vietnam. It was like that when Uncle Ed and Uncle Andy were fighting in the Korean Conflict, or so I was told. War leaves an impression on everyone; Navajo, White, Mexican, Black – everyone – sacrifice for our country and protecting our *Din4tah (our homeland)*.

Other than the things that were going on outside of the ranch, life was simple, hard, fun, and great. I had to guess that that was why Gramps and Gramma chose two places to live. Often my thoughts drifted..."balance and harmony, that's all you need," Gramps would announce during or after (mostly out of the blue) to those who were of listening range and often when no one was anywhere near enough to hear except me. Many times, Gramps would fold the paper down and say something that sounded like it was supposed to be profound after reading from *The Navajo Times or The Gallup Independent.* Cousin Chuckie, my cousins, and I would look at each other with raised eyebrows. Come to think of it, even Lucky gave his usual side-eye shifted at Gramps, as if. So, everyone would just let Gramps go on talking what he knew and what he thought...because we knew that's how Gramps taught us and that was the way he was able to deal with two of his four sons being outside of the *Din4tah*. Their sons sacrifice for service of country…

The week before each school year started, my cousins and I went horseback riding. I relished the freedom of the horse rides and letting the horse take control during our horse races. We talked about how the war had affected the whole family. From what we gathered, Uncle Benny and Uncle Leonard were classified as 'Eagle Eyes' or Snipers.

"That means they were marksman," Chuckie explained.

That made the rest of us feel better but still, Gramps would not act this way if he were not worried. "Heeh, Gramps sighed, I guess we're going to be going into Saigon for what the United States Government is calling the Tet Offensive. That meant Ben and Levi were getting closer to the front line. As I grew up, I remember many times my family came together in prayer, for they were helpless to the government demands.

The dishes cleared from the table and lunch packed, Grammas, Gramps went about their business making sure they had plenty of provisions, just in case. I went to take one last look at the small room I shared with Gramma. I sat on the bed, took a look at where the squirrel had been running along the beam, and the hole that he had disappeared into, and remembered the day when Chuckie and I had snuck up on Gramps in the barn singing his usual, "MEXICO!! MEXICO!! at the top of his voice. His voice drowned out, as he became aware of us standing by the door.

Gramps said, "Well, you might as well come on in and help roll up this bailing wire with me."

As we came into the barn, I asked, "Gramps, how come Uncle Benny and Uncle Leonard have to be at war?

"Grandchild, you don't have to worry about that, everything will work out."

I knew Gramps, too, was thinking of the War and how Uncle Leonard and Uncle Benny were doing overseas in the middle of the conflict. Gramma's expression turned from anger, then worry, when she listened to Gramps interpret the stories about the progress of the war he read or heard on the radio. The thing of it all is that life went on, the work routine never ended, and we never did find out why Gramps was singing about Mexico in the first place.

A deep breath helps me gather my feelings every year on this day for nine years. One last smell of my goat skins bed and the smell of Gramma's bedspread I laid back and cried. It never gets easier to leave my Stone Castle and Tohatchi Flats. "Get yourself together!" I had learned to say to myself, because I felt sure everything would remain the same when I returned. I slowly made my way out to the truck with my footlocker and tote bag filled with "the essentials"-- Lays potato chips, cherry jolly rancher popsicle sticks, apple flavored block gum, a couple of dollars for spending and the usual school supplies. Red Robin, the ranch truck, was ready with all the necessary items. Hosteen T0dich88nii lifts my footlocker onto the tailgate and pushes it into the bed of the truck. I'm always the last of the grandkids to leave Tohatchi Flats, and that had to be the loneliest feeling in the world for Gramps and Gramma. The Stone Castle seems to take a deep breath knowing that the sounds of laughter would soon turn to the sound of the whipping wind, insects, and sounds of cattle. The familiar scent and scene of home leaves an indelible impression on the day I had to return to the prison that is Red Sands Residential Dormitory.

Gramps gives his final instructions to the 'Hired Hands' and then the dreaded final climb into Red Robin.

"*H1gosh88 t['44honaa'47.* {eezh {ich77' go d4y1. (All right, we are going to be back tonight. We are going to Red Sands.)

Gramma and I waved at Harry T0d7ch'77nii as he backed *T4lii* (donkey) out of the corral and headed down the path. The sheep were already at the bottom of the ridge by the time he reached them and that was when Gramps "turned over the vehicle." ...as Uncle Andy would say.

Uncle Andy and his kids left earlier in the summer. They lived in Phoenix and were already in their second week of school by the time I left for school. All my other cousins left the week before me. I was the last one to leave Tohatchi Flats, and was the most affected by the departure, especially as we drove away and the vast desert that made up Tohatchi Flats became a distant speck and soon disappeared beyond the dusty road.

The drive was long. Just getting to the main road from the Ranch was 15 miles of ruts, water puddles and rocks, then miles and miles of pavement. Gramps was humming his usual Navajo song, and I could feel the lump crawling up my throat as Gramma put her arm around me. "*Tladoo'n7'cha Sh7 ylzh7.*" "Don't cry, Grandchild." I knew those Navajo words by heart. I did my very best to follow Gramps' advice to keep my chin up.

When I thought of it, Gramps had a lot of sayings and through these, he seemed to live his life...even though a traditional Navajo life can be harsh Gramps found a way to make my memory of life at Tohatchi Flats something to cherish forever and ever and ever. "Every episode in your life is telling you something about yourself. When you place meaning and attention to this, then your life will be fuller."

He used to say things like that to us while we were herding sheep or even when we were trying to listen to XRock80 from Juarez, Mexico on the radio... I think not many people could hack life out at Tohatchi Flats. Survival is a way of life. To Gramps and Gramma, it didn't seem to be much of a sacrifice.

I know that nothing Gramps said was a waste of time for listening. I learned to believe his sayings were true. "A child or even a person has to hear something 1,000,000 times to remember it." Lord knows, I have heard some of them at least a million and ten times!"

The courage of leaving the comforts of home leaves an impression on the Bureau of Indian of Affairs child. Gramps eased the truck into the Tohatchi 'Gas and Stuff.' His usual fueling place.

As he popped the hood, he said, *"G*o get some paper towels so we can check the oil." Then he turned and unlocked the gas tank and began to pump gas, while I jumped out and walked towards the store - all the while Gramps whistled his favorite Navajo tune, I have grown to love.

"Gramps, how come I have to go to boarding school and why can't I stay here and go to school?"

"It's not up to me, Grandchild. Your mother wants you to get a good education and besides, you go to Public School and stay at a dormitory. There is a difference between that and the old Bureau of Indian Affairs schools."

"Still, I want to stay, and my mother doesn't understand." I turned my head to hide the tears and began to open the hood as Gramps had taught me, so he could reach the dipstick.

Gramma was saying something to Gramps while he nodded and grinned. I studied his face so I could remember the lines on his face and how his large hands had seen his fair share of hard work. I looked over to Gramma and wondered how it was like when they were young, and what the "old" B.I.A. boarding schools were when my mom went there. They couldn't be any worse than Red Sands Residential Dormitory, that's for sure.

The difference between life at Tohatchi Flats and life at Red Sands Residential Dormitory leaves an impression on a Bureau of Indian Affairs child.

"Looks like we're going to need a quart," Gramps said as he tried to line up the dip stick with the hole.

I studied his large hands that had veins sticking out and his hazel eyes behind his wire frame glasses. A small tear came down as he wiped his face and shut the hood.

"We better be going," Gramps said, as he got back into the truck after paying for the gas and oil.

The long journey to Red Sands was enough to make me fall asleep and a few times, I caught myself nodding off. Then the familiar edge of town came in sight and that lump welled in my throat as I rested my head on Gramps' arm to smell that "Grandpa smell". I looked up and I could see tears making our way down Gramps' cheeks.

"Don't worry, Grandchild, time flies when you make use of it."

Every year, the same advice was given to me as if it was the only thing they could say so they would not all give in and take me back to the ranch. The words that were supposed to comfort me only made me dread another long year ahead. "Uh huh." I say solemnly. Sometimes I would say that just so he would know I was listening.

"Just be strong and remember you come from a good family. This part of your life will end and something else will happen. Your Mom has been busy looking for a good job, so you can stay together again. That takes time, and you have to use your time wisely, so it will go quickly." Gramps finished and turned to Gramma who was now wiping her tears with her cotton floral scarf.

We dreaded making our way down that gloomy, ugly, bumpy old road towards the entrance to Red Sands Residential Dormitory. I guessed it used to be new, once upon a time, but now it was old and shabby. Like, even a fresh coat of paint wouldn't improve the look of this place, I thought sarcastically.

"Well, it's a long way home so we better get going," Gramps said after he signed me in.

Mrs. Hobart, one of the nice matrons, surprisingly, took her sweet time checking me in for the year. The familiar hustle and bustle that goes on at the beginning of each year could be heard, as I glanced around to see if any of my friends had arrived yet. Mrs. Hobart finally came back with the necessary sheets, an army blanket and the rock-hard pillow some of us would never use. These were the usual items loaned to me for the school year. The smell that emanated from the government issues was so strong that Gramps, Gramma and I all gagged at the same time. Good thing my friends and I learned to get rid of that smell by taking the sheets and blankets to the old ranch house and smoking the ugly smell out with cedar we "smuggled" in from home. This activity became a ritual for many students at the beginning of the year. Next thing you know, the whole dorm smelt like a hogan. That was a great smell!

"We'll miss you, Grandchild. Here, I bought this for you last week, at the Gas and Stuff store." As he handed it to me, he said, "It's a year-at-a-glance calendar." Gramps had marked some of the days they would be doing stuff, like sheep dip, branding (which was almost done), and moving cattle to the winter camp. "I marked these days, so you'll know that the work doesn't stop, and to let you know that we will be wishing for your help, and we, too, count the days that you will be gone. Be strong and don't forget your prayers," Gramps said as his voice cracked. I kept all ten calendars Gramps bought me and often went back to remember the days when I felt sad. Each year, Gramps had to pull Gramma away from me, as they had to say the dreaded "good-bye, Grandchild," one more time.

As they slowly, slowly, eased away that fall day last August in Red Robin, Gramp's 1972 GMC truck, I remembered how I listened to the stock rack rattle so loudly this way and that, as it made its way out the entrance of the dormitory and on down the streets of Red Sands, until I could no longer hear or see it. I remember the first time I did my best to run fast to the farthest edge of the playground until the familiar sound had drowned in the usual sounds of Red Sands traffic.

"Please turn around! Please come back! Please Gramps!"

But in all my wishes, I knew that they were not coming back, and that I had to stay in this stinkin' dormitory. When I was younger, I would stand at the big window in Dorm "A" and watch for hours hoping my ride home to show back up. Eventually, I learned, in all the times I had wished Red Robin to reappear, it never did come back. It was a ghost of a memory…swept away in time..patiently waiting for another visit..wishing.. As I made my way down the dreaded descent towards oblivion, my grandparents made their journey back to the Promised Land.

Gramps and Gramma did all they could to keep going…but they never let me know. They knew that I was better off staying at the dormitory and going to school with white kids and taught by white teachers. They knew a public-school education was a good thing, even though they never mentioned it to anyone but each other.

As I got older, I quit thinking they would come back, knowing it took a lot of time and effort to get me back to school. The love of Grandparents patiently waiting, counting time leaves an impression on a Bureau of Indian Affairs child. Their hopes and dreams were in the hands of their grandchildren whom they prayed for so fiercely each day.

The yearly event of leaving the comforts of home left a lifelong impression on a Bureau of Indian Affairs child named Florence Arviso - me. These memories indelibly etched in the memories of a Navajo girl who began this journey at the tender age of five, now almost fourteen. What can a person say when the most important impression on my life has been sacrifice, patience, survival and keeping tradition, living here at Red Sands Residential Dormitory and in the name of a public-school education.

In the end, one day I will know what Mom, Grandma and Grandpa meant by sending me here so I can learn how this experience can impress someone else's life. In conclusion, I would say that the theme of my essay is patience is a virtue put upon the lives of all of us who wait out our time in a place surrounded by a seven-foot chain linked fence, like the cattle that waited for their master to open the gate.

The End.

It took all of me to write this essay…writing and rewriting and finally satisfied with the content, I turned it in, not caring about the grade, but about the comments Mrs. Gardner would write.

I had to write some poetry to think out my feelings in my notebook, where I kept all of my secret thoughts….thoughts I could not say out loud for fear of punishment – or worse yet, The Room.

Big Mac
So powerful, yet gentle
Buckskin beauty
Gracefully moves across the land
Easy, without hesitation
Without provocation
Click, Click, Full speed my stead!
Big Mac

Dormitory Food
The smell in the air
The smell is so delicious
Floating through the air
Like a flavor wind – suspicious
One bite and a stare
Plsph – dormitory food.

Clouds
Clouds roll across Tohatchi Flats
Crows dot the sky
Wishing for a little rain dance
To swat away these pesky flies
The thirsty plants plead
Praying for a little rain dance
Clouds – don't blow away
Clouds – slowly drift and stay …across Tohatchi Flats.

Grandchild

Grandchild, you are Dine'
Dine' do this,
Dine' do not do that.
Why Grandpa?
Shhh, don't ask questions,
Listen.

Grandchild, you are Dine'
Dine' always think of the good,
Dine' do not dwell on the bad.
Why Grandpa?
Shhh, don't ask questions,
Listen.

Grandchild, you are Dine'
The Holy People are watching,
The Holy People wait to bless us.
Why Grandpa?
Shhh, don't ask questions,
Listen.

One good thing to look forward to was that Ruby informed us that the state started building public schools and were being built on the reservations so kids could go to school from home. Those of us who still had to go to one of the Bureau of Indian Affairs Residential Dormitory and public schools away from home, had to endure and patiently count the number of years, days, hours, minutes, seconds. Waiting, waiting and waiting. Waiting for what? Who is to say what awaits us once released from this place? What would become of us; Clarice, Garnet, Ruby, and me?

We all knew Ruby didn't have to worry. She had it made. Even Ruby didn't make any bones about it. Ruby was at Red Sands Residential Dormitory simply because her mother just didn't have

0enough time to deal with her on a daily basis. Ruby was showered with everything she wanted, except her mother's time and attention, as it was an attempt to hide a guilty conscience. Meanwhile, Ruby anxiously waited for Friday afternoon, and, like clockwork, there came her mother or grandparents.

I knew there were kids at Red Sands Residential Dormitory who had families that did not await their return. They were the ones counting the hours, days, and minutes but they were guaranteed scheduled meals, and a routine in everyday life before they had to endure the hardship of home. These were the students I stayed with on any number of weekends. Most of them were loners who grew great imaginations in their solitude of patience.

It seemed like all anyone did in this place was wait, counting the days, the hours, the minutes and minutes and minutes that ticked by endlessly. They were the students who stayed every weekend, and the ones I learned to expect to be there with me. Over the years, it became a sad kind of familiar comfort.

The last part of the school year was agonizing for everyone. January made its pitiful way slowly through to March and finally to May. Living in the dorm was like waiting for a prison sentence to end with no possibility of parole, as Perry Mason would say as he ended many of his courtroom speeches every week. A prison sentence that for me and my friends would never end, unless something drastic happened to change fate.

Like clockwork, every Monday through Thursday after school, the kids of Red Sands Residential Dormitory who weren't in sports hung around the compound. We could roam around the 10 acres as long as we didn't go outside the 7-foot-tall chain linked fence….still prisoners of the Bureau of Indian Affairs continuous War on Indians.. Of course, there was someone at every corner to watch us loiter, but they weren't all bad. Sometimes they would look the other way when students wanted to run off to the store or movie. Mr. Laughter was one of the coolest guards at Red Sands Residential Dormitory. He always left the padlock unlocked when kids sneaked off to the movies. It was a good thing when the powers, that be, removed the spiked barbed wire, because Clarice and I could easily climb over the fence to make our morning run if the padlock wasn't left open by *mistake.*

When we were in 4th grade, Clarice checked out a book on how locks were made. We tried to pick the lock but never got it right… We had to beg the Guard on Duty to open the lock on most days. Usually they would, but if the mean white man, they called the Superintendent was in or around, they had to go back to following the rules for fear of being sent to *The Room.*

All the students at Red Sands Residential Dormitory loved music. Country Western, Rock-n-Roll, and Navajo songs. During the week the grounds would be filled with one type of music or another. Learning songs and walking around was one way we passed the time. The girls took the radio out to the compound and sang the songs, trying to achieve harmony.

We took turns listening to the lyrics, while someone wrote them down. Sometimes it took forever to get all the words down, because not all the lyrics are in Hit Parade. It was funny how we mumbled through the words we didn't know and then picked up when we did. Harry Billy always played the oldies, even though there was a mountain of new music available. Clarence and his boys were listening to a band named *Fleetwood Mac* that had a female singer with a beautiful voice.

California Dreamin' was a favorite and kind of set us in a melancholy mood.

…Well, I got down with my feels,

And I began to say….

….and the kids from Lupton would say…. I'd be safe and warm, if I was in Lupton, Arizona… And the kids from Lukachukai, Arizona would claim the song as their own. L.A…iss… followed by laughter…The kids spent their time changing the words to songs and making them their own. Listening to the boys changing those Country Western songs was so funny, that we would find a spot, within earshot, just to listen and get some giggles.

There were also a group of boys who kept to themselves, preferring to sing only Navajo songs. At times, they were seen as old-fashioned and an embarrassment. How awful this place made us ashamed of who we really were as Navajos. Our music should be a comfort and taste of home without the benefit of an open fire and traditional foods. Life at a Bureau of Indian Affairs Dormitory stripped our Navajo identity because the environment was not conducive to maintaining our way of life or our teachings as five-fingered people. Well, at least they couldn't take away our songs and prayers.

Chapter 12 – Killing Time

At the end of every week Ruby, Garnet and Clarice were picked up Friday afternoon and I was soon left to fend for myself. Sometimes this was a good thing, especially when the noise of a full dorm could get on anyone's nerves. I needed quiet solace, the kind found out at Tohatchi Flats. They said their good-byes and then silence…a familiar silence…a stinging silence yet, a welcomed silence.

By now, I had observed that when most of the students left for the weekend, this also left the same faces who quietly spent the time together, year after year. After all the commotion of the week, it was good for most of the students to exit the compound and disappear in all directions. The building took a deep breath, as the compound breathed out…and the wind gently settled upon the Earth.

In nine years, the weekend brought a peaceful calm I grew to long for during the noisy week. It's as if the building took a big sigh of relief letting out the breath through the cracks in the windowpane. This was going to be a windy weekend, but I was determined to go out. This weekend I had money, and that was a good thing and meant freedom to make plans. Now that I was older and was given more freedom to leave Red Sands Residential Dormitory, I didn't have to figure out a way to sneak out.

I made my usual way up the rocky hillside stretched, prayed, and ran the usual trail with a smile on my face and a prayer in my heart. "With this song I run. With this song I run." I ran out to the old Ranch House we used as a sanctuary for most of our childhood, finding comfort in its old wood frame. We stumbled across the old ranch by accident, on one of our early morning runs, and decided to make it ours. It was my weekend refuge and a place to collect my thoughts. Going to the old Ranch House was like visiting a long-lost friend - never changed and always welcoming us over the years. Sometimes it was so sad to be alone there at Red Sands Residential Dormitory that I made the old Ranch

House a place with the comfort of home, for my friends. One weekend Garnett and I swept the place of the red dust. We took the dishes left by the previous owner and added a tablecloth Clarice bought from Heap's.

Catching my breath and looking around the old Ranch House, at days gone by and memories of living and growing up alone, I thought of this place as a second home, a secret escape. A place where I would not get yelled at for stretching my voice and singing my favorite songs. It was a place to reflect on the future and look back on the past. "In my own time, nobody knew the pain I was going through…and waiting was all my heart could do…." Karen Carpenter knew what I felt. I guess I'm not the only one who had to wait…but for what? The question of my life.

A rush of northern winds pushed me back to the dormitory with an odd sense of urgency, as a tear slowly fell down my cheek. "Only yesterday, when I was sad…and I was lonely.." Spring was in the air and that meant March would either come in as a lion of whirlwinds and go out like a lamb, which wasn't likely. Judging from the dust storm we had last night; I would say that March was going to roar like a lion. At Red Sands, March winds did not do either…they did both. There was a strange sense of something hovering over the city lately, as I slowly made my way back to hell.. Exhausted from the early morning howling winds, I changed my clothes, deciding to make my way-out hell's gates and into a taste of freedom.

Roaming the streets of Red Sands was something to do to kill time before I had to march back to dormitory life, especially on Saturdays. This weekend, I decided to see what was "new" at Heap's Thrift Shop. Their *new* clothes arrived on Tuesdays but didn't get put on display until Friday or Saturday. I went out looking for something to wear for the last dance. Something with school colors, I decided…red or blue. Mrs. Heap knew our name and was always happy to see me and my friends. Mrs. Heap was a White woman of the Mormon faith and all the clothes in her shop came from Utah, so she had a little bit of the old stuff and a little bit of the newer fashions. She was always trying to get us to go to their church, to their ice cream socials, and Wednesday night activities for kids. Once, while I had to stay for summer school, I went there out of boredom but the only Navajo that was there was none other than Julia James, so I quickly said goodbye and went back on my way back to Red Sands Residential Dormitory. If it wasn't for Heap's Thrift Shop, I would have probably worn my clothes to rags.

"You got anything for a dance. I'm looking for something red, blue or both?"

Mrs. Heap looked up and over her reading glasses said, "I think I've got just the dress for you." Walking to the back-storage room, she flipped through the clothes rack to find the exact dress she thought I had in mind. These just came in on Tuesday, so no one has seen this dress yet. There it was - a blue dress with a halter top and open back.

My eyes lit up with delight. "That's the one!"

"This is chiffon materials," Mrs. Heap noted as she read the $5.00 price tag.

"Five dollars! Can I put it on lay-away?"

"Sure, Mrs. Heap got out her receipt book and said, "Let's see 10% is 50 cents".

I opened my coin purse to reveal a $10.00 bill and paid $3.00 for the dress. Somehow, I had to come up with the other $2.00 but I would worry about that later. I had snacks and my favorite Mexican food to enjoy. I decided I would borrow shoes from Ruby…yes,,Ruby…

I left the store with a smile and a skip in my step. Next to Safeway for munchies. With a heavy tote bag in hand, I stopped at Red Sands Park to read the latest *Hit Parade*. Mick Jaggar was on the cover. At the bottom I read, "You're So Unique." I took that as a message and decided to claim it! Too bad Harry Billy refused to play Rock and Roll songs! For sure, I wasn't about to mention Mick Jaggar to Gramps because most likely, he'll call him an old Galook, which meant he didn't approve of this fine singer. Sigh Oh,well. The older girls had a record player, and sometimes we would sit outside their Dorm B just to listen to the songs. I like the Stylistics....*There's a spark of magic in your eyes*!! Whoever wrote that song is a true poet!

Like sheep, we began walking back before the scheduled 6:00 P.M. curfew. The sun was setting, and I felt excited about my purchase. Deep breath, exhale, sigh....the darkness settled across Dormitory A and the few girls who had to stay drifted into sleep.

I often spent my evening watching this and that on television. The Ed Sullivan show was especially good with The Rolling Stones performing. Then there was Howard K Smith's "Family Hour." Sleep wisped me away to a faraway land and morning came all too soon. After my usual run, early Sunday morning was spent wandering around Red Sands collecting flowers to press in my flower book. I wandered past Mrs. Hamilton's house that seemed to be abandoned. Mrs. Hamilton always had the sweetest honeysuckle flowers and the most beautiful roses. The pleasant aroma drifted down the street even before I reached her garden.

I always stopped to pick a few sunshine yellow honeysuckles, enjoying the taste of sweet nectar. Mrs. Hamilton always left scissors in our secret hiding place, so I could cut a few flowers. A couple of big red roses and some pink buds were enough for today. I didn't want to take all the flowers even though that would be a wish come true.

Over the years, Mrs. Hamilton had grown into an elderly lady who after these eight years had passed, could be found sitting on her rocking chair on the wraparound porch. I watched as her hair went from blonde to snow white and noticed she didn't move around as much as she used to...kind of like Gramps and Gramma... She waved at passersby from her rocking chair, and as time went on, she started to offer me a glass of lemonade on hot days. In the spring, Mrs. Hamilton had the sweetest cherries her son brought from California. Mrs. Hamilton was one of the nicest white people I knew at Red Sands. I looked forward to seeing her on my long walks around town. It was sad to watch her grow old before my very eyes. Mammy Hamilton showed me not all white people were out to bring Navajos down, and she was always happy to see me.

The weather gradually warmed up before the summer months. This Sunday afternoon the wind lifted and swirled the dust around the compound. I did not feel like wandering around in the dust for very long, so I returned to Red Sands Residential Dormitory earlier than usual. Besides, in Navajo way, you're not supposed to be outside when there are dust devils as they are a warning sign. Another sign of change…hmmm even the wind knows…sigh. No wonder, Gramma listened to the wind, and Gramps whistled sacred songs as he worked. Instead of reading, I decided to open my crowded notebook and begin another poem about flowers and nature. I decided I would write some poems about the flower I picked, and about the nice old lady by the name of Mammy Hamilton with her milky white skin. Mammy always wore a crocheted scarf that hung over one of those flowered cotton dresses that went down just below her knees, woolen stockings, and brown penny loafers. Mammy also wore the pinkest lipstick, I thought it would look nice with my new dress. She had short, white hair, curled tight, and held under a net like the one the school lunch ladies wore. I flipped to the first empty page of my *Book of Flowers and Nature* notebook and wrote an ode to Mammy.

Mammy's Garden
There is this silly old lady named Mammy
The prettiest blue eyes
And soft milky skin
Spoke softly of days gone by
With a gleam and a twinkle
Her garden of honeysuckles
Golden Yellow and Honey Brown
Her garden of roses
Royal red to delicate pink
Sweetest smells for miles
Who taught you to toil so well?
Mammy, Mammy
Don't let that garden fell.

The flowers were stuck between two hardback books and in between white construction paper that I took out of the trash can in art class. They were torn pieces but that was all I needed to make a collage. The flowers would take five days to dry and would fit perfectly next to Mammy's poem. I smiled at my work. In the next couple of days, I would check them like I did so many times before, carefully lift the dried flower petals and glue them next to her poem. I smiled about how Mrs. Hamilton would laugh about my poem on a lazy Sunday morning. By noon, the wind picked up and soon the red sands tapped on the thin windows that rattled with each gust of wind. This kind of adventure had become my favorite thing to do on those kinds of days.

Sunday afternoon came and the usual hustle and bustle of life returned stirred up right after breakfast. My thoughts were on the dress, and of the dance that I did not know would end my years at Red Sands Residential Dormitory and close the chapters of my childhood.

"It's time for supper, you wanna eat?" Garnet Chee was standing at the edge of her bed playing with her long braids.

I pulled my face from the pillow and faced Garnet with red eyes and probably a red face. "Yeah, sure."

"I just got back from home," Garnet announced quietly.

Of all the girls, Garnet learned not to show emotion because of all the punishment.

"Smells like we're having beef stew and fry bread!" "Smells like we're having mystery stew again for the 10 billionth time!"

The hall that led to the cafeteria was filled with girls waiting for the dorm matron to give the signal to line up military style.

"Well, how was your weekend?" 0

"What did you expect, nothing happened? I took my usual hikes up to the Old Ranch House, roamed around Red Sands, and collected some flowers. How about you?

"Well, it's the same old weekend. I get picked up, drive my drunk parent's home, I take care of them, and my brothers, then turn around for them to bring me back to go for school."

"Garnet, you are one cool person. Tuba City just can't handle a chick who can handle all that stuff like you!" I remember meeting Garnet the day we entered Red Sands Residential Dormitory. We learned to seek comfort from each other over the years. Garnet, Clarice, and I were there for each other, to comfort each other, while we cried and cried and cried and cried and cried. Looking back, I realized being five in a place like this was really scary. Meanwhile, Garnet learned to be aggressive and often got into trouble because she couldn't help but voice her opinions, even though she knew she would get in big trouble! Now, it seemed to have hardened emotionally. I watched Red Sands Residential Dormitory take the very spirit out of the Garnet; I met what seems like a lifetime ago. Red Sands Residential Dormitory and the **B**urying **I**nnocence of **A**ll killed our innocent spirits as payment…like we owed them something, as if.

I always admired Garnet because she did not take the matron's cruelty. We had a favorite saying. "We're like two birds of a feather - and friends forever!" As the matron marched stiffly to her usual "ordering spot" at the entrance to the cafeteria. Her usual orders called us to line up from youngest to oldest. We learned to manage a smile so as not to call attention from the matron who was one of the meanest matrons. Even though Mrs. Lowell was a Navajo, she made life the hardest for everyone at Dorm A and Dorm B. She was the other Matron on Duty who made us line up on Sunday when Mrs. Hagga was M.IA. One by one, we walked to the beginning of the buffet; the cooks were ready to plop food into the compartments on our pink plastic tray. The cafeteria ladies were usually nice, but not in front of Mrs. Lowell.

Sometimes they would give me extra fruit and sandwiches because they knew I spent most of my weekends at Red Sands Residential Dormitory. I was being my usual self: loud and telling jokes trying to make everyone laugh. They all thought that Mrs. Hagga was going to be the dorm matron that night, but you couldn't count on Mrs. Hagga to be consistent with her attendance... So, there I was, carrying on when Mrs. Lowell lifts her voice through the noise, stunning everyone in sight. I was making one of my sheep herders' impressions and didn't notice Garnet trying to warn me when Mrs. Lowell marched down the aisle and planted herself next to me. I quickly made my way to my spot in the line right before Regina Henderson and after Loretta Cly. Garnett, Clarice, and Ruby followed Regina. Mrs. Lowell ordered me to her office later and assigned me to work in the kitchen doing whatever they needed me to do. I ended up mopping, sweeping, moving boxes around in the freezer, stocking the shelves and cutting up apples or oranges for the upcoming meal. Having been given that kind of punishment before, I knew exactly what to do. The cafeteria ladies were always nice to me and remembered how hard I worked, knowing I was punished for just telling a story...a story...

As we made our way to the girl's side of the cafeteria, we could not help but snicker as we passed Terry Wyaco and Clarence Begay -- Four-Eyed Geeks from Round Rock, Arizona. Clarence and Terry were usually acting as if they just stepped off the Geek mobile! The worst part of it was they liked me and Garnet and then made no bones about it. The usual rolling of the eyes as I passed by, while they hissed and made clicking noises with their tongues. Terry passed a note to me, and Clarence passed one shaped like a star to Garnet, then we hurried to dump our tray, and quickly headed down the hall before they were caught on the girl's side of the cafeteria. Clarence made sure Garnet never saw him pass a note to me, too... Terry never knew either. It was a secret we kept secret.

"Oh, brother, those two will never quit until we give in." "I ain't givin' in to them!" Garnet announced as she disgustingly opened her note, only to find another geeked out misspelled message professing Clarence's' adoration. I waited to read my note in the comfort of my bunk. I kept all of my notes at the bottom of my side of the closet in a shoe box tied with a piece of pink yarn. Garnet was wrong about Clarence. Terry was the one who was a geek alright and yeah, Clarnece also sent geeked out messages to me, but I wasn't going to say anything, because I really enjoyed reading Clarence's poems and secretly liked his attention in an odd sort of way.

Clarence's poem read:

Time
Just in time for a little time
With you, so fine, mine
Will it be me?
Will you see.me?
Just in time for a little bit of your time
Did I tell you, you're so fine? ..time?   smile..

Another good one...time... I smiled and tucked another one of Clarence's' poems in my little box of treasured words for the time being. Yeah, time is a funny thing. It was relished at times and hated at the same time.. Time.. Reality bites..deep breath, sigh..

Life at Red Sands Residential Dormitory was very regimented, like the military. For the past 2,190 days, the girls systematically made their way down the line of students waiting to eat mystery meals. There were two lines: one from the girl's dorm and one from the boy's dorm. Just about all the food we ate at Red Sands Residential Dormitory came from a can. Even the meat came from a can. The only thing that was cooked from scratch were the yeast rolls. For sure, a bright spot in our meals was hot yeast rolls with delicious crusty tops and fluffiness. Like chocolate milk, the golden-brown delight was savored and never shared or left on the plastic tray by anyone. After supper, it was study hall time, and the cafeteria ladies sometimes served milk, cookies, and other goodies during that time.

Mr. Saunders was our first Study Hall Monitor. He taught Social Studies at Red Sands middle school and moonlighted at

Red Sands Residential Dormitory for extra money. He was a good friend to all of us kids because he really enjoyed helping us with our schoolwork. Earlier in the month, the cafeteria ladies were overheard saying Mr. Saunders wouldn't show up for Sunday night Study Hall because he moved to Albuquerque so he could go to school and "get married". Mrs. Bell replaced him.

Mrs. Bell made herself out to be a groovy hippie in every way! She loved to talk about poetry and the arts, as she put it. She taught English at the local college and drove a bright yellow Volkswagen Van with stickers that told people a lot about how she thought. Stickers that read, "Peace Harmony and Love", "POW's NEVER have a nice day!" "Imagine" "No to War, Yes to Peace" "Give Peace A Chance!" "Come sit on my thing V.W." There were a lot of other ones that didn't make sense, because they were covered over by the new ones, she stuck on her banana boat. Before she arrived at Red Sands Residential Dormitory, we could hear her van at least five minutes before the banana boat appeared at the gate and encounter the familiar thump, thump, bump, as she entered the compound – it was worse than Gramps' stock rack. Chuckle. The boys made fun of her, because she didn't know how to drive a stick shift, and the engine often died at the stop signs. It was a stop and go fiasco!

We soon found out her name was Lilly. Lilly Bell's husband lived in New York, "for his own reason," as she put it with a far off look in her gray eyes. At first it was strange to see someone with gray eyes, but we soon paid no attention to them. Lilly wore chunky fake turquoise necklaces and bracelets, but she swore up and down they were real. We finally just quit trying to tell her they weren't real. She gave us a lot of hope about the world and introduced us to stories that Mrs. Gardner would never think of reading to us much less in the classroom. We ended up reading books like *"The Keys to the Castle,"* a romance novel about a woman who marries a French poet she hardly knows. He dies three days after they got married and she inherits Chateau Rondelais.

One thing that struck me was how Sara, the main character, was left to make difficult decisions and open her heart to change. I took a deep breath when we reached the end and thought even characters in a novel go through change.

Mrs. Bell played an indelible part of my life for her love of poetry. Mrs. Bell was one of Clarice's biggest buyers of jewelry, but for some reason she always wore that fake stuff...

Today, Mrs. Lilly Bell was late for some reason....but we waited patiently knowing she would arrive at any moment.

Finally able to talk, Garnet whispered, "Well, I guess it would have been better to stay here."

"Why, what happened this time?" I asked, reaching for my notebook, knowing the story would be the same.

Garnet's parents were alcoholics. As time went on, I guessed Garnet was one of the kids who came to Red Sands Residential Dormitory to get away from her home situation, and the results of alcohol. Red Sands was her place to stay without her parents getting into any trouble for being drunk with kids around. I thought, Garnett was at least getting an education...even if it meant having her travel back and forth to Tuba City every weekend. She was like a yo-yo. One place was good, and the other place could be dangerous. Garnet learned to be tough on the outside and on the inside. Deep breath..sigh..

"Oh, I just hate it when my stepdad gets drunk. He gets so angry and mean and I do not know what to do. My Mom just keeps getting beat up, and I do not know how long I can take it," she whimpered quietly, tears streaming down her olive-colored face. She pulled her brown hair from her face and wiped her tears. I don't know why I'm crying. You hear the same story over and over, Florence, it doesn't ever change. I already know when he's going to go into a rage, once the whiskey sets in, but Florence, it's scary because I'm beginning to hate him." Her sad eyes hugged the floor. Garnet did not like the word *hate*. We waited for her grief to pass in silence, as if it was going to make everything get better.

My heart sank because I knew that Garnet was calling this person "Dad." The reality was he wasn't her dad, but one of her mother's many boyfriends. "How can I think about home and the dread of leaving a place I love, when Garnet is thinking about a "home" she doesn't even want to visit."

Garnet slowly got herself together and started talking about the homework she had to make up for Science and English. We found a place to sit, because our usual study area was taken by some other girls.

"Florence you gotta help me with my Enlish…," aaay she tried to tease still wiping her tears. Garnet had to keep herself busy, so she didn't dwell on what her four siblings had to endure while she was safe at Red Sands Residential Dormitory. It was comforting to know that the neighbors were there to help. Garnet had no control over them except for the weekends. She was like their mother and worried about them constantly.

I was an only child and always wished to have siblings. Honestly, I don't know where I would be if I had siblings. I decided my dad would've probably behaved like any one of Garnet's "dads" and realized it was a good thing my mother made the choice to leave and never look back.

Meanwhile, Terry and Clarence sat strategically at earshot range as usual. I could see the concern in their eyes, and yet they never ever said anything about our conversations. The kids at Red Sands Residential Dormitory relished the opportunity to eat on the north side of the cafeteria and often tried to get there early so they could get first dibs. Keeping in mind that Garnet needed cheering up, I went into one of my "stories" while we waited for Mrs. Bell to show up. …and my storytelling began…

Kind of like the slop my Gramps cooks for the sheep dogs! I once wake up to a hip-delicious smell, only to find out that my Gramps is cooking leftovers, cornmeal, fat, and water for the sheep dogs!" I say, good morning, Gramps, how can you get me up so early with that hip-delicious smell!

Gramps would gaze at me with that, "what's with this 'hippy stuff? "look and says, "That's what you think!" I'll take some coffee, Gramps, I giggled at the thought, because I knew how Gramps felt about the hippies shown doing crazy things in the newspapers lately. He amusingly referred to them as, "those ole galooks."

I continued my usual story… "by sunrise, Gramma was up and cooking tortillas and eggs. She was busy packing our lunch and making sure we had enough water as usual." The whole thing was a routine I paused to read Garnet's face, that was engaged knowing the end of the story she had heard so many times she could tell it herself. "A rancher must think of a thousand things each day. The days start early, and every day ends late. As soon as the ranch work was done, there was the cooking. Everyone pitches in, peeling potatoes, roasting chili, starting the fire for the steaks, and making dough for tortillas. Everything was cooked on the grill.

All the food I have been craving ever since I have had to force down the "military issues" they give us here at good ole' Red Sands Residential Dormitory!" Eyes rolling, silent exasperation.

"Anyway, when it was time for eating Gramma prayed for the food, pass the water bucket around so everyone could get a drink and then the jokes would start. Any time my cousins or I did something wrong, one of my uncles would scold us, until we would learn how to work the cattle and sheep.

"Uncles, Aunts, Mom, Gramps, Gramma, and the rest of us gathered around a long rectangular wooden table equipped with wooden benches so that everyone had a spot, no matter how crammed in we had to get! Uncle Leonard would be the first one to start in on one of us that did something wrong. Once I steered my horse the wrong way and the cattle shifted to the other direction. Everyone was yelling, "The other way!"

Those were the times when Gramps cursed and that was the time you knew you were in big trouble! The yelling and cussing vanished when everyone gathered for our family meal. Next thing

I knew, Uncle Leonard started imitating me at the dinner table and everyone laughed – even ME.

I will bet the Red Sands Residential Dormitory workers could never get over a roasting by my relatives! Can you imagine Mrs. Hagga getting a tongue lashing for showing up drunk for the millionth time?"

Everybody exploded in laughter! Even Terry and Clarence, who were sitting suspiciously close, laughed uncontrollably.

"Shh, here comes the Matron on Duty!"

Quietly, looking down and pretending to study, I could see that my jokes were cheering up Garnet.

"Flo, you are my best friend and thanks for cheering me up! I just wished that I could have a family that can take a joke and have fun without drinking." Garnet gently nudged me.

"My silly and sometimes made-up stories were always the thing that makes this place bearable! I mean, just look how many times we had to eat Beans for Indians Always on the menu meals? Remember how Dorm A smelled for days? That stench lingered for days! Even burning cedar didn't help much! Not to mention all the mystery meals that smelled so good, until the first bite… I tell you, "Smells good" were the key words!" Yeah, we sure made Dorm A smell not good! Silent giggles. It was good to have everyone together after the weekend.

Garnet was an example of wanting to be there and not wanting to leave but having to leave and then coming back. It was hard to see her jerked around every weekend. It was hard to see her being responsible for her siblings. But when I thought about it who else would be responsible for them if it weren't for Garnet. Garnet was my hero.

Whenever Garnet was feeling bad, with my hand over her shoulder, I had no choice but to burst into song:

When you're down the wrong road
And you need help finding your way…
I'm right there..
And then Garnet, Clarice and Ruby would join in…

You can call me your friend….. end with, you've got a friend and tender consoling hugs. Times like these, songs spoke of everything we could not.

Suddenly, Ruby gave her usual exasperated silent stares at Terry and Clarence who had joined in without permission. Ruby continued her sarcastic look, while Clarice, Garnet and I scooted quickly to the end of the table. Clarence and Terry quickly looked down, pretending to be studying.

Hearing us singing, the Matron on Duty marched back into the cafeteria. "Shh!! You kits are not supposed to be singing!"

Everyone quickly put their heads down, pretending to study…secret smiles on our faces for pushing the limit one more time, for singing of all things.. yes, sing…

We, inmates at Red Sands Residential Dormitory routinely got punished for singing and telling stories – yeah, punished…relegated to the Manual Labor Guy for some dumbass reason to be punished. Our dampened spirits, let a collective exhale, maintaining the little dignity we had left.

I relegated myself to quietly write, it was a common thing I did to end my days…deep breath, exhale, sigh…. God, please bless my friend Garnet and her mom…mostly her mom.

Motherless Child

She's a motherless child—
A hurt little girl who stands so tall,
Yet drifts through the days,
Wishing for solid ground beneath her.

The arms that would welcome her hugs are gone.
"I will mother you,"
Whispers Mother Earth, soft and true.

Mother where are you?
Can you be found?
Today I needed you...
Caught a thought of turning homeward bound.

Each day I wonder—
Mother, do you ever remember me?

I grew up too soon,
Under sun and moon,
And time kept ticking,
June or July or just some other sky.

Now I've become
A childless mother—
Still searching, still yearning,
For what was never mine to hold.

Little Girls

Same faces from days of old
Same faces, little girls now grown
Now we have to face goodbye
And so I will say goodbye to
The day we met so long ago
The time we spent, so gold
Will I survive? Will you thrive?
Will I ever see you soon? Will I find you survived?
Remember our faces, from days of old when
We were so young, so young   Little Girls….all grown…

Memories
Beautiful memories
Beautiful times
Here in our forever hours, yours and mine to cherish
And I am gonna miss you so!
We came together at five
Now teens, I have to let you go
And you have to let me go
My quivering lips won't stop
My tears won't let me fight
And I'm gonna miss you so
Beautiful memories
Beautiful times
Goodbye, to the times,
If only in our minds.
Treasured memories..

Life in Solitude
In solitude's embrace, a child stood,
Left alone in the quiet neighborhood.
Echoes of laughter, a distance trace,
A tiny heart in a vacant space.

Tiny footsteps echoed in empty halls,
Loneliness wrapped in silent calls.
Abandoned toys and a vacant chair,
A child's world tinged with despair.
Alone, yet surviving, a spirit so small,
Facing a voice, an absent thrall.
In solitude of shadows cast,
Childhood memories slipping fast.

But within, a strength, a flicker of light,
A surviving heart in the quiet night.
Imagination blooms in solitude's domain,
Dreams unfurling, an irrepressible refrain.

Through the stillness, a lone child grows,
Navigating life's uncertain throes.
From the quietude, buoyancy is drawn,
A solitary journey, a new dawn.

Left alone, yet not truly lost,
For within, hardly embossed.
A child's spirit, steadfast and free,
In solitude, a survivor's legacy.

    The solemn air that lingered across Red Sands Residential Dormitory compound shifted its way into Dorm A as the golden orange sun set in the West and another day came to a close. Then the usual lonely solitude followed by the shifting and creaking beds when everyone took an irrepressible sigh and Dorm A gave its usual aging exhale.

Chapter 13 – Clarice's Story

"Line up, Girls! Line up!" Mrs. Yazzie demanded on Friday morning. This was usually an exciting day for Clarice because she knew she was going to be checked out for the weekend. No telling where she would end up or who would buy her jewelry. By now, Clarice had become a pretty good salesperson. Sometimes the selling could be so very boring between customers, so between customers, she drew what she saw in one of her countless sketchbooks. Some were charcoal drawings. Some were colored pencils. She often thought of her life as a traveling jewelry salesperson.

The reality was she had no real home…her home roamed from here to there and back again…it was no real comfort for a young girl. The room she longed for was sketched many ways, but it was just a dream for now. Her dream was a room of her own in a big house, in the trees of Cross Canyon where the Southern winds blew a beautiful song – sometimes warm, sometimes cold. Her room would be on the Southern end of the building to capture the cool breezes during the hot summer nights. Reality bites hard, because instead of a real home, she lived a life in a mobile home…a travel trailer that had only one room. She had to take the dining table out and pull out the bed where she slept, when she was with her parents. Her personal stuff was stored in a shed near her Grandparent's place in Cross Canyon because there was very little room in that 6x8 home-cum-jewelry store. In the travel trailer, she was able to store her belongings under the kitchen bench which also stored her thin roll-out mattress. It was even harder and stiffer than the beds at Red Sands Residential Dormitory. Sometimes she wished she was sleeping in her dormitory bed, no matter how it creaked at every move.

Clarice was thinking of her home and how long it would take her to get lonely during her summer vacation – living probably four hours into the middle of no man's land, as she referred to her home. Better go get some new sketch books before I leave civilization she often thought. Mr. Smith at the dime store often gave her a discount, because of the number of books she had purchased over the years. He even showed her a catalog where she could buy different kinds of pencils, paints, and paper. All kinds of different papers! Clarice was in heaven when she went to the Red Sands Dime Store.

Clarice's mother, Gloria, and father Jack Ashley made a living making jewelry, which meant they traveled all over the place. They were very traditional Navajos and never drank a drop of alcohol. Clarice was fluent in the Navajo language and knew the culture like the back of her hand. She was very reverent and never raised her voice. When Clarice was a child, her mother was barely literate and spoke broken English, but somehow managed to sell their jewelry. Jack was completely illiterate in English and spoke the most technical Navajo anyone had ever heard. The kind of Navajo my Grandparents spoke. He spoke only a few words of English, however his in-lay jewelry was known by many of the local Traders. Gloria was from the Black Streak Forest Clan and Jack was from the Towering House Clan. They had been together since 1953. Clarice was their pride and joy, after the heartbreak of a miscarriage. As time went on, Clarice learned to be the salesperson, and to closely manage their money.

Jack learned how to pound out silver to make the beautiful *názha* and silver beads. A *názha* is the rainbow shaped silver piece at the end of a turquoise squash blossom necklace…a signature piece on any traditional Navajo outfit. Jack was a patient traditional man. Clarice grew up sitting next to her dad learning how to make silver jewelry. Clarice never met her Nali's (her paternal grandparents), because they died of tuberculosis and were buried at Chí'įįdii Wash in a mass grave along with all the other Navajos who perished. Jack was passed from relative to relative while growing into the silversmith he was today. Jack was taught by Hosteen *Bééshłagaii's (Silversmith)* who he thought of as a father. Hosteen *Bééshłagaii's* died in the winter of 1939 at the old age of 110. Jack inherited all his tools and a piece of land somewhere in the woods of Cross Canyon. Some of the tools were fifty years old, some older. Clarice would inherit his tools and Hosteen *Bééshłagaii's* of his timeless stories.

Clarice never thought anything would come of that house, her father always talked about building. The best he could do is provide a life in a mobile house, mostly for its convenience, being a traveling businessman and all. Clarice had faith she could build a home for them some day. Every year, they took their travel trailer all the way to Albuquerque during the New Mexico State Fair. They made a killing from jewelry sales and Clarice was lucky to be able to taste the world outside the Navajo Nation. The carnival was like nothing she had ever seen. When Clarice spoke of all the Native American dancers and people at "Indian Village", it was something I had only heard about. Seeing how they dressed, their jewelry, their songs and dances, wow!

Meanwhile, Clarice's' dream of a real home in Cross Canyon stands still in time patiently waiting like the wind and the weather.

Gloria was from Klagetoh, the daughter of a military man –war veteran. Roy fathered 42 children by all accounts. Having spent some 11 years in the military, Roy still had children coming from all parts of the world, asking to meet their "dad." Once, his Japanese son, Yukio, traveled all the way from Japan to meet his Master Sergeant father. When he arrived, Roy was so whiskey drunk that Yukio stayed for only five minutes. Five ominous minutes to last a lifetime for a son born out of war. It must have been a sight to see the picture of a distinguished military man looking so old and small. Clarice couldn't imagine how that would have felt like for Yukio. It must have been heartbreaking. Needless to say, Roy didn't even remember Yukio's visit when his sister Marie told him about it.

Clarice knew many of her grandfather's kids were full-Navajos and the half-Navajos came from as far as France, Africa, Alaska, Korea, and parts unknown. Roy died a lonely man reliving his military days with the St. Catherine's Catholic Priest, who also shared his taste for whiskey. Rumor had it there are twenty-eight years of notebooks filled with his military adventures with sketches of people Roy met or served with, and of course the mothers of his children. His alcoholism was the very reason Gloria refused to drink and found a man who would never drink, either. She stopped the dysfunctional cycle with her family. Clarice never spoke of this part of her history to anyone except me. She said it's best to leave that part of her ancestry in the halls of history.

What a trip, Clarice once laughed! Can you imagine having 42 kids! Clarice's grandmother was Roy's first marriage, the second being from Chinle, by the name of Seraphina. Together they had six children: 3 sons and 3 daughters. By all accounts many of his children are about the same age and many share birth years and birth months. Gloria was in the middle of the group of forty-three, but she didn't know it until she was an adult. Clarice's mom only spoke of this part of her family when she thought Clarice was old enough to know all the answers to her nagging questions.

Gloria and Jack owned an old 1969 Chevy truck that had more than 200,000 miles on it. It got to be where they had to park the old clunker on a hill in order to jump-start it, especially if they had the travel trailer hitched on back. Clarice grew up traveling here and there but when she reached school age, Gloria was forced to enroll her at a boarding school so they could travel around earning a sparce living selling jewelry. Traveling from one tribal fair, county or state fair was planned for each year.

Sometimes their home was parked at Cross Canyon. Other times they would pull it to Klagetoh, their second home. Most of the time Clarice didn't know which place or town she would call home when she traveled home on the weekends. As time went on, Clarice became aware of the word "John." She heard her parents call that word now and then by Navajo customers. Clarice learned that the word "John" meant unschooled, illiterate Navajos by highfalutin Navajos. Imagine that Navajos putting down Navajo because they can't speak English, yet they speak technical Navajo. What's worse was doesn't "john" mean a pimp? Clarice had read that in one of the Rolling Stones articles she read while waiting for Florence to check in and out library books. Eyes roll, exasperation. She did her best to keep her parents safe from people by being their perfect English speaker, spokesperson, and cashier.

Clarice made it her mission to teach her parents how to be the "civilized Native Americans." She had heard one of her teachers read in one of her history lessons about the Dawes Act. Clarice was determined to educate her way out of this nomad life, and she knew her parents would be right there by her side. Over the years, she taught her parents to enough English to get by without her.

Red Sands Residential Dormitory life was good for Clarice in a lot of ways. She had friends and could spend her free time drawing or making new jewelry to sell to the local traders. Yes, last year, Clarice finally came into her own with the jewelry business making $150.00 on her first sale. She made unique pieces, and they sold in no time. The Traders were so interested in her jewelry; she had orders for more. Clarice often thought the one good thing about Red Sands Residential Dormitory is that it doesn't move, there was running water, electricity, and television. Best of all, she lived with her sister-friends.

At times, we would have to help her meet her orders by stringing beads instead of doing homework. "That usually cost some kind of food reward...chicken, hamburgers, whatever," Ruby demanded. Eyes rolling. Clarice was going to be a famous jeweler, maybe someday, but I thought her drawings would capture much more acclaim. Clarice shared her drawings with me, and only me.

Another good thing about Red Sands Dormitory was she didn't have to fold the table into a bed like her little trailer. The beds might be hell, but at least they were real beds. Ruby could complain about all she wanted, but Clarice knew how to rough it. At times, she wished she could stay at Red Sands Residential Dormitory for the weekends, but her parents depended on her to help sell jewelry in Gallup, Flagstaff, Farmington, Albuquerque, or anywhere there was something going on, like a powwow or fair.

Clarice often spoke of her favorite trip to a very hot place, called Phoenix. Even in March and April, Phoenix was hotter than hell, she claimed. She almost melted on the sidewalk in Scottsdale trying to make a deal. She had never been in such heat, but they had the most beautiful buildings and parks with grass everywhere. Clarice was in awe. She wanted to live in Phoenix but for the heat. The Heard Museum would be a good place to sell her own jewelry in the future.

They went to a park where they were having the annual Arizona State Fair Powwow. There were even people making frybread and stew! Imagine that, in the middle of this desert oasis. This was a time she wished Clarice could take me with her, but her parents didn't have permission to check me out. I tried to sneak off but worried about being A.W.O.L., so I never dared to go along. Clarice sketched the whole scene, cactus, dancers, the sunset, everything. Clarice just knew I would've loved this event.

Like the others, five-year-olds, Clarice was left at Red Sands Dormitory not knowing why she had to be away from her parents and not speaking very many English words. If it wasn't for Garnet, who spoke fluent Navajo, Clarice would've been lost. She had a difficult time learning how to speak English, but we all did our part helping her. I witnessed some of the teachers being really mean to the Navajo students who couldn't speak "proper English", and they spent a lot of time studying instead of going to music, or P.E.. Clarice thought it was a punishment, but she persisted. Garnet and I pulled together to teach Clarice how to read by the time we left First Grade. To this day, Clarice still has that Navajo accent when she reads. One we grew to love and know.

As time went on, she eventually taught her parents how to read, write in English and to do math. She taught to the point that the Traders couldn't cheat them out of money and soon paid for jewelry at market price without an argument. Clarice spent many summers traveling to cities like Phoenix, Albuquerque, Denver, and once even went to the Orange County Powwow in Los Angeles where they sold out!

Besides her beadwork, I watched her become an amazing artist! Early in the morning, Clarice would bring her sketch book on our runs, looking forward to capturing another beautiful sunrise.

"Here comes the sun, dodododo. Here comes the sun, and I said it's alright. Dododododododo." She would humm…her favorite George Harrison song while she endlessly sketched.

"You're late. Ready for our run?"

"Ready as I'll ever be. How you gonna carry that book?"

"I'll hide it." Stretching. Deep breathing.

Clarice began her prayer… "With this song I run….." Corn pollen, prayers for a good day, then run our hearts out.

What I didn't know was that Clarice took her ideas and color combination from the landscape of Red Sands. Just as I chronicled the time through writing, Clarice's sketches were forever frozen in time. They were spectacular and seen by a select few. Clarice took the time to lock her treasures in the heavy-duty model of footlockers…the ones that cost more than most of us could afford.

Clarice was also the most organized person I had ever met. She had all her beading supplies and things she needed to make her jewelry all labeled in different containers. She had a special box for her charcoal and colored pencils with the paper she had special ordered.

Although Clarice was quiet, she had a conviction. She only spoke up when she thought her words would be useful. When Clarice lets loose, watch out. Clarice roamed the streets of Red Sands looking for things that she wanted to draw. She spent a lot of time at the Allen Theatre drawing movie stars from the posters they had in their windows. She conveniently disappeared when things were getting too mundane or boring between her friends. Like all the kids at Red Sands Dormitory, she counted her time one minute at a time.

Unlike me, Clarice did not have a ranch to return to or grandparents who worshipped her. She was a nomad. She was a wanderer. All she needed was a flock of sheep and a *hogan*, then she would find true Navajo happiness around a pot-belly stove, spreading out some cedar making the place smell like home. Clarice, in all her creativity, had issues she never talked about, but if you look carefully at her drawings, therein lies the loner, the only child, the entrepreneur by necessity, and now by choice.

She listened as Garnet, and I found out we were not returning to Red Sands Residential Dormitory knowing she would be leaving as well. She didn't want to tell them because that meant she would be facing the fact that she would soon lose everything she knew. It was too painful and, so she spent much of 1974 finding reasons to be away from her sister friends…as if it would help her get used to being alone. Clarice was not the type to get caught up in the moment, but this year she felt impending doom. She felt something big was going to happen and the thought of separation was devastating. She never let on, her emotions always in check, pretending to be confident…like the salesperson she learned to be.

It sells jewelry – smiling does. She had lied to herself each time she thought of end of the year stuff because that meant she was alone.

Over the years, Clarice had to learn to live from the outside in, always searching and yearning for the almighty dollar after each show. Money was her comfort and her nemesis.

"It's your God given talent to be creative, Clarice. Do not be ashamed about the money you make from your hard-earned work! And don't forget we need our hard work rewarded with a bucket of crispy, hot, just out of sizzling grease, genuine Kentucky Fried Chicken. Romo's enchilada plate or taco dinner wouldn't hurt either. I have even thought of how delicious a perfectly cut steak grilled at Red Sands Park and Recreation would taste.!" I joked.

"Okay. Just look at my fingers all beat up from needles and such."

My exaggerations always had a way of making the most of any situation. There was always a smile and a joke, followed by words of advice and suggestions for a possible adventure. I mean all of us knew how to build a fire and grilling was a part of growing up on the Rez.

Clarice wondered what having a grandfather so dedicated to his wife, his family and his work would be like. She hoped she would find such a man and be as lucky to be together forever.

Clarice was turned on by drawing in second grade, but it wasn't until fourth grade that she was able and brave enough to wander the town of Red Sands with me. By then she knew many students walked around before returning to the dormitory after school. Their famous excuse was that they had to stay after school and do schoolwork. For a long time, the Matron on Duty never questioned them.

Like myself, Clarice loved black and white movies. In one of her visits to the city streets of Red Sands, Clarice saw the window of the Allen Theatre with the latest movies and the lead movie star painted onto the poster. She found herself spending hours sketching such actors as Clint Eastwood, Marlon Brando, Marilyn Monroe (her favorite), Judy Garland, Betty Davis and many more.

She kept a sketchbook of her jewelry designs too. She got the idea of keeping a journal from me after she saw my small collection of notebooks. Clarice flipped through the notebooks and was forever inspired.

"You drew all these? I marveled.

"Yeah, well, it's a start."

"Now let's see your collection grow!" That was all the inspiration Clarice needed...the rest is history.

Clarice felt ashamed for having felt so embarrassed by her parents' lifestyle. She did not like being transient. Who would? "I do have talent; she secretly told herself." I'm sure if she could, she would say, "I'm a badass artist," but that's Ruby style.

"Ruby, Ruby." Sigh.

As she thought about their life at Red Sands, Clarice realized she couldn't help but be Ruby's friend, because Mrs. Jones put them in the same group in first grade. Ruby was her seatmate and became a lifelong classmate. As it turned out, Clarice and Ruby were in the same class for nine years. This is where she learned to tolerate her verbal abilities, or lack thereof. All the while, Clarice wished she could be in my class but that just wasn't going to happen. Clarice saw Ruby as the annoying younger sister who constantly needed attention, or she might blow up into a million pieces or something close to that... Clarice often thought things like that but verbalized them to me during our morning runs.

In the meantime, keeping quiet was her M.O. She saw how loudmouth Ruby always landed herself in the Principal's Office or worse yet, "The Room." Nevertheless, Ruby was her sister and that was that...period.

Clarice always had at least two or three projects going on at any given time. She had to get out twice a week to get exercise and sketch the scenes of Red Sands in different ways. She probably has a thousand different sketches by now. There were drawings of the people who work on the Pacific Railroad. There were sketches of the people who worked for the county milled around the government offices. There were the myriads of people who sold just about anything to anyone in their "antique" stores. She sketched the retired people on their rocking chairs growing old on the porches of the old century houses on 3rd Street. Clarice thought those houses were probably built the same time the Old Ranch House was built. She wondered if any of the old people knew what happened to people who used to call it their home or why they decided to mysteriously disappear, leaving precious belongings.

Clarice found a bench where she secretly drew the Mexican workers who shoveled coal onto big buckets that were lifted into the train engine. Their faces drenched with sweat and covered in coal dust from head to toe. The railroad station had the prettiest carved wooden benches and wooden floors. The browns, yellows and blacks of the wood changed with the sunlight that came from a window on the south side of the building. She enjoyed watching the passengers enter and exit the train wondering where they came from and where they were headed. I joined her a couple of times, but it brought up too many fleeting memories that I waited at the library, instead.

One by one, Clarice sketched all those stained-glass windows depicting the Bible, at St Francis Catholic Church outside, waiting for me while I prayed for my release from prison to no avail. She talked about how right around 11:30, the sun hit the windows just right – as it filters through the vibrant hues, a dance of colors emerges, casting a kaleidoscope of brilliance within the sacred space. The intricate designs, once dormant, awaken as the sunlight breathes life into each pane. Images seem to sway back and forth while the prayers she heard drifted through the tiny cracks. Sunlight unveiled the intricate details, casting delicate patterns of light and shadow across the sacred scenes depicted in the glass. On hot days, the images wore a beam of white light that emanated from the inside of the Church. Clarice showed me how to look at architecture – the lines and curves. We were in awe at the time it took to cut and put together all those fragments of glass.

She had sketches of us in different scenarios. Our innocent eyes looking back at her and the pages of time. In her book of houses, she drew pictures of the type of home she wished to live in some day…all of them were grounded with no tires to be found. There was always some sort of fancy wrought iron fence with lots and lots of flowers of all colors in the front yard. Clarice said there would not be a wraparound porch for her to grow old, like those elders that faded then disappeared with the red sandy winds.

There was a special bond between Clarice and her art. Like my poetry, art was her best friend. She drew places where she wished to be but knew it was going to take a lot more money than she had ever earned. Peddling jewelry only brought enough to get by. The houses advertised in the newspaper all had price tags in the tens of thousands of dollars – more money than she could ever imagine. A girl can wish and make plans though, and that's exactly what Clarice set out to do – make her wishes come true.

Clarice and I enjoyed running to start our days in captivity. Over the years, I noticed she always had a new goal in her prayers as the sun peeked over the horizon. Of all the things at Red Sands

Residential Dormitory, losing me and our runs would be the biggest heartache. We found ourselves trying not to get choked up the last days as the time ticked towards the end of the school year.

Bending over and breathing hard from another long run, Clarice broke the silence. "Flo, what's going to happen to us? How are we going to make it without each other and living so far apart?" Silent tears trickled down her cheeks and her shoulders shook with grief.

"I don't know. I've been thinking about it since January. I never dreamed we would split up. We have to make the most of it – you know the time we have left. In the back of our minds, we always knew that someday we would split up. It was bound to happen – one way or another. We'll just have to keep in touch somehow." Deep breathe. Sigh. Hugs. Uneasy silence...priceless hugs...uncertain tears.

"Come on let's get back before the Matron on Duty gives us some manual labor..." smirk, giggle, rush.

"Manual Labor...caca de la menta!" Jogging turned into a race to the gate, with Clarice beating me by a hand.

"Manual Labor Guy..isss.."

One of a Kind
Clarice, Clarice
Delicate talented hands.
Bead one, then two, then a hundred
Out comes a necklace.
Pictures of this, unfinished sketches of that
Beautiful masterpiece
All of them.
Always one of a kind.
Clarice, Clarice
She is one of a kind.

The Pearl

I'm on top of the world
Feeling like a bright shiny pearl
I started out bumpy and confused
Life buffed it to iron out its confusion
Til it turned to understanding –
A smooth, perfect shine.
It's all mine, shiny pearl.
Life, for now – is all mine!
I'm on top of the world!

Chapter 14 – Change In the Air

At the beginning of each school year, I faithfully crossed out each day on the calendar, like Gramps taught me. There were only four weeks left. For almost nine years, this was how many students kept time, especially those who did not go home much, or not at all, for that matter. For sure, I could hardly wait to be back to reality, where things count, and every day is an adventure. I smiled at the thought of eating mutton and the sweet smell of tortillas grilled on an open fire and fresh coffee flooded the dry air. Like clockwork, the anxiousness floated through the air like the warm wind that sweeps across Red Sands every spring.

My eyes shifted to some girls, who were coming back from their weekend at home on a Saturday, then back to the year-at-a-glance calendar posted on the bunk divider I shared with Garnet Chee. Garnet was and will always be my best friend, but what would we do without each other?

Drifting in and out of a daydream, the afternoon sunlight glittered across the broken half-glued closet fixtures. The two flies that were trying to get out finally got tired enough to rest on the corner of the cold metal beam that supported the dormitory roof, painted Nabaho white.

Every day, I thought about how great it was to be out there in Tohatchi Flats or in the cool mountain… my sanctuary. A person could actually hear the buzzing noise in their ears because of how quiet and peaceful it really was. The tall pine trees on Chuska mountain used the gentle wind to sing songs to each other.

Red Sands Dormitory weekend noise left a different kind of silence, coupled with the buzzing flies trying to escape out of the tattered window. Like me, they seemed desperate to find a way out. Feeling sorry for them, I turned the rusted squeaky lever of the window and like magic they disappeared, and the din of the outside world blew in as if it had been trying to come in all this time. It smells like freedom.

"Ahh, cool breeze," I thought as the wind shifted through the stained windows and dried my face. "Not an *Asaayi* Breeze, but a cooool one indeed!"

I felt so lonely and emotional just thinking about how long I had endured being on my own. Why? Why didn't I have a mother who took the time to visit or check me out for a weekend of a holiday? Why? What was going on in my mother's life that was so important that I was forgotten? I turned and faced the pillow and cried until my head hurt. To make things worse someone just getting back from home turned on the radio and the song "Leavin' on a Jet Plane" came on KDJI.

The loneliness set in like an old friend…that feeling I felt when Gramps and Gramma left. Besides loneliness, my grandparents were the two people I could really count on. Many nights I cried myself to sleep and forced the dreams, dreams of going home. The reality of it was, even though I forced my dreams to be good, they were filled with a lot of this and that from my past and present, and possibly the future I couldn't tell, and then it was time to wake.

Countless nights filled with fitful dreams, strange visions, uncertainty. Tired. It was always a time for prayers and then to run. Sometimes at night, when everyone was asleep, when the dorm was quiet except for breathing, I would have the same horrifying dream. The one where they would all be sleeping, and a hundred elephants, gazelles, hyenas, and monkeys broke down the door and ran down the hall, trampling everything in sight, and there was always no way out and no one to rescue anyone. I would wake up stiff scared and wishing I would not have read that safari story, "The Strange Last Voyage of Donald Crowhurst." As I carefully inched my way to the edge of the bunk, I could read the clock at the end of the hall. I squinted as I tried to read the hands on the clock. 12:30 A.M. The dream ended almost always near that time…then it was another two hours before I could go back to sleep. Tired… Just a few more days of this awful place, just four more weeks…as I forced my eyes back to sleep land. I pulled the blanket over my head, so the darkness covered my eyes, but I continued the same dream. Although the eek eek, squeak of the bunk beds up and down the hall let me know I was not alone - I was alone.

In the morning, I commanded myself to get tough or I won't be able to handle being a ranch girl. I told myself: you lasted the entire year and now there are only a few more days, mere hours!! I reassured myself that I could manage these last days. Who knew that in all my time at Red Sands Residential Dormitory, these four weeks would be packed with so much more than the nine years put together? My instincts told me I was destined for change.

Funny how I never noticed some things in all the time I had spent here. Looking up I read "*Property of Red Sands Boarding School - Do Not Remove*" on the mattress above. As the colors of the morning lights glistened and danced through the window of Red Sands Dorm "A," I was thankful that the year had finally ended. This year I thought, I'm going to stay with Gramma and Gramps, and nobody will change my plans!!! I refuse to be the property of this god-forsaken place! I learned to take a deep inhale and slowly exhaled.

Red Sands Residential Dormitory was one of the many dormitories the Bureau of Indian Affairs built during the 1930's in many of the towns bordering Indian Reservations. I remember hearing stories of how awful it was to live at a B.I.A. Boarding School and how the treatment 'could be better,' as Gramps explained it. In all my thirteen years I thought, "When I was a very young child, I would never have thought I would end up here, in a B.I.A. Dormitory for this many years! Even though I went to Red Sands Public School, I often thought, I am still here, held hostage in a savage land. Like Louis Lamour would say in one of his stories of the rugged, savage territory out West. "Wherever that used to be."

The reality was the savage territory was the shabby building, military issues, and metal playground where we were made to grow up. It also represented another grim reminder of the age of Red Sands Residential Dormitory. All I knew was that I would be stuck here until twelfth grade unless some sort of miracle happened! To make things worse, I was only in eighth grade! The thought of another four years was too painful to imagine. I just knew what Clarice would say! "Fat chance! Flo."

The early morning sound of the Dairyland delivery truck every Sunday brought me back to the real reality of my life. I peered out the window to see if we would be lucky enough to have chocolate milk. "Wow!" "Chocolate milk this week!!" Seeing Chocolate Milk was like seeing your family at Red Sand Residential Dormitory! Every one of the students drank their chocolate milk really slow on those days. The Matrons on Duty would always know that things were going to be off schedule on these days, so they were ready to march around telling the students to hurry up and finish their lunch, so they could make it back to school on time.

It was time for me to stretch and get ready for my run and prayers. "I'll be glad when I don't have to wake up and see the sign that reads "Property of Red Sands", every day," I thought. Deep breath, exhale, sigh.

Chocolate Milk
Chocolate Milk is like gold
Every time we see it, we are sold
Sweet, smooth, thick
Drinking ever so slowly to the last drop
You just gotta to pick
Chocolate Milk, no one can top!

…relishing chocolate milk because it only came once in a while. Seeing chocolate milk was like seeing your mother or your grandparents, or your friends when they return from the Promised Land…smile…

As I ran up the familiar hill, thoughts of how Navajos name places by the way they look came to mind. There is Window Rock, Spider Rock, Rough Rock, Round Rock, Shiprock, Standing Rock, and the list goes on. They must've named this place because of how red the sand is out here. Sometimes, the rain would cool the mountain air, and the sand smelt good enough to eat. There is a shrub with tiny yellow flowers that smell so good after it rains! The frequent rain showers are one of the good parts of being here, besides being with my friends…things I will soon miss. I smiled with the anticipation of them arriving, and to be back as the sounds of life soon replaced the silence with another busy week. It was also the beginning of the end of a lot of routines and scenery. Someday these nine years will all make sense. I could count the number of times my mom visited me at Red Sands Residential Dormitory, and she acted nervous, like someone was watching her each visit. I hardly knew who she was and never or what she thought of. I didn't know what kind of life she lived without me. I turned to my poetry to find comfort, pass the time, and to say what I really thought.

Property of Red Sands
Bureau of Indian Affairs
Reads the sign as if to glare
Property of Red Sands
Do Not Remove!
Taken from the Promise Lands
One by one
From far across the vast land and into the sun
Scooped up in plain sight
Everlasting anguish and fright

It's in the Treaty
Western education brings us justification
So says the greedy
Civilization
Education

Property of Red Sands.
Do Not Remove!
Reads the signs   …as if…

Hearing familiar voices, I put my pen down and ask, "Garnet, wouldn't it be cool to smell boiling coffee on an open fire, and the sweet burn of the tortillas cooking on the grill?!" I was talking to the wall. I guess she's not back yet.

I continued thinking of how things would be out at the Ranch. By now, the golden orange sunrise that lifted the Holy Winds let the desert take a deep breath for another day. Ralph the Rooster would caw as he went about puffing his chest in front of the hens. The sounds of sheep made let everyone know they were ready to be released, and the horses circled around the corral. Gramps' faithful donkey would patiently wait for his Master to saddle him up for another day of sheep herding. Thoughts…imagination…that's all I had on most days.

Gramps would have already made coffee, for his love and the delicious smell of food meant for the faithful sheep dogs would linger through the air. Gramma would be busy making breakfast and Gramps' lunch so that he could soon make his trek for the day. Some things never change, or so I thought. I mused at the thought of drinking coffee since I was 5 years old. Hmm.. Wow. Coffee was prohibited at Red Sands Residential Dormitory and considered contraband.

Last month, Clarice and I were strolling down the aisles at Safeway when all of a sudden, I heard this shriek!

"Flo! Come here!"

Surprised, I looked up and thought the worst, only to find Clarice standing in the middle of the coffee aisle holding a bottle.

"What is it?"

"Folgers Instant Coffee!, Flo! We just have to add water, sugar, and cream!"

My eyes popped out and our mouths watered! This discovery was way better than chocolate milk!! The hot water at Red Sands Residential Dormitory came out hot enough to make a nice cup of coffee. We enjoyed our drink as we strolled to school the last couple of weeks. Clarice and I were the only ones that drank coffee. Garnet and Ruby preferred pop.

"Oh well, that's their loss," Clarice shrugged.

I don't know when instant coffee was added to the shelf at Safeway, but I could've used it years ago! From then on, I decided to check out what was stocked in each aisle, instead of heading straight for the snack aisle.

On many weekends at Red Sands Residential Dormitory, like clockwork, the maintenance men were seen fixing this thing or that. I remember asking Mr. Yazzie the maintenance man the name of the paint color. Replying in his usual hand on the chin feeling the whiskers pose, "Aaah well, lets see, dat's what you called da Navabo white," as he walks back to his painting job. "Hmm…wonder why they named it that." I had many opinions and knew it was better to keep quiet about them – or speak about them only when I was with my friends, or better yet, write them down between the lines of my poetry.

In my opinion, every wall was painted dirty white, which didn't match the dark Army green blankets, the cold gray metal beds or even the stark white tiles on the floor. Yes, I had a lot of opinions. If I had it my way, the walls would be bright pink, orange and purple – mixed up like those psychedelic clothes that were in fashion. Led Zeppelin, Rolling Stones, Michael Jackson, CCR, The Doors were so popular that everyone had Teen Beat Magazine posters and record covers we would have loved to put up, but we knew better than to do that. There would be posters covering the entire walls of Dorm A and B for that matter. Oooh, that would get on The Hagster's last nerve. The beds definitely need to be changed.

Posters of Tom Bee, lead singer for XIT, a Native American band, would be plastered all over the walls. XIT's latest hit, "Come and Get Your Love," topped the charts in 1973. Who would've thought a Skin band would make it off the Rez…, or off any Rez for that matter! Everyone at Red Sands Residential

Dormitory knew the words to every one of their songs. The one they liked the best was, *"Do yá'a'shon'dá, a Bilagána!"* which roughly translates to, "I don't know about these white people", or "don't trust the White People".....it was like a sacred gospel song sung by the prisoners of the Bureau of Indian Affairs in the fields of dirt compound and squeaky metal swings.

As I lay back down in the warm Sunday sunlight, I watched a huge black fly buzz in and out, in and out, out and back in the patched up open dormitory window. "Why would the paint company call a color of paint Navajo white, when all you can see is red mesas and brown people?" I guessed the name came from all the "not so white" things I could identify with the goat's pelt, the white corn, sheep wool or even the white horses that are rarely born. "That *must* be the white they were talking about – white but not so white." Sometimes I could relate to, Navajo, but not so Navajo.

Meanwhile, the broken patched up wall was just another remnant of Mr. Yazzie and his crew's handy work...all for the greater good.

Mr. Yazzie's job consisted mainly of patching things up and trying to make them look like us kids did not know or take notice that there had been thousands of holes that had been patched and re-patched, all in the name of keeping up the walls and roofs of Red Sands Residential Dormitory. There was not much sense in making things new at any of the buildings at this place, but he did what he could do day in and day out for 18 years.

All anyone would have to do is look around and see that Red Sands was a depository for all the things that people who feel sorry for *us* poor *little* Indians. The rocky trail that leads to the football field passes a yard full of all the discarded or donated Army issues. Everything was gray or military green. Yep, the maintenance yard was a veritable junk yard. Gramps would be in hog heaven thinking of the ways he could use this or that, I mused. "You would think they would just once send us something *fun* to do!" The sound of Garnett's voice recanting – "Fat chance Flo!" echoes in my mind when I knew very well that the bureau wouldn't provide it. By now, we were old enough to make some decisions and made it a point to make the most of this year.

I decided to make myself a secret cup of coffee while I waited for my sisters to arrive. I was glad to be at the end of the hall of Dorm A because I could prop the window open and let the smell drift into space. The poems were my comfort and my tongue.

Grandpa's Coffee
The smell fills the darkness
Like an old friend
Urging all out of bed
Get ready the day
It beckons.
Grampa's coffee
Made with yesterday's grinds
A splash of fresh Folgers
Water from the windmill
Perk, perk, percolate
Mix in fresh goat's milk
A splash of sugar
Grandma's cup, perfect!
The smell fills the dusty air
Like an old friend
From days gone by
As day breaks
Across Tohatchi Flats
Sheep beckoning in the distance
Rooster tells the time
Ah, Nothing like Grandpa's Coffee!!

Weekends
Some weekends are good,
Some weekends are sad,
Some weekends are bad,
All weekends are for poems
And perhaps another good book.

Da' Navabo White
There's a color
Like no other
It's called da' Navabo White
Only a Navajo can wonder
Like no other
What is da' Navabo White?

"..that was a sarcastic one but oh well.. Really? Who thought it was a good idea to name the paint color, Navajo White? We're *not white* or even *off-white*! It's as if we can't be recognized unless they neutralize our natural hue.

WORDS
The words you use,
Whispered from ear to ear to ear,
Will come back to haunt you.
Think about the words you use,
As they can be hateful
And you do not want to be hated,
By your own words.
The words you use,
To belittle, betray others.
Words meant to oppress,
Words meant to hurt the soul,
Are given back to you,
The rightful owner.

The Stone Castle
Dusty windowpanes whistle low,
Through cracks where old memories blow.
Time rewinds, a cautious glance—
Back to days of love's sweet trance.

Eyes burn like a longing child,
As Tohatchi winds howl wild.

A castle built on sand and grace,
Held by time, now lost in place
.

Gentle hands in sunlit rooms,
Drift like echoes, faint perfumes.
A past we knew would never last—
Now whispers in the desert's blast.

The panes still sing a song so slow,
Of long ago, and love's soft glow—
When Grandma's hands beat out the tune,
And Grandpa fixed things under the moon.

Tohatchi Flats still holds my might.
Some things fade,
Some things stay bright.
Some drift quietly into night

The Prison We Live In
There is a place called the B.I.A.
Where Indian children were led
Come here or else, they say
Indians enduring the time; day by day
Hour by hour; year by year, decade upon decade

That is the prison we live in…
There is a place called home
Reservations we were placed
 You stay in there, they say
Indians endure the time decade by decade
Year by year; day by day, minute by minute

That is the prison we live in
There is a place called imagination
A prisoner's sanctuary

We lived there day by day
Year by year, decade upon decade, second upon second.

Dormitory Life
I spent my life here
In these four walls
Cinderblock house
Red Sands, Chuska, Intermountain
All the same
Dormitory Life.

"Watch your words, Grandchild." Gramps' words echo in the back of my mind especially knowing my opinions ae kept to myself. At Red Sands Residential Dormitory, the walls have ears that had a direct link to the Head Matron on Duty, namely Mrs. Becenti. She tried to make us think we had no other future other than Red Sands Residential Dormitory life until we were somehow rescued, making us feel pathetic. It made me mad so many times.

Years later, I opened my eyes when I got out of the watchful eyes of the Bureau of

Indian Affairs. For my college Creative Writing class, I thought about the label, "Property of Red Sands", so I decided to rewrite that poem through the eyes of an adult survivor of Red Sands Residential Dormitory.

Property Red Sands
A sign declares in bold array,
Bureau of Indian Affairs, as if to say.
Belongs to Red Sands, heed the call,
A cautionary plea, "Do Not Remove" scrawled on every wall.

From the Promise Lands, taken away,
One by one, under the sun's broad sway.
Scooped up in plain sight, a stark reality,
Everlasting anguish and fright, a bitter decree.

Embedded in the Treaty, a solemn link,
Western education justifies, some may think
Spoken by the greedy, a civilization tale,
Education twisted, an unsettled trail.

Red Sands' possession, marked by signs,
"Do Not Remove!" as a silent line.
Reads the script, as if in glare.
A story etched, a history to bear.

    Closing my Notebook of Poems like an old friend, I thought of how writing always made me feel better. I thought about how my writing had improved over the years. It's like screaming from the edge of a canyon wall and the words echo back at you…and then you scream them again and they come back with more vigilance or rather defiance. I decided to take both at that point in time, just in case. Silent contemplation.

    In my Book of Lyrics, I tape lyrics of my favorite songs cut out from the *Hit Parade*. I also cut out pictures of the singers I love. "Leavin' On a Jet Plane" was an all-time favorite and always made me cry. My book of songs chronicled the times as society changed, but Harry Billy only played old timer songs on KDJI. At times, I was glad for that fact, other times, I wished he would play something new, but the Navajo public might not be happy about graduating to rock-n-roll. Issss…

    My favorite _XIT_ songs were kept in a separate section because I had to write the Navajo lyrics as I repeatedly played the songs in my mind trying to remember every word. I began to hum it while imagining the music, eyes closed… Hit Parade would never have an XIT or Redbone song in it. "Come and Get Your Love," was easy to get down, though.

    My mind escapes as if to fly over the vast lands with the beautiful oranges, reds, browns, yellows with dots and lines of black to define the depth. I could hear the hawk screech into the distance as it drifted over the canyon wall. The mundane life I lived at Red Sands Residential Dormitory had to be filled with imagination and possibilities, not impending doom.

Then, there was Jim Croce. Next Time, This Time

Time In a Bottle...always talking about time like there was so little of it, like it can be captured and kept still. Time, so much you don't know what to do with it after all. Now a kid of the dormitory life could relate to Jim Croce. Over time I hoped that time would make wishes come true...patiently waiting...keeping time in the pages of my notebooks so obediently waiting...for my own good! As if..

It took many years to understand how to express what "for my own good" meant. Years later in college, I took the time to reflect on my nine years at Red Sands Residential Dormitory. From time to time, I take this poem out, shed a few tears, and reflect on the history that is mine.

My friendly diary...another Sunday...time ticks by...still alive...longing for home and real food...waiting to ride a horse, and the smell of Gramps' yummy coffee. I decided to make another cup.

I decided it was also time to go request an XIT songs from our favorite D.J. Harry Billy, Crazy Injun #9 over at KDJI Radio Station! He will probably get reject my request, but I try... Sigh. I grew curious about the music of *Fleetwood Mac*, Clarence talked about.

For nine years, I wondered what "for my own good" meant. I went from confusion, doubt, resistance, and with age, eventual understanding.

For My Own Good

They said it was "for my own good"—
the leaving, the silence, the rules I withstood.
A wisdom they claimed, with a nod and a frown,
while packing my life in boxes, breaking me down.

A bed not my own, a voice not mine,
measured in prayers and punishments, time.
"For your own good," the words would repeat,
while I learned to survive on the edge of my seat.

I searched in the stitching of secondhand sheets,
in chalky hallways and cafeteria seats,
for the meaning that Gramps tucked behind his eyes,
a promise or lie, I still couldn't decide.

Years passed like wind through a broken screen—
shadows and sunlight, something between.
Maybe the good was not in the going,
but in the girl who kept growing.

Chapter 15 – Growing Up

It was another Sunday, and time was inching its way to May 1974. I lay on the steel grey bunk bed with my long brown braids dangling on the white tiled floor thinking about life. Father Paul's message was about life…about sacrifice and the meaning of life. For Lent, I gave up potato chips which was better than giving up pop, or my ultimate favorite green apple jolly rancher suckers. It's funny how I grew up alone and yet knowing so many people thought of me from a distance. Church and being with God was always a comforting place and another place to go to fill the time. These thoughts flickered in and out of the sunlight that shimmered through the windows that spanned both sides of Dorm A. The younger students slept in the bunk beds at the beginning of the hall and gradually moved towards the end of the hall as we returned each school year. This is where the double doors let in the shimmering morning sun through the iridescent glass. For me, moving to the end of the hall was ominous, because that meant I would be transferred to the beginning of Dorm B next year. I remember sleeping in the bunks down the hall, now my bunk was next to the East door, which allowed us a better chance of sneaking in and out.

I looked at the walls painted a shade of white, that in nine years and even in all that sunlight *never* looked clean. As I read the last pages of another friendly book, I spent that Sunday afternoon thinking of a life without books and of someone always looking into a person's daily life. Yep, George Orwell thought that eventually people would live a life of examination. Little did he know a life in the Bureau of Indian Affairs dormitory was much like the life in his book, "1984," which was only 10 years from now.

In the nine years I lived at Red Sands Residential Dormitory, books helped me travel all over the world and meet all kinds of people who filled hours of boredom that could easily make living at Red Sands Residential Dormitory a living hell… My friends, the books, kept me company on endless weekends when everyone else got picked up for a taste of the Promised Land.

"You just can't judge a book by its cover or its title. I hated it when Mrs. Smith was right about books," I thought shifting my slim 5'5" body enough to throw the book into the blue footlocker filled with a myriad of other books I was reading, finished reading or wanted to read next. Catching my reflection in the mirror taped on the lid, my big brown eyes, light brown complexion and the freckles that dotted my shoulders reflected back at me. The sun cast a golden reddish-brown shimmer on my long hair bringing out my Grandmother's Spanish side. I had her Navajo point of view and Gramps' temperament. One could say that I was a true mutt. My dad's Chiricahua Apache side made me as determined as, a warrior necessary when dealing with the reality of living in the white man's society. All the parts of me together helped me survive the place where **B**ullying **I**ndians **A**round was somehow for my own good.

I also experienced discrimination from the Navajo students who thought I was less than Navajo, because of my light skin color and Spanish features. That was when I experienced being alone the most…being different, yet the same. At times, I had to remember that *all* my fair-skinned, light-haired cousins suffered the same scrutiny, as did other kids experience a similar situation. It was as if I had to prove myself no matter where I went…little did I know it would last a lifetime – always living on the edge of indifference.

Disappointed with *"1984"*, I thought about my childhood excitement thinking what the year 2000 would really be like, with the possibility of flying cars and robots to do my chores. No such luck. *Orwell* never mentioned the fantasy future Gramps and I sometimes talked about that future as our imagination wandered into the air with glazed eyes. The future was very bleak and disconcerting, especially because in 1984, books were censored to extinguish people's knowledge, quite the opposite of what we thought the new millennium would be. Gramps must read this book! I gave it another thought and agreed to look for it at Zane's

Used Bookstore. A book for his reading pleasure…something to chew on while he's out herding sheep on those hot Tohatchi days.

And so it was, in 1974 I finally found myself with more control of *my life* at Red Sands Residential Dormitory. There is little a person could do to find comfort in dormitory living. The mattresses were old, overused, and the springs were so, so hard against my body. The speckled-tiled floors were buffed to a shine twice a week; it's a wonder they didn't buff them to oblivion. My once tender skin grew tough from years of shower water that spilled out 100 miles per hour, made to wash off all the Navajoness from me. It had been a hard life. I could feel the building creak from the agony called time. Sitting up and craning to see the clock on the wall at the end of Dorm A made me realize how hungry I was, and the smell from the cafeteria was promising - "was promising" being the key words…

Cafeteria food in the Bureau of Indian Affairs was brutally tasteless or overly salty to cover up the hideous atrocity that can come from a can or, worse yet, another meal of beans. **B**eans for **I**ndians **A**lways on the menu at Red Sands. It would be nice to have frybread or tortillas with those salty hamless beans, I sarcastically wrote in my About Food journal. Okay deep breath…smells like beef stew and fresh rolls. Reality bites!

Beans, beans, the more you eat; the more you fart; the more you fart; the better you feel – so by all means, please eat all your beans….. At Red Sands Residential Dormitory feeling better means swallowing all those beans. Geez, they could make them a little tasty. Swallow…swallow…sigh…reality bites! I remember a time when it got so bad that beans were served just about every meal! We thought there must be a food shortage somewhere! Red Sands Residential Dormitory must be on a budget cut, Ruby grumbled. Those were the times, I wished really hard that the mail would bring me some dead presidents to relieve my hunger pains because I could not eat another meal of flavorless beans. I think I even prayed to the Holy People, God, and the Pope to take beans off the menu! I should've rounded up the girls in Dorm A

& B to do a collective prayer, or better a collection of money so we could sneak in some real food.

Beans for **I**ndians **A**lways on the Menu meal also meant that the whole dorm would be flooded with the smell of bean fart. The stench drifted across our noses and lingered down the halls and into the Multipurpose Room. It got so every inch of the air in Dorm A & B was filled with bean fart! Something had to be done! Clarice decided that she couldn't stand smelling the smell of farts every night and decided to get a collection together for the cafeteria ladies. Dollar bills, quarters, dimes, nickels, and a whole bunch of pennies were donated, adding up to a total of $22.53 – enough to buy the necessary ingredients. Clarice was going to be a great leader and probably a Council Delegate in the future! When I suggested that to Clarice, she gave that look, and said, "I will do no such thing, Flo! And we both looked at Ruby, bursting into laughter! The four of us were rolling on the bunk with laughter! Good times!

Clarice set about buying onions, garlic, carrots, pepper, ham hocks (courtesy of Harry Billy), Blue Bird flour, Morrell's Snow Cap Lard, baking powder, salt, and of course 100 pounds of dried beans. We helped her secretly carry the groceries in our tote bags. We felt like we were on a mission! Like the mission to infuriate Mrs. Hagga with the blasting of "Bad Moon on the Rise"!! Clarice wrote the following message:

Dear Cafeteria Ladies,

We, the kids of Red Sands Residential Dormitory, are tired of your tasteless, meatless, spice less. breadless beans! We have taken up a collection and wish for you to use these items to make our Beans for Indians Always on the Menu meal. Some of us want tortillas but most of us want frybread, please. WE know you can make it brown and crispy just like you like it too!

Signed: ALL The Boys and Girls of Red Sands Dormitory

Boy, when Mrs. Hagga, the Matron on Duty, found out about the groceries and messages, she was furious at first but as she looked through the items, it only made sense that the kids wanted beans cooked the way they did at home. Surprisingly, Mrs. Hagga ordered the Cafeteria Ladies to cook the beans the right way and even the lunch ladies were so happy. They were probably tired of the fart smell that lingered throughout every last vent across Red Sands Residential Dormitory. HAHA!! Mrs. Hagga was puzzled about the carrots and left a message on the bulletin board, that read, "What is the carrots for anyway? Clarice responded with a note:

Dear Matron on Duty,

In Mrs. O'Connor's science class, we learned that carrots are known to take the acid out of the beans. It boils into the air therefore the eater will not get gas and Dorm A, B, C, and D will not be filled with smelly farts because it's been two months that **Beans for Indians Always** *has been on the menu!*

It was signed, "From, The Mouths You Feed."

Beans On the Menu
Beans for Indians Always on The Menu,
but please cook them right!
I know beans could taste so good
if only you would see the light!
A little onion, garlic, salt, pepper, chopped   carrots
Don't forget ham hocks and fresh bread
BUT we beg of you, please, Please NO MORE
Beans for Indians Always on EVERY OTHER Menu!!
T'ashoodi! (please..)!

It took us many years to muster the strength to protest, and it was another small victory because after that beans were cooked with carrots...fresh carrots that are *not* canned. As for bread, well, that's a different story. Most times they made us corn bread, which wasn't bad, and, of course, the delicious white rolls with the crusty brown top. That was a favorite of all students...just like chocolate milk. Every kid at Red Sands Dormitory was happy and the smell miraculously lifted out the wretched hallways, floating into oblivion. Clarice was a hero! We laughed and laughed for days after that. After all these years later, thinking of those times made me giggle. Beans for Indians Always on the Menu, will always make me smile when I see beans, no matter how... Reality is what you make of it. What a great time to share our lives with the Cafeteria Ladies, who were happy to serve us beans and frybread. although we never knew that at the time.,,,sigh.. I like to think they had a silent victory for us and future inmates of Red Sands Residential Dormitory.

It was another Sunday; the routine never ended at Red Sands Residential Dormitory. A couple of Navajo maintenance workers, in their dusty, worn blue uniforms, began pounding their heavy hammers, which made me turn my attention to the reality of life around Red Sands Residential Dormitory - "Home of the Roadrunners." Reality can be loud!! Louder than the thunderstorms that rumbled across Tohatchi Flats bringing much needed rain and hopefully the beautiful sunflower Gramma loved! Smile..sigh.. They were making their last pounds and using some tool I couldn't distinguish. They had to make their way out of Dorm A and proceed on to Dorm B which was adjacent and connected to my wing and then on to Dorm C and D which is where the boys were housed...all before 5:00 P.M. That was when the evening shifted to people began arriving for evening duty.

"Yep, there were people working and watching the students of Red Sands Residential Dormitory 24 hours per day, 7 days a week." sighed...deep breath...time ticked by second by second..sigh.. deep breath. "I can do this..I can do this.."

Although the students of Red Sands Residential Dormitory did not have a sports team, we cheered for the "Red Sands Roadrunners" because that was the mascot at school. The dormitory itself was built to house children from across the Navajo Nation in the name of education. It was where we lived while we were away from our families. Way back in the 1930's, 40's 50's and early 60's, a lot of Navajo kids were literally dragged, and *forced* to go to school – kicking and screaming…Mothers, Fathers, Grandparents crying as their children were swept up and never seen for days and years, and decades, sometimes a lifetime. When Chief Manuelito, Barboncito, Delgadito, and my great-great grandfather Jesus Arviso signed the Treaty of 1868, they never thought the children would be treated so badly in the name of education, sovereignty, and freedom from an unwarranted prison sentence. Bureau of Indian Affairs was another kind of torture,...the details are different, but the experience was similar at best.

A hundred years later, many students voluntarily came as far as Cameron, Arizona, Tohatchi, New Mexico, Shiprock, New Mexico, Tuba City, Arizona, Aneth, Utah and from the capital of the great Navajo Nation, Window Rock, Arizona. All of these places were at least a 4-to-6-hour drive away, but they came back every school year, year after year, decade upon decade…second by second.. sigh..

The students enrolled, withdrew, or were kicked out of Red Sands Residential Dormitory for many reasons. Some children were forced to be away from home by their parents in the name of a good education. Some children were there because their parents were too busy. Many of the children at Red Sands Residential Dormitory were there for their own safety, due to alcohol abuse that swept countless Navajo people into a life of hopelessness and early death. Many just had no choice. As I look back, it was what it was..good and harsh. And sometimes torture.

Gone were the days of living off the land. In one hundred years, a majority of Navajos could barely live off the monthly government welfare handouts guaranteed by the Treaty of 1868, the United States offered in return for what, our way of life? I never really thought of why the kids were at Red Sands Residential Dormitory year after year…second by second.. until now. At first, I thought were all here for our own good, and that none of us any choice about the whole matter…until now… I was the only one there, "for my own good.." words echoed in the back of my mind.. year by year, month by month, day by day..second by second... sigh.. "Reality exists in the human mind, and nowhere else." George Orwell said it right…Like clockwork, my friends, fellow Navajos, and myself came back to live here year after year – enduring another year regimented by the dictates of the almighty United States Government, and at the hand of Superintendent Levenstein and his right-hand Mrs. Becenti along with her faithful minions.

Chapter 16 – Reflections

Nine years, time had splashed scheduled and unscheduled events across the lives of four Navajo girls with an odd sense of longing, emptiness, and uncertainty certainty. Memories guarded in a capsule called time as it ticked, ticked, ticked ever closer to the beginning of another decade. We were left at the doors of Red Sands Residential Dormitory in August 1965, now it was May 1974. In those nine years, so much had happened in the outside world but life at Red Sands Residential Dormitory stood motionless. Yet, spring was a time when all its residence took a collective breath and a sigh of relief in the border town of Red Sands, Arizona, as change blew in the quiet desert.

I watched the news from time to time. I didn't like it if there was another war going on because the last one took my dad and his spirit from him and then us. President Nixon began his Presidency by announcing the suspension of offensive action in North Vietnam, which hopefully meant that the war was finally ending. It seemed like an eternity since this war started and everyone; Native Americans, Mexicans, Blacks, whites – everyone was glad it was over. The Hippie Movement was fading, and Elvis' Hawaii concert could be seen by millions on television.

The turmoil and news of the killings of the war weighed heavily on the minds of many Navajo families. Their sons were fighting for the lands within the four sacred mountains, first – America second. Navajos were not strangers to combat service for the United States. They joined all branches of the military during the European Invasion in an effort to protect their families, their people and most of all their sacred land. Even though Navajos weren't considered U.S. Citizens, many didn't think twice when called to serve – to protect their families and Diné bi'keyah. (*Our homelands*) During World War II, Korean Conflict, and now the Vietnam War, while the whole Navajo Nation said a collective prayer each sunrise and at sunset. Offerings evoked Holy People every day since the beginning of time and every inch of another war.

Meanwhile, on the great and vast Navajo Nation...spanning four states: Arizona, New Mexico, Utah, and Colorado... Former Navajo Tribal Chairman Raymond Nakai signed away the coal for ninety-nine years while current Chairman, Peter McDonald, an electrical engineer, promised economic development and jobs for Navajos. Water Rights, running water, electricity and health care were issues of the day. Thanks to the overturning of Plessy v. Ferguson and the Civil Rights Movement, the Navajo Nation and the State of Arizona were making plans to use state monies to build public schools in rural areas so that the children did not have to be separated from their parents and families anymore. Change was definitely in the air..

It was also a time when four girls began thinking about entering high school while our last year in middle school slipped away. Our childhood was a series of episodes where other people determined every minute of our daily lives. Once in a while, and just when it was needed, life threw in a dash of sweet times. This year brought a sense of wonderment and excitement that made them feel as if they were floating through time at Red Sands Residential Dormitory. Through his notebooks that told of their whereabouts, I learned the value of writing about our lives and secretly sending messages in poetry. I guess I did not want to forget our time together – to keep our memories dear to my heart because after silent words and countless pencils were all that kept me company. My observations were not just of dorm life, but of life outside the gates where the paradox of heaven and hell met and parted ways.

Thinking back, even as kindergarteners, I could see the difference in our lives and the lives of our schoolmates who were Anglos and Mexicans. Over time, as we were gradually allowed to roam the city boundaries the countless, boring weekends alone or with whoever didn't get picked up my eyes opened to society. The separation between us and the people who lived in the nice homes with the nice gardens and nice vehicles in their driveway was a glaring example of the racial unrest that was going on all over America – the land of the free, home of the Braves…and those of us who were forced to be brave. Those who had so much stuff; stuff that seemed to separate the students who lived in town and those of us that lived at Red Sands Residential Dormitory. Nevertheless, we all came together at Red Sands Public School…day after day, year after year. The minorities, Navajos, Mexicans, Blacks endured the subtle and often outright racial tension at school. It was as if the tension could simmer and boil, spilling over when they reached an apex of differences. I could feel the tension's ebb and flow with the tides. The fights were mostly between the boys, although catfights between the Navajo and Mexican girls happened more often than fights with the whites. The fights usually happened outside the school grounds, but everyone knew when one was going to happen. Then there was the usual name-calling. Navajos, Mexicans, and Blacks called each other names. Nevertheless, they were always called "a dirty this or that" according to the white kids. It was when we were in fourth grade that I noticed the white people lived on the north side of the tracks. Everybody else lived on the south side of the railroad tracks, and most likely worked for the Pacific Railroad, Red Sands Schools, Red Sands Residential Dormitory, or the local stores. Red Sands was a small town, packed with a lot of different kinds of people. Outwardly, the border town people lived their lives from the outside in…which was a peculiar thought in and of itself.

Then, there were those of us who lived on the West end of town on a 15-acre Bureau of Indians Affairs lot called Red Sands Residential Dormitory. A compound surrounded by a seven-foot chain linked fence meant to keep us separate from the other people who lived in Red Sands. One entrance also served as an exit. The little hut of a building housed the security guard who made sure no one escaped. On the east side were two gates that allowed the students to walk to school…boys through one and girls through the other. At the northeast corner was the gateway where the students used to attend football games. It was also a symbol of freedom whenever they could sneak up to the football field whenever it wasn't being used. The west side of the compound was used as a maintenance yard and a place where the employees of Red Sands Dormitory parked their vehicles. A separate fence covered all the "unusable" items taken out of any one of the four dorms over the years. We called it "The Army Graveyard" because all that unwanted stuff was a dull sad green.

Day after day, week after week, the children at Red Sands Residential Dormitory were routinely rushed to wake up, rushed to get ready, rushed to eat breakfast, and then rushed through the gate to walk into the outside world where it was a requirement to attend Red Sands public school. Until we reached 6th grade, we were required to eat lunch at Red Sands Residential Dormitory cafeteria. It was in 4th grade we got wise. We rushed back to the dorm for lunch, where we strategically put our unwanted slop in napkins that were deposited in our tote bags. By 5th grade we had this deception down to the seconds. When the lunch Monitor wasn't looking, we slipped the mystery meal into the tote bags we made in Home Economics Class. We learned to put our totes near our legs for quick disposal. We had mastered the way to make it appear we had finished eating so we could be released from "lunch detention". Those were the days we ran back towards the school, sneaking off to meet Juanita who was allowed to go to Romo's for lunch. She took our orders during recess so we could share the chili fries we learned to love. We also learned to slowly walk back to the dorm at the end of the school day. Romo's Mexican Restaurant was the closest thing to home cooked food. Our orders included burgers, or chili fries we had to scarf down before the bell signaled the end of lunch break. Maria, the waitress, began asking us if we were going to send Juanita to get our order so they could get our food ready.

"It's not good to eat too fast," she would jokingly scold us.

We decided on setting a schedule for those days. When we reached middle school, we did not have to go back to the dorm so on those days we rushed to Romo's for lunch and after school for delicious homemade food!

At the end of every day, lights went out at exactly 9 p.m., then slumber. The regimented life every student at Red Sands Residential Dormitory grew to know was much like a mouse stuck in a mousetrap, or a cute fluffy gerbil. Many children spent twelve years at Red Sands Residential Dormitory. Twelve years away from their families – stuck and trapped by time. For me, nine years was a life sentence.

Compared to the sporadic home life I came from, where there was relatively no anger and only a whole lot of hard work, Red Sands Residential Dormitory was either simmering or boiling over or somewhere in between. It was frightening to see so much anger and hate in the eyes of the kids fighting. It always scared me to see a fight, and we decided it was better not to show up. It was equally scarry to see the Matron on Duty's resentful glares and harsh tone. I decided to tune them out at a very young age. I had enough of that anger when I was very little!

For *me,* I had the sense that nine years of living in this bubble was about to change for good, or for bad…I didn't know. It was an uneasy feeling I felt as I took my morning run with Clarice. My life had some stability and some instability just like everybody that blew in, blew up, and then blew out of Red Sands Residential Dormitory. Nerves frayed and butterflies turned my feelings with uncertainty looming in the air.

There was a growing knot in my stomach as we traveled the familiar path from Tohatchi Flats to Red Sands Residential Dormitory, as Christmas break ended, and another New Year's Eve celebrated with family. In the back of our minds, there was a knowing we had only a few more weeks before the end of middle school arrived, and we would step into the world of high school. This also meant we would be moving to Dorm B where the "big kids" served their time at Red Sands. …some reward..tsk tsk.. What I didn't know was it would also be the end of my daily life with Garnet, Clarice, and Ruby – my best friends.

I often spent my time wondering what was happening at Tohatchi Flats. I anticipated a small note from Gramps that kept me informed. Knowing Uncle Benny and Uncle Leonard were coming back from years of fighting the Vietnam War gave me butterflies as I thought of how my family was handling the news. The four years they were battling for the Marines and Army were tough for my Grandparents. The happiness vibe knowing that the Vietnam War was over reverberated throughout Red Sands and the entire Navajo Nation. I learned to pray from listening to our Prayer Meetings and praying early in the morning with my grandparents. Clarice also taught me to keep the prayers alive. She kept me grounded. We started running when we were in 4th grade. Every morning, Clarice and I snuck out of Red Sands Residential Dormitory compound to run to greet the morning sun.

This is our special prayer:

> *As the Bluebird Sings at dawn,*
> *I breathe in the cool air to nourish my spirit,*
> *As I sing towards East to offer my Corn Pollen,*
> *I ask Mother Earth and Father Sky to rejuvenate my spiritual, physical, mental, and emotional health.*
> *Through the Blessing from the Holy People,*
> *I shall Walk in Beauty of love and happiness.*
> *The blessings shall always restore the unity of my family and community.*
> *It is finished in Beauty.*
> *It is finished in Beauty.*
> *It is finished in Beauty.*
> *It is finished in Beauty.*

We placed tá'didíín on the tip of our tongues, sprinkled some on the top of our heads, and sprinkled the rest in front of us as we faced East. "Sometimes prayers are answered," I thought. It was about time for my family, the Navajo Nation, and every United States Citizen to collectively exhale. "War sucks!" I boldly said to myself! Change was in the air.

Gramps' latest letter told me about preparations for the Enemy Way Ceremony necessary for my uncles to leave the war and battle on the battlefield. This was the same ceremony held for Uncle Andy and Uncle Ed when they returned from WWII and the

Korean Conflict. That was first on the list of things to do when I returned home. Come to think of it, I was sure that my father didn't have an Enemy Way Ceremony during the short time I lived at Klagetoh. No wonder he drank himself into oblivion; reliving all horrible acts a soldier must do to survive war ~ to be a *hero*.

Over the years, I found it comforting to spend my time writing my thoughts during endless weekends at Red Sands Residential Dormitory…thoughts I didn't dare to openly express for fear of, "The Room." The family was so far away, the burden and high cost of being away from the cattle and sheep weighed heavy on their minds. The oil crisis didn't help either! There was always some work to do and the sacrifice of driving over one hundred miles one-way was overwhelming for Gramps and apparently too overwhelming for my mother. I had to learn the quality of patience because, well, I just had no choice in that matter. I patiently waited for each and every precious letter from home.

For sure, the thoughts of Tohatchi Flats kept me from going insane while counting the endless minutes and buzzing silence. Time was often spent counting the floor tiles or the holes in the ceiling for the millionth time and always wishing I could paint over that Nabaho white paint with something more refreshing. The students at Red Sands Residential Dormitory lived in small capsules of time in the shadows of the dominant society and in the name of education – Indian Education, meant "to kill the Indian in him, and save the man,' as Pratt proclaimed in his assimilation speech decades in 1892, yeah, 1892…

I had a lot of thoughts about the regimented life at Red Sands Residential Dormitory and any dormitory for that matter. By the time I was in third grade, I knew better than to express my thoughts and decided to spend my time observing and waiting…waiting for what? I still didn't know what, "for my own good" meant, so I continued my search with no resolution.

My cousin Burton, aka Chuckie, was a good source of information, for he had been an invited and eventual uninvited guest at many of the area's Bureau of Indian Affair Residential Dormitories, although he never was a number at Red Sands

Residential Dormitory. I never knew when a letter would arrive from him, but it always had a few dollars...or dead presidents, as Burton referred to money. He was a free-spirited boarding school transient. Boys were typically the students that roamed from school to school. Although girls came and went from time to time...it was mainly because of fighting or not following the rules...or so we thought. I had observed that most of the girls, who were sent to the Promised land, were punished in the "The Room" first... it was a mystery to me as I fought the temptation to be rebellious. Besides, who wants to end up with that putrid stench Ruby often had to scrub off of her, having spent one or two nights in "The Room."

I was a thirteen-year-old with the mind of a much older and much wiser person. My Gramps and Gramma had instilled in the value of things and common sense some people just don't get or see. I learned to lean on and thank the Holy People, God, and the Pope for helping my mother find the courage to leave Klagetoh when she did!

Fun memories of Tohatchi Flats also made being alone bearable. I thought of days gone by, like how it was funny to watch my nine-year-old cousin, Chischilly who decided to take a short-cut but steeper route to the sheep camp up in the mountain. We all told him to go down the path with the worn indentations made by the wind and horse hooves, but he chose to move the sheep down a steep path. "He must think we're real goats!" We laughed before he made the big fall! To this day, Chischilly still carries the scar from that decision. Nobody dared to say, "I told you so," but we all learned to take the well-worn path instead of the short cut...common sense is a funny thing. I wondered if that's what Robert Frost meant by taking either the path well-worn or the one that is less traveled... Smile. Common sense is a funny thing as well. For me, it was just force of habit.

Yeah, I thought, those were the days I was free to run around and explore for hours upon hours. At Red Sands Residential Dormitory, I found myself watching and enjoying television just about every day. There is no electricity or running water out on

Tohatchi Flats but there was a large collection of Louis Lamour books and Time Magazines to read. Gramps had a special place where he kept the issue with the late President Kennedy on the cover.

If my grandparents knew I was sitting around that much, they would scold me. My guilty conscience sometimes got the best of me. Those times I would pick up a good story to read or reread. However, the vampires of *Dark Shadow* were my favorite, and each week I hurried from the high school football game before the turnstile slowed the crowd of spectators, so I could watch beginning to end.

My friends weren't always as eager to race back to the dorm to watch television but that didn't stop me. I also loved The Lucille Ball Show. How could this white woman get on television and do all those crazy things? Especially when most of the white women at Red Sands were so somehow...stiff or something...I never could put my finger on it. Anyways, television was good, and I was sure that Gramps would enjoy seeing Lucy, Desi, Fred, and Ethel being so silly in front of the world. The writing for this show was nothing like I had ever seen, and Cuban music was different from anything I heard Harry Billy play on the radio.

I learned to be very observant of how people said things to each other on television. Watching television made me think of how Ms. Larimore once said, "Someone wrote those words." Hmmmm...

Students at Red Sands Residential Dormitory were required to attend every one of the home football and basketball games. Baseball and softball games were optional. When one lives their life in a Bureau of Indian Affairs Residential Dormitory, time always revolves around a schedule. On the other hand, if things weren't scheduled, the students would probably go nuts, or so I mused.

I guessed that the experiences or misfortunes of life at Red Sands Residential Dormitory would not happen out on Tohatchi Flats. How could they? There was nothing to do but work work

work work work work! No television. No stores. The neighbors lived at least five miles away. Just the news and music on the radio and thoughts of the work that needed to be done were enough for the people out on Tohatchi Flats. Heck, just eating was work!

In their nine years together, all my friends knew exactly how to get to Tohatchi Flats. Ruby loudly proclaimed with arms emphasizing, as if! "To get to Tohatchi Flats, you have to drive east from here down Interstate 40 to Gallup, New Mexico...The Capital of Indian Country."

I rolled my eyes and thought, the reality was that it was more like The Capital of Stealing from Indians in this Country, I thought. But the whites chose to call it Drunk City, because of all the drunken Indians laying around in the alleys and streets...probably including my father. What they didn't realize was that there were drunken whites and Mexicans lying around inside their homes.

Ruby went on, "at Gallup you go North on the notorious Highway 666...the sign of the devil."

In all my years, I had never seen a devil while traveling on that road. A lot of people died or were killed on that road in head-on collisions. Instead of the devil, it's because of the crosswinds and the way the road was built so narrowly. I grimaced, remembering how Gramps cursed at the people who built it, before telling us to "hang on tight." The fact that there weren't even any shoulders to move off the road made Highway 666 earn its name. If someone has a bad alignment from the bumpy roads or if someone has bald tires – that could make them go off the road and make the vehicle flip. There wasn't anywhere for them to stop – so they either go back on the road or roll into a ditch.

Ruby always made things bigger than they were. "AND," Ruby continued in her best Gramps voice, "A lot of people are driving after they had a few whiskeys..." Ruby's voice faded into the distance while the three of us gave each other that look... deep breath, double sign.

All of Gramps' kids and grandkids knew how he felt about what a few whiskeys meant….so no one talked about it. I knew that whiskey was the reason Gramps didn't like my father too. "You don't know how to, or you forget to take care of your family with whiskey.." he would mumble under his breath…careful not to talk down about others in front of me, but I heard…every word.. U.S. Hwy 666 was somewhat straight but there were a few spots that the road from Gallup to Tohatchi, thirty miles to be exact, was a bit narrow and scary if you were driving in the dark. The sign to turn home was really not a sign. It was a tire hanging on the barbed wire fence and three big reflectors Uncle Ed had hammered to reflect the light at night. The eastward drive was fifteen miles of rugged dirt road, and it changed with the weather. All who used the road knew how to be prepared for anything. Flash floods poured down as the heavy clouds covered Chuska Mountains and eastward toward Tohatchi Flats. The tall sandstone mesa that hid the home provided much needed shade in the summertime. It also served as a shield from the raging dust storms and the blistering winter winds. It was a happy sight, and thoughts of the comforts of the stone house – our castle, our refuge, kept me going. The Stone House was built by Gramps and his young sons long ago, next to Gramma's dad, Charlie Arviso. Great Grandpa Charlie and Great Grandma Bah had a lot of children, and Gramma Florence was his favorite child.

There were three ways to get to the Stone House on Tohatchi Flats. One was from Sheep Springs to the north. That road was the one we used when coming back from the mountain and leads to the newer Cinderblock house, which was two miles north of the Stone House. Another way was the usual 15 miles off of U.S. Hwy 666, just north of the town of Tohatchi, where Gramps picked up their mail. The third way was just west of the town of Crownpoint, where many of Gramma's Arviso relatives live.

I guess I had talked about Tohatchi Flats so much that my friends knew about the Stone House and the newer Cinderblock House as my family affectionately called them. They also knew about the summer mountain ranch near Asaayi Lake, a beautiful valley of lush grass, juniper trees, high rock ridges and water. This was the place where my family grew alfalfa and oats for the cattle.

"I like the way I tell it!" I quietly thought, as Ruby ended with..." AND that's how you get to Tohatchi Flats..." finally making eye contact with the girls who were giving her that look. The one that made you feel awkward. Slowly sitting down; the conversation usually turned towards something else. Uncomfortable silence...sigh.. We had learned to let Ruby be Ruby. We had no choice but to burst into laughter, with Ruby joining in.

The reality was, if it weren't for Tohatchi Flats, the unnatural "home life" dormitory living and the experiences that inevitably came with it would try very hard to wash my Navajo identity away. For, while things were done on a schedule, it was okay if the schedule wasn't completed out at Tohatchi Flats, because there was plenty of time to catch up during the early day or late night.

Red Sands Public School had another routine. I grew up observing many things. Kids who didn't stay at Red Sands Residential Dormitory were different and their parents would show up at all school events. The white kids always wore the latest fashions from a big town called Phoenix. I could tell the Mexican kids got their clothing from either J.C. Penny's or Montgomery Wards because I saw them in the magazines.

At the beginning of my prison sentence, I felt pathetic because it was hard to figure out how to mix the five sets of clothes I owned, but by the time I was about to turn ten entering the fourth grade, the need to be groovy was all the rage! Mrs. Haney left the library to become our Threads Teacher. Our first project was to embroider a handkerchief. My friends and I began embroidering and adding beads to our clothes. With the few dollars my mother sent me, I learned to wait until the Matron on Duty was either drunk or taking a nap to escape and wander around Red Sands on another lonely weekend. It was then I found Heap's Gently Used clothing store on the main drag. I could stretch my money for "new" clothes and made them look hip with embroidery. I also learned how to sew by watching Gramma all those summer days. Hip huggers were all the rage in fourth and fifth grade! It wasn't long before we soon made a little business of our decorating project. Altogether each of us made forty dollars. For sure, $5.00 was a lot of money for ten and eleven-year-olds. Five bucks could also buy a lot of clothes at Heap's. Those memories are the ones I put down on paper, and the ones I held onto whenever I did them.

For me, my eyes began to view life with a new sense of reality in 1974. Maybe it was because I might have to start another year in a different school with older kids – high school. Before I paid attention to the details, now I was seeing the bigger picture my family talked about. Thirteen was a big year. There was a feeling in the air that something big was going to happen. Memories of advice and warnings whispered in my ear while I dreamt or ran in the early morning. Over the lonely years and empty weekends, I learned to tame loneliness and make myself feel better by sneaking out to run towards the rising sun. "With this Song I Run. With This Song I Run." I hummed the same song taught to me by Auntie Clara, all the while trying to beat my mark from the day before...before the sun reached the horizon.

Days were marked by the countless pencils I used to fill notebook after notebook of lined paper. Sometimes, I would take the time to read what I had written months or years before to bide the time at Red Sands Residential Dormitory. My favorite was about Tohatchi Flats.

Reality bites! What I would give to hear his order in place of the order the matrons issued.

"Get to your detail! Get in Line! Go to sleep! Get Up!" echoed throughout the hallways of Dorm A & B as students scurried to get the place "spic and span."

Yeah, life was work, work, work out on Tohatchi Flats. Here at Red Sands Residential Dormitory, it was wait, wait, wait...counting the months, the days, the hours, second by second.. waiting for time to take a deep breath...and well, be patient... hmmm..

I had a semi-traditional Navajo upbringing and Grandparent's wisdom prepared me for life. Turning away from the pages as the clouds cast a shadow across Dorm A. Yes, contrary to how the town people treated us, or what the Red Sands Residential Dormitory Matrons demanded, there was another way of thinking. As I grew older, the wisdom learned during the countless happy summers on the plains of Tohatchi Flats helped me patiently survive dormitory life.

Coming back to reality, I had precious words and stories to keep me from being lonely and to pass the time away, and yes, be patient…for what? On any given weekend, looking through my favorite journals or writing poems was my only company. Yep, this is definitely somewhere to escape to on days like this! I thought closing my notebook..endless deep breaths, endlessly waiting..

I took a deep breath during the harsh reality of the dorm life with the routine the noise of returning girls making their way down the 36-foot wide by 500-foot-long hall that was lined barracks style with our grey metal bunks where there was almost no room to do much of anything between bunks.

Every other day the tiles were buffed to a shiny sheen. The floor was so shiny that you could see the reflection of the bunks down the halls at certain times of the day, and a person could easily slip and fall down. If Mr. Benally did the cleaning, some of the older girls would cover the edges of each penny with pencil lead. When the matrons were not looking, they would roll pennies just to see how far they could get away with being defiant. The coins made marks crisscrossing the shiny floors, leaving black lines that crisscrossed across the hallway. Before the matron on duty could find out who made the mess, they quickly ran out the back door and onto the compound, looking all casual. They could hear the matron yelling from the thin walls getting mad, not knowing who to blame or who to send to the Manual Labor Guy. It was hilarious! Now that wasn't living from the inside out at all!! Sweet revenge was a sport, and I learned from the best!

All students knew that any Bureau of Indian Affairs dormitory was not a good thing. It was a place where the "**B**rutality of **I**ndians in the **A**mericas could be covered up and buried for centuries. I exhaled all this schooling in the name of *civilization*. So much for the "Glittering World..."

Thinking back to the day which came around every year - that dreaded day, was as painful memory burned into all the minds of the children schooled by the Bureau of Indian Affairs in one way or another. To be sure, we dreaded the day when we had to return to for the school year. Those days left an indelible mark on Native American children throughout the centuries and forever. Some children were ripped away from their parents, never to see their homes again, all in the name of education and the almighty dollar.

Throughout the school year, I was secretly glad I didn't have to go through the trauma of separation every Sunday. It was tough to see families drop off their children, listen to them cry, and watch them try to get back into the dormitory routine. When I was little, my Grandparents would pick me up for Thanksgiving and Christmas Break, but as I got older, I was only picked up at the end of the school year. My mother visited once in a while, but for the most part, I spent the school year isolated, waiting patiently for another cherished letter from the Promised Land. My journals and books were my friends as I marked one school year, after another, after another.

Gramps hung this quote next to the calendar, "There is no destiny that makes us brothers. No man goes his way alone. All that he sends into the lives of others comes back into our own." Charles E. Markham. I was thankful for the three friends that remained consistent companions in a path of questionable destiny. Surely our lives were leading somewhere...but where?...and why?...sigh...deep breath.., "Heh."

Chapter 17 – The Old Ranch House
Our Sanctuary

By the time Mrs. Gardner finished her paperwork and began her usual routine of handing back our journals, the bell rang, and it was finally time for a break. Everyone let out a silent breath of relief because there was not enough time to read to Mrs. Gardner. This could be very painful for the kids that did not know how to read, much less read the same sentence written in different ways, for others. I was relieved not to have to be questioned about my life at Red Sands Dormitory and vowed to have something to write about for the next journal entry.

It was good to get some fresh air and to see some of the people who a person would rather see in class every day, like Clarice. As soon as I walked out, the sun was a welcome sign of warmth and of freedom. Clarice was standing by the monkey bars waiting.

"You get your lecture on the CAT test?" Clarice announced to us as we headed her way.

"Yeah" we all said in a way that screamed "BORING!" We chimed in together.

"You think they'll cover the same thing from last year?" Garnet asked. "I don't know, probably."

"Hey, let's go up to the Ranch House after school!" Ruby suggested. "My Grandparents bought me some snacks, and I brought something special AND I feel like pigging out!!! What do you say girls?"

We looked at one another with raised eyebrows and agreed that would be the plan. We haven't been up to the Ranch House together in a while and it's always nice to be there.

Ruby always had a way of making the rest of us wish we had a parent who worked for the Navajo Tribal Government because she *always* had everything the rest of the girls could only wish for.

Clarice once asked out loud, "I wonder why she is at Red Sands. She seems to have everything at home, so why doesn't she stay there?"

Over time, we concluded that the mere fact that Ruby was attending Red Sands was a loud announcement that her mother was far too busy for her. She was one of those kids that came to Red Sands Residential Dormitory because her mother was too busy with her latest boyfriend who would soon be her next stepfather, or so she thought. Ruby had an older stepbrother who was already on his own, living in Phoenix, but she didn't really talk about him.

Yup, our group was like the fingers on a hand...no two are the same. I think that's why we click in and click out at times – but we always clicked back, like a magnet.

"Hey that sounds good!" Garnet said breaking the silence, looking like she started to forget the problems that were touching the surface from inside out.

"Yeah, girls let's go over to Safeway first and get some Pe-si and peanuts."

"Here Garnet, I will let you have my favorite flavor of laffy taffy – grape! That outta pull you back to reality, Ruby offered, while Garnet cringed at her insensitivity.

"That was Ruby – the pinky finger," Florence chuckled at her thought. We cracked up and the bell just had to ring and bring them back to reality.

"Come on; let's go wish this day to pass quickly!" Ruby sullen, walked down the sidewalk towards the west wing. "Here we go!"

"Okay, before we take the mathematics part of the test tomorrow, I want to do a quick review. Let's turn to page 249 in our mathematics books..." Mrs. Gardner's voice drowned in and out of my mind.

By now, I had finished all the problems in the entire book and the only thing she had to do was turn to the right pages. All those days cooped up in the dormitory with no one to talk to can make a person do insane things -- like, get ahead in your mathematics. I found a way to use the answers in the back to figure out the odd problems in the book and then worked backwards from the answer, it was not always foolproof, but it was enough to keep her B+ average.

Gramps claimed, "Grandchild, there is more than one way to skin a rat." So, I figured out my own strategy when it came to mathematics.

"Florence, Florence," Mrs. Gardner was trying to bring me back to the classroom.

Oh, yes, Mrs. Gardner.... ahhh what did you say? I stammered. Oh, problem #45 is a sample of the Pythagorean Theorem, so... ahhh, let's see.... I managed to solve the problem and was finally left alone. The rest of the kids had that; "PLEASE, don't call on me!" look. Science, Social Studies and at last Art...then the school day was finally over.

The last bell finally rang and to the relief of all the kids who were busy taking the first part of the Mosi' test. The students poured out of the school doors and went off in all directions. We found each other at the big elm tree on the south side of the school. That was our meeting place since 3rd grade.

"Hey, was that a boring day or what?" Clarice announced, as the girls walked to Safeway for a few items. The chatter went from subject to subject from the aisles of Safeway, through the back streets, and up the hill behind the football field.

"Yeah, I'm ready to groove my way down to the dorm and get my groovy snacks and hey, we're ready to go do some groovy munching!" Ruby said as the girls laughed, trying not to let their Pepsi and peanuts fizzle over.

"These snacks are like far out! Ruby." Garnet managed to say as she took a bite of the mutton sandwiches Ruby's mom packed for us.

"Wow, I haven't had mutton sandwich in ages! Thanks Ruby." I added while taking another bite of the delicious tortillas. Tortillas which cooked over an opened fire added to its crispy cracker effect were my favorite! There is a certain taste to tortillas cooked over an opened fire and I did not realize how much I craved such delicacies. How did you know I was dreaming of this? My eyes were filled with delight and my nose knew exactly how my first bite was going to melt in my mouth!

"Well, I thought since you practically don't get to go home, I'd treat you with a bit of home life." Ruby exclaimed.

Giving her the side-eye, I felt slighted, like Ruby was putting me down in a bragging way. Oh well, Ruby is Ruby. Quiet footsteps and mindful breathing, we trudged up the worn sandy path. On cue, we stopped for a moment to observe the wind shifting from South the East. Within fifteen minutes we were finally at the Ranch House, our friend and sanctuary.

We continued to savor every bite of the mutton sandwiches, washed down by Pepsi, and ended with delicious roasted pinions

"These were leftovers from last season...they might be a little stale, but I think most of them are still good.... My *Masani* (maternal grandmother) stores them in our cellar, so they will not get spoiled. We usually use them to cook winter kneel down bread, with the frozen Navajo corn we get from Shiprock farmers." Ruby explained.

Satisfied contentment, we cracked them open one by one looking into the passing clouds. "Our Gramma's do all kinds of things like that, huh," Ruby concluded, waiting for some kind of acknowledgement.

"We don't care; just keep bringing us these delicious reminders of our Navajo life and the Promiseland!" I joked.

More uncomfortable silence, followed by bursts of laughter. Those precious moments breaking bread and being free made living worth appreciating. Garnet looked at her watch and let us know we had about thirty minutes before curfew.

Descending towards our gated cinderblock home, I thought of the *All About Mutton* and other *Delicious Foods* notebook where she will write another Haiku.

Roast Mutton and Grilled Tortillas

Heavenly mutton
Grilled tortillas cooked crispy
The good life tastes good!

The satisfaction of the mutton sandwich and roasted pinion nuts made my passage to sleep easier...so nice was the treat that I did not wake on my usual 12:30 AM and when Mrs. Montoya announced that we had to "Get Up Girls!!", I busted out of bed and bumped my head. "Ouch!"

"Get up Girls, Get up! Get up Girls, Get up!" Then the sound of click, click, click, click, as the lights lit up Dorm A from one end to the other and another routine day at Red Sands Residential Dormitory began again, with the sounds of squeaking beds and the muffled sounds of girls filling the hall. Mrs. Montano and all the other Dormitory Matrons yelled the same command all year long and of course at exactly 5:30AM.   Same routine....another day....a few left to go...deep breath, exhale, sigh...

"Someday I'll make my own schedule," one of those old sayings I told myself so many times, I began to believe it.

Ever since the beginning of that week, time seemed to start speeding up! Pretty soon, there were only two more weeks, then one week, and a half. Sunday came around twice, as usual, and again I waited for my friends to return from the Promise land. This time we decided to stay, and finally the weekend was not going to be boring. Garnet was a special friend, and I just knew that she would be a friend forever. Garnet slept on the next bunk that weekend so we could talk at night and listen for the supposed ghosts that everyone talked about, but no one dared to investigate the eerie noises coming from the bathroom and showers at the stroke of midnight – the Wishing Hour. It's funny, because all we could hear were the memories of days gone by, as if to haunt our minds…month by month, day by day, second by second…sigh.. deep breath…exist.

"Hey, let's go up to the Ranch House again today," Garnet suggested as we made our way to breakfast Saturday morning. It smells like Mrs. Benally made her famous tortillas and scrambled eggs with a slab of ham!

"Yeah, finally at the end of the year, she breaks down and cooks us a real meal!" We giggled as we reached the end of the line. I have some money, so we can go to Safeway and get some munchies later. I snickered as we made our way to the north side of the cafeteria.

"MMMMM!" We moaned as we bit into the sandwich. A familiar silence fell over the cafeteria as everyone devoured these specially made meals that came far and few between.

"Rhonda Tsosie, Jamie Begay, Jennifer Benally, Florence Arviso, Garnet Begay, Jolene Yazzie," Mrs. Montano announced the names of the girls who received letters. My heart jumped with excitement! We looked at each other and went to collect our letters. Clarice and Ruby rarely receive letters. They were always being checked out and pretty much always knew what was going on in their homes. I was so excited that I almost tore open the envelope and the letter inside. Three letters in one week that was like seeing your Gramps and Gramma pull into the B.I.A. Compound! The first one felt like a greeting card, was from mom, the legal sized envelope with yellow paper was always from Gramps and Gramma...and the small envelope was always from Cousin Burton who was currently *exiled* to Shiprock Boarding Hell.

Yes, some B.I.A. Boarding Dormitories and/or Boarding Schools were miserable and dangerous. Any Native American child could be shipped off to Intermountain Boarding School, in Utah, Ignacio Boarding School, in Colorado and quite a few went to Chilocco Indian School, which was in Oklahoma. Most of the students who went there were a part of "trade" school and were instructed in the *art* of iron pressing so they could find work at the local dry-cleaning store, or they could be some sort of maintenance worker. Many girls ended up going to shorthand and typing classes and were trained clerk typists. I'll bet Ruby's mother went there after high school. As B.I.A. boarding schools go, the last place anyone wanted to end up was Ft. Wingate Boarding School, which in the 1800s served as an Army depot and the first refuge the Navajos had on their return in 1864. Now, there were probably really A LOT of Ghosts there!! Yíiyáh!

Then, there was Shiprock Boarding School, which was notorious for housing the radical Navajos of the day, even though the town was thriving, and even Biligáana's wanted to live there. Shiprock, New Mexico used to be green and somewhat prosperous but when the Bureau of land Management shut down the Helium Plant, the Biligaana's (white people), Mexicans, and Blacks who worked there packed up and left and Shiprock went down the drain. What the Navajos did not know was that the Bureau of Land Management also left the dangerous and lethal uranium mill tailings for the Navajo to inhale and drink. Knowing how dusty Shiprock can become from March to October, many people must have become sick with cancer. This health problem was not public knowledge, and many young mineworkers began to die off in record numbers. In time, we would learn about a community named Cove where there were absolutely no living Grandfathers. None. The men worked the uranium mines without the right equipment and were infected with a cancer that started in their lungs and rapidly took over their once healthy body. Shiprock is located on the New Mexico side of the Navajo Reservation and near the Four Corners. This is probably one of the few places Navajos farmed precious food and implements used in our precious Ceremonies throughout the year. It wasn't until I was much older that the thought of eating food produced with all those dangerous chemicals could cause sickness. Hmm. My thoughts went to Cousin Burton breathing that air and drinking that water. I felt like telling him to escape, but knowing Burton, he probably already had a Plan Z by then. (eyes rolling).

Meanwhile, the Ranch House was the only refuge we could go to get away without being considered A.W.O.L. or M.I.A. . . We would take turns explaining to the Matron on Duty we were merely going to the football field to run and study, and they would be back before lineup time for lunch or dinner.

"We're going to the football field to run, so you don't think we're trying to be A.W.O.L. or M.I.A.," Garnet would sarcastically announce.

Then they would run to the football field, wait a few minutes, look out and, one by one, race up and over the hill then hide behind the big red sandstone boulder, before sneaking the rest of the way. The Ranch House was not far from the top of the hill, but you can't see it from the Red Sands Residential Dormitory. From the looks of it, whoever used to run the farm just up and left. There were still old clothes, old furniture, and old dishes left wherever their owner left them last. When they were in the fourth grade, we would play detectives and scour the place in back and around the house to find footprints or signs of struggle. A mystery that would forever go unsolved. We often thought and guessed as to why the farmhouse had been abandoned. We agreed that what probably happened was they rushed to California to try and strike it rich in gold and oil or just moved to California to become Hollywood movie stars, or worse yet, they were the ghosts of Red Sands Dormitory A & B! After a year, we decided to go ahead and burn some cedar, say a prayer before we cleaned up the mess and use it as their official hangout – refuge from the prison sentence we lived.

When we were little, they would pretend to be a playhouse, but now they just hung out and talked and talked and talked...about life in the dorm, about boys, about who was sent to "The Room" this time. The Ranch House was our place to let loose about everything. When we asked Ruby about her time in "The Room"; she just said, "It stinks, and it's dark," with that accusing faraway look she put her hand on her chin up and turned to the left hiding her tears. Her eyes would squint and fist clinch, as she took a silent breath. We agreed not to ask her ever again because it always made her really angry and spiteful.

In silent contemplation, I thought about how much I would miss these times when I was at *St. stinkin James*. "Arrgh!" I did not know how I was going to tell my friends about the news. As much as I looked forward to letters from home, the one I had received was not the kind I wanted to receive, after all this waiting for my own good. Deep breath, sigh..

"Well, let's dive into these munchies - there's vanilla wafers, cherry and apple lollypop suckers, gum, sunflower seeds, chips and the ever-popular pe-si," Ruby announced as she began to line up the goodies on the old wooden table that was probably the place of a lot of conversations for the old homeowners, and now us.

Garnet was staring into space like she always did. I always wondered what she was thinking, but I knew that it had to do with her siblings and her mother. Garnet had a world of anguish weighing her down. Still, she persevered with a heavy heart and her sights towards a better future. That's one thing Garnet taught me – don't give up!

The noise of Ruby loudly eating chips with her mouth open always irritated us. She had no manners!

Eyes rolled with tolerant sarcasm. Clarice opened another Pepsi took a big gulp and said, "For Pete's sake, please close your mouth when you eat! No guy is going to want to take you on a date again after he sees your food rolling around in your mouth!"

"Yuck! I'm going to be so rich; I'll be able to buy my own dinner! Guys taking me out on a date…not gonna happen." There was no use responding to Ruby so, I chose to eat my favorite cherry suckers in silent contemplation...all of us had something on our minds.

Just then, a noise from the back of the Ranch House caught our attention. As we made our way around to the back, there sat Clarence and Terry with their faded cowboy-style plaid button-down shirts, weathered leather belts, and Levi jeans. We quickly jumped to their feet!

"You squatters! This is our hideout!" Clarice yelled.

Clarence and Terry dusted off their pants while looking at us with a surprised look, fumbling with words of exclamation. Terry shoved Clarence and Clarence shoved Terry.

"Go ahead, ask her," Clarence chided Terry.

"No, you ask her," Clarence said as he pushed Terry towards me.

I pushed him back, and my face was flushed red. I stepped back to avoid touching Terry. Clarence stepped sideways and pushed Terry so hard he almost fell.

"Umm, will you go to the last dance with me?" Terry stammered, voice cracking as he tried to look me in the face, but his eyes hugged the ground, hands in pockets, nervously turning his boot from side to side in the dirt.

It took all Clarence had in him to stay but he felt like running as far and as fast as he could. For sure, he did not want to hear that I would accept Terry's date.

"Ah, well, I'll have to think about it," I said to break the silence which dropped their jaws.

Clarence, who was surprised Terry actually had enough guts to ask me, also blazed a hole in my forehead with his squinted eyes.

"Aah, Okay, I'll write you a note tomorrow and you can answer me then." Terry said, as he nervously backed away from the girls, pushing Clarence in front of him.

"We'll leave you girls to talk your girl talk, but can we have some of your snacks. They really look gooder..*Clii*.."

We looked around at each other, then agreed to give them some snacks to get them going.

"*Ahéhee'lah*...you Cats are the gooderest!" Clarence awkwardly backed away with his snacks in hand while Terry smiled slapping Clarence on the back before heading towards the hill that led to the football field. Before we knew it, all we could see was the sun lighting up their greasy heads as they descended the hill and back to the football field.

"I knew there was someone around, I could feel it! Those geeks! Florence, you aren't going to go to that stupid dance, are you?" Ruby just had to say something first.

"I don't know, it's the last dance and I kind of want to go, even if it's with Terry." I was secretly thinking, poor Clarence…and my thought went to how I was going get my dress out of layaway from Heap's Thrift Store.

"Well, Clarice, you're going to have to lend me something to wear…not wanting to tell them I had already bought a dress."

"Here's an idea! Why don't all of us go, so I will not have to be alone with Terry? We can just get a table, and he can come over and ask us to dance every now and then."

"You can dance with him, I'm not!" Ruby said as she began to put the last of the chips in her mouth, crushed the bag licking her greasy lips. "We better get going or we'll miss supper," looking at her watch.

"We just ate!" We chimed in together.

Ruby made the demand as she forced her way past Garnet and Clarice, in true Ruby style. We stood silent, wide eyes, watching her, because this was like the 5,000's time, she acted that way. There was a certain amount of unsettled quietness between us that Ruby always managed to cause. I guess it happened so many times that we just blew it off and caught up to her as she stormed up the hill.

"Come on Ruby, ease down! You're probably gonna end up with a Council Delegate anyways.." Silent snickers, teeth grit, heavy breathing.

Clarice always knew what to say, even if she didn't say much. Clarice was quiet, but I knew she had a lot to say. Ruby managed to smile and joined in.. like she did 4,999 times before.

~ 216 ~

Change was in the air, but knowing the Ranch House would always be there was a bit of comfort, I thought taking one last look at the Ranch House before heading down the hill. It had become a habit for me, like saying good-bye to an old friend as the sun slowly sank beyond Red Sands mesa. If I could take a picture of the yellows, oranges, reds, and dark reddish browns that became the landscape at sunset, it would forever sit above my couch in the living room.

The Old Ranch House
We found you by accident—
leaning into the wind,
your windows dusted with time,
your bones still holding the past.

Abandoned but not forgotten,
you waited for us—
girls with too many questions
and nowhere else to go.

We swept your floors,
brushed sunlight back into your corners,
and called you ours.

You smelled of wood,
rusted tools, old rain,
like someone had just left
and might walk back in.

We read stories in your silence.
We left laughter in your walls.
You held our secrets
without ever asking for them.

Even now—
when the desert hums and the years pull away—
I think of you:
The Old Ranch House.
Still there.
Still ours.

…memories

The Old Ranch House
So, we stumbled upon you because curiosity
Always wins. We were so young, and you were so old. Yet,
Now, you are a friendly sanctuary. We
Cleaned you up, and made you cozy for
Those days when we needed a refuge. Like an
Undiscovered gem, the kind only the meek shall
Adore, you rose up to the challenge. Our harbor, our
Refuge. We will all miss you when our distance keeps us from
You. Our sanctuary, The Old Ranch House.

Red Sands Sunset
Red, Orange, Yellow
Casting long shadows across
Dark desert landscape

Chapter 18 – Mrs. Gardner and School

I settled into my assigned desk in the back of the room for the last month of my days at Red Sands Junior High School. I was relieved to have steered myself away from another dumb decision. Julia James will not be my nemesis anymore. I will ignore her.. She is invisible… Julia bleh!

Over the years, we watched Mrs. Gardner's blonde hair turn gray and were there when she became a widow while we matriculated from elementary to teach Middle School English. She taught at Red Sands Elementary for thirty years and was ready to retire after this school year. I watched her spend the year giving away her teaching materials to the new teachers and books to those who wanted them. She went from being our 1st grade Teacher, and then we had her again in 3rd grade. She was the Reading Intervention Teacher for one year and then decided to move up to middle school. Her favorite subject was English, so for the last three years, she taught English to 6th, 7th and then 8th grade to end her teaching career. A lot of us had her as a teacher in elementary or intermediate grades. Mrs. Gardner is one of those people etched in the memories of our childhood.

She looked worn out by the end of the day. I've seen that worn out look on many faces throughout my life. Mrs. Gardner was one of those people who will always be remembered because of her caring nature. She made learning fun and always gave the students different treats depending on the holiday. The most memorable were the treats she made for us when we were in elementary school. I remember for Halloween she made chocolate cupcakes with candy corn that were so sweet it melted in your mouth. I still have the Santa candy jar, she created from baby jars and filled with candy for Christmas Now that it was almost the end of her last year of teaching, and the end of the school year, she was planning her last cookout at her house – it had been Mrs. Gardner's tradition and all the kids wanted to be in her class so they could be a part of this event. This being her last year of a long career must be hard because we sensed sadness in her eyes as she gave her things away. She looked with far away eyes, while talking about the vacation in Hawaii, and, how during her "free time she would have to care for her roses and vegetable garden." "Oh, and let us not forget all those unfinished projects I have been wanting to get around to finishing," was another comment she made lately.

I guess everyone is going through changes this year I thought. Today, she was writing on the chalkboard as I shuffled through my tote bag for a pencil. "Get out your Journals, write today's date, then write about your weekend." You are to write at least five paragraphs with proper punctuation. That means a sentence begins with a ---- "Capital" retorted the students, "and ends with some sort of punctuation. Remember no floating letters and if you need help spelling a word, use your -- -"dictionary," retorted the students. When you are finished, you may place your paper in the basket...now you may get to work." Mrs. Gardner sat down back at her desk and began to take attendance.

Meanwhile, Clarence Yazzie was crossing his eyes, trying to make Gary Chee crack up with him. Mrs. Gardner stopped and began looking at Clarence over her wide-framed light brown Sophia Lorenz glass frame with that, "get back to work, young man" look. Clarence quickly shifted his body and put his head down while pressing his pencil so hard that everyone glanced at him, looked at each other and shrugged their shoulders. What they did not know, and what Mrs. Gardner did, was that Clarence was quite a Poet, a writer of all things. He did not want anyone to know, otherwise the boys might call him a "sissy", so it was his, Mrs. Gardner's and my secret.

Clarence had to live at Red Sands Residential Dormitory for nine years too. He too was a scared little boy wondering what happened to his secure sheepherder life, with all its freedom. I noticed that he was not picked up or checked out very often, because as time ticked by, the kids who didn't get picked up routinely showed up at the cafeteria on Saturdays, Sundays and the endless weekend. That's when we both realized neither of us got picked up very often, or at all. It was one of those things I would admit that we had in common.

"Think, think think!" I gazed out the window looking at how the tall cottonwood trees were moving slightly from the calm desert breeze. "Think, think think --trying to find a way to make a long uneventful boring weekend stretch into five paragraphs. Maybe I should write about life in the dormitory, about its ghosts, spirits who go knock, knock in the night or in the shower…right at 12midnight and ending at 3am..the Witching Hour...

"Nice clothes," Jenny Yazzie whispered. "Don't worry about what Julia says, they're not out of style, she's just jealous." "Thanks." Jenny was one of the shyest girls in our class.

I took an uncomfortable breath, shifting my weight in the hard seat, and glanced at the clock, realizing there were only thirty minutes to *Journal*, as Mrs. Gardner did for the millionth time in her career as teacher. I was finishing my third paragraph when, suddenly, Mrs. Gardner's voice broke the silent handwriting... "Now class, we're going to be taking the last portion of California Achievement Test at the end of the week, and I want everyone to get plenty of rest and don't miss any days, okay." When she said, don't miss any days, I rolled my eyes, took a deep breath, and continued to listen. Having taken the *Mósiyázhí (baby kitten)* test eight times before, I learned that a person needs to read a lot of books about different places and people in order to know what some of those words are or the meaning. Like the word /pail/. Navajo's do not use that word. They say /bucket/. It means the same, but the *Bilagaana's* (white people) want us to know /pail/ instead. It's no wonder so many kids fail miserably on that dreaded test. The part about getting enough rest at Red Sands Dormitory? "Yeah, right!" Mrs. Gardner should spend a weekend in Dorm 'A' or 'B' by herself and see if she'll be able to take a test after one night! I tell you the Dorms are *all* haunted, the *whole* campus is haunted! I sighed and began to write about dorm life. "*Mósiyázhí* isss," could be heard from the back of the classroom. No one liked that stinkin' cat at all!

The Ghosts of Red Sands Dormitory

By, Florence Arviso

Legend has it, the whole Red Sands Residential Dormitory and Compound was built on top of an old cemetery. In fact, most B.I.A. compounds were built on old cemeteries, because no one else would give up their land for schools built for Indian students. So, I'm sure if I looked up the old records, they would say that "Yes, Red Sands Residential Dormitory was built on top of the old Red Sands cemetery". This fact would tell me that I am not in the place that I should be, because Navajos are very wary of devils and evil spirits. Nevertheless, my friends and I have been living in that mire for nine years!

Some of the older girls said that Red Sands dormitory was built on top of a graveyard and that they could hear babies crying in the shower. They also said that they could see things moving around and some of their things were misplaced. They had all kinds of stories, and as the years passed and I have heard all of them. Some are unbelievable and some sound unidentifiably spooky. All I know is that when I got up at 12 midnight, last Saturday morning, I was too scared to go to the restroom, too scared to move because I heard something moving around in the showers. I heard the faucet come on by itself, and I heard babies crying just once, up to that point. My heart was pounding so hard that I thought everyone could hear it. There were only seven girls who didn't get picked up for the weekend. I was always one of the number of girls who didn't get picked up. None of them said they heard anything on Friday night. They all seemed to be oblivious to the ghost noises. On the other hand, maybe they were just as scared to move as me. Living at Red Sands Dormitory for the past nine years, I can say that I have heard things, but I have never seen a ghost. I know, my title doesn't fit my story, but there isn't really anything to write about, because it's the same every weekend, nothing changes – just the Matron on Duty.

Living in a Bureau of Indian Affairs dormitory is like living with people from all over the Navajo Reservation. This is groovy for me because I know people from all over the place. Living in a Bureau of Indian Affairs dormitory has its difficulties too. Some of the Dormitory Matrons would be nice and some were very mean. The nice ones allow us to watch television longer on the weekends and they always bring popcorn for us to pop. Sometimes, they would let us go outside to hang out at night, especially when it gets hot. They allow us to go to the store an hour before the sun set if we have our own money for movie night snacks. Then, there are the mean ones. Well, they always come to work grouchily. They must have a list of reasons why they do not like some of the students and always treat them badly by sending them to "The Room." The mean ones are used to ordering people around and do not do much of the work that they are supposed to do. Like, students in trouble would have to do all the laundry at night. Good thing I can get along with most of them and have never been sent to "The Room." Those that do get sent to "The Room" come back looking like zombies – all the life sucked out of them. I think we should change the name to "The Dungeon."

We live life by the clock. The students at Red Sands Dormitory have been on a regimented, strict schedule since it opened in 1937. For the past nine years, at precisely 5:30 A.M., I have been jarred out of sleep, whether I had enough or not. We have 30 minutes to get dressed and to rush to line up in the middle of the hall – shortest to tallest. Like trained mice, we eat breakfast at the cafeteria with all the other students at 6:00 A.M. and then we get to school by 7:30 A.M. This happens day in and day out - Monday through Friday. Saturdays and Sundays were the same, but we had more freedom. If you don't rush to get in line by youngest to oldest right away, the Matron on Duty will yank you by the ear and push you into line. One other hand, when the nice Dormitory Matrons are there, we just go down and eat in any order. The lights go out at exactly 9:00 P.M. and sometimes we get to stay up late during the weekend to watch television, but the lights still go off. Most of the time, the nice Dormitory Matrons would bring popcorn or snacks for those of us who must stay during the weekend. My Mother and Grandparents are too busy working that I am not picked up much, so I have learned to find ways to have fun like counting the number of tiles on the floor between the mountain of books that served as my friends these nine years.

The good part about living in a B.I.A. dormitory is that I have lifelong friends. I have friends that are funny and friends that are serious. I have friends that have problems, and I have friends that are spoiled rotten. Although, when we get together, it is as if we are all equal. The bad part about living in a B.I.A. dormitory is the things I miss from home. I miss my grandparents so much that I cannot stand it, sometimes. I miss my mother a lot too. I miss learning how to manage the cattle out on Tohatchi Flats. I miss herding sheep with my cousins during the summertime. I miss waking up to the smell of sheepherder coffee. I miss smelling the cedar wood as it burns to charcoal and the first smell of roast mutton on the grill. I miss the delicious flavor of tortillas cooked on the grill. A tortilla is round shaped bread that is like a cousin to fry bread. One is dry, the other is greasy. The things I am going to miss when I go home this summer are my friends and you, Mrs. Gardner.

In closing, living in a B.I.A. dormitory has its ups and downs. I have had some good times and some very bad times. I have met nice people and mean people. I have learned to become strong while learning to be patient. I have learned that the Navajo Reservation is a big place, and that people are pretty much the same, even though they identify themselves as: Western Navajos, Eastern Navajos, Northern Navajos and Southern Navajos depending on where they come from. There is not much to write about, because not much happened like the weekend before and the weekend before that one. I roam around Red Sands and often stop by the Catholic Church to hear the words of the Lord. This weekend, I did not see any ghosts but heard spirits milling around in the restroom. Hmm, sometimes I think, we kids will become the next Ghosts of Red Sands. Like those who have come and gone from there, we too will leave our childhood lingering around, *while others will think they're hearing spirits – it will be my imprint on this place… This is my journal entry for today.*

Mrs. Gardner read all our journal entries during lunch and recess. After lunch, she had a crossed look on her face that all the kids noticed but were too afraid to say anything. She gave a direct look over her glasses at me. Mrs. Gardner was not hot tempered, and nothing ever got on her nerves, so it was unlike her to curl her eyebrows. "I hope it isn't about my journal entry," I nervously thought.

What I would find out later was that this particular journal entry would change the lives of the children at Red Sands Residential Dormitory forever.

P.S.: Still no word on the most important person impression essay, from Mrs. Gardner…I should have revised it.

Chapter 19 – The Changes in the Air

Cousin Chuckie lived a tumultuous life and was systematically sent to different boarding schools throughout his seventeen years. Being used to change, he was now considered *overage*, which was a label given to students who flunked some grades and ended up older than their classmates. After each episode, Uncle Benny, Burt's dad, threatened to keep him from school, so he could work on the ranch. What a novel idea... I think that was probably a good idea, but he never went through with it, because Gramps refused to have any of his grandchildren uneducated. Burton always said he was getting an education on the streets, so he could be street smart... "Smart Alec. That's what you think," Gramps mumbled... Still, Gramma and Gramps had hopes for their grandson and prayed more for Burton than any of us...praying for a miracle. I prayed extra hard for Burton, too.

Gramps lectured on the importance of being able to live in both the Navajo world and the White Man's world, and that meant being educated. Burton maintained correspondence with me over the years, telling me about how Red Sands Residential Dormitory was heaven compared to this place or the other. I looked forward to hearing from him because he always managed to send a few dollars each time and kept me informed of what was happening with his side of the family. I never knew where he got them dead presidents, and I never dared to ask.

On days I receive mail, I always felt anxious. I didn't know, but it was a feeling of impending doom. Like many times before, I made my way back to my bunk, as did Garnet...Clarice and Ruby, feeling slighted, went outside to the playground to see who could blow the biggest bubble from the newly opened pack of green apple block bubble gum. Lying with my braids hanging from the edge of the bed with my feet propped up on the top bunk, I proceeded to carefully unfold the letter...something I did so many times before, because as the years came and went, the letters came less and less. I decided I would re-read the letter from my mother first and savor Burt's letter after. It was one of those cards that had a picture of a pink flower and a, "Thinking of You" message in fancy gold letters.

Dear Daughter,

I hope this letter finds you well. I miss you so much and look forward to the end of the year. The year has gone by so fast and all year I have been thinking about our future. I have good news! I got a job with the Arizona Department of Economic Security at St. James. I will be the one issuing out food stamps and general assistance to the Navajos who live near Interstate 40. Next year, you will be attending school at St. James High School because I finally bought a trailer house – our new home. Your Grandpa and Grandma want you to spend the summer with them as usual, and they look forward to picking you up. They always ask how you are doing when I visit. They are going to be picking you up on May 20, around 3:00 P.M. They have been talking about this for weeks. They cannot wait to make the trip. I cannot wait to see you too! I will be out on the ranch on Saturday with lots of goodies for you and your cousins. Your cousins, well most of them, will be dropped off that weekend too. I know you will have fun. I hope you will be able to use this $20.00 for yourself. Buy some supplies for your time at the ranch so you will be prepared. The rest can be your spending money. I will send you another $20.00 before school ends, so you can get some necessities when your Grandparents pick you up. I will tell you later about my new job. We will have more time to talk when we get to the ranch. Hello to all your goofy friends! Take care of yourself, Shíyázhí.

You're Loving Mother

I remember my surprise reading this letter. I wondered if this is how my prayers would be answered, but holy mollie, St. James?! THIS was the impending doom I was sensing from the beginning of eighth grade. Deep breath, change… Stunned, I put the letter back in to the envelope and carefully opened the letter from Burt.

This was NOT the change I had expected...but it could spell doom! I hadn't lived with my mother in nine years and hadn't seen much of her in all those years, days, minutes, seconds, waiting because, "it was for my own good."...sigh... Now, Cousin Burton's latest letter!

Dear Cuz,

Almost the end of the school year and here I sit at Shiprock Boarding Hell...exiled once again. My dad said this is the last place he will get me into before I have to figure things out for myself. Some threat! Shiprock Boarding Hell is okay...at least these guys understand the tradition. Good part about being here is there are some radicals that joined up with the American Indian Movement or A.I.M. We call ourselves, AIMer's, aaay! They plan on taking over the Fairchild Building to make a stand to these filthy white people who don't respect our rights and want to strip us of our tradition! I guess the workers are saying they aren't being paid enough for all the work they do for hours and hours and hours. Some of them work for twelve hours a day and make only $1.75 per hour! That's so cheap! Some of the guys have family working there and can't even buy a vehicle! They're barely making it while those white asses drive Cadillac's and wear fancy clothes! Shit man!

Anywayz, I joined them man! I finally found some Skins that understand me, man! We wear badass Levi jackets with AIM symbols all over them and I am growing my hair out so I can braid it and look like one of the gang, man! It's far out to hang with the AIMsters, man. They really know what they want to do! It's no use thinking about a future in the white man's world so I'm going to go Injun..kidding. Of course, this means I probably will not be making my grand appearance at the Flats right away...maybe not at all. Some of the guys are also planning on hitch hiking across our stolen lands going from powwow to powwow for the summer. Sounds groovy, man.. huh! Right now, we're making Anti-War signs like Peace Not War!, shii! A.I.M. Flag has a symbol of a peace sign with a red fist in the center. It's pretty cool man! Some of the Lakota brothers have been traveling down to give us their assistance and knowledge through the Sun Dance. I might even get my skin pierced if they let me. I'll check it out. I'm learning about their ways and learning some powwow songs and how to dance the two-step..shii! Aay Hok-a-hay! Even Marlon Brando, that guy who played The Godfather, supports us! Cool huh! So that's the plan man! As always, a couple of dead presidents for you and your punk friends, kidding! Peace. Your crazy Cuz, Burton. ☺ aka Chuckie.

Now, for Gramps' letter.

Dear Granddaughter,

It's been a long school year and here we are making plans to travel over to Red Sands Residential Dormitory. Just a small note to let you know that we're planning our long trip. Your Gramma is getting anxious about having all the Grandkids all over the place. ha! I guess everyone will be making their way to the Flats as usual. Also, try to get all your checkout things done right away so we can turn around and head back before sundown. Until then, enclosed is a couple of dollars.

I Remain, Your Loving Gramps.

Silently, hand shaking, I placed down letters, listening to my heart. I could feel the love sent with words. Over the years, I have read and reread their letters. I slid my fingers across the page to feel their hands and know they were written with love. I still didn't know how to feel. I knew things were changing but I never thought they would be this hard to take. Sigh… carefully resting these letters on top of all the other ones… the pages seemed to sigh as I closed the specially decorated shoebox. Taking a deep breath, and the words sent bewilderment across my mind. "Boy, I thought I was going to make a stand about staying with Gramps and Gramma and *now* Mom has a new plan, and I will be going to school at St. James - one of Red Sands Roadrunner's arch enemies! What a change of fate - Mrs. Gardner would say. Well, I guess I have something different and something new to look forward to after all!" That nagging feeling I had felt all year sent chills up and down my whole body. My mom had mentioned something about buying a home for us, but I had learned to listen to her promises and wait for them to come true. Not many did, maybe this one was the exception. I learned how to trust my gut feelings and just like that – I was proven right. The outcome of this letter would be shocking to say the least. I quietly tucked the money into the torn envelope, knowing that I had enough money to pay for the rest of my dress. On the other hand, I wasn't shocked about my favorite cousin who seemed to be going bonkers in Shiprock! American Indian Movement? Sun Dance? Powwow Trail? St. James? Ugh!! Sometimes changes just doesn't make any sense at all...sigh... Reality's gonna make Gramps, Gramma and Uncle Benny really angry.- man!! haha!! Man... For sure, the thing that stayed the same was Tohatchi Flats, or so it seemed.

Chuckie was always gettin' into the latest craze or fad. Now, he was getting into something that Gramps called, *old galooks*, and that could not be good at all! Gramps said, AIMers were no good and made the rest of us Indians look bad. Nevertheless, Chuckie was always trying to make sense of his life, the government, and so far, they ain't done anything for him so why should he abide by their idiot rules as he called them. I hope he does show up at the ranch otherwise, I'm going to have to babysit my punk cousins who are at least six years younger, and without my pal. Geez, this is just not good news at all! Another bit of bad news...good to hear from him again, though. Pow-wow trail? hitchhiking? St. James? she sighed. What is Chuckie getting himself into now...AIM, guns, hostage! Geez! Rolling her eyes. Uncle Benny's going to hit the roof when he hears his son is a radical AIMster! I pulled out my notebook and began to write Burt a letter. How could I get him out of this crazy thinking! He *must* come and help with the ranch work. Chuckie was always drawing and not much help. Russell and Timmy just wanted to take off with the horses all day. Darrell and Ben, Jr. were most likely going to order us around like we were at boot camp! Chuckie kept the place even! Some things have got to change…for him!!! Man.. Ugh!

I put those letters away and knew this was a turning point in my life. I had to think long and hard about the news. "St. James.", "Of all the places, I never thought I would end up there! What would happen to my sister-friends, what would happen with our lives?" I knew there was going to be change; it is just that I did not expect *this* kind of change…AND never ever did St. James cross my mind!! I didn't even know where it was!

"I don't know! Right now, I just cannot believe that I am going to move to another city, another school – worse of all, our rival school…ugh! What will going to that school and living in that town be like and what about the other students. I just can't believe it!" The only good news was I had money to get my dress out of lay-away, finally. A message in Gramps' handwriting always brings a tear to my eyes followed by that far off look, with Tohatchi Flats on my mind..he'll never change! I could count on that, for sure..maybe..

I pushed the beans on the menu around my plastic tray, not saying much…taking the millionth bite of **B**eans for **I**ndians **A**lways on the **M**enu meal was especially hard to swallow. We nervously looked at each other and quietly ate our portion of mystery meal…hard swallow. "Change sucks!!" I quietly announced. "Turns out, I'm not going to live with Gramps and Gramma… My mother said I'm going to live with her in St. James..yes St. James!! Can you believe it?" The girls gasped, deep breath. Ruby almost choked on her food. They didn't know what to say…unsettling quiet. This time the food actually *looked* like chili beans and actually *tasted* like chili beans, and the corn bread was fluffy. The Cafeteria Ladies used our recipe after all!! None of us could enjoy the meal with the news. Nevertheless, we knew that it was part "real food" and part USDA government commodity food issues. Putting our trays in the proper military receptacle, we walked out towards our wing, silently contemplating the future. In an instant, we realized that this was the beginning of our last days together…forever.

Getting a grip on my emotions and news of change, I had no choice but to make the most of things. Wiping up my tears of joy, tears of sadness, and wondering what to do about Chuckie. Once he's on the powwow trail, how will I get a hold of him and know how he's doing? We finished our meal and went outside where the little girls were on the swings, having a great time on the teeter totter with no worries in the world. I had to take my mind off this grim news. "Hey girrs, let's study for the last part of the CAT test tonight." I suggested. Weird stares, awkward silence.

"Or not!" Ruby sarcastic eyes glazed over each of us.

The boys were playing basketball on one court, while a team of girls played on the other. The little kids continued to play on the merry-go-round and slide. Some were on the swing. The nights were getting muggy in the dorms, and most of the kids enjoyed the weather outside. That, and the fact that boiling beans for 400 kids made the humidity smell like beans and by midnight, Red Sands Residential Dormitory would need some serious air freshener! I knew I should study but couldn't concentrate so I decided to go take a break. I'll go for a little bit, but the only way I'm going to do good on the test is to study.

"I thought about wearing hip-huggers to the dance, but I guess I should get a dress and borrow some shoes. What do you think about pink..." Garnet chattered on as we straightened up before heading to the football field. Garnet shared her famous juicy fruit gum. Inspecting herself in a small mirror. "I look fabulous," she giggled.

"Better not let anyone see you with that," Ruby warned. "Else you'll end up in The Room. Or, Mrs. Hagga would find out and there will be hell to pay. Contraband, Sister! Contraband! AND, hip-huggers? NO, you have to wear a dress!" Ruby was on her podium, as if.

"We all have to deck-it-out before we leave here for good." Garnet chided. We took a look at each other, sighed a deep breath, and walked out around the track.

"Remember that time, a couple of years ago, Mrs. Hagga came to work so drunk and in a rage that she broke all of the mirrors so no one could get a good look at themselves." Ruby hated Mrs. Hagga with passion.

After that, we wished her bad luck for seven years.

"I guess, the "Almighty's wanting to pass along their bad luck to us, with all these broke mirrors…She added. "That smart gal Jenny, from Chinle got it the worst, sent to The Room and then just like that, she was exiled to the Promised Land. Once I saw her at Gallup and she said she was going to Shiprock Boarding Hell. She seemed to like it there…guess it's not that bad. Shiprock Boarding Hell was also known as a haven for girls who found themselves pregnant and then transferred.

"Wait, did Jenny get pregnant?" Awkward silence.

"Endless Bureau of Indian Affairs dormitories throughout "Indian Country"…ugh! Garnet finally let it out that she too was going to be going to another school. "Chuska "stinkin" Boarding School. Florence, I might run away to your ranch – it's close enough."

"Sure, I will tell Gramps to keep an eye out for you". Awkward giggles. Garnet sighed, knowing our time was ticking by…deep breath..sigh…

The night before, Garnet secretly explained, her mother had enrolled her there for high school, and to be closer to her brothers. They, too, would be attending Chuska the following school year. The news of Frank's death, her mother putting the boys at Chuska made Garnet think that there was another man in her mother's life and that she would begin drinking again, but that was far from the truth.

What really happened was Garnet's mother, Daisy, checked herself into Rehoboth Rehabilitation Center for one whole month. It took her one whole year to be cured of her thirst for alcohol and to understand the dysfunctional family life she grew up in and the one in which she immersed her children. She fought off the cravings, anxiety, but the thoughts of her actions while she was disabled, kept her from going down the depths of an empty bottle. It was a harsh reality, but Daisy finally realized that she could change things for her children now that Frank was gone. Garnet was forever grateful for the way things turned out after eighth grade. It took 6,750 prayers for The Holy People, the Pope, and God to finally hear her..finally…finally…

"Oh, Flo, you always want to do the right thing! Come on! Delfred, John, and Terry want to meet us at the football field tonight! Flo, Terry wants to talk to you, and he wants to get an answer about the dance. We need to have fun before it's time for *US* to go home for the summer! I think you should go with him to the dance!" Ruby said, with such great enthusiasm, that everyone knew she was trying to get somebody, anybody, to do what *SHE* wanted to do.

We made our way out to the vast wasteland that was the Compound, passed through the gate and made our way up to the football field.

"Oh, some of the kids are already at the football field," Clarice pushed her way over the last step, and into the turnstile that led to the track.

I did all I could to not look over to their direction on the football field, but caught a glimpse of Terry's crew cut, with the little lock of bangs neatly curled. Clarence looked directly at me, too. My face began to feel flushed and red as I quickly turned towards the girls.

"Ooooh, you are blushing!" Garnet and the rest of them giggled, and I was sure they would die laughing, and so I decided to join them before I died of embarrassment!

Ruby would be the one to want to get out of studying, but then again, I felt obligated to at least spend some time with them and the group before I left this God forsaken place with at least some good memories…I agreed, secretly knowing Clarence and I had a think. But they really didn't know what kind of thing. It was just like one of those friendships. He saw me from afar and sent secret messages of his interest. Nothing ever came of it, mostly because both of us were just too shy… Oh well..

In my mind, I thought of how things were going to be….the new environment. The new school and then all I could hear was the silence buzzing, pretend smile, unsettled happiness. Deep breath, sigh.

Chapter 20 – The Race

My memories often went to the last time we ever spent at the football field. It was one of those sweet innocent times when young love blossoms or rages. I find myself smiling and occasionally shedding tears each time I reminisce about that day and the days that followed, leading up to my departure from Red Sands Residential Dormitory for good.

"Let's walk up to the track and get some laps in, girrs. It could be the last time we can be up there before they start repainting and getting the fields ready for next year." Clarice was right, so we took no time to join her as she walked up the well-worn path. As we ascended, I noticed how our middle school footprints now eclipse the fading imprints of our younger selves from years gone by. The thought of how many little feet had made the same trek before us and how many would after we left, sent chills up my spine.

Delfred, Clarence, John, and Terry were waiting for us on the bleachers. A mountain of sunflower seed shells had already begun to grow under their feet as their eyes peeled upon us. The fresh grass had just been watered so sitting on the grass was not ideal, so we opted for the bleachers instead. The boys sat goggling at us. "Awkward!" Ruby directed her loud words toward them, and they chuckled with that usually, "clii." The sound is made by making your mouth wide, placing the tongue behind the front teeth, and then forcing air to make that clicking sound that grated on my nerves! Ruby turned around and ordered them to clean up their mess, as if. Clarence was the first to go up and the others followed them moving to the set of bleaches across from the girls. They left the pile of sunflower seed shells where they dropped.

"Honestly, Ruby, do you have to be so harsh?" Clarice bent forward to face Ruby.

She replied, "Did you see them eyeballing us? Did you see them making a mess?" She turned her head and popped her gum the way we learned to tolerate, just a little. The three of us took a deep breath, knowing how her bunk area is always a mess. I wondered if we would miss Ruby. Long exhale, yes, we would..

We sat on the bleachers watching kids running or just fooling around. Four high school boys were set up to practice for an upcoming state relay race, so the rest of us had to be mindful to stay in the outer lane. This was the time of year everyone was let out of Red Sands Hell to spend time at the football field. You didn't have to ask us if we would take the opportunity to escape from the dorms, even if it's just for a while. The pressure of not getting in trouble or having to sneak in and out allowed us to have real fun. From the bottom of the bleacher, Terry turned and looked directly at me.

"So, are you going to the dance with Terry or not" Delfred teased Terry patting him on the back. Clarence turned and glanced at me, taking a noticeable breath, then hung his head. I was startled and embarrassed. I had not seen them strategically move to the bottom of our bleachers, because I was busy watching them set up for the relay race.

"Gosh, let's get right to the point why don't we," Ruby chortled.

"Well, she never responded to his note," Delfred grinned, while extending his hand palms up, high-fiving Terry.

"I think I'll go if Terry can beat me around the track one time", I challenged. I couldn't believe I was being so bold, what if I lost! Not a chance.

"You're on," Terry puffed up. "Sko-den." The boys following him to the starting line, patting him on the back, giving him some pointers. I took a deep breath hoping I wasn't going to regret this bold decision, then I looked back and the girls who were crossing their fingers for good luck.

"Okay, on your marks! Get set! GO!" John yelled. I was off to a solid lead, but Terry was close behind. I better stay ahead all the way so he won't get a chance to hold my hand or dance with me....on the other hand, I'll stay ahead and then pretend to struggle slowing down so I *could* hold his hand and dance with him….but what about Clarence….? Before I knew it, Terry was beginning to pass me on the outside lane. Clarence, John, and Delfred were cheering him on from the sideline, saying; "You want this!! Yeego, Yeego!" Meanwhile, the girls were standing at the finish line, wondering what I would decide because they knew very well that I could beat Terry hands down.

The kids were standing up cheering us on from the bleachers, while some were standing along the track. The high school guys stopped what they were doing to join in. My legs were ablaze with exertion, yet my determination fueled each step. With every stride, my arms pumped vigorously, my legs leaped to the next step as the wind blew my hair into a tangled mess. The sound of the cheering crowd drowning out my labored breath. I turned slightly, hearing the panting of Terry and his every step pounding the track. From the corner of my I eye, I watched Terry, and I crossed the finish line neck and neck! It was a tie! Panting, hands on knees, he was about to throw up the chili beans they overserved the boys

"TIE?? Sheeesh!…what does that mean?" Ruby chided. "To go or not to go, Flo? That fickle girl will give in at the last minute – she's just being difficult!"

I gave Ruby a dirty look. "You don't speak for me, Ruby!" Clarice and Garnet pushed Ruby aside, telling her to shut her mouth!

"Whose side are you on anyway, Ruby?" Clarice scolded. Ruby's wide eyes turned to Terry. "You have to flip a coin then!" "Okay, I pick heads." "Tails it is," Terry gripped his thighs, panting because he was completely unprepared for a foot race. He found himself struggling to recover and almost threw up the sunflower seeds, instantly regretting all that salt. I kicked myself for not speeding up when I got my second wind in the final yards. "DARN IT! I shouldn't have looked back!" Delfred quickly handed a quarter to his bro. Terry threw it up in the air and we held our breath as we watched it flip in the air, flatten out thin air fall flat onto the asphalt.   Everyone except me jumped up and down with celebration!

"Get your blue suede shoes on, 'cause you're going to the dance, Terry." Delfred danced around like a fool while Clarence, disappointed, aimed directly at me.   He gave a small smirk. "Next..." was all he could manage to say.

"You're up next." John stared at Terry. "What? This is your deal. I'm already going with someone." "No, you're not," Terry responded eyebrows curled. "Clii, you don't have a date, yet..don't lie.." Everyone burst into laughter.

"Come on. You know you want to go with Ruby because you said you would treat her like a real lady." Clarence teased.

"I don't think you could outrun me, Johnnnn" Ruby challenged.

All of us turned to Ruby with that surprised look. "Put your money where your mouth is, Ruby!" Garnet lectured. John was up for the challenged and readied himself at the starting line, all the while Clarence and Terry looked at Delfred and then at Ruby, surprised that they never knew there was a "thing" there until the end of the year.... "On your marks! Get set! GO!!" yelled Clarence. Of course, John won easily with Ruby huffing and puffing about 10 yards behind him. We just shook our heads. Joining the challenge, Clarence's cousin-brother Delfred wagered his chance to race Garnet. He knew that Clarice was going out with that white guy named Kyle Rodgers, but he wasn't sure about Garnet...the quiet one. He didn't need to put her through a race to ask her out, so he got a wind of braveness and approached her.

"And, how about you Garnet? Will you go with me to the dance? You don't need to race me, just say, "Yes." Garnet was so embarrassed. She couldn't breathe.   She was Delfred's classmate in Mrs. McKenzie's room but that was three years ago. Might as well, she thought. I could be stuck here with no friends at all. Better to have a boyfriend or a friend that is a boy than no one at all. "Aah, okay, since everyone else is going. I'll go too." Garnet committed.

John, Delfred, and Terry left the field with a content smile. Clarence followed in quiet contemplation with his hand in his pockets, he looked back to meet my eyes, I leaned my head on my shoulder and looked away. Clarice had already accepted an invitation with Roy Begay, who was from Indian Wells, because Kyle would never be allowed to even enter Red Sands Residential Dormitory compound. We stayed at the field a little longer and then remembered the studying we were supposed to do for the achievement test. It had been two hours of excitement that turned into nervous contemplation. Clarice and I had no problem with the test. In the back of Garnet and Ruby's mind, there was a bit of apprehension about taking tests, any test. We had taken the Mósíyází tests for eight years but would never see the results. We would not be there to see them when our teachers posted them outside the classrooms. No matter what kind of test we had to take over the years, those were the nights we tossed and turned trying to find sleep, on a stiff mattress covered with as many blankets we could manage to soften our dreams.

Ruby walked several feet behind the group as we descended the hill. She kept her sad feelings to herself, for she too would miss her sisters. In just a few days, she would be traveling into a world of new people and a different life. At Red Sand Residential Dormitory, she had learned the terror of being helplessly alone, and for the first time she admitted that fact to herself. Ruby had grown thick skin after years of being the target of evil. What would life be like at Window Rock? Would she spend her summer babysitting and not liking the school? For sure, she would NOT MISS, "The Room!" She kept that horror to herself and only herself. Ruby resolved to forget the trauma that she endured and leave it to roam the halls of Red Sands Residential Dormitory.

In the last days, we took a collective sigh and thought for now, this was normal....yawn, restless sleep.

As I looked back on the days that followed, after the races at the football field, everyone went about doing their own thing. I had to get my dress out of layaway and agreed with Mrs. Heap's suggestion to have it dry cleaned. I remember walking the aisles at Safeway, trying to kill time and pretend to be shopping. I went from one aisle to the next, not paying attention to the people. As I pretended to check out the selection of pinto beans in a can, I heard a familiar voice. Looking up my eyes caught Clarence talking to himself. Just then he glanced at me and stopped in his tracks. He took a pause and decided to approach me. I stood there frozen in my tracks. "Hey, whatcha doing here?" Clarence stammered while looking directly into my eyes. "I'm just looking at the many selections of pinto beans in a can – all two of them!" We chuckled to let the air shift, as I took a quick look down the aisle for fear the Matron on Duty would send spies to catch me in the act of escaping jail, or something! I looked for the closest EXIT sign but couldn't find one. "Umm, did you escape jail or are you spying on me?" I said suspiciously. Clarence chuckled, "Clii, spy iss. Eugene the Manual Labor Guy is on duty this week, so it was easy to sneak off because he has all those Manual Labor Job slips to organize." He let out a loud laugh and I quickly shushed him! "Terry snuck in his office and messed them up so us boys could just sneak off for a little while. Delfred kept Eugene busy talking about new ideas for Manual Labor jobs." Right then and there, I knew the boys in Dorm C had their own shenanigans going on.

"You want to get something and eat it over at the park?" Clarence was a year older than me but because he started school late, we were in the same grade. I decided it wouldn't hurt anyone to kill some time and enjoy the park with someone else. I paid for my Frito's corn chips, bean dip, cherry jolly rancher lollipop, and Pepsi. Clarence bought peanuts, Pepsi, grape gum, and Lay's potato chips. We took the alley so no one would spot us, like Mr. Sells, the Truancy Officer.

"I wrote you a poem. Do you want it?" Clarence was shuffling in his pocket to present it to me. He took me by surprise, and I really didn't know what to say. I was a shy girl, deep down. Fresh off the Rez…aaayy.. I unfolded the star-shaped paper, revealing an acrostic poem that read:

F is for the fresh flowers that bloom when I see you.
L is for your lovely hair that blows like a kite in the wind.
O is for if only you would look at me, like I do you.

    I could feel my face get hot and then flush. I had an idea of how Clarence thought of me. I did see him watch me. "Well, it's a start. I didn't have enough time to finish your whole name, but you get the idea." Clarence was quick to fill up the silent air. A slight breeze blew my hair in my face, and I just started laughing uncontrollably. "That bad, huh?" Clarence ate the last of his chips. His face was beet, red. "Well, it's okay. I didn't know you felt that way about me, Clarence. I don't know what to say. Thanks! I guess I like the way you see me." I didn't like how my hair whipped around covering my face in a tangled mess. We both laughed. Clarence claimed his poetry was getting better and I should have noticed with all the poems he had sent me over the years. We pretended to window shop and let the noise of the traffic help me "not hear him." "Look, it's the new 10CC album! "Yeah, my black friend Tyrone lives on the other side of the tracks. He has all the latest hits and some oldies! I don't know why Harry Billy never plays the latest hits, always oldies! AND, what's with this everlasting, "Leavin' on a jet plane?" Crazy Injun Number 9, isss" I felt a little abashed because I had been the one to constantly ask Harry to play that song. I thought I was the only one who listened. It never occurred to me to think about what the boys were doing while I was wandering around Red Sands, let alone have friends who weren't Red Sands Residential Dormitory prisoners. Next thing I knew, Clarence proceeded to serenade me! "The things we do for love!" Passersby turned back to see my embarrassment.   I turned my head with curled eyebrows and rolled my eyes, took a deep breath, and moved on. "Clarence! Stop!" There was an uneasy quietness. Let's walk over to the library before it closes, I suggested.

    I walked ahead of Clarence, to shake him off. I wasn't sure about his poem or the lyrics or that song. I knew he liked me, and that he wasn't picked up on the weekends, because he is one of those kids I started to recognize at a very young age. From then on, I started to notice him, and his gang were always lurking not too far from my friends and me.

Here, "100 Best Poems of all Times" is just what you need! I giggled while Clarence eyed the title. "Ummm does this mean you didn't like my poem?" No, you just need a little help.. I giggled. I'm going to be looking at mystery books." I picked "The Hidden Staircase" with Nancy Drew. I read all kinds of mysteries that took me all over the world and in different time periods. Clarence pretended to flip through books.

I smiled remembering how from the 4th grade, Clarence dedicated a lot of time writing poems about everything, including me. He always found a way to get them to me without anyone knowing. It was our little secret. Two years had passed, and his poems piled up in two shoeboxes. Once Garnet spied them out, but I kept them secret, and my footlocker was always locked. My mother said I was not allowed to have a boyfriend until I was 18, so Clarence's affection was just us being friends. From then on, Clarence and I happened to bump into each other at the store or library on most weekends. Clarence spent time with his friends on the weekend when they didn't get check out, so that's when I would not see him out and about. I did notice his attitude changed when he was around his older friends. That's how our friendship started and how it continues. Getting poems from him was like hearing from an old friend because he was able to say all the things he couldn't say out loud. The fact that Clarence didn't ask anyone out for the last dance and walked away looking dejected at the football field made me feel bad.

It wasn't until after the football field race that I got the courage to ask him why he didn't get picked up. He shrugged his "shoulders and hung his head down. "You don't want to know." Yes, I do." "Ok, well I'll tell you why I don't get picked up. First, my mom is busy working. Second, my grandparents live one hundred miles from Red Sands Residential Dormitory, so it was too far for them to visit all the time. So, we write letters to each other. Also, everyone said coming to Red Sands Residential

Dormitory was for my own good. I am still waiting to understand what "for my own good" means. It's been eight and a half years and it's still a mystery.

"Well, my mom is busy working, too. My dad works for the railroad, so you know he's traveling around the country. So, I'm stuck here. Right now, my mom is living in a motel in Gallup, so she can be by the railroad. Our truck is old and can't go very far. She sends me money in the mail and a few words about her work and my dad's whereabouts. I haven't seen him face to face since I was seven years old. I think he forgot about me, by now." He took in a big gulp of his drink that let me know that there was more to that story, but we sat there in silent contemplation.

The church bell rang, signaling Saturday afternoon Mass. That meant it was 2:00 and time for us to meander back to Red Sands Residential Dormitory.

"Let's go down 3rd Street. I want to get some honeysuckle flowers," I suggested.

"Ok. Um Florence, please don't mention what I said," his eyes peered into the distance.

As we walked, the smell of spring showers filled the side streets of Red Sands with the promise of moisture.

Chapter 21 – Letting Go

The dreaded last part of TESTING WEEK came with the smell of freshly sharpened pencils. The smell of fresh ink used to print the booklets emanated throughout the classroom, as though to say, "Here I am Students!" We carefully peeled off the seal and opened it to READING COMPREHENSION PART II. "You have forty-five minutes to complete this portion of the examination," Mrs. Gardner said, as she read the instructions from the Teacher's Manual. Okay, this is the easy part, I thought as I dove into the reading. Meanwhile, Clarence sat nervously shifting from one side to the next, playing with his pencil, which he purposely broke, disturbing the class. Some kids snickered, while some looked back at him with that look, the one he was used to seeing. Mrs. Gardner gave him the usual annoying look we had grown to expect. As I gazed around the room, some students sat with their foreheads curled and some worked through the problems with ease. The discrimination was clear, by the way were seated, even by my favorite teacher. The white kids were in the front row Penny, Suzie, Francine and Gina, Randy, James, and Kyle. Next, were the Black kids, Trevor, Mary, Bernice, Charles, and Claire. Juan, Maria, Gracie, Santiago were the Mexican kids who sat in third row. Then there was us, the Navajos. We were in the back rows, *all* of us. While I gave praise to Mrs. Gardner, this realization gave me a new perspective on whether she deserved to be called my favorite teacher anymore. The test was very regimented, like Red Sands Residential Dormitory life – all calculated and timed. Next was the second part of the Vocabulary Test, which was another forty-five minutes, lunch, recess and then a regular day in the afternoon. Tuesday, we took the Problem-Solving test, which was two and a half hours. On Wednesday, we took the Mathematics Problems tests, which were also an hour long and finally on Thursday, was the Spatial Perception, which was scheduled for one hour and thirty minutes. Luckily, I had mastered these kinds of puzzles over the years, and it took all but fifteen minutes to fly through them and check my answers twice.

Thursday afternoon was spent taking down Mrs. Gardner's bulletin boards. She kept everything so organized in neatly marked boxes so that it would be easy to take out each year. She taught me how to be organized without even knowing it.

Only this year, she had two boxes: one labeled "Give Away" and the other "Throw Out." By the end of the day, the whole room was taken down and put into one box or the other. Mrs. Gardner had a table where she put stuff she didn't want and let the kids choose what they wanted. She had some boys take her "Give Away" box of teacher stuff to the teacher's lounge. After a thirty-year career, yeah, thirty years, it was time to let someone else take her place while she took a deep breath into retirement. Thoughts of all the years seem to flow out of her, as I watched her rifle through each item contemplating which box to place them. It must be very hard to part with time. What a novel thought. Mrs. Gardner seemed to sense me watching her, because of the look she gave me over her glasses and gave me a caring smile I would not soon forget. Imagine one look could tell so much! I learned that by watching Gramps make that same glance and quick smile over his glasses.

The pressure finally turned off and the week was almost over. Friday, Mrs. Gardner had a substitute by the name of Josh Greer, a young red-haired white man, who let us play board games or play outside. One more week and the school year is over. That thought has been on our collective minds since the news of going to other schools next year came to put a wrench on our foursome.

"Hey, how did you do on the *Mósíyázhí* test?" I asked the girls as we shuffled into the Multipurpose Room to rest our brains. "Oh, it was harder this year, and the math problems were sort of hard to understand. I guess I should've studied more." Garnet glanced at me. "Yeah, we should've listened to you instead of going to the football field." Clarice admitted, passing out juicy fruit. "Ahhh, Juicy Fruit!"

Clarice and Garnet were B students, and I knew very well they didn't have to study to pass any test. Sometimes, Clarice would disappear for hours, and when she finally reappeared, we knew that by the filled denim tote bag that she was at the public library with Kyle, a white boy in my class and the guy who had to secretly like Clarice. Sometimes he would give me that weird look when I would score higher than he did on a spelling test, or worse yet, a math speed drill. Seems like white people are always trying to be the best or beat out their opponent... I enjoyed besting them, all of them, because after all it's a dog eat, dog world...and whiners always end up last. We didn't mind Clarice going to study with a white boy, but Clarice knew that she could never take him home, or that he wouldn't even think of taking *her* home....as if!

Clarice really liked Kyle because he didn't see her as a Navajo. He saw a beautiful smart girl he had a crush on since 4th grade. The time they spent together came when she snuck off to the movies, or he strategically sat near her at lunch, and they would walk around together after school until it was time for her to return to Red Sands Residential Dormitory. He gave her small trinkets and whispered sweet nothings into her ear while sitting on the benches at the city park. He even took the time to find out that her name meant, "clear or bright shining and gentle, famous." It was perfectly innocent. Clarice shared with him that she wanted to study art and become a famous artist. She shared the dreams of her future. He already had plans to go to the UCLA School of Business, because that's where his dad and grandfather went to school. It was a family tradition, he claimed. Clarice and Kyle knew very well that this friendship was just a passing phase in their lives. He told her that his parents expected him to do what was on their plan...he would attend school in California and live in the big city never to return to Red Sands, Arizona. Kyle didn't have the heart to tell Clarice that his family were already packed and ready to hit I-40 right after the test was complete. He made it a point to have his friend Raymond give Clarice a small package on the following Monday. Clarice opened the package and found a silver chain and one half of a silver heart. His note read:

Dearest Clarice,

I'm sorry I could not tell you I was leaving because I knew it would break both of our hearts. When you read this letter, we will be half-way to our new home in Los Angeles, California. That means I probably will never see you again unless there is some kind of miracle. I want you to know that I enjoyed our time together and will never forget you. I have enclosed one half of my heart, and I will keep the other half close to my heart. I will not forget you, Clarice. I hope you will not forget me.

All my love, Kyle*

Clarice had opened the package and read the note in the bathroom. She shuttered as she tried to keep the tears from gushing. She admired the half heart necklace, and slid her hand over his words, as if to touch his hand one last time. She put the necklace on and did not take it off for many years after that fateful day. When Kyle left right after the CAT Test, Clarice knew that their friendship was a chapter in her life she had no choice but to close. Too bad for both of us, Kyle would say out of the blue. Yeah, too bad.

Most times, the whites at school separated themselves into their little group. The majority were too good to talk to us or be our friends. The rest were just as poor as Navajos and did not care either way. The Mexicans and Blacks pretty much stayed in their own groups too. It was a simmering pot with all these different groups. The kids didn't know it but, they had a lot of common family issues as the kids at Red Sands Residential Dormitory. Some of the kids would rather be at school, because it was better than being at home. There were many fights between the Navajos and the whites, the whites and the Mexicans, the whites, and the Blacks – It was as if the whites were always fighting somebody about something. But then again, there was fights between the Navajos and Mexicans and they both fought each other. Over the years we have seen many combinations of fights over things that really matter.

Anyway, after the Career Fair 8th graders were required to go to last month, Clarice made plans to go to college at Haskell University, which was in the State of Kansas. The lady from their booth was nice and made it sound like a great place. I once asked her Clarice if she would be able to stand it out there, where there were a lot of tornadoes and flat plains. "You better take a picture of the mountains, so you'll remember what they look like!" I exaggerated after hearing of her plan. I spent the whole time talking to the people at the University of Arizona booth. I wanted to be the second to go where Uncle Andy had graduated with a degree in accounting, years before. Naturally, I chose to study Journalism and Education. "You should think about going to Tucson with me. If we're going to be separated from now on, we can still meet up in college," I suggested. Clarice took a deep breath. "Yeah, in the meantime, let's make sure we write to each other, okay! Let's not lose touch with each other, my sister. I'm also thinking about going to the Art School at the University of New Mexico in Albuquerque. Tucson is a much better place because it's not a long trip to get back to the Promised Land." Awkward silence, deep thoughts. " Flo, you know that Tucson is much too far for my parent's poor little 19 and 69 Chevy pick-up truck that has more than 250,000 miles to travel even one way!" Clarice exaggerated. Well, you have four years to save up for your own vehicle. And how do you think they're going to make it twice that far to get to Kansas," I asked? I took a deep breath and wondered what life would be like without her? How will I be without her by my side? Who will run with me?

Moving away from my sisters at Red Sands Residential Dormitory was going to be harder than I thought…harder than all of us thought… Clutching her half-heart, Clarice let out a sigh…"letting Kyle go was a close second." deep breath..sigh.. "You know that relationship would never go anywhere," I whispered giving her a side hug.

For the past month, it seemed like the whole compound took a deep breath, as the buzzing of the swamp coolers tried to hush everyone's uncertainty, blowing out an unnatural breeze that smelt like wet hay.

Like Mrs. Gardner, I felt the need to start sorting the things I wanted to keep and the things I would give away, and the things I would throw out. The space under my bunkbed was filled with the last year of my prison sentence…I couldn't imagine thirty years. For sure, I don't know if I could decide what to keep, what to give away, and what to throw out if I had to choose.

Chapter 22 – The Wrath of Mrs. Becenti

Startled to reality, I heard her familiar harsh voice getting louder as she brought me back from the loud ringing and burning sensation from running of my dream. It was a long hard run, but I couldn't remember where I was running or where I was at. It felt like an enduring run away from fleeting emotions of separation anxiety. My golden skin glistened with sweat as I caught my breath, bolting and facing reality with my sheets crumpled around me. "Gee what were you dreaming, you're all sweaty! I've been trying to wake you for three minutes! Get ready. Let's go, Flo." "Ok." Bringing myself out of deep sleep was rough and my eyes were clouded with junk. "And who in the world is Jose?" Clarice chuckled. I thought Mrs. Becenti was chasing me and some guy named Jose. She was even infiltrating my dreams. That was definitely not a good sign. Still sleepy, I got myself dressed and was ready within minutes. Time was always of the essence when we had to sneak out to get in our morning run before it was too late. Trekking down the familiar path, the two didn't speak a word as they made their way to the top of the hill, turned around and went back. Clarice took out her tádi'díín pouch just as the golden sun peeked and then spanned across the top of the red sandstone hill. "I'm going to remember this sunrise." There was unsettled silence as we understood our lives were going to change in a matter of days. We rushed down the hill and by the time we slipped inside the gate unnoticed we could hear shouting coming from their Dorm B.

"Shh! What is that noise? They peeked through the door window and saw Mrs. Becenti marching around like she knew how. The wrath of Mrs. Becenti showed itself one last time but for what?

Panting and out of breath, we could hear, "Line up Girls, Line up!" Our eyes raised, not knowing what was going on, we quietly snuck in hoping we weren't late. "It's too early for her to be lining us up." When we neared the hallway, we could hear Mrs. Becenti yelling off the top of her head at some high school girls. Everyone was just looking at Mrs. Becenti as she got redder and redder. Even though her skin was dark brown it was a peculiar shade of red that day. Rumors whispered from ear to ear that Laura Walker had snuck in some beer and had a little "end of the year" party with some of the other girls, *and* they snuck in a couple of guys. Reports were whispered from bunk to bunk. Laura was the only one to get into trouble. Clarice and I quickly dressed and snuck into the line and waited for the torment to end.

"For sure it's a trip to "The Room", and she's never going to be seen again," Ruby whispered as we stood like statues in a straight line. At that point, I wondered why some kids were sent home after they were let out of "The Room."

"Get your footlocker packed and clean out your closet. You're going back to reservation life where you belong!" Mrs. Becenti chortled at the top of her lungs. "We should've gotten in trouble a long time ago, so we could have gone home too," Clarice whispered. "Shh, here she comes." "The rest of you need to get to breakfast and on to school before you're late." Mrs. Becenti commanded as she stormed past us in her starched blue matron uniform. She smelt like grease and smelly body odor sweat…yuck! "Hmmm, she must've finally found a way to get the Dippity-do to tame her rats' nest, Ruby covered her mouth and chuckled to herself. "Shhhh.."

Mrs. Becenti's wrath came in waves. I saw her pull girls by the ear so hard that her jagged nails drew blood. We watched her throw Jenny's clothes onto the floor and made her put them back, just because she thought Jenny was hiding something. Contraband, like make-up or worse yet, a mirror. I remember a time several years back when Mrs. Becenti was going to get her way. A high school girl from Dorm B named Leilani was busy every morning trying to braid her three-young sister's hair in Dorm A. Mrs. Becenti cling clanged her starchy matron on duty outfit with pounds of keys all the way down the hall and the next thing we knew, Mrs. Becenti was yelling about how long it took to braid their hair every day. Next thing we knew, those little girls were matched into Mrs. Becenti's office. They came out crying, their long hair gone. The jagged scissors used left an uneven bowl cut mess. Leilani and her friends tried to even it out. It was really sad because those little girls were just innocent and they had beautiful long hair, as a Navajo girl should have. For many days after that, there was an unsettled silence that made us hate Mrs. Becenti even more.

At night, we could hear them crying and wished that this could all end, and we could be treated like real human beings. Once their mother found out what happened, she told Mrs. Becenti off for cutting her daughter's hair without permission. Mrs. Becenti almost got herself beat up, because Leilani's mother was so mad that Leilani had to keep her mother from hitting Mrs. Becenti. There was a lot of yelling and cursing and then Mrs. Becenti threatened to call the police. That is when Leilani, the little girls, and their mother took all their stuff and left, never to be seen or heard of again. The story would live in the halls of Red Sands Dorm A & B forever. Mrs. Becenti was hated even more but she showed up like clockwork rain or shine...like it or not. The children at Red Sands Residential Dormitory endured Mrs. Becenti's wrath for decades.

That scene left the rest of us with the understanding that if we got in trouble, maybe our parents would stand up for us and take us away from this living hell. Or maybe not. A strange and sad quietness settled over the girls in Dorm A when something like that happened. It was as if we were all praying for each other to survive the pain that we heard and felt so many times in the halls of Dorm A & B. The emptiness that those little girls were unbearable and all too familiar. All the girls, young and old, hated Mrs. Becenti. Patience was really difficult in times like that. Patience my ass!

By all accounts, all it took was a high school girl to threaten Mrs. Becenti like Leilani and her mother did for Mrs. Becenti to back down. Although that was a sight to see and hear, in the end Mrs. Becenti wasn't as powerful after that scene. Some students taunted her by asking if they were spending too much time fixing their hair just to aggravate her or get her mad. Some of Leilani's high school friends wore a bowl on their heads in protest. Mrs. Becenti was never the same.

My Hair
My hair is my family, my values –
  Honoring my elders, my lineage.
My act of survival
  and resistance...
My path to Hozho'
I grew from birth and forever
Never to be cut – protected from birth.
My hair carries my thoughts, prayers
  Our lineage to my ancestors – our memories.
My hair holds memories and prayers!!
My hair is who I am -
Dine'

Vanity was something Mrs. Becenti thought a sin, endlessly professed that she was a staunched Catholic. She said, Jesus thought girls who spend too much time in front of the mirror were destined to be cast into the depth of hell upon death or probably as soon as they even thought of being beautiful. Mrs. Becenti was always quoting and interpreting the Bible. Instead of dealing with her, the girls learned to rush to school to fix their appearance. Imagine that, making such a fuss over a simple mirror! The high school girls would rush to school with their mirror and make-up. They made sure their faces were washed before they entered the compound on the days Mrs. Becenti was on patrol. The girls had to hide their mirrors, make-up, and anything that represented vanity when Mrs. Becenti was around. On etiquette lessons days, we could hear her shouting, "You have to "Sit up straight"! You have to "Keep your stomach in and da feets flat on da floor"! "Make sure you don't drag your feets or leave the black marks on da clean floor!" "If you don't, I'll sent you to the Manuel Labor Office for da' punishments. Order upon order...always with the consequence of manual labor.

If a student got the consequence of manual labor, they would be ordered to go to the Manual Labor guy. Eugene stood behind a large window with a small rectangular opening at the bottom thinking of manual labor jobs and waiting to hand them out. When anyone was ordered to do manual labor, he would say, "Are you here for da' manual labors?" Then he would hand you a piece of paper so you could write down your name, B.I.A. number, precise time of offense, circle type of offense and explain why you did what you did…Then it took about five minutes for him to read your form and write down when your Manual Labor Duty was to commence. How ridiculous is that? I thought with a sarcastic laugh. "Yeah, Option 201: please give me some manual labor for the sin of being human." I decided to collect manual labor jobs in wrote in my "Give Me a Break!!" Journal.

Are you here for the manual labor? I wrote, "No, I'm here to see who has manual labor." "No, I'm here because I want to sign up for manual labor just in case." "No, manual labor is my favorite." "Oh, I had some ideas for manual labor." OF COURSE I HAVE MANUAL LABOR! THAT'S WHY ANYONE WOULD EVER COME HERE!!!!" IDIOT! I burst out into laughter. "Are you here for da' manual labors?" HAHAHAHAHAHAHHA! That was a good one!

Mrs. Becenti's circle of keys pounded as her hard black shoes stomped down on the tiles, making them appear to stomp back in retaliation. Even the building didn't like Mrs. Becenti. We watched her violently grab Laura by the back of her neck and marched her down the hall towards the Multipurpose Room and then to her office. Laura was having a hard time lugging her footlocker and all her other things. We winced, wanted to help her, but we knew all too well that we would be reprimanded. None of us wanted to be sent to, "The Room". So, we stood in silence as we watched Laura struggle with her stuff. Seeing a smile and a smirk on her face, let us know she knew she was going to be free in a matter of hours. Free to go home, free to go to the refrigerator and eat whatever she wanted! Free to come and go in her own time! Free to make choices about her life without someone always breathing down her neck in judgment! "Yep, we should've all gotten in trouble a long time ago!" I thought. The only thing was my family would be upset with me if I got into trouble again. No, not a good idea… For sure, I did not want to herd the sheep over the mountain as punishment, ever again! As the students began to mill into the cafeteria, everyone whispered about the incident. Some of the boys were talking about the guys that were drinking with the girls. "I guess one of the boys is also going home today, too," Promised Land time…was on the minds of all the students who knew what happens to those who got in trouble – especially for drinking beer. One of the girls was overheard saying, "Why do some kids get sent home and some kids get sent to "The Room" and then home." Ruby's eyes hugged the floor, she swallowed hard and whispered, "Count-down to Freedom.." AND, YES..there was a "Room" in the boy's dormitory too.

"Well, they get to have summer vacation one week early." I commented. "And we only have one more week together," Garnet reminded as we shuffled our way to the cafeteria trash to dump food from the plastic trays. "We need to shower Clarice…get this sweat off…don't wanna smell like Mrs. Becenti." We quickly headed for the restroom before Mrs. Becenti caught us being vain. Mrs. Becenti was too busy with Laura to notice the noise from the shower. Even our showers were scheduled, as if..

"Well, we should be getting our final grades this week then. Remember how they let us have a free week during the last week. My voice trailed off as I reached my bunk realizing that in a few short days, hours, and minutes all that I knew would become a memory that would be indelibly etched in my soul forever. All the fun, exciting, and good times I could remember as if they happened yesterday. Then there were the bad, hateful, sad, lonely, and depressing times that I could just as well forget. In time, all of it gave me a kind of strength that would carry into my new life at St. James. A place I could sense would also be challenged with many difficulties. Very shortly, I would be immersed in the never-ending work of a Rancher. This would replace my scheduled life at Red Sands Residential Dormitory. The life I endured would soon drift into history...forever. Yet, I knew it would follow me for the rest of my life.

"Please The Holy People, God, Jesus, and the Pope: Please let just this time go slow." I decided that by adding God, maybe my prayers would be answered in short order...maybe. After years of asking them to make the time go fast...I found myself asking time to slow down, if only for a few days, minutes, seconds. There was an unsettling quiet hovering over Red Sands, Arizona as we walked out of the 7-foot chain-linked fence, and down the sidewalk that led to Red Sands public school for the last times...forever. Mother Earth could feel our heavy hearts silently break and tried to hug our steps in understanding support. Heavy silent hearts pretended to be happy with quiet uncertainty... deep breath, quiet sadness...sigh.

Our nine years of regimented life, scheduled seconds, commands, orders were about to cease being a part of our daily lives. Innocence is lost - courage and strength taking its place for so many children, for decades and even centuries. Small victories and happy times helped keep us from losing all self-esteem. The Holy People, God, Jesus, and the Pope brought us together, so we wouldn't be alone. I found myself reciting John 1:1 "Ask me for anything in my name, and I will give it to you." All they ever asked for was hope, strength, dignity, and love. We found those things in each other. Sometimes the answers to your prayers hide in the words of your friends, but you must listen carefully.

Chapter 23 –Red Sands Public School

Mrs. Gardner's *Absolutely Last Day* of Teaching:

As always, on the last day of school, Mrs. Gardner handed her students a small gift and some work to do during the summer. This year she gave everyone a word search book. She also gave all of us a choice of two new books that she ordered. We had a choice of "Where the Sidewalk Ends" by Shel Silverstein, or "Alice: The Story of the Andes Survivors" by Piers Paul Read. Clarice and I chose Shel Silverstein. Then we all walked to her home, which was two blocks from the school, for her end of the year party. Mrs. Gardner had one of those little houses that had a great big back yard filled with roses of every color. Even Mr. Burrow, the Principal and some of the ladies who worked in his office, were there. We started with a water balloon fight and pin-the-tail on the donkey. We got in two lines with blown up balloons, and one by one raced across the yard to a chair, then sat on the balloon until it popped. The next person would run to the chair in the other direction and do the same. The group that popped all their balloons first won. That was a lot of fun! Mr. Burrow and a couple of office ladies grilled hamburgers and hot dogs. Some of the parents that could attend the party were there to help. Mrs. Gardner always had the best party ideas! Everyone had a smile on their faces. Despite knowing that some of us were leaving that day, and some of us were leaving the next day, and the rest on Saturday, gnawed on the back of my mind. I tried my best to enjoy the day.

"Okay, boys and girls, gather around," Mrs. Gardner commanded in her soft usual tone. She wasn't a harsh teacher by any stretch of imagination. She was a kind person who felt pity for us Navajos and learned ways to keep us interested in learning. "As you know this has been my last year, and today is my last day of teaching, her voice quivered. For the past thirty years, I have taught many, many students, probably even your own brothers or sisters. In the years, I have never seen a finer bunch of students.

You may become the leaders of this town. You will grow up to be leaders of the great Navajo Reservation. Some of you will go on to be doctors, lawyers, teachers, moms, and dads. Please remember to take time to smell the roses. My backyard is filled with roses so that I can remind myself to take time for myself, as well. Take time to appreciate life every day. When you get to be my age, you will understand what I mean. Don't wait that long." She glanced at us over her wide-brimmed eyeglasses – giving us that look that meant, listen to me. She went on.. "I have had a momentous year teaching all of you. Some of you I had to teach more than others, and some of you taught yourselves. Some of you taught me a thing or two with your writing," she said, looking directly at me. I blushed and put my head down. "We all learned this year, didn't we?" The Kids cheered, YEAH!!!! She went on, "now if you will be coming back next year, be sure to stop by and say hello." By then our stomachs were hungry, but we patiently sat on the grass feeling like it was the last day of the world. The summer sun blasted heat on our drenched hair and dried our wet clothing. It was finally time for hamburgers and hot dogs, but not before some more words of wisdom.

"Now I shall read to a quote from Aristotle," "For the things we have to learn before we can do them, we learn by doing them." "By that he meant that up until now you have learned the basic skills you will need to use in high school. You have four years to appreciate learning what you want to learn before entering your adult life. Please try new things and perfect what you have learned thus far. Boys and girls, you have made my last year of teaching a memorable one, and I will always remember each one of you. Thank you for a great year!" Tears trickled down her delicate face.

Mr. Burrow quickly gave her a tissue as she maintained her composure. We had never seen Mrs. Gardner get so emotional like that; her commanding voice trembled all the way through her speech. All of us just sat there quietly, not knowing what to say. Finally, Clarence stood up and started clapping and the rest of us chimed in with loud cheers and whistling. Mrs. Gardner made our last day and last year at Red Sands public school memorable and we all knew she genuinely cared for each of us white, Mexican, Black, and yes, us Navajos.

Mr. Burrow took over the show and presented Mrs. Gardner with a plaque showing how much they appreciated her teaching at Red Sands public schools. He told us how blessed we were to have been taught by such a dedicated and hard-working individual. He handed her a gift wrapped in shinny paper. She carefully opened it to reveal a Ganado Red style Navajo rug that he bought from one of the peddlers who often stopped by Red Sands Administration Office to sell their wares. Mrs. Gardner gasped in delight. "Oh, thank you, thank you all!" He handed her a card signed by all the employees at Red Sands public school. Tucked inside was $500.00 cash for her well-deserved trip to Hawaii. "Oh, I couldn't. This is too much!" she protested, but Mr. Burrow wouldn't allow her to refuse the money. The staff, teachers and parents at Red Sands public school are very appreciative of your years of service to this community and we are going to miss you! Have a wonderful retirement and stop by to see us sometime." Mr. Burrow left it at that. Dabbing the corner of her eyes, Mrs. Gardner pulled herself together. The teachers and parents dried their eyes, while lining up to give her hugs and more gifts. Mrs. Gardner was indeed the gardener of our lives, and we were the seeds that somehow thrived. Once again, Clarence stood up and started the standing ovation for our dear teacher, Mrs. Gardner.

"And now for the Academic Presentations," Mrs. Gardner announced with a shaky voice and teary eyes. The students looked at each other with questioned looks wondering, academic? Mrs. Gardner opened her file folder where seven neatly inscribed certificates sat. "The first award is for academic achievement in science. Randy Evans, would you please come up." Randy was a hefty white boy, was a brainy guy and loved to do experiments, so that was an easy one. Randy was all smiling when he shook Mrs. Gardner and Mr. Burrow's hands as he received his certificate. He turned to the crowd and took a bow. All of us cheered and whistled.

"The second award is for academic achievement in Social Studies. Penny Smith would you please come up." Penny was another white kid that loved to be the teacher's pet. She never once spoke to any of the Navajo students and she sat conspicuously separate from us, careful not to touch us. Social Studies, isss.. "The third award is for academic achievement in writing. Clarence would you please come up." Clarence? Everyone looked around at each other in disbelief. Surely, there was a mistake because I thought *I was the best writer in the class.* Mrs. Gardner announced that the Weekly Reader would be publishing some of Clarence's short stories and poems, and she immediately began to clap. All the students clapped, but I sat there, dumbfounded. I instantly regretted giving him that "100 Book of Poems" as a joke. Teachers always know when to rescue students in moments like this. Clarence held up his certificate and yelled, "Right On!..." Everybody laughed. Clarence sat down with a big grin on his face staring at his certificate. The pride he had in himself would last a lifetime because Clarence never found himself in the spotlight until today. The fourth award is for academic achievement in English. "Florence would you please come up." I blushed and felt embarrassed after being so jealous of Clarence that I almost tumbled down as I managed to stand up. Everyone laughed as I made my way to Mrs. Gardner and Mr. Burrow. I was ready to bolt out of the spotlight when Mrs. Gardner said, "Stay up here. This young lady also is the recipient for academic achievement in Reading. Miss. Arviso has read well over 1,000 books this year alone. Well, done. Florence!" "Two certificates!" All I could think of was how proud my mom, Gramps, and Gramma would be to know I won awards in these areas. Gramps taught me to love reading, and it paid off! Grinning from ear to ear, I firmly shook Mr. Burrow's hand and Mrs. Gardner gave me a hug. "Good luck, wherever you go, Florence," she whispered. Her hand was so soft and delicate; something I never noticed. The sixth award is for academic achievement Mathematics; Kyle is not here to accept this award, so we will be mailing it to him." Mrs. Gardner reported. The seventh and final award is for Overall Academic Achievement and that goes to Florence Arviso." My eyes grew wide with shock at being given that award. I knew my grades were good, but I was sure the white kids scored higher, although I never checked. Stunned, I had to be pushed by my classmates to go back up to receive the certificate. "Thank you so much, Mrs. Gardner. I will never forget you." I hugged Mrs. Gardner as I looked at her loving hazel eyes for a long time. "You will go far, Florence Arviso." Three certificates!! Groovy, man! All those lonely days paid off in the most unusual ways. Clarence watched as I passed, beaming with pride for "his love,"..as if. "Clii, his love, isss.." He stood up and led the kids in a cheer for me! "Go Florence!!" Shy Clarence wasn't as shy as he pretended to be, after all.

The parents lined up one side of the tables to serve the students. We chatted while we were scarfing hamburgers, hot dogs, chips, soda, ice cream and cake. There were tables lined up in three rows and everyone talked, ate and there was a lot of laughter in the air. Before long, it was time to clean up the party. We were escorted back to the school where the buses had already lined up to take the bus riders home.

I gathered my belongings and scurried out the door to find my friends. Clarice had already left to meet Garnet and Ruby. Then, I thought twice and turned around to find Mrs. Gardner alone in her classroom looking around at shuffling paper here and there. "Mrs. Gardner, I just wanted to thank you for everything. I'm not going to school here next year, so I won't be around to say hello when you get back from your trip." She made her way around her desk to give me a tight hug and a card assuring me that I would be just fine, to keep up the good work, and always continue being a good student…the kind of things a teacher tells their students. I somehow knew you would stop by when everyone was gone. I have learned to look forward to what you wrote, Florence. Keep writing." Tears of sadness, tears of days gone by, tears of separation, those are all things a child should never have to go through, Florence. Believe me, I prayed the hardest for you over these years." She looked up in the air…"what has it been, almost ten years?" I nodded. I remember your sweet little face when you arrived in kindergarten, and look at you all ready, for high school. I stood there for a moment, tears streaming down my face. I gave her one last hug and asked if she needed any help. "Thank you, but my son will be here any minute to carry out these boxes." Mrs. Gardner had narrowed down what she would take with her to three boxes. I took a deep breath and bid her farewell.

Mrs. Gardner was the Guardian Angel I had always felt watching over me. She would forever be an inspiration for me.

I decided to sneak down to the kindergarten hall and peek into my first classroom. Everything was taken down and the children had already gone home. This was the beginning of my journey at Red Sands Elementary School. I made my way to my 1st grade class, remembering learning how to read and write. The image of a little girl turned to look at me, smiling before vanishing into time. I peeked into my 3rd and 4th grade classes, where the teachers were packing up their classroom. I was careful not to make any noise as I drifted down the double doors. I pulled the door to the 5th and 6th grade wing, but they were locked. I took a deep breath, wiped my eyes, and wondered if this is what, "for my own good," looked like.

Mrs. Gardener had made a full circle with me. We ended this part of our journey together. Mrs. Gardner was ending her career, and I was about to embark on another journey. Our paths would probably never cross again. I decided it was good to take one last look at the places that became my refuge when I was allowed to legally escape Red Sands Residential Dormitory from the age of five to what felt like a hundred and five. Destiny or irony? I circled back and left my handprint on the window of my kindergarten classroom, turned around to find my friends - my sisters.

"Well, how was it? We get cafeteria food, and you and Clarice get cookout food. Not fair!" Ruby chided. Excited, I changed the subject. "Look! I got three certificates for academic achievement in Reading; English and I got the Overall!" I jumped up and down in girlish delight. The girls passed the certificates around inspecting the calligraphy Mrs. Gardner must have taken hours to write. Each oohing and awing. "Cool, Flo!"

~ 263 ~

"Okay, let's go to Safeway and get munchies to celebrate!" Ruby sarcastically chimed in. We made our usual trek from school to Safeway. In a matter of minutes, we were busy dropping peanuts in our Pepsi bottles, trying to prevent the mixture from bubbling over. Little did we know these events in our lives would soon become a faded memory.

As we sat at the metal table behind Safeway, an unsettling quiet seemed to hover over the town of Red Sands as the cirrus summer clouds drifted overhead, casting an eerie shadow of change over the four of us. The familiar sinking sun painted another landscape of gloom, with golden glimmers of a hopeful future. We knew that our lives were never going to be like this again. The reality was that this moment would have to stand in time. It was the beginning of the end of our times together and we all knew it. Even though we were excited about freeing ourselves from Red Sands Residential Dormitory, we began to have separation anxiety.

Ruby was busy carving her initials in the table that was covered with other initials, which claimed they were here. We looked at each other and rolled our eyes before Ruby blurted, "Now, we have to get back to *the halls of hell,* so we can practice wearing our high heels. We must know how to wear them for the dance tomorrow night. Wouldn't want to show up lookin' like a ... never mind." I never knew if Ruby was being sarcastic or being her true self. The strange thing was that most of the time her sarcasm made sense. "Good idea, Ruby," Clarice added.

That night the girls helped each other style their hair this way and that, trying to figure out what style to wear. Ruby suggested we look at <u>Seventeen</u> and <u>Teen Beat</u> magazines to get some pointers. I was nervous about dancing with Terry. I was nervous about what the future would hold. Restless thoughts, fitful dreams as the kids in Dorm A tried to find deep sleep. It seemed like everything was already different. Mrs. Gardner won't be there next year. My friends and I were uncertain about what the summer months and new schools would bring. As I lay on my bed, I remembered the card.

I carefully opened Mrs. Gardner's card. The cover was beautiful honeysuckle flowers with two bees searching for nectar. "Honeysuckles, my favorite." Smile.

Dear Florence,

What great words you write about your experience at Red Sands Residential Dormitory. I never would have known what you kids go through but often wondered. Your paper made an impression on me...just like you wanted. Tohatchi Flats sounds like a good place to live even with all its struggles. I'm sure some day you will be able to get your work published. Keep writing! I would have liked to meet your Gramps and Gramma. I know I would love a cup of morning coffee percolated over an open fire, too! Follow your dreams, Florence. Have a wonderful summer and future.

My regards, Mrs. Gardner.

I touched her words and hugged the card. I would never really understand what kind of impression I made on Mrs. Gardner through my writings. I felt safe expressing myself with her because writing was between the teacher and the student. Little did I know that the impression Mrs. Gardner had made on me would help me through the days and years to come. Little did I know my words would also help others in ways I would never have known.

Fitful dreams, bodies wrestling, bed springs squeaking throughout Dorm A. Even the walls seemed to creak with impending silence. The end of the year was scheduled like every part of our lives at Red Sands Residential Dormitory. Every year at this time, the girls' anxiety can be felt through osmosis. Not a word had to be spoken, because we could feel them. Everyone felt the annual change was about to commence. But for Clarice, Garnet, Ruby, and I, we knew it was going to be our last days together – forever.

The days got slower once we knew the end was coming. We didn't pack like girls going home – we packed like ghosts. What do you carry when you don't know who you are anymore? What do you leave behind when you're still trying to remember where you began? I wrote something down the last days. I didn't know if it was a prayer or a scream, or just a whisper to remind myself I existed.

Children of Oblivion

Hey—
have you heard of me?
I'm sitting in the face of oblivion.
Another year, another second
spins past like a torn page
on the calendar of life.
I was careful—
so careful—
but still I slipped.
Been waiting for a day
to reclaim my soul.
The wind calls my name—
echoes in an empty hall.
Time tries to trick me,
make me wonder
if I was ever here at all.
Left alone to wander,
I'm the child of oblivion—
the one you used to know.
But I'm not done.
Gonna hit the pavement soon.
Gonna fly up to the moon, out of oblivion.

Chapter 24 – The End of Year Dance

I got up early, skipped my morning run, and rushed to collect my dress. No one knew I had bought my dress weeks ago, or that I had it cleaned and pressed, just in the nick of time, by Mr. Huang, who owned H & H Dry Cleaning. For the first time in history, I raced back to Red Sands Residential Dormitory. I placed my dress in the closet, snuck in through the back door of the cafeteria, and casually joined Garnet, Clarice, and Ruby who were already trying to figure out what we were eating. "I don't know," maybe we should sneak out and get some read food," Clarice suggested. We agreed. Like clockwork, we waited for the right time when Mr. Benally wasn't looking to make our way out of the compound. "Let's go to Romo's for some Mexican food." Garnet loved Mexican food! Maria let us choose our booth and took our order. "I hope the smell of Mexican food doesn't stick to our clothes, or we'll be busted for sure," Clarice thought. We just chuckled. "Who cares? What's the worst they can do? Send us to 'The Room'?" I said before thinking. "Sorry, Ruby. No offense." Ruby gave me that look I had learned to mean shut up! Garnet chimed in, changing the subject to how delicious the food tasted. We decided to get some munchies before heading back to get ready for the dance. I felt a little nervous for a lot of reasons, but mainly because I kind of thought I was betraying Clarence. "It's just a dance." Clarice seemed to know my thoughts. "Smile! We're going to have fun! Let's have the time of our lives before we leave this god-forsaken place!" You're right, as usual.

"Well, is everyone almost ready, doz Boyz are just waiting for us fine looking Rez-Dollz!" Ruby announced suddenly changing her tone. "It is so hard to accept that soon us City Girlz will be on their own, without the comfort of our BEST GIRLFRIENDS IN THE WHOLE WIDE WORLD!" Ruby fell and began to pretend to sob at the thought of her best friends scattering to the winds. The others looked at her with pity.

"Stop! You'll mess up your make-up," Clarice kidded

"Gee, can a girl express herself?" Ruby was always so extra! "You've been expressing yourself all this time, Ruby!" Garnet chimed in.

"I ain't no Rez-Doll," either Ruby." I joked. We just laughed at her dramatic scene. Ruby, Ruby, quite contrary.

The end of the year dance had us busy helping each other with our hairdos. I borrowed black high-heeled shoes from Ruby. "You think I'll be too tall for Terry?" Snickers, followed by silence. Clarice started laughing, and we had no choice but to join in. "Too tall for Terry, isss!" Nervousness overwhelmed me as I thought about Clarence..sigh..oh well.. I decided that I would pin up my hair into a braided crown with small white honeysuckles tucked here and there. Ringlets hung on both sides of my face and around the back of my neck. I was amazed when I looked in the mirror. Ruby, you did a good job with my hair! Clarice presented us with one of her beautifully beaded bracelets designed with sparkling beads. We ooo'd and aww'd, as we prepared ourselves.

Clarice had bought herself a cream-colored sleeveless dress with fake pearls sewn into the bodice on one of her Saturday meetups with Kyle. His eyes lit up when she stepped out of the fitting room. He smiled and gave his approval, but they knew it was the only time he would see it on her. She sighed knowing he was shipped off to California as soon as school was close to being over – after testing to be exact. They never got a chance to say their goodbyes or exchange addresses. It was heartbreaking to hear her cry, but we all knew that there was no way she could ever be with him. It was a sad day for Clarice, but she knew better than to think their friendship would amount to anything. Her deep depression showed in the way she moped around, the days after he left. Nevertheless, she reluctantly agreed to go to the dance with Roy.

Ruby's grandmother had made her a dress from silk fabric that one of her Council Delegate friends bought her from a trip to Japan, years ago. It was breath taking to watch the turquoise blue fabric flow in the breeze as she walked. Her black shimmering black hair was pulled back with a silver barrette that had rhinestones. She curled long ringlets and had two on either side of her face.

Garnet wore a pink and orange chiffon dress that layered and hung straight on her slim figure. It was even more gorgeous with Garnet's dusty brown hair, looking stunning in a bun held together with a gold band and baby flowers placed here and there. This was all thanks to Ruby..yes Ruby.

When we were finally ready, we strutted through the crepe paper streamers, into the cafeteria dance floor. Everyone turned and gasped. A few Wow's!, and lots of smiles. Some of the boys clapped and whistled, embarrassing us just a little. We were on top of the world in the nicest clothes we could have ever worn at Red Sands Residential Dormitory. We quickly found a place to sit, as the DJ put on Paul Simon's "Kodachrome" to start the dance. We snickered because the next group of girls to enter the cafeteria got the same Wow's and lots of claps and whistled too…humble pie..

I found myself thinking, the time has come, the time is now, Terry Wyaco *better* be a good dancer, otherwise I will fade into the wall like one of those wall flowers that showed up at dances. He came up to me in his brown polyester pants, blue checkered long collared shirt. His brown belt was at least 4 inches wide. I didn't know what to think, but oh well. I took his extended hand and let him lead me to the dance floor. Roy walked across the dance floor practically dragging Clarice out onto the dance floor, and she finally started having fun.

Everyone looked up and around to see the amazing decorations. Earlier that day, the older girls and boys had decorated the entire cafeteria with soft blue and white plastic. There was a mirrored ball that rotated rays of light from the middle of the dance floor out to the wall that lit up silver tinsel shimmered everywhere. There was a flashing light casting little rivers all over the room. Martinez DJ Machine set up their own lights around their turntable, and they had the biggest speaker anyone had ever seen.

They had a mountain of records organized in bins. Their set-up took almost the entire West wall.

It was hard to see the details of people's faces, so Mrs. Becenti demanded they turn the lights up – just a little. As soon as she left the room, the lights were immediately dimmed. It was a sight to see, having been in this room for the study hall, to eat and to be lectured by Frankenstein at the beginning of each school year. The DJ put together the sound system with record players and huge speakers so that you couldn't hear anything, except for the bass. We moved to the other side of the cafeteria where the music sounded better. The cafeteria workers went out of their way to make four huge chocolate and vanilla sheet cakes, with fruit punch and sugar cookies. They also had sandwiches that were cut up so a lady could easily eat in front of her gentlemen friend in a gracious way. Delfred showed up in his multi-colored psychedelic shirts and blue polyester pants pressed with a crease that almost turned my stomach, but I had to acknowledge the effort he put into his dance moves. I wondered where Clarence was and felt bad, I didn't accept his invitation to the last dance. I now wished I had run faster and won the race too. Nevertheless, all of us secretly practiced dancing in our dorm rooms for days, trying to imitate those dancers on Soul Train. As the age when rock-n-roll and free love pushed Elvis out of the limelight, and new songs and sounds like _Smoke on the Water_ and _Your Momma Don't Dance_ reminded us of how times had changed with music. Even Harry Billy finally started playing songs from _The Rolling Stones, Led Zepplin, and Elton John._ "Go Harry!"

Just as Terry was leading me onto the dance floor for the second time, Clarence showed up with none other than Julia stinkin' James! Of all the people he could've snuck in, he brought her! I felt my face flush with heat and anger and quickly made its way to my squinting jealous eyes. How could he do this to me? Did I think I would be able to dance with both Terry _and_ Clarence at the same dance? I never responded to his date request like I had planned. In fact, except for Mrs. Gardner's end-of-year party, he pretty much ignored me for the last week, and I did the same. We took special care to pretend not to notice each other. It was an awkward moment at Mrs. Gardner's backyard party too, with him winning *my* writing award. Julia just had to wear something a glamour girl would be seen wearing on the cover of Seventeen magazine. Julia wore a light blue chiffon dress with puffy see-through sleeves and silver sequins sewn all over the thing. It sparkled with every move. I was full of hate with the sudden sharpness in my squinty eyes. If she wasn't the enemy, the girls would be down with it! Clarence proudly escorted her onto the dance floor in his dark blue polyester suit with a light blue fake silk shirt, he managed to buy from one of the second-hand stores downtown. He even replaced his pointy black Beetle shoes with 4-inch platform shoes. "Looks like he finally woke up," my snide remark was made under my breath. "Traitor!" I thought! "Let's dance!" I yanked Terry's hand so hard he almost fell but managed to get his feet working. Grace Slick and the Jefferson Airplane resonated through our ears. Like a fool, I proceeded to tear up the dance floor. Poor Terry felt like he was dancing alone, as he watched me give it my all. Garnet and Ruby danced their way, flanking me on both sides trying to get my attention. "Flo! Settle down!" Garnet yelled. I was in my own world, and when I opened my eyes, I noticed Terry had a look of disgust as he grabbed my hand and took me off the dance floor. "What's wrong with you? Are you trying to embarrass me?" he questioned. "No, I just thought the song was so moving that I wanted to groove my way around the whole dance floor. How come you didn't follow my lead?" I hissed through my teeth, *Yádísh*! Geez!!

Terry said, "Boy, Clarence showed up with that city girl, Julia.James...isss. You know, the one you and your friends don't like. How did he sneak her in here? *Chi'įįdíí'né'*" (that devil!) I tried to ignore him as the music turned to a slow song by Roy Orbison. "Come on, let's dance," I commanded never answering Terry's question. It was all Clarence could do to keep his hands off Terry's neck, touching his girl and standing so close! He knew that bringing Julia James would create a scene, but that's what he wanted – a chance to profess his love for Florence. Judging by the look on my face I would have nothing to do with Terry or Clarence. "Timing is the key." Mr. Seiler once told the boys in his health lectures about boy things. The girls got the same lecture from Mrs. Rodriguez during Health class. "Okay, so I have to be patient, and yeah, watch my timing..isss" Clarence thought. Smirk.. Nervous sigh..

Delfred, Garnet, Clarice, and Roy saw the whole thing as they sat on the opposite corner of the dance floor. What Garnet and Clarice caught themselves doing is trying to get a look at the Boy's Wing – just to see how it was over there. John and Roy made fun of everybody. They made funny remarks in Navajo about how the guys were dancing.

Unbeknownst to everyone, some boys were given the assignment to open the back door when the lights dimmed, so that Julia James could make her appearance. Ruby and John sat hand in hand, as if a couple for a decade, while Clarice was careful not to touch Roy. John wouldn't let Ruby's hand go, even though she protested and finally gave up. I, too, watched as Clarence plotted his moves, and I brushed them off. Terry was clueless, or so he seemed. "Cake and punch for the loveliest looking lady here?" He offered. I looked up and saw Terry in a new light. Too late, I thought. I won't be here next year and for all I knew I would never see Terry, John, Delfred, or Clarence ever again for that matter. Sigh.

I glanced around to find my friends sitting and not dancing! Terry took charge, ordering John, Roy, and Delfred to get up and dance. "Shíyáadíí!! Get out der and dance!" He said, it was almost sounding demanding. His request magically brought the whole crowd onto the dance floor, as shyness seemed to dissipate.

This was his last chance. Clarence got up and nodded his head towards the bathroom. He headed that way, with Terry following. With the door closed Clarence asked if he could dance the last dance with me. "Go for it!" Terry agreed, not knowing the extent of the feelings between the two of us. "She might go nuts again on the dance floor, just to let you know…clii!" As the D.J.'s or disc jockey's turntable plopped a record on top of the previous one, Stylistics *"Betcha By Golly, Wow!"* came on. Clarence made his way around the back of the tables towards me and my friends.

"May I have this dance?" Clarence offered his hand as I turned in shock to see that it was *him* – standing where the shimmer of the mirror ball touched his face every few seconds and made him kind of look handsome. "Aaah." I looked at Terry. "Do you mind?" "No, go on ahead. I'm going to enjoy some cookies and punch before it gets thrown down the drain, isss." Terry got up to join the line that had formed at the goody table. "Okay, I'll dance with you." Deep breath, my eyes hugged the floor as we made our way to the dance floor. For sure I didn't want him to see me blush with embarrassment.

"Where's your date, Julia?" I growled.

"She had to go home, her dad said she could only be here for forty-five minutes," Clarence answered, as he held my hand, trying to pull me close by the waist. It was something he had longed to do for the last couple of years. He often dreamed of kissing her full ruby lips. "Timing is the key," he wrestled with his emotions. "I love this song. The singer sounds so desperate and so sad in this song." I whispered as we swayed with the music. Just then, I noticed Clarence began dancing towards the back door.

"What? Where are you taking me?" I gasped, trying to head back inside.

""It's okay. The guys will open the door when I give the secret knock," Clarence whispered as he pulled her towards him, trying to French kiss me. I slapped his face so hard that he didn't even see it coming.

"How *dare* you show up with that enemy? I thought you were a friend." I pushed Clarence away, but he pulled me towards him.

"Guess what, I'm going to be going to school at some place called St. James," Clarence announced.

"St. James?" shocked at his news, I stepped back.

"So, I have only one chance to tell you how much I like you and want to be more than a friend. May I kiss you, Flo? I've been wanting to for the longest time you know."

For me, I secretly wondered how it would be kissed by a boy, any boy. Without hesitation I moved towards him with lips puckered, eyes closed. His lips were smooth and warm, and I liked it until he started to put his tongue into my mouth. "Stop that! That's gross!" I pushed him back again and it was over. "Do your secret knock so we can get back in there!" I demanded. Clarence could've kicked himself for going that far! His timing was way off. Mr. Seiler made it sound so easy. Exasperated bliss!! We rushed back in when Terry gave the danger sign. The guys kept old lady Becenti's attention away from the door as we slipped back in.

Where are my friends? I thought. They were busy helping divert Mrs. Becenti's attention, so we could slip right in without her knowing. No one ever noticed we went outside. I was glowing and my face flushed. I was secretly delighted that I wouldn't be alone at St. James after all.

Next thing we knew, the DJ announced, "It is time for the last song! Get up boys and girls! He let his DJ light flash all over the room creating the mood for dancing. Let's Dance! He said dropping the tonearm and the silky sound over the vinyl record signaled everyone back onto the dance floor partner or not. "I'm so excited! That I just can't hide it! I'm about to lose control, and I think I like it!!" The Pointer Sisters blasted around the walls of the dance floor. For a moment in time, there was utter happiness at Red Sands Residential Dormitory. Music has a way of doing that to people. We danced so hard, our hair turned to a hot mess, flowers, and all. We looked at each other and howled with laughter! Mrs. Becenti stood there with her resting grouchy face scowling at the sight of us having fun. The Cafeteria Ladies moved to the beat of the music, careful not to let Mrs. Becenti see them having fun, too.

"Witchy bitch!" Ruby said under her breath. "Shh!!!" We ordered, giving her that look with eyes opened wide.

Before the lights were turned on, Clarence gave me one last look, "Don't forget me, Flo. Okay?" He passed me the usual folded star paper and rushed off, disappearing down the hallway that led to Dorm C & D. "Write to me!" echoed in the hallway as I looked for his address…there wasn't one.

Little did Clarence know, he would be seeing *me* at St. James High School – Home of the *Redskins* -.of all things. One by one, after the lights were switched on, and true to form, Mrs. Becenti was ordering everyone around. She commanded the cleaning crew to hurry up, clean up, and stand at attention all at the same time. Mr. Yazzie, the Dorm Man, just looked at her, knowing not to utter a word, set about taking the decorations down. Mrs. Becenti deflated everyone's bliss with a brazen hiss and a stomp of her clubfoot!

St. James *doesn't* look so bad after all, I smiled. "Well, how was it?" Clarice whispered.

"How was what?" I stammered looking here and there…no eye contact.

"You know, with Clarence." "You knew?" "Yeah, are you into him? I mean, even Julia set her pride aside so that Clarence could win your heart."

"Oh, my god! She did what? You guys did what?...and everyone knew about it?…oh how embarrassing!"

Garnet and Ruby leaned in for my response, giggled while pretending to sweep, and I stood there feeling more and more like a fool…a fool in love…

"Momma said this would happen one day…she just didn't think it would be him..." Ruby teased.

I glared at her then joined in with the laughter. "He's just a friend."

"Sure…" the girl chimed in.

Just then, we could hear the pounding of keys that rocked back and forth Mrs. Becenti's wide hips. Our eyes quickly hugged the floor as if we were not trying to get sent to the Manual Labor Guy, or worse yet, "The Room". She always had a way to diminish our last glimpse of happiness.   All the signs of our happy time disappeared right before our eyes. When all the lights clicked off one by one, the cafeteria tables waited for the daily routine to continue the next day.

For once in their 3,000 days at Red Sands Residential Dormitory A, no amount of noise or ghosts could keep us four from having the best night's rest since stepping into our cinderblock house – the God forsaken place we called hell one minute and home the next. It was a love-hate situation. A peaceful quiet, drifted down the hall as slumber took all to dream land. The squeak, squeak of the metal beds didn't wake us, not once. Blissful sleep…finally. St. James, here I come.. smile, sigh, deep..breath…sleep…change isn't so bad…maybe hmmm…

Tables Turn
That moment of uncertainty.
Clouds lift, tomorrow's sunshine
Tables turn, again.

Chapter 25 – Last Days, Sad Days

The last two days we spent time on our bunks talking about the time we stepped into Red Sands Residential Dormitory and how scared we were and how we found comfort in each other as scary beginnings turned into lonely days and nights, into month after month, and year after year. We promised not to let them fade into black and white memories. We found ourselves wishing now for time to go slower, and slower, and slower, realizing time ticks by no matter what we thought. Alas, we knew that this would be the last couple of hours, minutes, seconds, we did our best to make the most of it. Realizing we would no longer be at each other's side, and that our bond as sisters, friends, enemy... you name it, was going to be a big part of how we would look back on our childhood. We found ourselves in constant flux from the beginning. From day 1 to now, day 3,064. Day 1 echoing from a distant lifetime, with cries followed by laughter. Yes, I was going to miss each one of those moments, days, hours, years...all of them and forever. "Me too," Clarice sighed. "Me too," Ruby, chimed in. "Me too," Garnet wrapped her arm around Clarice. Ruby and I joined in. We took a collective breath, trying not to cry.

Our teary eyes looked at each other as if that would be the last time. Memories lingered in our minds; of school dances, of school parties, of talking about our ups and downs, of growing up in an unpleasant environment for most of our lives. Through it all, we had each other. The grief and happy times we lived together flooded our collective minds with the pain of impending separation. What mattered was this was our forever family. We stuck with each other from Dorm A to kindergarten class and on into the halls of junior high school, to right now.

As we got older, we looked around and saw the oppression and talked about the way we were treated by some of the white people we encountered at school, and when we ventured into the streets or stores of Red Sands. Not all of them were bad but those that were awful! Thanks to Chuckie, I learned the word oppression and understood it all too well.

There was one place that had no oppression at all, a place that always welcomed us with open arms, was the old Ranch House. So, we decided to spend one last day there: each taking something to remember our days growing up at Red Sands Residential Dormitory. We each left a note of thanks to our sanctuary. Our notes would stand in time. Messages understood only by our friend, the old Ranch House and us. She kept our dried tears, our secrets, and our wishes. I went first. I decided to read write poem called, "A Place For Us".

A Place For Us.
You stand patiently waiting
For the sound of our voices
You light up to hear our presence.
Into your tattered worn space
Listening carefully to hopes, wishes,
And secret plans. (chuckle)
You were a special place for us
A place called optimism and
A place to count time
A place that was our refuge.
Thank you for being a place for US.

Please don't forget us. See you someday, Love Flo

I'll go next, Garnet, stepped forward and read her letter.

Dear Ranch house, our Friend.

Guess what? I'm going to miss you so much! You were a friend when we needed a place to go. You never told our secrets, and I could tell you were glad we came over the hill to see you. Now we must leave you. Until next time, Garnet.

I'll go next; Clarice read her note.

Thanks for everything, everything! I will miss you forever! Love, Clarice.

Your next Ruby. She read her note.

Dear Old Ranch. You will be missed forever by 4 girls who visited you for many years. Thanks for the shelter. Ruby

.

Clarice said the Navajo prayer she always says before we left the old Ranch House. She said thanks for this place to be a part of our life at Red Sands Residential Dormitory, which included prayer for bad spirits lingering around, not follow us when we left. She gave thanks to the Holy People for helping us find such a place to call home. She passed around her *tá'di'díín* pouch and each of us gave an offering of corn pollen. Each of us took one last look around and, one by one, we slowly walked out the door.

Of course, Ruby had a sinister plan. We turned with the clicking sound of her opening a switchblade, as she announced she would be carving her name first. We just stood there with our jaws dropped, mouths opened, not knowing what to say. We looked at each other wide-eyed as we watched her finish. "Where did she get that switchblade?" Garnet whispered to Clarice. "Walt's Hardware. They sell anything to anybody." "Who's next?" She held the knife in the air. Garnet looked at the two of us and decided to take the knife. She carved her name below Ruby's. One by one we carved our names. At the bottom, I carved 1965 – 1974. Peace!

"Hey Clarice. You've got a friend." "Huh?" "You know, you've got a friend." Yeah. "When you're down and troubled and you need a helping hand...." Garnet and Ruby joined in as we made our way out of the old Ranch House and up the dusty red trail one last time. The wind picked up the dirt as if the old Ranch House gave us thanks and a wave goodbye.

As we reached the top of the hill that looked over Red Sands, we looked back one last time. The old Ranch House began to crackle and the eerie sound of wind blowing through the broken windowpanes, as if to say "Farewell." The distant clouds that rumbled east of Red Sands would soon be followed with the smell of a spring shower. "How fitting," I thought. "I guess the wind is chasing us away, like an in-law. Chuckle. Farewell, you old house and refuge. Farewell." The wind picked up and the smell of rain took the place of sadness, and we knew it was time to let the old Ranch House stand still in time – another family leaving its imprint and perhaps another taking our place.

Before the black cloud of thunder shifted its way over the old Ranch House, the sprinkles began, and the girls were already past the football field. "Our last taste of mystery meal awaits," Ruby yelled as we began to run before the rain poured, washing away our footprints. Ruby will always be Ruby and by then, that was just fine with us. We rushed to the porch brushing ourselves off before entering the back door. "Whew, we made it just in time!" "Yeah, we would've been drenched!" "Excellent prayer, Clarice. You sure know how to bring on the rain! It's like a cleansing before we walk down our new paths." We walked to our bunk and changed into dry clothes.

Suzie came to give Clarice a message. "Clarice, they want you at the Multipurpose Room." Clarice's parents unexpectedly showed up to rescue her from the hell that was Red Sand Residential Dormitory and the promise of **B**eans for **I**ndians **A**lways on the menu meal, just for old time's sake. We watched her walk between the row of bunkbeds to the end of Dorm A, Clarice said, "Well, I guess this is it." We took a deep breath and gave her a big hug. "Let's help her take her things," Garnet said picking up two of her boxes. As we carried her belongings to her parents' brand new 1974 Ford F-150 pickup truck with a newer, better trailer hitched on the back, I understood that Garnet, Ruby, and I would also leave one by one

"You all have my address…I want us all to keep in touch. Don't ever forget what we went through together, okay." Clarice managed to stay strong though tears poured down her cheeks as we hugged it out. I handed Clarice a box carefully wrapped with the prettiest wrapping paper I had ever seen. The beautiful purple and pink flowers lined with gold shimmered in the sunlight. "Don't open it until you leave Red Sands," my sister, my friend. I hugged her one last time. Tears quietly flowing silent words, knowing that at some point we might eventually forget to keep in touch. There would come a time when all we would have to rely on was our memories, memories…soon to fade into yesteryear…minute by minute; second by second. Our years together, replaced by years apart.

Clarice's parents waited, not saying a word, like Navajos do. They couldn't bear the heartache their only child was going through and had to bite their tongue, so they would not start crying too. *"Tį' Shíyázhí,"* Let's go my child, her mother took her by the shoulder and guided Clarice to the truck. The tears blurred her view of us as she slid in the middle and looked back, waving while her dad slowly drove the truck to the entrance that led to freedom, with a thump, thump bump…and we ran down the road until they couldn't see her anymore. "Please come back! Please come back!" Our shoulders shrunk as we slowly walked back to Dormitory A in silent reverence. Goodbye my sister, goodbye…forever.

Remember Me
Will you remember me?
   -tomorrow?
   -the next day?
   -forever?
Will you remember our times?
   -tomorrow?
   -the next day?
   -forever?
I will remember you
   -tomorrow.
   -the next day.
   -forever.
Goodbye my friend, please remember me.

For one second, we fell into a painful silence as we watched her truck slowly make its way down the same driveway where Gramps, Gramma, and countless other parents had taken to let the almighty Bureau of Indian Affairs rule their children from August to May. Every second counted, silence…now freedom.!! "One down, three to go!" Like me, Ruby also thought of our impending departure. Deep breath, silent wonder.

In my mind, I thought that the saddest moment in my life was leaving Gramps and Gramma, but now, I had something to compare. Silent reverence. The rain moved across the sky as the time seem to slowly tick by and soon the clouds parted ways to let the bright sun cast its hopeful golden rays across Red Sands…The wind rushed the clouds East and drifting into the horizon… And there you go; Clarice is gone with the eastern winds...

True to her words, Clarice waited until there was no sight of Red Sands Residential Dormitory to carefully open her gift making sure not to rip the paper. There was a book covered with dried flowers she was sure came from Mrs. Hamilton's Garden. Inside were a collection of poems I had written over the years, ones she had read and some that were new. Florence would become who she dreamed – a writer, Clarice thought. Clarice often wrote in her journal about how she learned to be strong from watching me, and the lessons she learned from my Grandparents…in many ways they were her Grandparents too. Clarice was honored to read poems written just for her. I had also purchased a sketch book and a set of pencils which I labeled – Clarice, Famous Artist and Best Friend Forever…. Her parents looked as she went through the gifts, glancing at each other..careful not to show their tears as their only child's heart broke… Her mother hugged her, "Ta'adoonícha' (don't cry) Shíyázhí..shhh.." Like a true gentleman, her dad handed her his handkerchief.

Instead of eating one more **B**eans for **I**ndians **A**lways on the menu meal; we decided to sneak off to Romo's Mexican Café this time for cheese enchiladas and beef tacos…eating in silence…the Pepsi burning down our throats. That evening, Ruby, Garnet, and I played cards and Chinese Checkers trying to pass the time as we remembered some of the fun times we had. Other students were also playing board games laughing, happy they too would be going home soon.

Garnet reminisced about the time we played a joke on Mrs. Hagga. We had boiled some Navajo Tea and black tea so that it was a dark brown...like the whiskey she enjoyed. Then, we poured it in one of those old Tokay bottles we found on one of our walks to the old Ranch House and mixed in some X-LAX. Mrs. Hagga came in drunk as usual. So, we waited until she was good and drunk, then we decided to con her into giving us the key to the snack machine for the bottle. We made off with a bunch of snacks, and Mrs. Hagga in her blackout, never could figure out what happened to all those snacks. AND, don't forget it was also because she had spent most of her working hours on her porcelain throne, she decided to let the incident go. Poetic justice...

"Remember, we hid the snacks up at the old Ranch House, the next day?" I admitted. Stealing was stealing, but that one time was sweet revenge!! Truth is a funny thing sometimes...Gramps words rang always true. Man, that was funny watching Mrs. Hagga think that the tea was whiskey. Hagga, Bagga, Sagga... laughter! Her reality was a porcelain throne! Laughter, followed by quiet uneasiness.

Ruby changed the subject, remembering the time we used honey, peanut butter and chewed up gum to get back at Julia James. We took a trip to Petrified National Forest. On the way back, Julia fell asleep. We were all prepared before we got on the bus. We spent most of the trip to the forest chewing gum so that we could carry out our plan. Julia was so mad when she woke up with the mixture all over her hair. "Remember, Julia came to school with a new haircut that Monday morning. She glared at us for months until she finally got tired of guessing who had actually done the dirty deed!" We laughed remembering the mess we had made out of Julia's long black hair. "Oh well, it didn't take long for her hair to grow back!" Ruby howled as we chimed in. "The good thing about hair is, it grows back!! HAHAH!!" True, Ruby!!

"Remember when we broke into the kitchen and took all that fruit." I added. "Man, we had a fruit feast and paid for it later!" "Yeah," Garnet remembered. "We spent days on the toilet, because of all those oranges!" "We must've been nuts to do that!" Ruby chortled. "Good thing we didn't eat all of them carrots!" Laughter.

Before we knew it, we were all sniffling again remembering that Clarice was slowing down that wretched road only hours ago, minutes, seconds that seemed like an eternity. We were on an emotional roller coaster. We fancied our necklace and knew we would forever cherish the jewelry Clarice made for us. We found the matching necklaces placed under our pillows after she left. "She must've felt like Dorothy making her way down the yellow brick road, finally leaving Oz." Garnet tried to lighten the mood.

"How many times have we seen that scene?" Ruby just had to get pro-Indian and radical on us one last time. "How long do our people have to be made to go against our tradition and culture? We put our head down for almost a decade! Why? We know that it was up to us to get a white man's education, in order to be seen as human beings with a brain and a right to choose our destiny. Civilization bites, Tradition rules!" Ruby finally made sense...yes Ruby...dear Ruby. She even sounded kind of like Chuckie. Rebellious. snickers.

How did we survive Red Sands Residential Dormitory all alone, yet together? We counted days, hours, minutes, seconds – together...somewhere in time, at a place called Red Sands Residential Dormitory A. For sure, we tried to live from the inside out in this unnatural place, we somehow learned to call home. Gramps always made sense. Deep breath, sigh..

Chapter 26 – Time to Part Ways

Ruby was the first of the three to *try* to leave at 9:45 A.M. She decided to get the usual check out started before her mother showed up to whisk her away from Red Sands Residential Dormitory, one last time. We got ready so we could walk through the agonizing check-out process with her because we weren't able to with Clarice.

In true Ruby fashion, she sarcastically handed in her pillow and bedding, saying "Here, these things should probably be burned and replaced with something that is not so abrasive to the tender skin of the poor soul who will inherit them next…but oh, I forgot, my skin has become so tough from that freakin' water hose of a shower! On second thought, take them and burn them!" Mrs. Becenti, their last and final Matron on Duty, yanked the pile and Ruby's grabbed her Checkout sheet. She scribbled her initials so hard you could see the imprint on the back as she threw the Checkout sheet at Ruby with a scowl. *"Chi'įįí'shá'! Diigis!"* (You stupid little devil!) Ruby had learned to cuss under her breath so she wouldn't be sent to "The Room", but on this last day, she said, "You're the devil and you are the stupid one!" In the Navajo language, that's about as bad as one could throw words at another. She scowled. Then she barked, "Now, you have to go check out with the Manual Labor office to see if you have any manual labor hours to make up! *Nówehji!"* (Get out of my way!) Mrs. Becenti had to maintain her behavior because parents started to file in the Multipurpose Room. Some of them watched the whole scene in horror. Ruby, all puffed up, claimed, "I am not ever coming back, so go straight to hell, Mrs. Matron on Duty!!" Smirk, smile… "I take back my life, my innocence, my reality! Mrs. Becenti's hateful reality no more!" Ruby really wanted to say something about "The Room" and Frankenstein, but she strutted off from the Linen Check-in table and strolled on to join the line formed near Manual Labor Guy's window. We followed close by. Ruby sure stirred up a commotion. I didn't understand because she had been checked out just about every weekend for nine years, not to mention all the holidays. "I'm so excited! After all these years, I'm minutes to complete freedom.!" Ruby went back to the Linen Check-in table with eyes squinting and told Mrs. Becenti, "*Judge not*, lest *ye* be *judged*. For with what judgment *ye judge*, *ye* shall be *judged*: and with what measure *ye* mete, it shall be measured to you." Ruby followed that by saying, "Matthew 7:1-3. "I'll bet you skipped over that Scripture in your wretched Bible, she announced glaring at Mrs. Becenti, the self-proclaimed Bible thumper. Mrs. Becenti turned red with anger, and for once in her pitiful life didn't seem to know what to say…. "She is one nasty biddy I do not want to ever see again!" Ruby announced at the top of her voice to anyone who would listen! Raised eyebrows, awkward silent agreement. The other Matron on Duty watched in case something else happened, but it didn't. There were giggles all the way down the hall and around the Multipurpose Room. Ruby's words would live on in the halls of Red Sands Residential Dormitory

Mrs. Becenti pretending not to be fazed and sensing her authority was diminished raised her voice and her keys jingled as she continued to order around the girls in the room, "Once you leave here, go to the cafeteria to make sure you don't have any cafeteria duty for naxt year. You can clean up or help with dishes tonight, so you don't have cafeteria duties when you come back from da summer breaks. Thannn, when yer der, you need da nitials of da Study Hall Monitor to make sure you don't have any books checked out. Oh, your current address needs to be on filing… just in case there is something we forgotted." (eyes rolling) Mrs. Becenti made the *same* announcement *every* year for *nine years*. We didn't need to be told what to do – anymore.

Garnet and I stood in silence watching the whole thing. We almost clapped but decided to play it cool. "Ha!" Ruby said. "I won!" "Naxt year," iss.. that fat blob needs to go to Red Sands Public School again! She didn't even learn anything, ober der," she said with her lips pointing. Sarcastic Ruby is, as sarcastic Ruby does. Some things just shouldn't change," Garnet's eyes and mine met and we silently giggled.

We passed the little girls, sitting in a line of chairs placed against the wall, waiting to be checked out for the summer break. Their eyes twinkled with wonder as they looked at our Check-out Sheet. I left the Multipurpose Room imagining myself with that same look of wonder and sadness in my little face all those years ago. I stopped and said, "Just follow the yellow arrows with the numbers, go to number 1, then 2 and you're done when you get to number 5 and you're back in this room." The little girls looked at each other and giggled, stood up and acted like it was a game. I took a deep breath and hoped they would find a way out of Red Sands Residential Dormitory without much damage. "Please, Holy People, God, Jesus, and the Pope..take care of these little girls and boys," I said under my breath. The commotion and endless waiting in this line or that one, was routine for every end of year checkout time. Only this time, it was to check out of this prison and finally go home. Sigh, deep breath…

"Imagine that, going to the Manual Labor Guy so he can forward any of punishment time to next year!" Ruby's nagging voice had a way of reminding everyone how much they wanted to be anywhere but Red Sands Residential Dormitory. "At least you and I can get some of our Check-out Sheet signed, so it wouldn't take forever when it's our turn to leave." Garnet's gentle voice always calmed Ruby down, and for that, I would always be grateful. Even though Ruby was the oddball of the group, she was still our sister and spending these last minutes with her might be the last time. In all our days at Red Sands Residential Dormitory, I never witnessed Ruby get so mad, and I may not never know what her time in "The Room" was actually all about.

Eyebrows raised, made our way around the milling students. We laughed before getting to the Manual Labor office where there was a long line of students moving, ever so slow, to meet Eugene, the Manual Labor Geek. "Dang, Ruby. Where did all that anger come from?" Garnet asked, while I nodded. "It was time to let that old biddy knows how I feel, and you know you feel the same way, too! We all do! Every one of those kids in Dorm A & B!!" Her eyes started to water, but she brushed them off. "Yeah," we chimed in. We patted her on the back and gave her a high-five. "When did you learn scriptures from the Bible?" Silence.

She led the way out of Dorm A and onto Eugene, the Manual Labor guy. There actually were kids who had Manual Labor hours forwarded to next year! We watched some of them who did their best to claim that they already did their manual labor time, to no avail. Eugene looked like his usual greasy, goof ball self, but he could be ruthless. I decided to get back at him one last time.

"Hey, let's write a list of the top five manual labor jobs for the Manual Labor Guy to issue out next year!" I suggested pulling out paper and pen…"Okaaay!" Ruby sarcastic responses did not end. Eyes rolling, deep breath. "Looks like we're going to be waiting in line forever! We might as well make fun of him one last time." Ruby was on a roll. "We're going to be leaving, too, Ruby, and we're going to miss you…not matter what comes out of your mouth." Garnet was finally making her voice heard. Maybe, it was because she wouldn't be at Red Sands Residential Dormitory either and it was about time Ruby got a few words of advice. Or maybe she was as nervous as the rest of us, or maybe Ruby needed to be given a good tongue lashing before we sent her to The Great Navajo Nation.

Raised eyebrows. Uneasy silence. Impending separation anxiety. Sigh.

"Okay, we'll start with…I redirected…

Dear Manual Labor Guy,

We have been here for nine years, and we have had to put up with your lame ass consequences to our innocent misdeeds, because you know; were just kids. Instead of issuing orders to pick up rocks no smaller than four inches and no bigger than eight in three hours… Instead of issuing orders to spit shine the windows in Dorm A, B, C, or D with chemicals and no gloves in two hours. Instead of issuing orders to run 100 laps around the football field… We would like to offer you these harsher punishments for your reading pleasure. Besides, we spit shined the windows of Dorm A, B, C, and yes D so many times, for so many years; they're *liable to crack right open and finally the **B**ureau of hating us Indians of America will have to buy something new.*

We, the victims of your manual labor, have compiled a list of five that will change the world of manual labor at Red Sands Residential Dormitory forever! Good luck in the future and please be creative with the kinds of manual labor you issue next year and years to come. We would like to tell you a secret. There are only so many rocks and twigs that can be found here, and I'm sure by now we have picked all of them. As you can see, the compound is virtually bare. Even the dust devils have fair game on the compound! Picking up rocks and twigs as a manual labor punishment needs to be retired. We have kindly listed them below, because we know you're as deegis (dumb) as Mrs. Becenti who is probably your Auntie!!

We hope you have a great year next year because we will not be here! We will never ever be ordered to go to, you Eugene, The Manual Labor Guy (that's you) to do manual labor ever again!

Laterz!
The Girrlz in Dorm A

On the back side of the paper, I wrote: Here is the list:

Manual Labor #5. Congratulations, you get to spend one hour sweeping the dirt at the playground. If there is a rainstorm, you must reschedule your Manual Labor duty....Garnet added. Giggle, laugh!

Manual Labor #4. Congratulations, you get to spend three hours sweeping the bleachers at the football field with a toothbrush. "Ouch..what if he does that one?" "Poor souls.." Laughter.

Manual Labor #3. Congratulations, you get to spend one-hour peeling potatoes in the cafeteria with a dull ass knife… "Ruby! Don't get carried away!" "You know a dull knife can't cut good.." her voice trailed off. By this time, we were the next victims to face the Manual Labor Guy. Kids were either happy to have no

~ 289 ~

manual labor, or very angry they had to re-serve their manual labor because goofy Eugene couldn't figure who mixed up his filing when he was on Dorm Man last month. 'Hmmm… wonder who did that?" We laughed! There was *no* justice without revenge at Red Sands Residential Dormitory! "Ok, final two." Garnet and Ruby huddled around me to quickly get them written.

Manual Labor #2. Congratulations, you get to spend one hour picking Mrs. Hagga's coarse witch whiskers without waking her up from her drunken-stupor. Laughter. "Yeah, that's a good one!" AND DRUM ROLL!!!

Manual Labor # 1. Congratulations, you get to spend two hours re-taping all the cracked windows inside and out. This one is rain or shine, no questions asked.

I added: P.S.: By the way, I really love collecting rocks, so that one is not such a good consequence, and I was very happy to serve this in particular manual labor punishment so many years ago. Smile.

Returned laughter. Giggles. "Okay, how shall we give it to him?

Deep breath as they stood at the office window with their Check-out Sheets. Time was ticking by, and we knew that time would win. Standing in line…one last time…together forever…

Garnet was the last to get the Manual Labor Guy's seal of approval of a clean record. "I never seen you here." Smile with his missing front teeth. Cringe. "That's because I'm not stupid enough to get caught!" She snatched the signed Check-out Sheet out of his hand, to his surprise. With a sinister smile, she handed him *the list* and told him to read it later. He smiled, and shrugged his shoulders up and down, as if…

Next, we went onto the cafeteria and another line of waiting. Ruby was first to get her Check-out sheet signed and just had tell the nice Cafeteria Ladies, "I'll send you a cookbook!" Ruby could damper a special moment. "Well Ruby is Ruby." I knew these ladies as aunties who always cared enough to think of a little girl who spent time at Red Sands Residential Dormitory. The Cafeteria Ladies didn't pay Ruby any mind. I waited for a moment for her to step away.

"I won't be here next years." "Oh.." they all stopped what they were doing to listen to me. I could tell this really annoyed Ruby. "I'm going to St. James to live among the *Bilagánas* (whites) and *Nakai's*" (Mexicans), I teased. It was harder to say goodbye to the Cafeteria Ladies, than I thought.

Gladys took a deep breath, and was first to speak, "We've known you since you were a little girl. Now you're a young lady. You study hard and get a good education. You'll go far." She said this while gesturing her hand in a path forward. Smiling with that familiar twinkle in their eyes, they nodded in agreement. "You stop by to see us sometime." Susie, the tall skinny Cafeteria Lady said, smiling that beautiful smile I will miss.

"Thank you for everything," was all I could manage to say, fighting the tears that were welling up in my eyes. Gladys handed me my Check-out sheet and shyly turned around.

That would be the next to last I saw the ladies that saved my life, feeding me all those weekends. The Good Lord, God, Jesus, the Pope, and above all, The Holy People had always taken care of me, just like Gramps promised a lifetime ago.

At the west end of the cafeteria sat Miss Lilly Bell, the Study Hall Teacher, in all her fake turquoise glory. Her bangles clicked and clanked with her every move. Rumor was that she left and came back from New York, a single woman. The line of students that were at the Manual Labor Guy were patiently waiting while the Cafeteria Ladies served red punch and cookies. Every now and then, a student was sent back to the dorm to look for a checked-out book. I took one last look around. Memories of our first taste of mystery meal, study hall, Miss Bell, and the last dance flashed across my eyes. I headed down the hallway to the noise of the Multipurpose Room, where many parents and grandparents patiently waited to collect their precious children. Deep breath, sigh. Some things change, and some things will continue after we're gone.

We took our check-out sheets so we and handed them in at our last stop, Mrs. Montano, who had been our favorite Matron on Duty. By then, Mrs. Becenti was locked up in her office, eyebrows curled, unhappy as usual. Mrs. Montano gave them the final signature of release. I was happy to see her once last time. When it was my turn to have her sign my check-out sheet, I whispered thank you for caring for me all these years, and that I would not be returning. Her gentle brown eyes and beautiful smile looked up at me, "Where will you be going, Florence?" I told her about St. James and living with my mother." Her head nodded as she smiled, "Oh, that will be nice! No more, Red Sands Residential Dormitory!" She said with a sigh. "Yeah, for sure. NO MORE!" She held my hands inside hers and squeezed them. She stroked my hair and gave me the best side hug I didn't know I needed. "I will always miss you, Mrs. Montano. I will think of you, every time I eat popcorn with extra budda." I looked at her and we smiled. It felt bitter-sweet realizing that we were the same height. I took a few seconds to remember every part of her face and her voice. We were so relieved to finally complete our very last Check-out sheet as unwilling participants of the Bureau of Indian Affairs Residential Dormitory experience.

Ruby quickly raised her voice, as if! "Free at last! Free at last!" Eyes rolling, exasperation, chuckles. Garnet, who was last, joined us at our bunks.

"Whew! That took forever! We had fun writing that Manual Labor list, don't you think, Ruby?"

"Yeah, it's only 12:00 and my ride won't be here for another hour," she replied.

I was kind of glad Ruby would be leaving before Garnet. At least we would have some time alone before forever started. Our only wish was to have spent this time with Clarice. She would've had fun with the Manual Labor Guy's expense! We spent the time playing board games and talking about the past. Ruby paced back and forth, looking out the window. At times, she went outside to check the parking lot. Students and parents were crowded in the Multipurpose Room. Some students were still in line somewhere and parents were patiently waiting. One by one, the students from Dorm A & B hugged their friends and took the exit for 100 days of freedom from Red Sands Residential Dormitory life. I wondered how many, besides the three of us, opted never to return.

Suddenly Ruby startled us, charging into Dorm A and announced in a squeal, "It's time for me to leave, my sister friends!!" Ruby hugged us so tight, whispering promises of keeping in touch and don't forget our times. Ruby was ready to start a new life. She wanted to forget all that she secretly held in so much more than Clarice, Garnet or I ever knew and would never know. Secrets she would never reveal to anyone for but me....Ruby had taken back her life...forever. The sad part is that her family will never understand how much pain she experienced for the better part of 5 years.

We helped her take her belongings to her mother's vehicle. "Well, I guess I'm on my way to Window Rock." Ruby managed to stammer through her tears. Garnet and I hugged her for the last time and the flood began once again as we sadly saw our childhood sister make her way into the passenger seat of her mother's 1974 gold Impala floater. It wasn't long before, her mother backed up and turned around, easing towards the exit and left onto Eerie Street. The familiar thump thump bump before being released from hell's gates... That road that took her and all of us to the Eastern part of Red Sands and Interstate-40, led to the capital of the Great Navajo Nation.

"Did you notice her mother didn't even acknowledge us?" Garnet whispered. "That's ok. She's probably mad that she must take care of Ruby 24/7." Silent exhale followed by giggles.

As she left the grounds of Red Sands for the last time, breathing a sigh of relief, Ruby was no longer afraid of what the future held, no longer a victim of "The Room" and Frankenstein...freedom...silent reprieve. Thank you, Holy

People, God, and The Pope – I made it out of hell and now I create my paradise. Little did Ruby know that that kind of damage would last forever in her mind.

Ruby's mother ordered hamburgers and soda at the Dairy Queen, and they ate as she drove east out of Red Sands. After she had finished her hamburger, Ruby watched the passing landscape in her thoughts drifting. As she spent her last days at Red Sands Dormitory, Ruby remembered all the good times, all the bad times, all those times that shaped her life in many ways. She remembered always being an outcast, being in a group and being ever so lonely. The one thing she would forget forever; was "The Room" and Mr. Levinstein - Frankenstein.

Would another wonderful group of girls ever accept her wherever she ends up next year? Her future was uncertain at that very point in time and she was uncertain about returning home full-time. Tears flooded out of her eyes as they made their way down Interstate 40 while her mother talked endlessly about what was going on with whom??? Yes, the Great Navajo Nation. "Well, at least Merwin is waiting for me, smile, sigh. "Free at last, Good God Almighty, I am Free at last!!" She knew what Martin Luther King meant. Ruby pretended to go to sleep, so her mother would stop talking and turn up the music. "She's a butterfly in mid-July who just can't wait to try on her brand-new wings.." Johnny Cash said it all as she fell into a fitful sleep.

"Well, I'll bet you a jolly rancher sucker, you will be the next one to leave," Garnet broke the silence.

"I hope we both leave at the same time," I replied as we wiped our tears. Let's go get some real food for the last time. We still have time Garnet, and I still have money to burn, girl! Walking to Safeway was surreal. At this point, we didn't even try to sneak off, we just left. It was like we were walking in time, and time knew very well that it would never be the same. Scenes of days gone by flashed throughout our final trek to Safeway. The food kept our thoughts from spilling over and the pop burned unusually hard.

"I bet I can blow a bigger bubble than you, Garnet challenged, even though she knew better than to go against the chewing gum queen! We unwrapped our green apple and grape gum blocks. "Ready, begin!" Straight away, we began to chew the gum hoping to reach the right softness first. Practice bubbles were allowed but when the competition began, it began. All gloves were off when it came to bubble gum contests. Like a thousand times before, I beat Garnet and both of us popped each other's bubble...innocent laughter shadowed by impending separation.

"Do you think we'll be able to heal from this experience?" Garnet's serious side showing up after losing yet another bubble-blowing contest. "

Of course. We've already started healing, just look at how we tamed Ruby!"

We laughed until we rolled over on the park grass nearly choking from the big wad of gum still in our mouths. Missing Ruby, yes Ruby; we did our best to save Ruby from "The Room" at least we tried. Not forgetting, Clarice has been gone a full 24 hours. "I wonder what Clarice is doing right about now?" Garnet thought out loud.

"Seriously." "Yes, we learned enough to last a lifetime and we're going on fourteen, well almost fourteen..." We'll be alright. "You think?" "I know." Silence. Deep breath, heavy hearts impending separation.

"Let's go over and say goodbye to our good friend Harry Billy and good ole' Mrs. Heap our fashion source." Thinking I should say goodbye to as many people I will never see again, or for a long time. The good part is I'll be able to hear Harry Billy's voice on the radio. *Smile.* "Okay, we have enough time to kill." Garnet glanced at me knowing their close connection would somehow end today. Having driven her drunk mother and "father" all over the Great Navajo Nation, she knew that the miles would make visits difficult, and letters would have to suffice. She knew that our daily talks, walks to school, and daily everything would end today.

"Florence, I have admired you for so many different reasons. You are a person of strength and confidence. Honestly, I don't know how you survived all these years practically by yourself." Garnet was looking down as we walked down the sidewalk. "You never showing how lonely it must've been staying at Red Sands Residential Dormitory nearly the entire nine years." Garnet told me how she secretly wished for a Gramps and Gramma like mine. She told me she wished for a place to miss like Tohatchi Flats too. Garnet, you gotta do what you gotta do. Besides, all of this was somehow supposed to be for my own good. I'll keep you posted when I find out what that actually means. Chuckle. " I couldn't have made it without you. You are so strong to drive yourself and your parents to safety and still make it back to Red Sands Residential Dormitory. You don't know how much I prayed for your safety, Garnet!" Hugs.

As we walked, I took the time to admire the stained-glass windows at the church I could confess all my disgust about Red Sands Residential Dormitory, Mrs. Becenti, Mrs. Hagga, and how much I hated **B**eans for **I**ndians **A**lways on the menu. I remember Father Paul laughed so hard when I confessed about tricking Mrs. Hagga with x-lax, but he made sure I said 10 Hail Mary's and promised not to do it again. After each confession, and there were a lot, Sister Mary Louise was aways there to offer me cookies and punch and reminding me to be careful and come again. Chuckle..

Harry Billy was chopping another fine piece of meat for a white couple, so we loitered around the market pretending to shop. Finally, free, we stepped towards his infamous meat counter with the thick curved glass window that covered that fresh meat odor. The familiar smile he gave all his customers before he asked if it was a meat order or a song request, even though he knew very well whom was there, for what… Music was also his passion. He had been reporting the news for KDJI in the Navajo language for 20+ years. Everyone tuned in to KDJI when they came within signal range.

"Well, we came to say goodbye Uncle Harry. We're not coming back to Red Sands Residential Dormitory next year. I stammered. "Oooh, you are moving on. They all do dat..the kids. They all come and go. It's gon be ok...you see." Uncle Harry's smile of assurance was just what we needed. "Well, thank you for coming to see me. I remember seeing you - that leavin' on the jet plane girl"...pointing his lips at me. Blush. "Yeah, those were the days, huh." Embarrassing! "The music is not the same these days, but I still play it when you kids request it. Stop by and see Harry Billy or listen to Crazy Injun Number 9 on KDJI...I'll be here."

Garnet chimed in, "Uncle Harry, you're the best! We will miss you and yes, we will listen to you on KDJI...Crazy Injun Number 9!"

"So long and just for you," he pointed his lips at me, as he cleaned his hands and walked over to his turntable, and within seconds, "All my bags are packed, I'm ready to go..." drifted through the air and chills ran down my spine. This time it was me who had packed my bags and yes, I was ready to go. Hold it together, Flo! As we made our way towards the door, we took one last look at our friend, Harry, who was already dealing with another customer. He waved as we closed the door, and left that part of our past right there, with that song. "I'ma leavin' on a jet plane..." Smile.

Saying goodbye to Harry Billy was harder than we expected. Though we barely knew him, there were tears of sadness knowing we would also be leaving Harry Billy today. Leaving him was closing another chapter in our lives. Unsettled silence...deep breath...sigh... "So kiss me and smile for me...tell me that you'll wait for me..." The music faded into the air, drifting into the bustle of traffic.

Mrs. Heap was busy doing her thrift shop work with her team of three. The place had grown so much that she had to hire help. The doorbell signaled our presence and Mrs. Heap looked up with a smile - that familiar smile. "Well, hello! Now what can I do for you two ladies today?" Her usual greeting. I don't think Mrs. Heap ever had a bad day!

"We're here to see anything you might have that's new," I responded remembering I had money.

"We just received these here on the rack. Some are priced and others are negotiable as usual... I'll be over here if you need anything." Mrs. Heap was busy with the monthly delivery from Deseret Industries

Garnet and I always went for the granny clothes and told each how good they would look on each other. I found a humungous short sleeved white polyester shirt with big red and black circles dots plastered all over the thing. "Hey, this looks like your style." I joked.

"Oh, no...*black* is definitely your color, Flo."

Nobody called me "Flo" except my friends and that was something I unexpectedly missed. Sadness. I bit my lip, turned my back holding back tears.

"I found the perfect night gown for you, Garnet!" She looked up looking up to see a granny house dress with faded blue flowers and white lace. I held it next to my neck and put on a silly straw hat that had fake pink flowers. We laughed so hard, Mrs. Heap cleared her throat and asked again if we needed help.

"Umm, no, we're good." Garnet chuckled... I turned my head and silently chuckled. I put the house dress and hat away and went shopping. I mean, serious shopping.. Giggle.. I ended up spending $15.38 on three not so worn jeans, a couple of button-down shirts, and six white tube socks, so I would be ready for the ranch life I would be waking up to in a matter of hours. This should get me through the summer, I thought. Garnet bought two pairs of jeans, a couple of T-shirts with butterflies and hearts, and some hair ties. I looked at Garnet, knowing that yes, in a matter of hours our lives would become a new normal, and those memories were all that we had after today.

"Let's make sure we listen to KDJI, at the same time! It'll be like we're together!" I quietly said.

"Come on Flo, we gotta get back." Garnet was an even-tempered person who suddenly turned into an opinionated person on the last day of our lives together. I knew it. I knew that Garnet was secretly harboring all these pent-up opinions but never expressed them. She would be okay.

We never went back to Heap's Thrift Store again. It would be nice to think that Harry Billy would always be our guiding voice on the airwaves, but that was just wishful thinking.

Our walk back to Red Sands Residential Dormitory would be our last walk together…our last talk together…our last moments as wards of the almighty Bureau of Indian Affairs…expected silence, deep breath..relief..followed by sadness Sigh.

We were hanging around on the swings, not more than ten minutes and the next thing we knew we spotted a gold Impala driving through the entrance. Behind her was what looked like Clarice and her parents' truck! My eyes lit up Gramps and Gramma in a brand new 19 and 74 GMC pickup truck. I knew it was them because the stock rack was ladened with a ball of bailing wire hanging on for dear life! I smiled, "Look, my new ride home!" Garnet's mother and little brothers were the last to drive in. Garnet smiled…we would leave together…as it should be… Four vehicles caravanned through the entrance each with a thump, thump, bump making their way off Eerie Street. My dreams have come true! Clarice!! I thought I would never see you again, or at least for a long, long, long time! And how did you get away from not going through the check-out? I screamed as I practically yanked Clarice out of her vehicle.

"Turns out we stayed in Red Sands to get jewelry supplies and ended up staying the night at the Wigwam motel. That was a weird experience! Anyway, I was so heartbroken that my parents thought of the idea. Today, we sort of waited at the Hwy 77 turn-off until we spotted Ruby's mom. We waved her down. It wasn't more than ten minutes that your Grandparents went by, then we followed them all the way here. We just happened to see Ruby's mom gassing up at Shell station before they went onto Interstate. We stopped by and asked if they wanted to follow us back to Red

Sands Residential Dormitory, one last time." Clarice was out of breath with excitement, as she hugged her sisters.

"I didn't sleep a wink last night! I thought when I saw you disappear down the street Clarice, that, that was it. I am so relieved, right now!" Garnet chimed in.

Gramps and Gramma were met with unexpected hugs from the girls…and I stepped forward waiting an eternity for that familiar smell, those familiar hands, familiar "Hello Grandchild." I was home…finally.

"Gramps, Gramma, these are my sisters…we've been here together since kindergarten."

"Yea, we know exactly how to get to Tohatchi Flats, too!" Ruby announced.

Gramps hazel green eyes peered down over his glasses and said, "That's what you think." Gramps told Ruby. Then he chuckled. Gramma smiled. We burst out laughing.

Ruby blushed and said, "Yah that's what I know." Ruby red faced…yes Ruby being Ruby. Gramps gave me a slight glance, and I just shrugged my shoulders.

"Get your luggage…we have a long way to travel Grandchild." Gramma shook hands with the parents and began conversating in Navajo.

The foursome ascended hand in hand, one last time up the cement steps and into Red Sands Residential Dormitory and to the end of Dorm A. The end of the year bustle greeted them one last time…forever. We collected our belongings. In true Ruby fashion, she pulled out her switchblade and announced she would leave her imprint! "

"Ruby, put that weapon away! Why would you want to leave any of yourself here? Bad enough, our innocent spirits have to linger around here because we won't forget our time here." Clarice's wisdom was on point.

"Oh, NO! I'm not leaving my spirit here! I already gave this shit hole enough. You're right!" Ruby snapped the switchblade shut and tucked it in her pocket.

"Ruby, lower your voice!" Garnet demanded. The few girls that were waiting stood up to listen to the noise. "Ok, Ok, Ruby was just being Ruby."

As we made our way into the familiar Multipurpose Room, we could not help but be flooded with memories of our childhood. The moments that would burn forever in our minds, and those we chose to forget and never repeat. We thought of the times that would always be precious and would last a lifetime. "Well, I just had to take one more look at the place where I spent my childhood and remember never to put my kids through anything like this," Clarice admitted. Ruby, Garnet, and I nodded in agreement. "For our own good," I added…our eyes met.

The smell of tonight's mystery dinner emanated from the kitchen as we carried out the last of our belongings. "Poor souls who have to eat that tonight," Garnet lamented. "On the other hand, we might wish for mystery food once we get home…maybe…probably not."

"NO fuckin' way", Ruby professed!

Together we let out a "RUBY!!" Heads shaking followed familiar laughter…and then a deep breath that shuttered through our veins.

One last time, that unmistakable feeling fell upon us, a solemn, reverent cold shudder crept over our minds when the heavy metal double prison doors slammed behind us, releasing us, as if we belonged to the number they issued us nine long years ago, and forever. That sound would echo in our minds like day one had just turned to day two, a lifetime ago. The prison sentence was over, and life would begin anew!

We hugged each other one last time. We climbed into our vehicles with a sense of sadness and relief. Sigh. One by one, we caravanned out of Red Sands Residential Dormitory compound with a thump, thump, bump onto Eerie Street and into the future.

To her amazement, what Garnet discovered was a sober Mom who converted to Mormonism, and another marriage. Her brothers, who seemed to have shaken off that scared look, happily sat in the back seat, ready to be a family. "Ready to go. Anybody hungry? How 'bout some Kentucky Fried Chiggen?" Her mother suggested... 'No! It's gonna be McDonalds, with the special sauce!" Garnet demanded, surprised by her boldness. The boys cheered singing, "Two all-beef patties, special sauce, lettuce, cheese, pickles, onions on a sesame seed bun!" Garnet felt good for once in her life, *and* she didn't have to drive home. Maybe she could be the kid, not the adult – finally.

I sat in my cherished spot between Gramps and Gramma. Their smiling eyes met as Gramps eased over the exit with a thump thump bump – stock rack shifting this way and that while hanging on to the familiar ball of bailing wire for those just in case moments. Even though I was a teenager, I nestled myself next to Gramps, like I did so many times before. I couldn't believe the time was finally here for me to actually step into the change I had been feeling all year long and finally learn why this was for my own good. I fell asleep while Gramps whistled his usual song and Gramma crocheted in silence. Comfortable silence...freedom. It was pitch dark, except for the stars that twinkled over Tohatchi Flats. The moon hid behind rain clouds, illuminating a glowing outline. The air was crisp as the Holy Winds would hoover over Mother Earth, until the rising sun beams of light grew in the eastern horizon. When Gramps turned the pickup truck onto the bumpy road signaling, the last 15 miles to Tohatchi Flats, I woke up. I was so restless and anxious that the whole day was exhausting. "We thought you were going to sleep all night, the way you were snoring." Gramps teased. "Gramps! I do not snore, I'm a lady." Smile. Gramps let out a big laugh and explained to Gramma what I had said. "*Nádinii*" "She always says that.." We made the familiar turn around the hill. The smoke was drifting into the darkness. The light of the moon slowly brightened the dark shadows to reveal the Stone House, my castle! I am truly home, finally home. Gramma giggled, stepping down from the truck. The smell of cedar wood burning and a slight breeze. I could hear talking and laughing coming from the Stone House and when I stepped in, where my mom, uncles, and aunties were planning for the weekend. My cousins were milling around in the Shade House. I looked around and of course, nothing had changed. "Mom!" I dove into my mother's arms while my uncles and aunties gathered around. Tears of joy, relief, uncertainty. Home. Finally. I'm home...

Each of my sisters arrived home with a whole lot of emotions, knowing we made it out of Red Sands Residential Dormitory – Dorm A- "Home of **B**rutality on **I**ndians of **A**merica". While we had no choice but to serve a nine-year sentence, we realized we had to look toward our future. A future without regimented schedules and asinine punishment dished out by Eugene, the Manual Labor geek. Sadly, we soon realized our future would be walked without each other by our sides.

For me, I realized Red Sands Residential Dormitory was a testing ground for what was to come, but for now, I was going to relish my time with my beloved mom, Gramps, Gramma, and family. Time spent nestling in the little castle built with love, out on Tohatchi Flats. It took several years for me to overcome the feeling of anxiety I felt at the end of July knowing that was when I would've had to return to Red Sands Residential Dormitory. In the end, trauma and separation anxiety never seem to heal.

Chapter 27 – Life After Red Sands
Residential Dormitory

Sometimes life lets you experience reality, even though it was kept from you, "for your own good." For me, life at St. James was like stepping into another world – the "real" world. The town was full of whites and Mexicans. Whites on the West side of the town and the Mexicans on the East side. The road that separated them led south to a small farm town and on to Morenci, a silver mine The Mexicans were of the Catholic faith, lived in what looked like the stone house, built a 100 years ago. When I walked down 2nd Street it was easy to tell who lived where, by the homes in which they lived. The majority of the whites were of the Mormon faith and lived in the two-story homes with the nice lawn and white picket fences. The rest of them, who were not Mormon lived in modest older homes on the North side of town, near St. James Rodeo Grounds.

St. James was in the middle of nowhere! It took an hour to drive the only road that led north out of St. James to I-40 and east to Gallup, New Mexico. Ther one road that went through the town from west to east. I found a pamphlet in Charles Grant's Gas Station that told of St. James' history, and of how in 1872, Spanish pioneers traveled along the Little Colorado River in search of gold. Eyes rolling. It seems like everywhere the Spaniards went, they always left behind a huge stone church with stain-glass windows, and the word of their Lord and Savior. Before them, people like Juan de Onate traveled north in search of the Seven Cities of Cibola, with no avail. He would later become the first Spanish governor of the colony of Santa Fe de Nuevo Mexico, in 1605. It took two hundred years for Mexicans and whites, mostly Mormons, to squat on Native lands in what became the four corners. The people from Mexico who settled in St. James farmed and raised sheep. Yes, sheep.

My mother and I lived in a three-bedroom 14'x70' used trailer she purchased, and had it parked at Grant's Mobile Home Park, on the west side of St. James. I found Mr. Grant and his family were good people. I had neighborhood friends that were white,

Mexican, and Vietnamese. It was weird living in St. James. My mother seemed to like her job, but it required her to travel all over the Promised Land, which was a 60-mile drive one way...that was, if she just went to Lupton Chapter House. Otherwise, a one-way trip could be as far as 150 miles. When she arrived home, it was usually late, and I was sound asleep. I had to get used to being alone, really alone, in my 10'x10' shoebox of a room.

I deeply missed my friends. I rushed home to see if I had received a letter from them. At first, the letters came often, but as time went on and the girls became busy with their own lives, and the letters showed up occasionally, even though I wrote them all the time. For months, I was miserable. If it weren't for the weekend trips to Tohatchi Flats, I would probably go insane with loneliness...a different kind of loneliness. I missed being able to walk around and visit different stores at Red Sands. They didn't even have a Radio Station and absolutely no signs of Native Americans existence, except my mother and me. St. James was a different story, because there was one main road and side streets full of houses and government buildings. St. James Market was the only grocery store and Cleveland Street spanned from West to East and became Route 191 which led to I-40. After a week of staying in our trailer watching endless "continuing stories," as my mother referred to Soap Operas, I resolved to find some friends at church...yes, church.

Having spent the month of June and the 4th of July out at Tohatchi Flats, my mother thought I should get used to St. James, and so it was that I stepped into another world, the one that she promised me a lifetime ago. The world I always longed for with my mother, the one I always imagined while imprisoned at Red Sands Residential Dormitory, was far from the imaginary life I encountered in real time, here at St. James.

Breathing a sigh of discontent, I thought I had to get out of the confines of that small trailer called home. I now knew what Clarice complained about, how ironic. Walking down the sidewalk, I couldn't believe that I even missed Red Sands Residential Dormitory compound. In the middle of town, there was a small market called Turley's Mercantile, and a Mobile gas station. Across from St. James High School was Mom's Café where I learned to love the green chili French fries and Mexican food. The St. James Motel housed the other restaurant in town. It was more like a Diner with a wrap-around counter and blue vinyl stools with silver legs. Several small square white tables with the same silver legs were placed along the vast curved window that spanned from the ceiling to the half wall below. Everything was blue or light blue and off white – Navajo white of all things! I thought my eyes deceived me when I saw that color and then felt sad as memories flashed across my mind and how I never thought seeing that color would bring some kind of comfort. Red Sands Residential Dormitory will never leave me. The big windows could blind a person if they looked straight at them in the morning hours. It's a miracle the early morning reflection didn't bounce off like a magnifying glass and ignite a fire somewhere... Da Nabajo white probably kept the place cool and from burning down... hmmm.chuckle..

I found comfort at St. Mary's Catholic Church, founded in 1649 by Franciscan Friars. The church was made of red stones with wooden pews that were used by three hundred years of parishioners. Like at Red Sands, I found solace at church in times of loneliness, and I soon began attending Wednesday religion classes after school to kill time. Sister Teresa always had a welcoming smile and a gentle hand to guide the class to understand the Scriptures. St. Mary's was easily a mile from Grant's Trailer Park and was the last building on the east end of St. James, just before you reach The Little Colorado River. It was once a river that flowed year-round, but with the invention of plumbing the water soon dried up. Now, it is only filled with water whenever there was a downpour, which only happened during the spring and summer. The vast flat land that followed was filled with sagebrush and juniper trees. The sand was red and had lots of red and a few black rocks that protruded along the hills. It took an hour to drive to Interstate 40 and another 45 minutes to Gallup, New Mexico. The road that seemed to span for miles west out of St. James led to another Mormon "founded" town of Show

Low, which also led to the big city of Phoenix. For some reason, my mother and I never traveled down that road. I found a map at Grant's gas station and discovered where the road led, and that was where Phoenix was - the capital of Arizona. There was another road that went straight down the map to Tucson, where the University of Arizona is. I once asked my mother why we never went to Show Low or Phoenix. She stopped for a minute while doing her paperwork at the kitchen table, and responded, "I don't have any business over that way."

I decided that my mother was a boring person who lived a mundane life. I vaguely remember how she used to always in a good mood while music filled our Tennessee home. I dared myself to ask her to cook neck bone, collard green, buttery grits, and southern style pinto beans. Her eyebrows quickly curled, as she gruffly claimed, "They don't sell that kind of food here." That was the end of that period. I also didn't dare ask her about my dad. It had been a decade since I saw him, and by then I had forgotten what he looked like. For the longest time, I refused to think of the time in my life that started with a long bus ride across America and into oblivion.

Father Gonzales had a strong deep voice that made anyone believe in the words of the scriptures and there was something to learn in every sermon, like the pieces to a puzzle. At times, I heard Gramps' wisdom coming from the mouth of Father Gonzales, and he learned to greet me by name, always ending with a nod and the symbol of the cross and a "The Lord Be With, You, Florence."

St. James Cafe was where I learned to love to stop, after church. My order of a slice of apple pie and a cup of coffee became routine. Katie, the blonde waitress, looked at me weird when I ordered coffee, being so young and always alone. She soon learned to expect the order, adding an extra scoop of vanilla ice cream from time to time. Katie had never met a Navajo before and was so interested in hearing about the Wild West, and I sometimes made things up to keep her happy with intrigue. At least Katie helped me not to feel so lonely, and I found myself looking forward to seeing her each Sunday. From time to time, my mother and I would race back from Tohatchi Flats early Sunday morning, so that I could attend afternoon Mass. Otherwise, I would have to go to the evening Mass, which was more serious and all in Spanish. All the widows showed up in their black dresses, with black lace covering their faces, which was kind of creepy and sad at the same time. It was weird that all the whites went to the Mormon church, and all the Mexicans went to the Catholics church.

The thing that kept this knock-about town alive was that St. James were the government buildings, along with the usual police and fire department. Pioneer Elementary went from kindergarten to 6th grade. Kids went to St. James High School from 7th grade on up, because there weren't enough students to have a junior high. I decided to join the Thespian Club and Choir during the years I was in St. James, but I never felt like I belonged there. My mother never saw any of the plays we put on, because she was forever out of town. I loved singing in the choir, led by Mr. Allen who was so dedicated to tuning our voices. St. James Honor Choir won State in 1975, after being runner-up two years before. That was a good feeling. Joining these Clubs also meant I didn't have to sit around the trailer and hear the silence buzz in my ears. I had to keep busy, or I would go crazy!

Gramps had told us one way of knowing how to live in both worlds is to understand what they believe in and to know our sacred Navajo prayers. I treasured his words as I learned to live on my own, there in St. James, Arizona. I heard Gramps' voice repeat my favorite story, the Creation Story and all the lessons the black, yellow, blue, and glittering world taught. The one lesson that started with, "It's for your own good, Grandchild," remained a mystery, at this point. His voice, stories, and wisdom swirled into the wind, like the way smoke swirls into a circle, dissipating into the ages. Like many years before, Gramps talked about preparing for the beginning of the school year prayer for all the kids. Ceremonies and weekends were always something to look forward to, and I began a new reason to count the days, hours, minutes… old habits are hard to break. Smile, sarcastic sigh. "For your own good…isss" Ha! For sure, I had to keep busy, so I would have some great stories to write down and send to my sisters.

Mr. Tillotson, my history teacher, assigned the students to write something about the history of St. James or the State of Arizona. So, I decided to write about how religion and the search for gold, was the main reason St. James became a town, and Arizona a state. One of my paragraphs read, "Conversion to Christianity crept onto Navajoland and other tribal lands in the Southwest, from as early as the 1600's. With the onset of the Spaniards who brought Catholicism, and their greed for the silver and yellow metal, were sent from Spain with the blessings of the Catholic Church and the support of Spain's King and Queen. For a long time, Catholicism was the only religion besides respective traditional Native American beliefs. They always managed to find a way to build huge churches, with forced labor or from their converted native parishioners. There is no record of them finding the Seven Cities of Cibola where claims of riches and gold were buried. By 1868, and the end of the Navajo imprisonment at Ft. Sumner, many religious societies such as Pentecostals, Baptists, Methodists, Holy Rollers, Mormons, and others sought parishioners among the Navajo, Apache, Ute, and Pueblo people. There was a definite need not only to civilize Indians but to Christianize us…as if… 1868 was also the same year that the U.S. declared any Hispanic born in the United States a Citizen with all the rights. Two reasons why Mexicans settled in St James in 1872 was citizenship and the Dawes Act which allowed non-Indians to claim land that belonged to Indians since the beginning of time. As time went on, Navajoland has become riddled with many different religions. If one drives across the reservation, they will see at least five different religions represented in very small communities. My paper went on to talk about how the State of Arizona was established and how people had learned to live side by side here in St. James, Arizona.

Mr. Tillotson questioned me about my sources, but when I produced documents sent by the University of Arizona Library, he quickly gave my essay back with a big fat B+! I refused to accept the grade and waited after school to approach Mr. Tillotson. I could tell he didn't like me by the smirk on his face. I showed him the places where I found my evidence. I even showed him the envelope that the documents were sent in. He had no choice but to change my grade to an A+! Little victories like that helped me gain confidence.

My school bus trip to Phoenix was another experience I will never forget. Clarice was right! Forget about these small towns, Phoenix was huge! I couldn't believe how big the shopping mall was with all those stores in one place. I was sold. I made up my mind to move to Tucson after high school, but first I had to take a trip there to see it for myself. The brochures in the counselor's office showed a little bit of the campus, though. I was undecided if I wanted to go that far away from home. In the end, I decided Tohatchi Flats would always remain the same, …well maybe.

Even though I honored my traditional side, and I followed Gramps' lead, I also was a member of the Catholic Church. I dedicated my time to church every Wednesday and Sunday at St. James. All those weekends I spent alone at Red Sands Residential Dormitory also included one or two hours at St. Francis, rain or shine. St. Francis had a lot of stained-glass windows and a huge old wooden cross brought from Spain. For centuries, Jesus' sad eyes merciful looked down at them. It hung majestically from the ceiling, behind the huge wooden podium. Here, St. Mary Catholic Church was older than St. Francis. It housed the traditional pictures of the 10 Commandments, statutes of Our Lady of Guadalupe, baby Jesus, and Joseph, Mary. Father Gonzales wore a long brown robe with a thick white rope. He preached from a book that was much older and bigger than Father Paul's and probably was converted into English a century ago. The original Spanish version of the Bible brought from Spain had been used for centuries at St. Mary's. Father Gonzales took special care to place this Bible in a glass case to keep the words from fading into history. Everything about St. Mary's was old, even the adobe fence that surrounded the whole compound had been mended for three hundred years. It reminded me of how Mr. Yazzie and his predecessors mended fences at Red Sands Residential Dormitory for decades. Every Sunday I woke early and quietly got ready, careful not to wake my mother. I rushed to beat the ringing of the old bell that reminded me services would begin in 30 minutes. It rang so loud everyone across St. James could hear it for miles around. I noticed that after the last ring drifted into the wind, the roosters cawed, and the cows mooed. By fourteen, I had lived in Tennessee, in Klagetoh, in Tohatchi Flats, in Red Sands, and here St. James. I decided to accept the life I had had and vowed to find a way to make it better when I was on my own. I could hear Clarice say, "What do you mean, Flo? You are on your own!" Smirk.. It took me a while, but I soon learned what Father Gonzales was saying when the sermon was in Spanish. I even learned to sing some of the songs in Spanish. Life was as good as I made it.

I often wondered what my sisters were doing. They used to write every week and after two years; I only received a letter from Clarice and Garnet every now and then. Ruby must be keeping herself so busy that she didn't have time to write to any of us. The promises we made were just that, promises. I thought Clarence was supposed to move to St. James, but he never did, so I learned to live with a new kind of normal – by myself.

Then, at the beginning of junior year, Clarence moved to town…yes Clarence. When Clarence and his parents moved to St. James it was much better for me to bear. Even though I never really gave him the attention he wanted at Red Sands Residential Dormitory, I secretly kept all his notes…notes from days gone by. I soon learned to enjoy his company on a daily basis…which was a strange thing in and of itself. Clarence and I were the only Navajos attending school at St. James High School – Home of the Redskins, although we were the only "Redskins" there. In fact, Clarence, his family, my mother, and I were the only Navajos living in St. James or anywhere in a 50-mile radius.

Gone were the days of living among Navajos and the regimented schedule with people hovering, watching, recording our every move, in the name of the almighty dollar. What was striking to me was that even though I lived with my mother, I still felt alone…days, minutes, seconds…always alone. Never once, while living at Red Sands Residential Dormitory did, did I ever think I would long to return to that life! Reality bites.

Amidst the racism and snide remarks, I outsmarted and outscored the white kids during high school years. It was funny to see all those white kids ask each other who the kid was that scored the highest grade, because grades were posted by our school number. I waited until after school to check my grades. High school was easy, because I was so disciplined by the regimented life at Red Sands Residential Dormitory. While my classmates enjoyed athletics, partying, and dating, I spent my time staying ahead. I couldn't help but feel sorry for Clarence, who was not able to adjust to St. James. I spent many hours at the library helping him with his schoolwork, so he could stay in school. Influenced by his Mexican friends, Clarence soon began to drink and do drugs…yes drugs…the evil marijuana to be exact.

Many of Clarence and his new friends partied at the Concho Reservoir where the winding road caused many of them to drive right into the water, drowning them. I prayed he wouldn't end up at the bottom of the reservoir like decades of teens. Suicide by water was something the Medicine Men couldn't undo and spirits who succumb to that kind of death wandered endlessly in between the living and the dead. Nobody wanted that kind of death. So, I prayed every day for Clarence, although I knew that some prayers would never be answered, and only prolonged the inevitable.

Nevertheless, Clarence was constantly showing up at my house drunk, high, and acting like a fool. The neighbors complained to my mother, and I finally told him not to come around intoxicated or *I* would call the police.

Clarence professed his love to me many times and eventually we became a couple, but the evil alcohol and marijuana drew him down a miserable spiral. He left St. James by the beginning of summer, never to be seen by anyone again. I would think of him often and knew that his life was leading down the wrong path. I would think of us growing up at Red Sands Residential Dormitory…how innocent we were…how things would have been different if we could have stayed at Red Sands Residential

Dormitory. No, that wasn't going to happen. Destiny was destiny. Sadly, Clarence left his whole soul at Red Sands Residential Dormitory...he would never recover..

We did have many fun times together at St. James, but, within one year Clarence's dad quit his job at the generating plant, and got another job with Pacific Railroad, so they moved to a small house in Manuelito, west of Gallup. Clarence found new friends who weren't any different from the ones he left behind at St. James. He never finished high school, sadly becoming one of those "drunken Indians" the local news had the nerve to exploit. But it was true. Any day, any time, you could find him in American Bar or in the alleys passed out...like my dad...I hated Gallup for many reason – but mostly that..

Meanwhile, life at home with Mom was not what I had expected it to be. My mother had a life of her *own* and pretty much left me at home alone for the whole week – every week....where did I experience that??? No wonder I never got picked up. At times, she would come home from work enraged, because the laundry was not washed, or her work clothes were not pressed just right - just like Mrs. Becenti. It didn't take long for me to understand what, "For your own good" meant. Gramps and Gramma never spoke a negative word about any one...they just tried to teach us all by example... How naive I was to think my new-found freedom was a good thing. Some things need to be experienced firsthand, even if they weren't good...for my own good... deep breath, sigh...carry on..

These were times I was severely beaten with a hanger or a belt. For the first time in my life, I was physically abused. In all those years of wishing to escape the abuse of the Red Sands Residential Dormitory, I found myself wishing to be back there, but that wasn't going to happen. Within the first four months, I remember beginning to miss Red Sand Residential Dormitory's regularly scheduled meals and regularly scheduled events. I even missed the nights sleeping on that stiff cardboard of a bed and hearing the occasional squeak of the metal bed frame. There were no ghosts I could detect here like at Red Sands Residential Dormitory. No noises to keep me guessing where the creaks and knocks were coming from… I realized that the noises we heard were from Red Sands Residential Dormitory aging right before our ears and eyes…and the ghosts were probably the sad memories of past students who left Red Sands Residential Dormitory for their own good or not. Irony bites..

Most of all, I missed the company of my sisters. I spent my time sitting in my room reading, and re-read the letters they had sent talking about their school and new friends…yes new friends…deep breath…sigh…Code3: Jealous.. sigh..

I never made any real friends at St. James High School. My only friends were my library books and when he was sober, Clarence. After he left, I found myself taking adventures to 17th century France and far-away places in the many romance novels I found at Mr. Garcia's Thrift Store. I kept many things bottled up until one day Miss. Larimore, my English Teacher, counseled me about life and how I did have control over it. She talked about how I needed to think about my future because it would come knocking at the end of senior year, ready or not…and that it's going to be a good life or a life of struggle. "The road to success is education", she ended our conversation, and by my senior year, I was determined to reach my new goal. Miss Larimore sounded just like Gramps who imparted his infinite wisdom every time he dropped me off at the doors of Red Sands Residential Dormitory a lifetime ago, ending with how it was for my own good. Until then, I never had a teacher talk about having control of my own life once I got out of high school. Miss Larimore must've had a Gramps like mine… smile…reality doesn't have racial bias when it comes to life's lessons… I thought of a lot of things on my lonely walks home..deep breath, silent tears. Irony. Books never left me, they never argued, and they never abused me. They were just words stuck in a time capsule; waiting for gentle hands to open the first page; the reader captivated to the end. The only thing was I had to return the ones I checked out from the library. Those books were my borrowed friends. Gramps was right again, "Grandchild, a good story never dies, it just lingers in your mind until you read it again with new eyes."

There came a time, during my sophomore year, when I had had enough of my mother's abuse; I finally challenged her and almost beat her up. I could not believe all the rage and that I actually slapped my mother...Gramps and Gramma would not approve of such behavior, period! "Watch your words, Grandchild..." I had no choice but to make it stop, for my own good.

After it was all over, we never spoke about it. My mother began to treat me like a young adult, giving me the keys to the car, and more spending money. Control. I wrote and wrote and wrote...just like always. I discovered a wall of honeysuckles and just about every yard had different flowers along the path to school. These were neatly dried and added to my Flower Notebook. Sheets and sheets of my ideas, of the world, of anything. My mother often complained that my writing was taking up too much space, but that did not stop me from writing. After a life of living alone, I realized my mother didn't know me at all. It hurt to know she didn't even want to get to know me - her only child. Maybe she was embarrassed or felt guilty that she abandoned and neglected me. Maybe my mother saw the man she loved and hated in my eyes. It could be the way I spoke that made her roll her eyes. All I knew was that I didn't know my mother at all either.

I began to store my writings and secret manuscript, underneath the trailer in those plastic storage boxes, because there was no more room in my bedroom or the old hayloft at the ranch. Gramps made my uncles reinforce the floor because it began to sag from the weight. Gramps insisted that the footlockers stay there until I was ready to pick them up. In those sheets was my life and my identity.. .my soul.. the one I left at Red Sands Residential Dormitory. It was my childhood and memories of days gone by, when I lived in a place called Dorm A and then moved to a strange town called St. James, "Home of the Redskins"...where I was actually the only "Redskin" that attended school there... chuckle, deep breath...Irony.

Chapter 28 – Senior Year & Learning My History

During my senior year, I drove out to Tohatchi Flats alone to hand deliver an invitation and graduation picture to my beloved grandparents. As I turned off U.S. 666 and onto the fifteen mile stretch of dirt road, I stopped to stretch my legs. I turned west to face Chuska Mountain, as cars whipped passed going north or south. The warm anabatic winds warned me that a dust devil could whip up at any moment. As usual Uncle Leonard's tractor work made driving easy across the dusty fifteen miles. I looked across the desert plains and imagined the field of sunflowers my Gramma loved to remember. Passing the windmill that slowly rotated with the wind, my mind went to carefree days of endless playing and exploring with my cousins. Our laughter echoed as the windmill cranked endlessly, pumping water for the thirsty cattle, and served as the source of our water fight. I finally approached the friendly mesa, went around the familiar sandstone hill, and there stood my Stone Castle. The Stone Castle stood still the test of time. Gramps was milling around the corral, looking up and waved. His truck, "Bluebird," waited outside loaded down with the stock rack, which meant they were preparing to travel up the mountain with the horses, to their ranch at Asaayi. He took his time walking towards me, as I parked. I noticed that Gramps was limping, and his breath was labored. His once dark hair was almost completely white. I took a deep breath. At that moment, it occurred to me how small the Stone House, my castle, really was.. Gramma peered out the window and greeted me at the door. "*Yá'át'ééh Shíyázhí, dá'ó'sá'.*" Hello, my child, it's time to eat. "Hi, Gramps! Gramma!" I was greeted with the same hugs, same loving faces, and I knew I was home. The decisions Gramps and Gramma made for me saved my life. Same smell, same hands, same, "Hello Grandchild, how have you been?"…same hazel green eyes looking over his glasses. Always happy to see me…some things should never change…deep breath. Sigh…Home.

As I entered the one-room home, the heat and smell of cedar wood hissing and crackling, while the light of the fire danced along the newly painted walls. Gramps, what color is this paint? "Nabaho White." You gotta be kidding me!! I laughed out loud. Gramma didn't seem to understand, but years ago, on one of our drives, I read Gramps my poem. It was an inside joke. The smell of Folgers coffee..perc, perc, percolating, fresh goats' milk, fresh mutton stew and Gramma's delicious tortillas greeted me…it was as if they had waited for my next return to Tohatchi Flats. My grandparents, waiting in time, kept the fire going– waiting for a visitor was more than I could bear. I set about scooping up bowls of stew, and pouring coffee for my grandparents, as they did for me a lifetime ago. I wished this time would never end, but I knew it would, it had to. Gramma's rugs took longer to finish…Gramps labored in his walk… The love remained the same. Deep breath…sigh… I noticed the pictures I had drawn for them, still posted here and there on the wall, along with my cousin's artwork. My Grandparents lived for our visits, but over time, few of us did. Gramps carefully opened my graduation announcement with a proud smile and interpreted its content to Gramma, who also smiled. "You did good, Grandchild. Education is the path to a good life." I beamed with pride. Everything I did was for their approval. Every award was earned on their behalf. We spent the night talking about my plans for college, about the horses that needed to be taken up to the mountains, about the new ones that needed branding, about the sheep that needed to be sheared…everyday life…that was Tohatchi Flats.

I maneuvered the roll away bed and got ready for bed. Grandma still smelled like cinnamon and vanilla. It didn't take long for me to fall into a deep sleep into the night. Peace….in the Glittering World, Monsters Slayer, well at least for that day.. different Monsters to be sure… sleep… The next morning, after I cooked breakfast, we took an hour to visit before I left to return to St. James. To my surprise, Gramma handed me a beautiful gray, white, and black diamond designed rug. She shuffled inside her small pink suitcase and pulled out a beautiful silver bracelet with three turquoise stones. She said some words in Navajo that I couldn't understand. Embarrassed, I looked at Gramps for an interpretation. "Your Gramma had that made for you. She said, she better not ever see either of them at the pawn shop." We both burst out laughing. "I will cherish these forever, Gramma and Gramps! Thank you so much!" Exchanged hugs and a few tears shed. Gramps burned some cedar and said a protection prayer for me, for my trip back to St. James, and for my plans for college.

Hózhó Nahasdlii..
Hózhó Nahasdlii.
Hózhó Nahasdlii,
Hózhó Nahasdlii.
It is finished in Beauty.

The Tohatchi winds had shifted with another door to step through, in my path of solitude. Inevitably led to more choices, my choices. "Grandchild, you study hard. We'll be there for your graduation." More tears, hugs, and goodbyes.

As I reluctantly traveled away from my Stone Castle, I had to face the reality that my Gramps and Gramma had grown old, and I knew that the next time I returned to Tohatchi Flats, things would be different.

In May of 1977, I was the first Native American to graduate from St. James High School. For a moment, I thought Clarence should be graduating, too. Graduation night, I looked into the crowd for my dad, and for Clarence's friendly face, but they were nowhere to be found. They put two tables together for us at Mom's Mexican Restaurant. The food was delicious! My mom, Gramps, uncles, aunties, and some of my cousins took turns telling me how proud they were, and each gave some words of wisdom. My cousins were happy to scarf their enchiladas, tacos, chips, and salsa! I felt great! I felt like I finally had control of my life, and the next decisions were up to me – but then again, weren't they always up to me? There were other students and their family's celebrating graduation. Momma Rodriguez had hired Mariachi Azteca De Oro to serenade us. They came to our table and sang a song of celebration called, "Mujeres Divinas", which translates to divine women. I felt very special that day! One of the singers started speaking Spanish to me, but I replied, "No habla Espanol, mi Indios." He laughed and said, "Oh, I thought you were Mexican!" "I know, I get that a lot. Thank you so much for the song!" I gave him a $10.00 bill, like I saw the other people do, after they sang. By the end of dinner, we were stuffed, and I could tell my grandparents were tired from the long drive and excitement of the day.

What I didn't know, was Clarence had hitch-hiked the 84 miles from Gallup the night before and stayed with his Mexican party friends. Too embarrassed and drunk, Clarence crept around, in the dark shadows of the crowd, and in the parking-lot watching as I walked across the stage to receive my diploma. He watched as we celebrated. He lurked like a coyote and then disappeared back into oblivion. I remember the first couple of months after his arrival at St. James, I tried relentlessly to get Clarence to go to church with me. I tried to get him to quit drinking and doing drugs, but the bottle always took control...like my dad.

I followed my Grandparents and relatives to St. James Motel and helped them check into their rooms because our trailer was too small for all of them. I waited until I was alone with my Grandparents. "Thank you, Gramps and Gramma for coming to my graduation, for everything! Gramps, all those times I wondered what "for my own good" meant. I want you to know now I know; everything *WAS* for my own good!" "You will learn as you get older, Grandchild" Gramps translated for Gramma and they both nodded their heads. Their eyes gave that knowing look, revealing what I knew now about my mother. "All those years by myself taught me to rely on myself, just like you both rely on each other and on the livestock that keep you busy. Now, I'm ready for the world!!" Hugs, tears, smiles...tired eyes... And one last time, Gramps looked over his glasses with his hazel green eyes and said, "That's what you think..." Some words will last forever! Smile.

When we returned home after graduation, my heart skipped a beat, because there was a gift on the doorstep. I just knew it was from Clarence because I recognized his handwriting, and the feeling of his presence at graduation were right. As I unloaded the truck, my mother gave me one of those looks I learned to ignore. She took her tired self to bed and before long snored into dream land.

I settled in my small room took a deep breath and opened his gift…knowing I had sensed him at my graduation. Inside the box were poems professing his love for me…words I would cherish forever. Deep breath, sigh…

There was an envelope with the words, "For my Love, Florence." Eyes rolling, sigh. The cover of the card had a graduation cap, trimmed with red roses that had silver tips. It read, "Congratulations, Graduate!"

Dear Florence.

How proud I am of you! I watched you from the time when we were little kids to now. You always had that light around you, like you always had a plan. I watched you graduate tonight, too. Please forgive me for everything. Have a great life. I will think of you forever. I can't express myself like you, but I wrote you some poems over the years. My words are my gift to you because that's all I have to give. My love for you, always – Clarence.

I ran my fingers over his words. I took a deep breath and thought I caught a glimpse of him in the crowd but there were so many people. Now I knew. Then, I thought of how he better not show-up tonight, especially if he was drunk or high. I got ready for bed and began to read some of his poems…poems he had written on napkins the bartender puts under your glass at the bar, different sizes of paper that had a faint odor of marijuana and alcohol. Eyes rolling.

Funny Bunny
It ain't funny honey
The way you been acting funny honey
I thought I was your love bunny
I thought I was your honey bunny
Let me be your buckle bunny
Baby, you're just a funny bunny.
Honey…

…she giggled…buckle bunny..isss He must've been hanging out with some cowboys listening to Buck Owens or Waylon Jennings.

That Smile
Was I dreaming or was it real -
that lovely face,
like a reel to reel?

That friendly laugh,
that gentle light,
the smile that carries me
through the night.

I've been on the road
for miles and miles,
but still I see
that lovely smile.

Please tell me now –
was it real?
or just a memory
I still feel?

Abandoned
You abandoned me
There's no turning back now.
Before you know it,
you'll realize –
life without me.

Who will you turn to
when things go right,
or when things go wrong?
who will you turn to when I no longer exist –
the way you wished?

But I abandoned you, too.
I can't turn around.
Before you know it,
I'll realize –
I didn't need
A life with you, either.

I turn to myself.
I turn to me.
And I never look back.

Goodbye.
…….abandoned..

I unfolded the paper, my fingers brushing the crumbled edge. The words blurred for a moment – from the stains, That one on had yellow whiskey stains that told me he was drunk when he felt abandoned. **Evil whiskey!..** I folded the paper back, slower this time, and set it aside.

Nothing New
This is nothing new
There's a full moon tonight
stars sailing across the sky -
it's all just
nothing new.

It's nothing new
That my heart still belongs to you .
It's nothing new
That my dreams are still about your.

The full moon shines so bright,
And I know
You're with him tonight.

But that's nothing new.

He must've wrote this when he was mad.. I could almost hear his voice slurring through the lines. That old moon, still pulling at hearts that had nothing new left to break.

I turned the slip of paper over in my hand, the words still humming in my chest.

Navajo warriors creep though the night,
Chasing the spirit winds.....

Navajo Warriors
Navajo Warriors creep through the night,
chasing the spirit wind.
Their songs echo through our minds –
a drumbeat,
a memory,
a call.

Someday,
I will find my spirit again
when I chase the warrior wind
      Hey ya, hey ya, hey

I turned the slip of paper over in my hand, the words still humming in my chest.

Navajo warriors creep through the night,
Chasing the spirit winds.....

It felt different from the others – less angry, less bitter. This one felt old, like something from before the pain, before the whiskey. I closed my eyes and imagined him under the moon, singing to a memory neither of us could name.

Someday I'll find my spirit again.

I felt my throat tighten. It wasn't just his longing. It was hers, too. For all they'd lost, for all they'd left behind.

I whispered, soft as breath:
  Hey ya, hey ya, hey….

And for a moment, I wasn't alone.

<u>Into Oblivion</u>
The sun creeping over the horizon,
greasy face, greasy hair -
another day spent in oblivion

Been waiting for a chance
to redeem my soul,
if only for one day,
one hour,
one minute

Ten thousand miles
 for twenty thousand beers
Nobody never mind,
Nobody can seem to find me.

Makes me want to cry -
what kind of man am I?
The one you used to know
if only
in my dreams

And the sun sets
into oblivion..

I folded the paper slowly, my fingers pressing the creases tight.

Ten thousand miles for twenty thousand beers…

Evil whiskey, I thought again, and this time, my chest ached.

Lost

I've been lost
on the Red Sands Highway,
searching for that light
that shines forever bright on you,
dimming on me.

The colored light
fades to black and white -
Mom and Dad
so sad.

I've been lost
on the Red Sands Highway,
waiting for the time,
waiting in time,
for the light
to shine on me.

Too bad-
I've been lost in time,
my lonely soul
drifting down Red Sands Highway.

Tears trickled down my cheeks, as I looked at his handwriting, some perfect, all of it sad and dark. Shaking my head, never imagining what the boys at Red Sands Residential Dormitory went through, knowing what I saw and lived. There were a lot of other poems written on napkins with food stains, the back of envelopes, and scraps of paper. Whew, I sat in silence, no more tears could drain out of my eyes. Clarence was just one victim of the Bureau of Indian Affairs Dormitory life meant to save the man, while killing the Indian. Sadly, they killed both. It is no wonder that alcohol and drugs would comfort their abandoned souls. Those are the souls that lingered aimlessly into history and crept up and down the halls of Red Sands Residential Dormitory. I felt sad that Clarence went down the wrong road. All I could do was cherish his words because his soul and his mind belonged to the devil at the bottom of each bottle. I carefully tucked the poems back into the box, closed the lid, turned off the light, and accepted the future that waited. Deep sleep…finally.

Clarence was dropped off at Red Sands Residential Dormitory with his cousin-brother, Gerald. They were just six years old and never knew anything about what was going on around them. They were puzzled about the place where they had to sleep and why they were forced to be there in the first place. His mother and grandmother would threaten them that he would be "thrown in" the Boarding School if he was naughty. The reality was that Helen was on the brink of poverty and could not take care of Clarence. Clarence's father was off working the railroad in Riverside, California and barely sent enough money to manage. Clarence never knew that his mother had no choice, but to give him up to the Bureau of Indian Affairs. Clarence grew up thinking he had been sent there because he was naughty and unworthy of his mother's love.

I just knew Clarence had to be a victim of "The Room" and Levinstein's wrath. Every time he took a swig of whiskey reminded him of that putrid smell. Like countless friends, Clarence learned to find ways to get away from breaking the rules without getting caught. He spent many, many endless weekends passing the time and at the age of nine, he quit expecting to be picked up by his mother or family. By twelve-years-old, he even forgot what his mother looked like when she happened to pick him up for summer break. When he got home, he found that he needed to herd sheep while everyone went on a trip to the Crow Fair powwow in Montana. They were gone for a month and came back with great memories. Clarence felt deeply hurt but never showed his feelings. He had grown up alone waiting to be part of his family, but after that summer he knew he was alone. He watched Florence spend time alone. He saw how she went running, or how she went to church – alone. Clarence thought that if she could do it, he could too. But he didn't have a Gramps or a Gramma or a Tohatchi Flats to wait for..he had no one. His friends Terry and Delfred were his family.

On one of his weekends roaming Red Sands, he went into the library and saw me sitting there reading. He thought I read too much, but maybe he could kill time reading too. I never noticed him watching me and he didn't want to seem like a stalker or some shit like that. He waited for me to leave and then picked up the book I had left on the table. The title read, "Family Pictures," by Gwendolyn Brooks. He sat down and flipped through the book. He saw that the author was Black. "If she can write poems and publish a book, then I can do that too," Clarence told himself. His hobby of looking for coins on the ground for snacks, took on a new reason. He needed money for paper and a nice pencil with a big eraser. One thing that Gwendolyn Brooks wrote struck him deeply. She suggested that a poem doesn't do everything for you. The poet brings experiences to life with rich words. He copied her poems and read them whenever he needed some inspiration. It was also then that Clarence began watching, observing everything around him, including me. I would be his muse. Mr. Yazzie their "Man on Duty" as he was called, always said, "If at first you don't succeed, try, try again." So, Clarence kept trying to write poems that made sense or spoke with rich understanding. Much of that precious paper had been written on, erased, written on again and then usually ended up in the trash. Terry and Delfred made fun of him but pulled the paper out of the trash and read his poems when he wasn't looking. Terry made a comment when it was time to take out the trash. He said, "You should keep these poems, they might be worth something later on in life." Delfred chimed in throwing Clarence a box saying, "Yeah, here's a box for you to keep them in." They made fun of Clarence using Navajo jokes, but threw their arms over his shoulder and said, "*Hóó ádishni, Shí'naai!*" "Come on Clarence, we're just kidding you! Your poems aren't bad. Who is your O'shí-heart?" Terry always had to be nosey, Clarence thought. He would never tell Terry he liked me, because by then Terry and I were kind of a thing. It became a secret thing for Clarence to send me his love through poems by folding the paper into different shapes on one of those weekends when all the kids were playing outside.

His first poem was folded into a stealth plane and flown right into my lap as I swung on the swing. He watched my facial expression as I unfolded the airplane and read his words. He has written and rewritten his first poem to me and finally decided on the acrostic style poem written on the folded lines inside that airplane. His heart was beating so fast as I opened it and began to smile. He knew he was on his way to becoming a real poet. He watched me look around wondering who "C" was. That's when our eyes met as I quickly looked away. A little confused, I wasn't sure how to handle having a boy take interest in me, I took his attention as a joke. By then, my mother didn't discuss anything about boyfriend girlfriend situations. I figured I would end up living by myself for fear of experiencing what she did all those years ago. I re-read the poem:

For Florence -
F is for the way your fine hair flows like a gentle rhyme.,
  like a gentle song only the wind knows.
L is for the way you lean on your friends,
  Finding strength where the hard day ends.
O is for the way only you
  can stay on my mind the whole day through.
R is for racing the sun in the sky,
  your laughter rising as the world flies by..
E is for how easily
  you outshine the dawn and light up me..
N is for Navajo- .proud and true.
  a strength I see in all you do.
C is for coffee, strong and bold,
  like the girl whose heart I wish to hold.
E is how easy – easy on my eyes,
  the kind of beauty that never lies..   *- From "C"*

Years later, when I came across this poem, I remembered that was the last time I would see the real Clarence, before he succumbs to alcohol. Our secret communication began when I caught him throwing a paper airplane, trying to land it on my lap, again. Those were fleeting memories. I began to see Clarence in a different way. I learned to secretly relish and privately cherish his words. In the back of my mind, I thought there were some things I didn't need to tell my best friends, and this was one of them. Clarence, too, made sure he didn't tell anyone who his poetry was for and kept that secret along with his tortured experiences of" The Room", to his early grave.

In my junior year at the University of Arizona, I received mail from Gramps. Inside was a newspaper clipping from the Gallup Independent. Gramps, wrote a short note that read, "Grandchild, I thought you should know about this. I'm sorry, *Grandchild*." I opened the folded newspaper clipping and read how Clarence succumbed to hyperthermia in Gallup on a cold, cold January night in 1980 at the age of 22. Irony bites again, as that was my favorite number. I cried and cried, remembering all those innocent times at Red Sands Residential Dormitory and St. James…feeling guilty for giving up and pushing him away…what would have happened if we had all stayed together in the comforts of Red Sands Residential Dormitory…yes comfort. Clarice and I spent some time reminiscing about our times, the race at the football field, about our times at the old Ranch House. "You never told me you and Clarence had a thing. When did this start?" I don't know, it just started. He went to school at St. James for a while, then his dad went back to the railroad. After that, I didn't see him again. Curious silence…unspoken secrets.

How would Gramps know anything about Clarence? I tried to remember if I had mentioned him but couldn't think of that time. Maybe he found one of his poems that just so happened to fall out of one of my plastic bins in the hayloft.

What Gramps didn't tell me, until much later, was that Clarence made the infamous trek out to Tohatchi Flats, the place that he had heard about so many years ago. He met Gramps and Gramma.

They served him a meal and Gramps prayed for him. Gramps decided to give him a ride to Highway 666 while giving him some of his advice. As they began the trek towards Highway 666, he turned around to take one last look at the Stone Castle Florence always spoke about. The one he wished he grew up in… The Stone Castle I loved so much and longed for as my eyes remembered my times there, while I pretended to be happy walking the streets of Red Sands, killing time. It was the short time he spent with Gramps and Gramma that told him why I always waited months, weeks, days, and seconds to be out on Tohatchi Flats. Before he jumped off the truck, Gramps handed him a few dollars and sent him on his way.. Gramps kept his promise never to tell me of his visit. Gramps kept his word until he thought I was ready to hear them.

As he hitchhiked towards Gallup, the orange sun glowed and slowly drifted behind the horizon and yes, he actually felt Chuska Mountain exhaled across Tohatchi Flats..just like I tried to explain. Deep breath, sigh..... "She'll never know, huh, she didn't need to know," he thought as he made his way back to his drinking friends and in no time, found his way back to oblivion.

Clarence deserved that reward, and he deserved a better life. Damned that evil alcohol! Damned that evil marijuana! Damned the **B**laming **I**ndians of **A**merica dormitory life! Cherished words….lost life…wandering soul…abandoned at the steps of Red Sands Residential Dormitory… Every now and then, I would find some time to open up all those paper shapes and re-read his poems. I would smell the paper, but the scent of High Karate was long gone. Thankfully, the smell of alcohol and marijuana had also disappeared, just like Clarence wrote – into oblivion. When drunk Clarence felt bold, he would tell the other drunks how he got an award. He would bring that worn out academic achievement award for writing from his worn leather wallet, unfold it and proudly show it to his drinking buddies, saying "You guys are nothing but a bunch of shit" usually followed by a fight for his life. He spent his days roaming the streets of Gallup, sleeping in the alleys or in the ditches near the railroad dreaming of becoming famous. I wouldn't be able to recognize him even if

I tried to look for him, which I thought about but never did. It was a slow but eventual death. Why?

The irony of it was after his death, Clarence's mother found stacks of steno tablets in his room filled with stories, poems, drawings; she never knew her son was a talented writer, and wondered who Florence was... All she saw was what society labeled as *no good*; and the guilt of ignoring and pushing him away made her an old grey-haired woman before her time. That's how people end up when they live from the outside in. What she would never know was that Clarence was not a bad soul. He had a big heart that society turned bad. What made him give up? His mother would never know what Clarence would never tell anyone about his abuse at Red Sands Residential Dormitory.

Clarice, Ruby, and Garnet sent me their graduation announcements, but I did not attend, because I spent my last summer out at Tohatchi Flats. In the end pictures, cards, were all that I had of my long-lost sisters. As time does, we drifted apart and had lost touch in many ways, but it was ok, for we had spent so many seconds, hours, days, months together...a lifetime ago in the walls of that cement home called Red Sands Residential Dormitory - Dorm A.

Shortly after graduation, my mother and I started packing for our move from St. James to Uncle Benny's home site in Sawmill, where my mother and her siblings grew up. It was a long trip following the moving truck haul our trailer home from St. James, down I-40, up a two-lane dirt road and finally reaching the small mountain town, called Sawmill. The small community nestled at the edge of the Defiance Plateau brought distant memories of Klagetoh, a place I thought I had forgotten. Tired from endless miles of traveling, my mother retired from the job at the welfare office and soon found a job working at the Hewlett Packard Company in the Shipping Department in Ft. Defiance, where she worked, eventually retired a second time. Stung by a tumultuous marriage, she spent her life as a single woman. When I was in college, my mother used my dad's Veteran's benefits to build a small two-bedroom home that didn't have wheels. She lived in that small home in Sawmill where she keeps the temperature at an even 100' degrees all year long…the way she likes it. Some things never change.

A weeks after we unpacked and the mobile home energized with electricity and hooked up with the coldest tap water, I decided it was time for me to spend one last summer at Tohatchi Flats before venturing into college life…and another new world. My younger cousins Ernessa, Michelle, and Cheryl took over our spot on the hill, waiting for each other to return for a summer of fun, work, and freshly salted onions. Ernest Ed took my place next to Gramma and Gramps. Cousin Chuckie never returned to Tohatchi Flats and eventually quit writing to me, his favorite cousin. I figured he didn't have my address, but I felt his spirit around me now and then. Life out at Tohatchi Flats would never be the same…the memories will live in my heart forever…deep breath…sigh… During the weeks I spent with Gramps and Gramma, I learned so much about my Navajo people. Gramps waited until I was old enough for me to hear this part of his story.

The Navajo way of thinking is where people pampered themselves from the inside out through prayers, good thoughts, and songs passed down from generations. "A person without spirituality is penniless in a sea of stuff," Gramps professed as he herded one hundred sixty-five sheep while religiously whistling the songs that came in fours, always in fours. After the day's work, Gramps went to his hogan to practice singing his sacred songs, praying those prayerful thoughts. I remembered as a child, those were the times Gramps did not want to be disturbed. We could listen but we couldn't say a word, for those were sacred songs and we had to act sacred, think sacred, and be very, very still.

Hogans are for living and are often used for religious purposes. For this reason, Navajos usually have two or three hogans. The one-room hogan used for religious purposes has a dirt floor. Mattresses, covered by wool rugs or Pendleton blankets, line the walls, and a potbelly stove in the middle puts out enough fire and heat to make everyone red with sweat. It was like we sweated out our prayers, our sins, and just about the very life out of us when we were young children.

The dirt floor was hardened by sprinkling sacred water, and using a straw broom carefully swept it to a uniform level. Now, I knew where mom learned to make the floor at the Klagetoh hogan smooth and hard. Inside my cousins and I sat on the left side with Gramps in the center facing the doorway that opened to the East. Visitors sit to the right. Like his dad, Cousin Ben, Jr., kept the fire burning so he sat next to the doorway. He was our "Fire Chief." At times, my cousins and I could not keep quiet or still and were eventually chased out by Gramps, who was trying hard not to laugh at himself. It was hard to be spiritual in all that heat.

Gramps was a working man who announced orders about what needed to be done, to anyone within earshot mainly his grandchildren and the pubbies. His voice would cause big waves across Tohatchi Flats. "Eight Hours Work for Eight Hours Pay! Now get to work!" Even the dogs, sheep, horses, goats, birds, and cats all stood at attention when Gramps was using his yelling voice. After a series of orders, Gramps fired up his 19 and 75 Chevy pickup truck with the over cab stock rack. The truck was filled with odds and ends and, just in case, stuff. Gramps was a collector of things.

Gramma maintained the house cooking up a storm and wove another beautiful rug. Grandma did her share of the ranch work too. Grandma was the favorite daughter of her father, Charlie Arviso, who was known to be a cattle baron owning hundreds of acres where his beef master steers, quarter horses and churro sheep roamed freely. I learned that he was a wealthy man. Charlie Arviso spoke, Navajo, Spanish, and English, in that order. He always wore a three-piece gray wool suit with a matching Stetson hat. He was a very distinguished man, and I know now where Gramma got her soft-spoken voice. All my Arviso family were soft-spoken, and I discovered not to let that fool me, by any means. Mr. Manley would say, "she is soft-spoken, but be careful, she also carries a sharp stick." That was Gramma. At times, the wind sang a lonely song, other times it whispered of cold winters to come. Gramma could always tell what kind of weather there would be by the way the wind blew her skirt. Every morning when the weather was supposed to change, she would stand outside and let the wind tell her how to plan for the day. I found myself doing the same thing throughout my life. Funny how some things stick with you like the glue that keeps your spirit together. I learned over the years that when the wind began to change and ease its whistle through the windowpanes, I knew it was about time to return to school, leaving uneasiness in all our hearts.

The wind blows something fierce at Tohatchi Flats but those who lived there welcomed the wind. The ranchers who dotted the Checkerboard area were either related or long-time friends with Gramps and Grammas. Our closest neighbors were Grandma's siblings: Martha Barney and her family. Nearby were the Manuelito's, who were related to Grandma through our Honeycomb Cliff Dweller Clan. We are born to the Tsin'ji'kini' Clan ~ Honeycone.. I like that!

Grandma and Grandpa lived in two different places depending on the season. During spring and summer, they lived in the cool Chuska Mountains near Asaayi Lake, and during the cold winter months, they lived on the dry windy flats of Tohatchi. Most of the summer and on weekends, the whole family could be at one ranch site and then go miles away in any number of road conditions, to the other ranch site on the same day depending on the work that needed to be done. It was a really rough and tough rancher's life; Gramps would not have it any other way. He had a three-year stint hauling logs with his brothers, John, Oscar, and cousins, forming Damon Trucking Company. Ranch work in all its duties beckoned him, leading Gramps towards Tohatchi Flats for good.

The days started very early, and the work never ended. Gramps and Gramma had ten children all working in one place or another in Tribal Government, Bureau of Indian Affairs, or the State of Arizona. Every summer his grandkids, eventually all 32, would help with the livestock and herd all the sheep, sheep, and more sheep. It was the responsibility of the older cousins to initiate the younger ones on how to brush and saddle the horse. Putting the bit and bridle on was another thing Cousin Chuckie would have to do for us. It was his duty and a pleasure, being the older one because that meant he could order us around, too. We had to learn how to herd sheep and give commands to Lucky and the other sheep dogs that came and eventually left for the Spirit World. It was a happy time for me because I walked on the open land from the crack of dawn 'til the stars were so bright, my cousins and I were sure we could touch them, especially the little ones. The time we spent sitting on top of the sandstone hill gave the adults time to talk about adult stuff. As usual, Cousin Burton and Benny Jr. would sneak down to get as much intel as they could. They would move like soldiers sneaking up the hill and report to the rest of us anything that was of importance. Most of the time, it was just news of the upcoming work that needed to be done, like the yearly sheep dip event. I often wondered if they ever talked about fun stuff.

Like me, many of my cousins were routinely "dumped off," at, Tohatchi Flats for the entire summer. Always, always there was a welcoming smile and a "Hello Grandchild…ready for another summer of work?" Gramps would be toiling around the ranch getting ready to do something or just about being done doing something. That's how living on the ranch was; something always needed to get done, and "by-cracky" Gramps was gonna get it done.

Gramps was a storyteller, and his grandchildren loved to listen to him. His giant 6-foot structure and resonating voice with the gentlest hazel eyes that hovered over his reading glasses, made us think he was kidding when he got mad. Gramps was a happy person by all accounts and was serious about work. I thought that was about the only times Gramps got mad; when the work wasn't done, or when we did what he called an "H-A job," that was another story. It was those times; we knew he wasn't kidding because he would say, "Jish cha'dá mą'ii yázhí!" (darn you little coyotes) and end with a "Yáadilá!" (good grief!)

Like clockwork, on the weekends, my mother, aunts, and uncles would drive the long road home. Work like branding horses and cattle, transporting water, shearing sheep and other repair work took place when there were stronger hands. I would think of how sore I would be in a matter of days, just from getting used to all this work and sitting on a horse once again. ALL of us would sit up on top of the ragged surface of the sandstone mesa top that stood West of Gramps and Gramma's house. There, we took turns guessing whose parents were coming by the headlights.

It took some distance (about 5 miles), but eventually the lights would slowly 'eke their ways up the last hill towards the ranch house. We would see who guessed right, then race down and give everyone hugs. We would collect some cousins, and race back up the hill and wait and watch for the next pair of lights to make their way down the dusty road.

The fifteen miles of dirt road were riddled like a washboard, some smooth and there were ruts everywhere. My uncles spent a lot of time driving the yellow tractor called, "Yellow Fin", with a metal plate trying to flatten the road. It was a relentless job because the condition of the road was a never-ending story. These memories travel in and out of my mind so many times traveling down that fifteen-mile road. The weather played a big part of getting home. In so many different types of weather and so many times in my mind, we all made our way to the Stone Castle.

That yellowish dusty hills top that never changed over the years would remain a very special place and memory for all of us. We carved our names into the yellow sandstone, and over the cold winters, the bitter winter winds eventually blew the names into obscurity until the next summer, of course.

Family gatherings were an important and routine activity. It was as if we didn't need anyone but ourselves. There is a special memory I have of Charlie Arviso. I remembered a time driving the long, treacherous road leading East to Torreon, Great-Grandpa Charlie Arviso's second Ranch. Hanging on for dear life in the back of Uncle Benny's overhead camper, the road was so muddy that we flew back and forth wondering if we would make it. It had been rainy and, eventually, we were stuck in the mud. It was hilarious to see the tire spinning with mud spraying all over Cousin Burton's face and front. When Uncle Benny stopped accelerating, Burton stood covered with mud. Everybody took one look at him and burst into laughter. Burton had no choice but to join in. When we finally made it to Great-Grandpa's ranch Chuckie was the first to get off to face the outdoor shower. Good thing we always carry an extra change of clothing. Imagine a bunch of Navajos singing "She'll be coming around the mountain" in the middle of the New Mexico desert! What a hoot!

There it stood as we rounded the bend, nestled in the high red cliff mesa and many tall cottonwood trees in the midst of several hogans and two rectangular ranch style homes with the long porch in the front. Of course, it was another stone house that would weather the time and last forever. Rocking chairs and an assortment of chairs lined the veranda beckoning visitors to stay a while. Old Man Charlie, as he was referred to by my uncles, came out with Great-Grandma Bah, smiling and waving us in with a "Wóshdę́ę́' Shí awéé' (Come in, my family).

Bah was a respected and well-known Medicine Woman and was so reserved in certain company. One wall was lined with shelves and countless jars of herbs and wild tobacco from the mountain gathered during the summer months. Around her family she lit up and was a funny, happy person with a peculiar laugh and, of course, that soft spoken voice she passed on to Grandma and onto me. There were at least a thousand Hereford steers standing in front of the door all over the place. It was like a minefield. My cousins jumped down and walked through them with ease. I was so terrified that I decided to stay in the camper until someone came to get me. At times, the steers would rub themselves against the truck, which scared the wits out of me. I thought they were after me and scratched their backs against the truck like they wanted to tip the truck over. I sat petrified in the camper until the coast was clear and the cattle meandered towards the coral. Gramma and Gramps took the treacherous trip to visit often during the summer as the winters were too dangerous. Those were days filled with singing and eating. The kids all scattered along the red stoned mesa mindful of the snakes and desert critters - not wanting to disturb their routine. One time we competed in a couple of contests. Kids had to eat five crackers and whistle. Whoever won got $1.00. It was anybody's guess who would win, because we couldn't stop laughing while cracker bits flew out of our mouths. Another time there was a foot race between the girls and boys. There was always some kind of competition, and every visit was an adventure.

As time went on 80-year-old Great-Grandpa Charlie began using a cane to get around. His eyesight was going bad, but he was still a feisty man to the end. Charlie Arviso died at 104 years old a wealthy self-made man. I remember Gramps telling me stories about Gramma's side of the family when we herded sheep. He explained that Gramma had five sisters and five brothers, with Juan and Anita being twins. Twins are a major deal in the Navajo culture. Bah, their mother, gave them their Tsénjikíní Clan. Bah made sure they knew which herb to use for any number of ailments. From childhood, Gramma was taught to be an expert weaver through years of practice and watching her own mother. With her 5-foot stature, Gramma's ability to break a horse and run the cattle was impressive. Grandma was so busy with the family cattle she only attended school for a few years. She didn't really need Western education anyway. She communicated only in Navajo using a few English words. She spoke the Spanish language that her grandfather, Jesus Arviso taught the family after the Long Walk Era. Gramma could talk to horses. Without hesitation, they followed her commands, with very little effort on Gramma's part. As I look back, I could see how Gramps took a liking to her ability to be gentle and tough at the same time.

One adventure I would have liked to have been a witness was when Gramma took control of her rights. At that time some cattle rustlers stole horses and cattle from the ranch and tried to sell them at the Gallup Cattle Auction. As soon as Gramma found out she had missing cattle, she demanded Gramps take her to town. There, they were waiting for her in the Gallup Cattle Auction corral. She got out of the truck with rope in hand, climbed that fence and gathered up her stolen horses and steers. The auction owners and cowboys were amazed. Gramma told them in Navajo that these were her belongings, and she came to get them back. Gramps had the papers, of course, and the markings matched, so they couldn't say anything. That scene was talked about for years at the Gallup Cattle Auction. It was amazing because she was five-foot tall. In her lace up brown cowboy boots and straw hat, she opened the gate, standing among all those horses, and with a click of her tongue, one by one, the horses just put down their heads, accepted the bridle, and climbed into the horse trailer without any hesitation! Gramma broke most of the horses with her sons and daughters and taught them to be amazing cattle and horsemen! The horses gladly followed their master towards the gate. Gramps smiled as he remembered that day. "Hehh" he expressed as he looked into the past.

I remember Gramma's hands always amazed me. They gracefully pounded out another beautiful saddle blanket. She is a weaver who perfected the double weaving technique that is used in making saddle blankets. Her loom took most of the northern wall of the Stone House and was big enough to make a queen-sized rug. Like her father, Gramma was always dressed well. She cut out and sewed one-of-a-kind matching outfits without a pattern. I remember hearing the sounds of the needle pounding up and down while her feet paddled back-and-forth early in the morning and knew that Gramma and her paddle Singer Sewing machine were hard at work. I learned to always stand guard, ready to rethread her needle and watch her sew the summer days away. Gramma's fluffy soft tortillas served hot off the grill, melted in my mouth. In her special way, Gramma enjoyed cooking and having her grandchildren around.

She enjoyed listening to Navajo Hour and Father Cormac's Sunday sermons on KGAK, and to hear the latest news. During summer visits, I learned that Gramma loved yodeling. When she heard a yodeling song on the radio, she would cry. I never knew why but it was a sad thing to see Gramma cry. Maybe it reminded her of the times when she was a young girl. That was the time, the wind, the animals, the clouds, and all life out at Tohatchi Flats stood still when Gramma cried. Sigh… Gramps has had his work cut out for him from the start. The sparse arid desert of Tohatchi Flats required patience, dedication, and perseverance. They made the routine manageable and for that reason there was some time for fun.

I never met my great-grandfather Jesus. Grandma's dad, Charlie, was one of Jesus Arviso's many children. I learned that he is referred to as "The Spanish Interpreter" during the Long Walk Tragedy and on the writing of the Treaty of 1868. Jesus Arviso was an instrumental part of the delicate negotiations in which Chief Manuelito would speak in Navajo and Jesus would interpret it to the Spanish/English Interpreter who would then interpret it in English to the U.S. government people. They proudly represented the Navajo people when they traveled to Washingdon and freed the Navajos from four years of starvation and humiliation. The Navajos who were not captured hid out on Beautiful Mountain near Lake Powell and strategized the release of the People. Countless prayers and ceremonies were conducted by powerful Medicine Men, like Manuelito, Bighorse, and many others. They knew the mountain like the back of their hands and could outsmart any of the white soldiers or their Ute trackers, who were paid to hunt down the Navajos.

Gramma would always ask Gramps to tell us the story of her grandfather, Jesus Arviso. She would tell us that we needed to know who we were and where we came from and of course, that we come from good people and good blood...both side of our families. So, Gramps would begin, his eyes looking as if, peering into the distant past... Take a deep breath and begin... The story goes, that way back when the Europeans were coming to our land, lots of Spaniards from Northern Spain ended up in what we used to call Meshico...Senora, Meshico. Now they call it Mexico. That was where your Gramma's grandfather was born.

The story passed down is that around the 1840's, Jesus Arviso and his flock of goats were captured by a Band of San Carlos Apache near what is now the Arizona/Mexico border. He lived with his Apache family, he affectionately referred to them, for about two years when he learned the Apache language. Then one day, for some reason they allowed him to return home of Sonora, Mexico.

Not too long after that, he was herding his flock of goats and they were once again captured, but by a different band of Apache. This time he went further north near the Chiricahua Apache land. Apache raids were common because of the Blue Coats riding along the Chiricahua Mountains in the quest to take the land for themselves. After about two years, he was traded to a Band of Navajos for a black stallion horse. By this time, he was about 16 years old. This Band of Navajos treated Jesus like a son, and soon he married a Navajo by the name of Bah Spearman who was originally from Tse Ho Tso, which is now known as Fort Defiance, Arizona.

Sometime in 1862, as the Navajos were being rounded up, he was sent out by his Navajo father with a piece of goat skin to tell the Army soldiers that they were peaceful and were not doing any harm to anyone. The Army went across Navajoland burning our crops and murdering our beloved sheep, horses, and cattle. They literally starved us into submission. Lots of Navajos had no choice but to surrender at Ft. Defiance because that's where they were told they would get food. It was a trick.

At that point, Jesus was trilingual, something that wasn't common at that time and in the area. Of course, the Army guys didn't know any Navajo words at all, so now they had a way to order our ancestors around. The Army saw the value in Jesus as an interpreter and the rest is history. Anyway, Jesus interpreted for both side along the trail to Hwéeldi (Fort Sumner), with all the Navajos who were forced to walk about four hundred miles. They had no choice. They were prisoners. Many Navajos died or were shot because they couldn't keep up. Mothers were shot giving birth to babies, like the elderly who were too old and sick to walk. Many Navajos of all ages who were not allowed on a wagon or rode horseback drowned trying to cross the Rio Grande River.

The four years imprisoned at Hwéeldi was miserable thousands died of starvation and disease. Many perished from hopelessness. I'm not sure how Jesus and Ta'deez'bah met but they became a couple in those tumultuous times. When the Navajos were freed in 1868, the two made a home near Church Rock, New Mexico where Jesus continued to serve as an Agent of the U.S. Army at Ft. Wingate. Over the years, Jesus had several wives, but he eventually settled with a Mexican wife who bore him more children in the Cubero area. He died an old man around 86 in 1932 and is buried next to the Catholic Church in Cubero, New Mexico. Gramps took a deep breath and said, "That's the short version."

I had heard the story of my gramma's side of the family many times. I also was told many times the story of Gramps' side of the family, as well. It seemed that storytelling just came natural to me, and writing followed. The words used to describe the people and vast lands, adventures…it all made sense to me, why I became a storyteller.

Gramps grew up in Old Sawmill, the son of a half white and half Navajo man named Charles Sumner Damon and his Navajo wife Hazbah. Gramps was also the grandson of Anson Chandler Damon, a Veteran of the California Calvary.

Anson Chancellor Damon's parents, Mary and Isaiah Damon ancestors came from County Kent, England. Isaiah's great grandfather emigrated to America in the early 1600's, but by the grace of Lord Almighty, Gramps would say, he made his way to help our people.

Anson told of being a stow away on a ship in Calais, Maine sometime in the 1850's. It sailed through the Isthmus of Panama finding on its way to California where Anson joined the California Cavalry. He was a butcher during his four years with the U.S. Army as a member of Troop H California Cavalry. and by order of the ruthless President Andrew Johnson. Anson found was stationed at Bosque Redondo by way of Ft. Lowell, which is now Arizona. Ft. Lowell was eventually changed to Tucson, or Tukshone, a Tohono O'odham name for their homeland.

Being a humble man, Anson helped the starving Navajos he watched die day after day. He sharpened a spear made of ocotillo cactus and in the early hours of the morning, he forced the spear into the backside of a steer, which eventually died a slow death. Anson was careful to watch so that the dead steer would be found just in time to butcher it and serve it to the starving Navajos.

During that time, cattle were dying of diseases; so Anson quickly reported that the steer must have died of disease, and he requested permission to cut it up and feed it to those Navajos, which was quickly granted. This is how many Navajos survived the four-year death camp. The Navajos were held captive at Ft. Sumner from 1863-1868.

Ft. Sumner is where he met Ta'dezbah. She was born to the Bitterwater Clan. There was a lot of commotion when the two of them got married, just like Jesus and Bah. It is a family story how Anson and Jesus were jailed for marrying Navajos but that's another story, for another day. Gramps took a sip of his coffee and continued. After the Navajos were freed, Anson and Ta'dezbah moved to Ft. Defiance, where they raised seven sons and one daughter. Anson named his seven sons after presidents. Nellie, their only daughter married a white man by the name of Alexander Black. Her brothers took Navajo wives and lived their lives as Navajos by all accounts. Like Charlie Arviso, Anson understood the obligation of a family. Ft. Defiance Trading Post was built and owned by Anson C. Damon for a period of time in the late 1800's and early 1900's. Anson's sons settled the land between what is now Ft. Defiance and Window Rock and raised the Navajo Damon family. He later sold the Trading Post to Sammy Day.

Gramps' dad, Charles Butler Damon married a woman by the name of Hasbah, who was born to the Mud Clan. Gramps, his older brothers Oscar, John, and younger sister Nettie were abandoned by their father when they were very little. Charles eventually settled, married and raised another family in the Tohatchi area. Hasbah was said to have been a mean, stingy woman. Navajo tradition requires an available brother to take the place of father for children of separation. Thomas Jefferson Damon, who had lost his Ute wife to tuberculosis soon joined

Hasbah and began raising Gramps and his brothers and sister. Anson, Susie, Togo, Virginia, and Mary were born to the two. Gramps had eight siblings! Gramps never let on that he had such a heart-breaking childhood, being a spiritual humble man. None of us grandkids knew that Gramps was a sad boy or had to be separated from his dad. It wasn't until I was thirteen that my mother and cousin Chuckie told me the story of Gramps and Gramma. As a young man, Gramps eventually began visiting his father, who had relocated to the Crownpoint area and built a relationship with his father's family.

Not many people know this story, and Gramps is not the type to go around boasting about his family history. Like him, I didn't go around telling everyone that I was part White or Spanish or Apache for that matter! I remember when I graduated from high school, I found out by accident that my father was half Chiricahua Apache – but that's another story. Meanwhile, drifting back to reality, Gramps drew in a deep breath, exhaled his usual, "Heh." The story of my mother's family never got old and helped me in more ways than anyone could ever imagine.

Now that his grandchildren were growing older, it was time for Gramps to talk about life. Last summer Gramps explained, "Living from the outside in, seems like an easy life. Lots of Navajos go to the city and live the white man's life but they long for their native roots. You see Grandchildren; living from the outside-in is a hard thing for Navajos to do because you can't control other people or the outside environment. A lot of times, people become angry and give up. It's best to be true to your Navajo self and your family. Being a Navajo means you have to think from your heart about the things going on around you, and then you make a decision about how you can steer away from evil words, thoughts, and actions. That way, when you need help, others will be there to help you and your family. That's thinking from the inside out. Watch your tongue! Bite your words if they are too harsh."

At times, when brushing my reddish-brown hair, I would think of how the Navajo people starved and had to live in dugouts for four years! I thought of how they prayed and prayed for the future of the Navajo People, all the while starving to death and enduring freezing winters and sweltering hot summers. There was some hope that not everyone was against the Navajos. Besides, as big as the reservation was in those days, there could be radical Navajos causing trouble in Ft. Defiance and the folks in Western Agency would not know a thing about the incident. "Why?" Because it would take them at least ten days by horseback or wagon to get to Ft. Defiance and, by then, the commotion would be over. Or the news would take fifteen days if it hit the trading post gossip circuit, which was the most reliable at time, Gramps once admitted. Gramps and Gramma established a hard-working family from those roots. I often thought, if Navajos could survive walking 400 miles, starving, freezing; I could make it through anything.

Last summer the gang sat under the stars up on the hill. It was pitch dark except for the kerosene lanterns glowing from down below. Cousin Chuckie told the story of how Gramps had met Gramma during a summer ceremony called Enemy Way ceremony. It didn't matter that Gramma was a cowgirl rancher, who barely attended the white man's school and refused to speak English, preferring Navajo and Spanish. So, when Gramps began writing her letters, she asked her sister Anita to interpret and write back to Gramps. How romantic!

As Chuckie reported, when Gramps asked Great-Grandpa Charlie for her hand in marriage, he approved even though Gramps only had a herd of goats. Needless to say, Gramma brought with her a large amount of cattle, horses and sheep, and the two settled as husband and wife. I was taught by Gramps and Gramma, and the rest of the family, we were her family, and no one could take that away from her. Even these people who work for the almighty Bureau of Indian Affairs; better known by many names. That place, Red Sands Residential Dormitory tried to bring me down, but I knew I came from "good people and good blood".

Four years of high school at St. James High School flew by and the memories of nine years at Red Sands Residential Dormitory was a testimony to our strength and the so-called resilience, many anthropologists credit Native American with possessing in order to live in *their* world. It all flew by and before I knew it, I was headed to The University of Arizona in Tucson, Arizona to study Journalism and Education, just like I told myself I would – the time came and went.

An Era of distinction passed as we moved into the 21st Century. I remembered how Gramps always wanted to live to see the year 2000 arrive. As children, he helped us imagine flying cars and all kinds of robotic things like in the cartoon The <u>Jetson's</u>. As children, he helped us understand who we were as Dine' and how we came to live in the Glittering World. As an old man, he showed us that life is what we make of it…if we live from the inside out. Gramps also taught us this, "If you don't have your health, you don't have anything." This is truth!

As time went on, Gramps and Gramma took their time moving around and spent most of their time in thought…eyes growing old, time spent listening to KGAK, reading the newspapers to Gramma. Their routine and chores didn't change, but time did. Everyone grew up and slowly drifted away from the ritual of summer out at Tohatchi Flats. It was unthinkable, but with the hustle of making a living, their routine had to change with time. Sometimes we have no choice but to change.

Chapter 29 – Travel to the Future

After the long years enduring St. James, the time came for me to fill out my admission application and all the other documents needed to get some kind of scholarship. While Mr. Heap, the Counselor for Seniors helped us, I had to ask my mom for my birth certificate. She kind of got angry, but I insisted that I could not go to college without it. I heard her digging through the boxes of things I was not allowed to touch. I often wondered what was in those boxes and often thought about riffling through them when she was at work, but I never did. After what seemed like two hours, she gave me an envelope, got her keys and purse and told me she was going to get some groceries.

After she left, I opened the envelope. The top of my birth certificate read, Mongomery County Hospital – Clarksville, Tennessee. My eyes went down to read my name – my real name, Florence Ann Brown. Brown? All these years, I thought my name was Florence Ann Arviso! I read my mother's name and then my father's – Harvey Brown. His occupation read, Retired Military. At that moment, I remembered Gramps' words. "You'll learn as you get older." I'll bet this is what he meant. My mind was full of questions.

I heard the horn honk to let me know I needed to come out and help her with the groceries. I placed my birth certificate back into the envelope, got my shoes on, and didn't know how this conversation was going to turn out. My mother was probably going to be mad, but it was my right to know all the answers to my questions. I tried to smile as I went down the steps towards the truck. In silence, I began to collect the groceries. My mother took her time bringing in the last load.

Umm, why is my last name Arviso and not Brown? Why did you keep this from me? When were you going to tell me the truth? How could you do this to me? I was so angry that I raised my voice enough to make the neighbor's dog bark. I pushed my birth certificate in her face and made her read it. Why did you lie to me, Mom?

"I didn't lie to you, Shí awéé'. Sit down and let me tell you now that you are old enough to know. When I left your father, he came looking for me and then you. He saw me on one of my trips to Gallup the first month after we left Klagetoh. Do you remember the day we were rescued?" She didn't wait for my answer. "He threatened to take you away from me. He threatened to kill me! He would have done that if I wasn't with my cousin Roberta. She helped me get away from him and we quickly left Gallup. Anyway, as usual, he was drunk and was a passenger driving around with his brother Roy. His brother tried to tell him to stop, but the alcohol was too strong. I had no choice but to change your name and hide you at Red Sands Residential Dormitory. It was for your own good and safety. I had no choice, Florence. You have to believe me, I wanted to tell you so many times, but I guess now is as good as any time. You're old enough to know." We stood there in silence.

"Is this why you never visited me?" I asked, fighting back tears. "Yes, it was for your own good."

I didn't know what to think. My mind was racing because I often felt like something was being kept from me; unspoken words I could feel. "Well, I'm not keeping his last name. I'm changing my name to Arviso. You should have told me when I left Red Sands Residential Dormitory. Is this why you took a job in the middle of nowhere?" "Yes."

OK, so why didn't you teach me my own Dine' language? She took another deep breath, looked in the air, before letting her breath out, just like Gramps did when he was going to explain something that would take a while. I waited.

"When I was fourteen, I was sent to school. I am the oldest of ten siblings, so I had to take care of them, your Aunties and Uncles. Your grandparents were busy with the cattle, so my schooling began late – really late." I took a deep breath and shifted on the couch. "I went to Albuquerque Indian School. I didn't speak very good English, so I was ridiculed by the white people who ran the place. A lot of us Indians didn't speak very good English. Some were Pueblo, Apache, you name it. If we were caught speaking our own language, we were punished. Soap was put in our mouths; some were chained to the basement without food or blanket, and more. A lot of us were punished, but we found ways to be who we were – Children of the Holy People. Eventually, I learned how to speak better English, while keeping my Dine' language. When I graduated, I met your father. Your grandparents were not happy about that, but I thought I was in love." She looked down in shame, took a deep breath, and continued. "We eloped and I followed him to North Carolina where he was Stationed at Ft. Bragg. It was an experience you will not believe or understand. I saw how your father and his Indian comrades were treated. Your father was a daredevil and jumped off planes in the warzone in France, Germany, and other places. I don't know. I just read his letters and prayed, like the rest of us Military wives. When he came back after the war ended, things between us were different. Your father was transferred to Ft. Campbell, Kentucky. When we moved to nearby, Clarksville, Tennessee and you were born, I made the promise that you would speak perfect English, so you would not be punished by the white people. That's why I didn't teach you our Dine' language, but there is still time to learn."

I got up and hugged her, and for the first time, I had answers to questions. "I'm sorry Momma. I guess this is as good anytime to hear your life story. Maybe someday I'll tell you about my experience at Red Sands Residential Dormitory, but that would take 500 pages!" We shared an uncomfortable laugh and set about getting dinner ready.

The theme song of a rerun of Star Trek filled the air as we contemplated what was, and why. Oh well… Momma's Southern style chicken sizzled, while the collard greens boiled in butter, and let's not forget we need some buttery grits to top off dinner. The dessert was strawberry banana Jello with whipped topping. There was an unusual moment of silent contentment…like all that the right time.

I finally broke my stunned silence and asked why the teachers referred to me as Florence Arviso, and not Brown. "My supervisor, Mr. Enfield, talked to the principal."

"Well, is there any way to get my name changed?

"Yes. We can go to the courthouse and request a name change. I did that when I divorced him years ago." "

Wait, your last name is Damon, and mine is Arviso. Why is that?"

That's your grandmother's family name, Arviso. It fits, don't you think?"

"YES!" By the end of the week, my name was changed and a new birth certificate with the right name came in the mail. That was the last document I needed for my admission to college. I guess I, too, divorced my dad's identity because it was for our survival! My mother and I never talked about my name, my dad, or decisions she made for my own good ever again. But that didn't make me stop thinking about him from time to time. I mean, I *am* or *used to be* his *"Little Stone."* Maybe someday I'll go look for him, maybe.

As I look back on the moment, I remember it took several days for me to figure out how to think about this news. I was sure Gramps and Gramma and everyone else knew. It dawned on me that hiding me at Red Sands Residential Dormitory and making me live in St. James *was* what they meant – " for your own good, Grandchild." Faded memories of my dad's drunken rage, and hearing Garnet speak of her mother's so-called husbands', helped me to realize why I was left to live alone. It made sense why my mother never visited me. I couldn't imagine how she endured it. As for me, I counted time thinking the worst. I finally understood why she became a bitter woman and never remarried.

After graduation, and spending my last summer out at Tohatchi Flats, it was time to travel to Tucson. I had patiently waited for my admission papers and scholarship amount to arrive in the mail. The day finally came when a large white envelope with the

University of Arizona address on the top left, addressed to me; Miss Florence Ann Arviso. I had gone to the Post Office so many times that Mr. Lewis was happy to announce that I indeed had some mail. He handed me my mother's mail placed on top of the large white envelope. I was careful to open the envelope, as if it was a precious gift. There was a letter welcoming me, along with information on important dates. The next page surprised me! I received a full scholarship for tuition, room and board, books, and necessities. I thought, I'm guessing *board* meant food.?

I had saved a little over $1,000 from birthday gifts over the years, and graduation money from my relatives. I decided to buy a Polaroid 1000 camera; the kind that produces a picture within minutes. I thought of how handy this would have been while couped up at Red Sands Residential Dormitory. Oh, the pictures I could have captured! For now, I took pictures of my grandparents, Gramps on Teli' (his donkey) with pubbiess. I took pictures of my Stone Castle, and my view from the top of the hill. I took pictures of the cattle that served as my audience when I practiced learning to read thirteen years before. I made sure to take a picture of Gramps' pickup truck; loaded with the stock rack, and the ever-growing ball of bailing wire that always hung on for dear life. I just had to take a picture of Gramma while she was weaving another beautiful masterpiece, and her magnificent hands! I had Uncle Ed take two pictures of my grandparents and me. One for me and one for them. Gramma was amazed to see our images slowly appear. I could not take them with me, and it was triple the distance from Tohatchi Flats and Tucson, so visiting either way was hardly an option. I was so grateful for the instant pictures that I was sure would keep me company, while I spent more years away from my family, in the name of education, that would be good for me!

The pile of envelopes was mostly for my mom, but as I shuffled through them, I discovered Clarice had written to me! I was always happy when I received a letter from my long-lost sisters.

Dear Flo,

HEY!! How's it going, girl? I hope your summer out at Tohatchi Flats is going good! I know you are happiest when you are there! Tell Gramps and Gramma I said, Hello! So, I went to check out Haskell. Girl, you were RIGHT! Once we left Colorado, and traveled east, it was all flat land! Haskell was nice and the tour was great! My parents kept looking around with question marks. On our way back, they let me know they didn't think I should be so far away from home. I was kind of disappointed, but I remember you suggested that I meet up with you at the University of Arizona. So, here I am waiting for an answer from admissions! Wish me luck! Have you heard from Garnet or Ruby? I haven't – in a while. I hope they're doing ok. Well, I'll let you know as soon as I know! Fingers crossed, my sister! I've missed you so much! Write back! Sending hugs!

Your Sister - Clarice

Wow! Well, that was an unexpected turn of events! I decided I would pray that The Holy People, God, and the Pope would help Clarice join me in Tucson. I walked up to Sawmill Dam to take in the summer breeze and enjoy, *"The Goddess of Mavisu"* one of the Harlequin romance novels I found in a dusty old box on one of our trips to Asaayi. I decided one of my aunties left them there and understood the role model my Gramps had been for them, as well. These novels took me to France in the 1700's. I traveled to Spain, in *"The Spanish Husband"*. I thought guys should read these novels, because they sure don't know how to treat a lady like these guys did! Chuckle..

Once again, there came a time when I had to leave my mom, my grandparents, my relatives, and Tohatchi Flats. In late July, we had our yearly Native American Church meeting held for kids and relatives who were beginning another year of school. By now, I had toughened up and was ready to suffer through the departure and the impending excitement of college life. I wasn't going to fool myself that things would never change, because I witnessed the subtle changes over the years. Gramps gave me the usual, "Grandchild, study hard. Make sure you write to us! Send pictures, too! We'll be here." I looked at his tender hazel eyes that had grown old, and assured them I would study hard, write, and send pictures.

The first weekend of August 1977, my mom, grandparents, and Uncle Ed were there to help me put my luggage in the undercarriage of the Continental Trailways Bus in Gallup. I looked at my mom and said, "Remember when we got off the bus here, a long time ago? I always wanted to get back on that bus and head back to Tennessee. Here I am, getting on another bus to parts unknown."

"You shouldn't talk about the past. The future is in your hands." She replied, with her eyes hugging the ground.

"My whole life has been in my hands," I mumbled under my breath. Our relationship started out rocky at St. James and we spent the next four years on a roller coaster.

Gramps cleared his through and said, "Well, Grandchild it's almost time for the bus to depart." Gramma handed me a plastic bag that held a Blue Bird Flour sack that held her famous tortillas and roast mutton sandwich. Gramma was always making sure I was fed. Some things will never change. Deep breath, sigh. I bit my lip and managed a "Thank you, Gramma."

The Bus Driver walked out of the Bus Depot announcing the bus would depart in 5 minutes. "Well, it's time for me to get on the bus," mom, Gramps, Gramma, Uncle Ed." They hoovered around me with hugs, and I took in one last whiff of Gramps and Gramma. I could smell my mom's Bird of Paradise perfume. I did my best to assure them I would study hard and make them proud before the river of tears rolled down our faces. By then I was shaking. I took a good look at each of them. I gazed into Gramp's and Gramma's weary eyes, the ones I had counted on. I smiled at my mom who never seemed to be satisfied. I asked a stranger to take our picture before I gave them one last hug and climbed five steps into the next journey in my life – alone.

I settled into a seat next to the window so I could watch them fade into the distance, as the bus driver closed the doors and the din of the bus took over the sounds of the city. I waved goodbye to another chapter in my short life. I watched my family wave at me, put their heads down, and slowly retreat to their vehicles. Our images became clear in one of our last group pictures. I decided I would protect this picture the most.

Familiarity reached into the distant memories of a four-year-old whose life was upended and changed forever. Like 14 years ago, there were children that ran up and down the aisle of the bus and the smell of dirty diapers filled the cramped air. There was a Black family of five that sat in the back, several Mexicans who were dressed in black, and couple of Navajos. The rest were white people, who boarded first, and took the seats in the front of the bus. By the time we got to the first stop in Sanders, Arizona, I felt hungry. I decided to eat the mutton sandwich my Gramma had made for my trip. I opened the plastic bag and pulled out the Blue Bird Flour sack that was neatly wrapped around the sandwich. I felt something like cardboard at the bottom. I smiled, more tears. Gramps had bought a mini-sized calendar. He had marked all the important dates, just like he had all those years ago. Folded in the back of the calendar was a small note from Gramps that simply said, "Grandchild, study hard. We will miss you. Don't forget to write. Spend your money wisely!" There was also a folded hundred-dollar bill tucked inside. Some things never change and that was my Grandparent's undying love for each other, their children, grandchildren, and all that inhabited Tohatchi Flats. Cherished memories.

The bus ride took us through Holbrook where we made another stop. I looked around at the things that stayed the same and the things that were new. St. Francis Catholic Church stood silently waiting for its parishioners. The Diary Queen had the usual line of children waiting for sweet treats I learned to crave. I craned my neck to see if I could see Red Sands Residential Dormitory, but it was too far. I decided that I had seen that place far too many times and it didn't matter because everything would be the same each time. I decided to keep the good memories and the rest on the pages of my notebooks that wait for me, in repose.

When everyone boarded the bus and we headed towards Show Low, into the Tonto National Forest, down the Salt River Project, to our next stop, Globe, Arizona. We got off the bus after the scary descent and ascent of the Salt River Project's winding roads and hours of sitting. Right away, I noticed the heatwave that hit us when we got off the bus. As we headed the last hundred mile stretch to Tucson, the pine trees disappeared and were replaced by shrubs that hugged the land, probably thirsty for water. There were cacti of all shapes and one that looked like a tall fork, called a Saguaro cactus. Tucson was filled with thousands of homes, stores, and tall buildings I had seen in Phoenix during our high school band trip! I was amazed and scared at the same time!

When I got off the Continental Trailways I was met by Grace and Charlene Davis from the Native American Student Services. They introduced themselves, gave me a big hug, and loaded my luggage into their station wagon. They took me to Coronado Dormitory that was 6 stories high! After all the check-ins, we took the three flights up in an elevator, where I found Room 322. Grace and Charlene watched me hold the rail in the elevator so tight that my knuckles turned white.

"Don't worry, you'll get used to riding up and down the elevator."

I looked at her as it kind of shook as it ascended to each level. The elevator stopped with a ring of the bell as the heavy doors opened at the end of a long hallway. They helped me carry my luggage down the hallway, explaining so much information that I just wanted to sit down and get settled in my dorm room. Charlene had a brown envelope the held some paper and the keys for my dorm room. I unlocked the door and smelled freshly painted walls. Yes, my old friend Navajo white was there to greet me, as if. Somethings become weird friends like paint colors. I smirked and then smiled. I took a deep breath that Grace and Charlene took as a signal to assure me that everything would be "ok", and they were there if I needed anything. There was a door that led to a bathroom that joined another door room on the other side. Grace said they would be back at 5 p.m. to take me to dinner and the activities planned for Native American students.

After they left, I started to cry because I was in a dorm room once again, and I was alone, again. I decided to try to make myself comfortable in that small cubicle with the twin bed. I sat on the bed that didn't squeak. Snicker… There were drawers underneath the bed, a desk, chair, and a small closet. I could hear other girls settling into their dorm rooms. I decided to unpack and make this place my new home. I set up the mini-calendar and ate the rest of my mutton sandwich. Deep breath, here we go.

As I look back on that day, I chuckle, because I was what you would call, "fresh off the Rez", as we tease each other about nowadays. In those days, Clarice, Ruby, Garnet, and I tried to keep in touch throughout our high school years and slowly drifted apart with time. Clarice and I made a promise to keep in touch, I had no idea what was going on with Garnet or Ruby. The last I heard they were doing good, missed me, and would write. Promises I learned to take with a grain of salt.

Well, Clarice, smart as she was, met up with me at the University of Arizona enrolled as a student of Art. She too, checked into Coronado Dorm but was assigned to Room 248. She told me of driving hundreds of miles to see Haskell Indian Nations University, she knew it was not for her. Besides the flat terrain, it seemed too far for her parents to travel. So, she decided to go the route I had suggested so many years ago. Our times in Tucson were some of the greatest times. We got to enjoy the yearly Spring Fling, Arizona basketball, and Arizona football games, and all the events centered around Native American activities. It didn't take long for us to be loyal Arizona Wildcat fans and alumni. I loved the times we traveled up Mt. Lemmon because I could pick cedar, listen to the trees sing, and the mountain breathe. Mt. Lemmon was high enough to have snow during the winter! There was a sky lift we rode for fun, snow or not. The Sawmill Run Café had the best burgers and the softest chocolate cookies! Mt. Lemmon felt like home. Clarice and I found ourselves asking other students who had vehicles to take us up there every time we could, especially in the excruciating heat. We found ourselves spending a lot of time in the Main Library where there were thousands upon thousands of books in every language you could possibly think of. I was amazed!! I knew Gramps would have been quite content sitting and reading all day at the Main Library! For the first two years, we decided to take the advice of our Advisors and stay in Coronado Dorm. Our last two years of college were spent in a big one-bedroom apartment at University Park Apartments. There we could cook out, swim, or play ping-pong. We decorated the walls with Clarice's artwork. We laughed to find the walls painted a familiar Nabaho White. Something has GOT to CHANGE!! It was super hotter than any summer at Tohatchi Flats, with temperatures climbing as high as 116!! It didn't take long for both of us to turn dark chocolate brown! We learned to get our business done early in the morning after our early morning runs, or in the evening when it got cooler. Well, if you think 98 degrees at 7p.m., is relatively cool. I remember the Native American Ambassadors who gave us a tour of the university, talked about the temperature and how to survive. WATER, was the key! I decided living in Tucson was actually when we really experienced freedom for the first time in our lives. We made our own schedule that suspiciously looked like the one Mrs. Becenti set for us. Habits are a funny thing. We talked about our lives at Red Sands Residential Dormitory, but we decided to put that chapter of our lives in history for now. Besides, it was too sad, and we usually ended up crying.

We eventually graduated in 1981. The greatest part about the whole ceremony was when Dr. Schaefer, the University of Arizona President said, "Will the graduating class of 1981 please rise." It was the greatest moment in our lives to see and hear all those people cheering U OF A!, U OF A! The steamers, the red and blue balloons, the laughter, the happiness – Navajo, White Mountain Apache, Papago, Hopi, Northern Tribes, White, Mexican, Blacks, Foreigners, they were all there together in celebration. A happy moment, happy times, happy memories…the ones they dreamed of in the small town of Red Sands, Arizona, three lifetimes ago. It is possible to live in both worlds, just like Gramps taught me – for my own good.   That brought chills to me for so many reasons.

Clarice became a well-known artist and painter. Her one-of-a-kind jewelry creations won 1st Prize at fairs and found a place in the Heard Museum, yes Heard Museum. Clarice married a man by the name of Richard Yazzie, but when they found out she couldn't have children he soon left her for another woman. She now serves as our Auntie Clarice and all the kids love her dearly. She still gets up early in the morning and runs up Summit hill, rain or shine.

From time to time, Clarice wondered what ever happened to Kyle, her first love…and she would never know that he too often wondered about his first love. He never returned to Red Sands, Arizona and lives in San Francisco, California with his wife Mary…secretly harboring memories of unrequited love for Clarice. I remember seeing her take out her half of Kyle's necklace, pressing it to her heart, knowing it is what it had to be. Deep breath. Sigh… I remember the time Clarice planned a trip to Mt. Lemmon during our senior year. She rented a car and just the two of us traveled to the top and parked near the ski lift.

Clarice took a deep breath and said, "well it's time to let things go." I was puzzled but remained quiet as we both got out of the car. Clarice reached into the trunk where she stored a small shovel. I followed her a short way down the north side of the mountain where we usually prayed before each semester. There was a quiet rustling of leaves and a cool breeze in that area that we enjoyed. I watched my friend start shoveling a hole in the ground. When it was deep enough, she pulled out a small white satin pouch that held her half of the heart necklace, pressed it against her heart and said some words I could not hear. She kissed the pouch and placed it into the hole, carefully covering the hole until it was filled and packed down. I placed my hand on her shoulder and said nothing.

As tears streamed down her eyes, she whispered, "It is time to let go of my childhood love. I've kept it safe all these years, and here is a good place to bury what could never be."

~ 358 ~

We stood there looking towards the Promise land, wishing for a time this time and longing for them. Irony stings. In true Clarice fashion, she said a different prayer – the one we say when we cut ties to the past. Just then the wind shifted and whipped her hair across her face. She looked at me and we laughed so hard. We took a deep breath, gave an offering of tádidíín, and we knew it was time to go. The mountain exhaled in acceptance of Clarice's treasure. We never talked about that time again.

Clarice's parents retired from their mobile life and settled in Cross Canyon. Clarice had a home built for them in a place where they enjoy the mountain breeze and endure the harsh winters. Clarice finally had her wish, a home that didn't move, and a home with a foundation. Her home was built next door. It was the one she longed for and was designed just as she had drawn in the pages of her youth. The worn paper that held her floor plans was framed lining her hallway, as a reminder, never to give up on her dreams. For sure, NONE of her walls were painted "Navajo white." Sigh…

Ruby graduated from Page High School of all places. As it turned out, her mother accepted a higher paying job with the City of Page, so naturally Ruby went along with her. Merwin, in all his fashion glory, moved in with them and eventually went to the Art Institute in Phoenix, where he perfected his designs enough to join Phoenix Art Museum. His designs were adorned on manikins that staired into space in area museums. Ruby's grandparents grew old and passed into the Spirit World…her grandmother, leaving first. Ruby and her mother took care of her grandfather while he battled dementia talking nonsense about what the Navajo Nation should or shouldn't do. On a cold winter day, he drifted off to sleep and never woke up. No more Council Delegates invaded their home, and the Navajo Nation was run by younger Navajos endlessly discussing what they should or shouldn't do. Some things should never change.

Ruby went to trade school in Las Vegas and remains today an accomplished welder and pipe fitter, working as a supervisor out at Page Generating Station, making the bucks no less. Ruby had two tumultuous marriages, which resulted in three sons and one daughter. They are spoiled rotten just as she was in her youth. They attend Page Public Schools and live in one of those beautiful homes near Lake Powell on the Navajo side, thanks to their great-grandparent's life insurance. Ruby's mother retired and lived in the apartment in their basement, with her boyfriend half-slash husband James Bodie. Yes, some things don't change because old habits are hard to kick. Giggle.

Leaving Red Sands Residential Dormitory, Ruby thought she had gained her freedom but for decades she was tormented with the memories that affected her life in negative ways. She realized she wasn't the butterfly Johnny Cash sang about, but a wilted rose that had almost all its petals ripped off, barely able to bloom each day. Her anger turned to thorns, as she pushed away any kind of love over the years. There came a time when Ruby found the courage to finally tell a therapist about her deep dark secret and is now in recovery for addiction to the prescription drugs, she used to help her sleep. Ruby met a lawyer by the name of Raymond Sandoval, who she reports is *just* her boyfriend, but every time I call, he answers the phone so, go figure. Ruby finally found happiness…finally. She gave up being sarcastic, but she never quit cussing.

Ruby's therapist said it best, "The one thing about a rose bush is that when it sheds all its petals and hibernates for the winter, it will grow anew in the spring and more beautiful roses will bloom. You are that rose, Ruby." She learned to break down that wall that housed all those horrible memories, the tormented dreams, the smell of whiskey, and the white monster who stole her innocence in the halls of Red Sands Residential Dormitory.

After months of therapy, Ruby looked at herself in the mirror as she brushed her long black hair. She had never cut her hair, but in a moment of clarity, she began to cut her hair. She cut away all the memories, of that evil person stroking her hair, and that evil woman yanking it, and the awful stench of "The Room." She decided to take the half day trip to our sacred mountain to the east, Mt. Blanca also known as, *Tsinaasjini* or Dawn Mountain. Her hair and the history it held were carefully placed in a buckskin. Ruby was never taught the Navajo traditional ways, but it seemed fitting that she would start a new way of thinking by giving her past an offering for her future. She placed the bundle in the ground and said the prayer she had heard Clarice say many times. Yes, Ruby was listening all that time. As she gave an offering of tádidíín, the corn pollen gently blew into the air and the mountain seemed to take a deep breath. Ruby buried her horrible past and the horrible memories that her hair held for a fresh start. It was time. Ruby had no choice but to leave the spirit of her childhood at Red Sands Residential Dormitory.

One early Tuesday Morning in October of 1983, we got the not so shocking news that Garnet had married a white man by the name of John McQuaid, of the Pennsylvania McQuaid's as he introduced himself. We all knew it was her destiny when we heard about him for the first time. I saved the news clipping announcing married at St. Augustine Catholic Church. Yes, Catholic. They lived in Scottsdale, Arizona where he earned a living as a civil engineer. Garnet did what she set out to do and earned her Juris Doctorate degree in Criminal Law from ASU and was a Partner with Flake, McMillian & McQuaid Law offices there in the valley, helping those less fortunate. Garnet was true to her word.

The three of us gathered for Garnet's graduation in Tempe. At her party, Clarice and I joked, *"Well, somebody has to go to ASU...haha!! Kidding!!"* Garnet glared, smiled, then laughed.

"1981 would be a year like 1974, a turning point. A milestone each of us would cherish." Garnet, always the optimist. Ruby called to send her congratulations, and that a gift was in the mail. We took turns passing the phone around to say hello. When the call was finished, we looked at each other and took a collective deep breath. "It looks like we made it." We gave a toast to history, then we gave a toast to survival.

We somehow knew that Garnet would spend the rest of her life outside the reservation, and we understood. They had two daughters and a son. She gave up being a Mormon after her foster parents, Marlowe and Sally would not accept her marriage to

John. John being a devout Catholic insisted they be a part of the Catholic Church. Garnet, the pleaser, switched religions for her mother, then for her love, John McQuaid, of the Pennsylvania McQuaid's. I sighed..

I chuckled thinking all of us Navajos have been baptized at least three times to different churches in our lifetimes. It's the lucky ones who find the path back to our traditional ways. – the Corn Pollen Path.

Daisy, Garnet's mother, maintained her sobriety and eventually landed a secretary job, when her youngest son, Cedar, entered Mountain View High School. Like she promised them, she was able to take her sons back from the Mason's care. They helped saved her children from the Bureau of Indian Affairs, and she was ever so grateful. Having been foster parents to many children, they retired and moved back to Filmore, Utah. They spent their lives serving the Mormon Church in different ways.

Garnet's brothers grew up, vowing to never return to the Navajo Nation, preferring the city life…can't say we blame them. In the end, Daisy kept her family together and each found their way out of poverty. Prayers spoken by a little girl of nine years old, driving her drunk mother and her numerous half-slashed stepdads 150 miles home in the middle of the night, were heard.

I never knew what happened to Terry, Delfred, or John as they disappeared into the Reservation Wind exiled to the Promised Land never to be seen or heard from and never to return to Red Sands Dormitory after that school year. Or so I thought. What is ironic is that what I thought was a turning point in just *my* life, turned out to be a huge turning point in the world around me, the people around me, and my understanding of the life that Gramps hinted of. The understanding he tried to teach me about is found in listening and learning from his and Gramma's wisdom. When I learned about metaphors, similes, and personifications, in middle school, I started to read people between their lines. Poets say things without literally saying it. They hide the meaning in their words. I liked that! I loved studying poetry at the university. Now, I love teaching poetry to my students.

I will forever be grateful for them and my days at Tohatchi Flats, and for making the right decision to hide me at Red Sands Residential Dormitory so I can get a good education. After I graduated the University of Arizona, I decided I would at some point take out all the notebooks and write about surviving Red Sands Residential Dormitory, and then I leave my childhood memories at Red Sands Residential Dormitory...for that is where it belonged, and no child should ever have to endure what we endured those nine years. Day in, day out – minute by minute – a lifetime ago.

In 1986, I married my college sweetheart, Robert, bearing our four sons. It was touching to hear Gramps recall his days to my eldest son, Tommy. Tommy was captivated with his life stories, listened, as Gramps repeated story: "Great-grandchild, our Dine' culture began in *Ni'hodilhil* - the First World. It was surrounded by four clouds columns...." Gramps recalled the day when suddenly, fifty F-16's flew over Tohatchi Flats heading West in 1942, and when he helped establish the Native American Church of Navajoland, and when he walked me down the aisle when I married. It was so special to watch the magic in Tommy's eyes as he listened to Gramps...just like I did so many years ago...three lifetimes ago...out at Tohatchi Flats...home.

"Wow, Great-Grampa, you're so smart!" And Gramps, in true Gramps fashion, peered over his weary hazel green eyes twinkled and said, "That's what you think." Some things should never ever change, but they do and will...smile, deep breath...sigh... I cherished the sparkle in his eyes that had dimmed over time, but it was still there.

As time went on, Gramps and Gramma took time moving around, spending their time in thought, eyes growing old, listening to KGAK, reading the Navajo Times to Gramma, and waiting for Father Cormac's sermon. Routine and chores didn't change, but time did. Everyone grew up slowly drifted away from the ritual of summer out at Tohatchi Flats. The hustle of making a living, their routines changed with time. Sometimes we have no choice but to change – time, distance, jobs, responsibilities. Silence...

Chapter 30 – The Family

As time went on, and time *did* go on, Gramps began sleeping more and more and forgetting more and more about the present and drifting into the past. Gramma slowed down and didn't wander too far from the house. The family decided to build a home for them in the mountain because it was close to where my mom, aunties, and uncles lived and worked. Gramps' mind often slipped back into the days of his youth slowly drifting back to reality every now and again. He became melancholy and preferred living in *his* Hogan, where he spent his days, practicing his Native American Church songs and praying. He even moved out of his room in the trailer house.

"My thoughts keep stopping at every corner! I need to stay in the *hogan*!" Gramps angrily protested.

Gramma spent her time weaving and worrying about them and their health, always wondering about the whereabouts of her children and grandchildren, with no power in their comings and goings. Time was silently passing by. Gramma often spoke of her late mother who would have had the right herbs to help them. She watched as her children and grandchildren drifted away from them, never understanding why. She often told Gramps' "Why do our children think of money first?" To which he would reply, "That's how it is now-a-days. Everything costs so much, and they have no choice but to work." Not many people can live on sheep and livestock." Silent contemplation.

In time, frequent visitors stopped visiting Tohatchi Flats for the summer and we had no choice but to live our adult lives. The family didn't gather as often as we used to unless there was a wedding or the passing of a loved one. Now, Gramps was getting too old to do much. Gramma's once strong hands could hardly thread the yarn in and out of the loom, but she kept at it and finished every rug she started.

One day, that inevitable day, the time came when Uncle Leonard had hired a sheepherder to herd sheep, but as usual, Gramps was out there at the crack of dawn getting things ready for him. When the sheepherder didn't show up for a day, Gramps went out there and saddled his télii - donkey. He was determined to do what was right for the animals. He could have put hay in the corral and waited for the sheepherder to show up but what's the use; he's probably drunk in Gallup with the money Uncle Leonard paid him, Gramps mentioned in times like these. The sheepherder was an *old galook* Gramps refers to, for sure!

There was a strange wind whipping through the mountain tops. That was the day Jackass got spooked and bucked Gramps off. He herded sheep and maintained the cattle and horses until the day Jackass changed everything. Jackass had replaced his faithful Téllii. Our beloved *Téllii* died of old age five years before. I remember Gramps' took the time to write informing me of the death of his beloved friend and companion and how they made sure Téllii had a special burial out on Tohatchi Flats, where he belonged. After that, Gramps was never the same. His strong healthy body grew frail, as his quick mind dimmed. His hazel eyes lost their usual sparkle, and his hugs became strangely hollow. At each visit, I knew he saw me, but knowing he couldn't remember who I was, really hurt. It was the most unbearable experience I had to endure in my life.

The family had no choice but to admit Gramps to an old folk's home, where he could be taken care of by nurses and doctors. It became obvious that Gramma was not able to take care of Gramps alone, and he needed daily care from the doctors and nurses at a nursing home. It was a painful decision for the whole family, and it made Gramps very angry, while Gramma's heart silently broke. Uncle Leonard and Uncle Ed were busy working and could only be there after work and on the weekends. Everyone was busy with their lives, even me. The closest decent place was in Gallup, but Gramps longed for Tohatchi Flats and ran away from there several times. Eventually the nursing home wouldn't take him back. So, the only decent place in the area was in Santa Fe, New Mexico, a good seven-hour drive from Tohatchi Flats. Each time relatives visited him, Gramps would ask, "Are you here to take me home?" Each time, Uncles and Aunties had to fight back the tears, and Gramps would just stare at the wall. He often asked Uncle Ed,

"Are you here to take me home, son?", followed by "I'm sorry dad."

Gramps waited until his visitors left to let his tears roll down his sad face. He was a number there for three years, always dreaming and wishing to return to his beloved Tohatchi Flats and the company of his beautiful wife. Sadly, Gramps never returned home, spending his time lost in his thoughts of a distant past. Gramps lived to be 89 years old and died of pneumonia on September 30, 1992. We buried him in the mountains beneath the same cedar tree we used as refuge while herding sheep near *Asaayi* Lake. A place where Gramma could see him from her living room window, where she spent her time weaving another beautiful rug.

After sixty years of marriage, her new life began at the age of 84, and although her eyesight was failing, she sat about four inches away from her loom and wove another double-woven diamond stitch rug. Like so many times before, Gramma paced the floor, occasionally looking out to the place where her beloved husband spent his days and imagined him riding his trusted steed with his dog Lucky trailing close by. When her sons took him to live hundreds of miles away from her, she had no choice but to learn how to live without him and knew she would never look into his beautiful hazel eyes or hear his voice explaining everything. She imagined him whistling or singing his favorite songs with every beat of the drum. Each day she took a deep breath, looked at his pictures that lined the wall remembering family gatherings as if they were yesterday. She secretly prayed the Holy People would call her home too.

After Gramps passed into the Spirit World, a lot of our way of life drifted into history. On a summer night in the mountains, Uncle Ed was wakened by the most "God awful sound" as he put it. He walked down the hill to the corral and fired off a shot into the air. The sound of dogs running echoed across the cliff as they ran towards the mountain. When he flashed his flashlight around the corral, all he could see was a bloodbath of carnage and dead sheep everywhere. A pack of wild dogs attacked the last twenty-nine sheep that Gramma would ever own. It took a whole day for

Uncle Ed, Levi, and cousins Benny Jr. and Brayden to bury the sheep in a mass grave further up in the mountain. Uncle Leonard thought of how angry he became, when it was time to do this or that for "the love of those damn sheep," instantly felt guilty knowing how much they meant to his mother and dad. That chapter in their lives was closed forever. Heartbroken, they had to convince Gramma that if they bought more sheep, they would also be killed again, because there wasn't a reliable sheepherder to watch over them. The worst thing about the whole incident was that Lucky, Gramps' faithful companion, was also killed valiantly trying to protect the last of his flock.

In her last days, Gramma spoke of her beloved sheep and the horses she loved to ride. At times, you can be in the early 1900's listening to her stories as if they happened yesterday. All her stories are told, in the Navajo language of course. Gramma learned to communicate as best she could but preferred the Navajo language over English. Gramma still cried after hearing a yodeling song on KGAK…and the Earth always stood still when Gramma cried.

In the years after Gramps stepped into the Spirit World, Grandma visited her mountain home and traveled between her children's homes during the wintertime. Every Sunday she turned on the transistor radio to listen to Father Cormac's Padre Hour and reminisce about how Gramps would faithfully listen to the word of the Lord. Father Cormac read his Sermons in Navajo and over the years his voice helped her be close to her beloved husband, if only for one day, one hour every week. Gramma became a lonely woman but kept her tears for the times when she was alone. Although the two of them never talked about dying, because that was a taboo in Navajo culture, Gramma secretly wished for a sign that he was ok.

On a spring afternoon, shortly after Gramps died; she encountered a flash of bright light that bolted from the sky. It happened so fast that she couldn't believe her eyes. In the middle of the bright light stood Gramps surrounded by the outline of relatives she could not distinguish because of her failing eyesight.

He held his hand out to her, like he did so many times before, but she knew it wasn't time to go. It was a sign from Gramps, to tell her he would always be watching over her – true love. Gramma still had her four sisters, all of them in their nineties. They visited and talked of days gone by as if it were yesterday. They talked for hours on the phone Uncle Ed eventually installed. They too drifted into time. Eventually, Gramma had to move in with her daughter Mary. Most warm sunny days, Gramma could be seen sitting in her rocker, crocheting on Auntie Margaret's porch. She lived the rest of her day with Auntie Margaret, never returning to her Stone Castle that silently waited out on Tohatchi Flats. Gramma did not return to the ranch in the mountains until we laid her to rest next to Gramps. After suffering a heart attack and failing health, our matriarch and loving Gramma walked into the Spirit world on June 25th at the age of 101. June 25th was also the day her first grandchild, Darrell, was born. Sometimes things come full circle.

Gramma outlived all her sons too. Uncle Benny died in 1975 leaving behind eight young children and our Auntie Clara. Benny Jr., Shreeve joined the Mormon Placement Program while the younger siblings followed soon after. Cousin Chuckie eventually joined. Some things have to change, and they will with time. Years went by and they too, hardly went to Tohatchi Flats after Gramma joined Gramps in the Spirit World. Sadly, this included me.

Uncle Andy died in 1979 at a private hospital in Phoenix. His kids, my cousins, have lived in Phoenix all their lives and now rarely visit Tohatchi Flats. Uncle Andy made a few visits home to see Gramps and Gramma, and the rest of us years ago. I remember one time, as I finished washing his white GMC truck with the overhead camper, he told my mother something that I will never forget. He said, "The city stole my children away from me." He, too, worked for the Bureau of Indian Affairs as an accountant in Phoenix. I often thought, the white man's world stole all of us from Tohatchi Flats. Red Sands Residential Dormitory did the rest by stealing my childhood. Uncle Andy was laid to rest at St. Anne's Catholic Church Cemetery in Tohatchi. The family tried to make sure Uncle Andy was laid to rest near Uncle Benny, and with time I watched my family dwindle into black and white memories.

My heart broke into a million pieces when my favorite uncle, Uncle Ed died in his sleep in September of 2002, the same month as Gramps but, ten years apart. He was buried next to Gramps and Gramma. Uncle Ed was a classy man. Everyone who knew him made that comment of him with sadness and condolences in their eyes. Unfortunately, he never had children, although I know he would've made a great father, like his dad. After decades, he finally retired from Bureau of Indian Affairs Housing Department and moved back up to Sawmill, just six short years before his death. My sons affectionately called him Uncle Ed and that made him feel young. When he settled into mountain living, he remarked, "I never thought I would return to live in Sawmill, but here I am." Uncle Ed spent his youth in Sawmill and vowed to never return when he was Honorably Discharged from the U.S. Army. After the Korean Conflict, he spent many years in California and in Chicago, sporting a 1955 Harley Davidson, black leather jacket, and aviator glasses. Uncle Ed always wore his handlebar mustache, neatly groomed like Wyatt Earp...aaayy.. Every one of us missed his smile, the gentle hazel eyes he inherited from Gramps', and his gentle ways.

Uncle Leonard spent decades working for Peabody Coal Mine. He spent much of his free time tinkering under the hood of tractors or the truck they used to haul water. The only one who helped Uncle Leonard was his only son, Brayden, and of course, Ben, Jr. Together, they did their best to keep both homesites alive, like Gramps and Gramma expected. Ben, Jr. followed Uncle Leonard into the mining business as a heavy equipment operator at Peabody Coal Mine. After Uncle Ed died, Ben, Jr. would be up at the mountains trying to start Uncle Ed's dump truck, but the fuel line had air bubbles. Being the mechanic he is, he knew what to do but the gas pressure had built up and backfired on Benny Jr., who was severely burned. Luckily, Uncle Leonard was nearby, rushed him to Ft. Defiance Indian Hospital and from there he was flown to a burn unit in Phoenix. In the traditional way, some people say that Uncle Ed's spirit didn't want anyone, I mean anyone, messing with his property while he made his way over to the Spirit World. Navajos say that when a person dies their *chi'įįdíí* or bad spirit, wonders around in confusion, causing havoc because they wanted to remain Earth bound. As Ray James, our family Medicine Man, prayed for Benny Jr.s' recovery, that message was what was revealed in the charcoals. While Ray James's prayer helped Uncle Ed's chí'íídíí to move on, the fire cackled and whipped up when he sprinkled cedar over the flame. The flame let out a loud hiss as the smoke rose out the smoke hole of Gramps' hogan. Ben, Jr., was in a coma for one month, and it was a miracle that regained his strength and was able to return to work. Sometimes prayers come true, but at what cost? Sigh..

As usual, Uncle Leonard and Benny Jr. went on tinkering around under the hood of their vehicles up in the mountain. Uncle Leonard had retired from Peabody Coal Mine. It was a beautiful fall day in August 2006, when he just fell over and died. Agent Orange, gout and other health problems followed him out of Vietnam, but he died doing what he loved and knowing his family was taken care of and left them in the hands of their Lord Almighty, and the Holy People.

As for AIM'ster Chuckie, he actually did what he said he would do. With his AIMer friends, he hitch-hiked across the United States attending all the different powwows all right. He wrote to me about how Navajos shouldn't complain, because it's twice or three times worse on other reservations he visited along his travels. After two years of traveling around, his mother, my Auntie Clara, convinced him to finally settle down and joined the Mormon church. He finished his schooling in San Diego, earning advanced certification in Equipment Operations and was known to groom soccer fields for the kids. He lives with his wife and three kids in San Diego, and hardly ever came home at all. I missed the letters he used to send. The ones that kept me company when I thought I was a hostage. Sadly, in time the letters would not arrive, so I had to enjoy the ones he sent me, so many years before. Sigh..

The rest of my cousins scattered to the wind with their families and jobs that kept them busy. Tohatchi Flats was never on our busy schedules, but always on the back of our collective minds...

Over the year, my mother found herself passing the time with friend, Ella, driving from casino to casino living off their hard-earned retirement. It was just like when we lived together in St. James when she was never or hardly ever home. Her job always required her to drive all over the reservation as a caseworker advocating for the welfare of others, leaving me at home, waiting for her return. Now, she was never home in her retirement. Some things just make you shake your head. At those times, I think about the wisdom of my Gramps. "Grandchild, you never know why people behave the way they do, they just do." A deep breath and a sigh must suffice on those time. I found myself secretly thanking my mother for my stubbornness, my tenacity for not giving up, and for everything else.

My Beloved Stone Castle:

The Stone Castle Gramps and his sons built out at Tohatchi Flats in the 1930's, the Stone Castle I once sat in the wee hours of the morning drinking coffee with my beloved Grandparents, sits abandoned and worn from the many windstorms that smoothed its once strong grainy stones. Most days, the Western winds eerily make its' way through the cracks of the windowpane; blowing gusty waves, making the whole experience appear to be a dance of dust. The first time back to Tohatchi Flats after Gramps' death made me fall to my knees in despair. It's until we grow up that reality shows us how everything looks gigantic when you're a kid and so small when you grow up. Perhaps it was because the kerosene lamp seemingly made Gramps' shadow span the 10-foot walls ceiling made him and everything appeared larger than life to my little eyes. I sat outside looking around at this once vibrant homestead. The wind whistled and whipped around the hill, greeting me like a long-lost friend. My hair blew up and I just knew as the clouds would grow, it signaled the impending thunderstorm bringing much needed moisture to this desert. I had to face the fact that the usual, "Hello, Grandchild. It's good to see you! Your Gramma and I have missed you," would not greet me ever again. The smell of cedar, Gramps' freshly brewed coffee, Gramma's delicious mutton stew, or fluffy tortillas would have to remain a distance memory, the kind I learned to rely upon

Who am I, really? By now, it felt like I had floated through my childhood, college, and into my life as a mother and wife with a lot of built-up trepidation. I took a deep breath, dabbed my tears, and decided to take in what they left behind – precious memories that held so many stories of our times together.

There was a padlock guarding the door with the aid of a few rusty hinges. I looked around and spotted the faded Folgers can sitting inconspicuously to the left. A spare key was always kept under the can, just in case. I lifted the can to reveal the faded medal key that welcomed me home. As I carefully pushed open the door to our Stone Castle, I looked around and instantly felt heartbroken and guilty at the same time. The familiar warmth of a family's love no longer lived there. I took one step on the dusty floorboard that creaked as if to welcome me home. "Gramps, Gramma, I'm so sorry this is how things were left," was the only thing I could think. After all the years of watching out for others, the family neglected to do the same to save our childhood home. As I looked around, the sounds of distant memories flashed before my eyes. There on the wall read the words of John F. Kennedy. "Change s the law of life. And those who only look to the past or the present, will surely miss the future.".

Gramps was still sending his wisdom and telling me how to live after all these years later. Thanks Gramps. Deep breath…wishing for that familiar smile, those familiar hands, familiar, "Hello Grandchild…" and of course those beautiful hazel green eyes peering at me over his glasses saying, "Grandchild here's another interesting story. I've been waiting all year to read it with you."

At that moment, flashes of Gramps sitting on the floor next to the blazing crackling fire, his shadow emanating across the walls while Gramma patiently listened, brought a smile. It was then I realized Gramps long legs sacrificed sitting in a cramped area each year, to tell us our favorite story. Love is having strength to endure uncomfortable times for teaching what is important. Gramps was still teaching me.

All these memories will forever linger in our Stone Castle. I prayed to The Holy People - please don't let this house fall." My palace was in shambles and in desperate need of repair. That potbelly stove that kept us so warm was still facing south but now, it looks like a person could never survive the winter living there with all the cracks in the walls.

The table I sat at and ate delicious food held the salt and pepper shakers, waiting for another meal. And the roof didn't look like it would shelter anyone from the snowstorm or withstand the desert heat. Nevertheless, spiders and other critters made the place their home. The transistor radio with its wire antenna extended towards the window, waiting patiently to be turned on. Everything was left there as if they had just up and left like the people who lived in and mysteriously left the old Ranch House at Red Sands. The worn calendar tacked on the wall, marked time and year of 1990, the last year Gramma and Gramps called the Stone Castle their home. The dusty velvet picture of Jesus looking up with his thorny crown still hung next to the same velvet painted picture of Gramps' beloved President Kennedy's picture - still smiling, underneath all that dust. A black and white picture of Martin Luther King, Jr., was pinned next to President Kennedy. All of them waited patiently for Gramps and Gramma to return and bring back life to the little room they called home.

I spotted some papers neatly tucked under some Life Magazines. I brushed the dust and cobwebs away from the top magazine and found an original 1961 Life Magazine with John F. Kennedy on the cover. Next to his portrait it read, "Any dangerous spot is tenable if brave men will make it so." I think Clarice, Garnet, Ruby, and I were in a tenable spot for nine years. Eyes rolling. Under the magazine top were the pictures I drew for them so many years before. I smiled knowing they kept everything, I mean everything! My finger traced my kindergarten signature trying to recall when I drew each picture. A whole lifetime flashed before my eyes, even though I had tried to tuck those days in the folds of history. I was surprised how quickly my mood went from sadness to sarcasm. Underneath the pictures was a stack of calendars for every year they lived there. I don't know how the weather didn't damage any of these treasures!

My thoughts startled by the wind that began to whip up and rattle the aged door. I decided it was a sign that it was time to leave before I started cleaning, as if anyone would stop by to visit after I left. I thought of opening the drawers where the dishes were kept. There, on the top shelf, sat her favorite coffee cup. I lit up and thanked Gramma for somehow forgetting to take her special cup. Maybe Gramma left it there for me to find, somehow sensing they would not ever return to live there, once they left for the mountains. Maybe.. I collected all the dishes left behind, the transistor radio, the calendar, some Time Magazines including J.F.K.'s, and of course, my pictures. I remember a friend telling me, "A gift given and returned is twice blessed." Deep breath.

I opened the other two drawers and found white, black, and gray balls of wool, spun by the ladies at Two Gray Hills for Gramma a lifetime ago. I picked each up and smelled them to find the faint odor of cinnamon and vanilla. I smiled. I took one last look around, promising myself I would return soon. I spoke to Gramma and Gramps, thanking them for everything and for always looking over me. I slowly backed up towards the door, took a deep breath and one last look before I stepped out, closing the door to my refuge. The click of the rusted padlock sealed our memories for as long as my Stone Castle stood. I placed the rusty key under the Folgers Coffee Can, just in case.

The weathered barn where hay was stored, sheep were shorn, folds were born and served as a hide-out during our summer days, stood still in time. The adjacent bare roof chah'a'oh' (shade house) where we had so many happy meals and played cards into the summer nights, waited patiently for our return. The distant sounds of happy family times, and the smell of roast mutton and Gramma's fluffy fresh tortillas flooded my mind. In our innocence, we never thought our home out on Tohatchi Flats would ever change and would somehow always be there for our return. We just never returned.

I walked down the hill and saw that the sheep coral was still there and of course showing signs of the mending that Gramps and his sons worked on year after year. It looked like it was in shambles, but that is how it always looked, but back then the sheep knew very well not to break through. The fencing was in need of repair, but the animals that called the land to their home were no longer there, so why bother. The few cattle that were left were taken to the mountain for the summer. The vast land is now being tended by Cousin Ben, Jr., Cousin Brayden, and a few hired hands who seem to come and go with the seasons. Gramma's brother, John, built and maintained the stone house next to our Stone Castle, until he passed into the Spirit World, too.

Several years before, I decided to retrieve the 5 footlockers Gramps' protected for me, like he promised. I just couldn't read the contents for a long time, but one afternoon, I decided to look at what I had stored there. The footlockers held fleeting memories that had too many times. I decided to close that part of my life for now, and until I was good and ready to understand, as if there was an age we were supposed to understand everything...

Charlie and his wife Ann still live there to this day. They have their own cattle that keep Tohatchi Flats alive. Cousin Raphi, their daughter, and our many Arviso cousins share memories of our times out at Tohatchi Flats. Many still travel the dirt road to spend time visiting Uncle Charlie and Auntie Ann.

I remember it was always a treat to have Arviso relatives visit during the summers I spent with Gramps and Gramma. Those were the days Gramma lit up. Gramma's sister, Martha Barney lived southeast near the town of Tohatchi. Her sister Anita lived in Albuquerque. Theresa Bowman lived in Gallup. When they got together, it was a good day out on Tohatchi Flats. Meanwhile, their husbands, including Gramps, went about doing ranch work. A delicious feast followed days of hard work and ended with bittersweet goodbyes until next time. I never thought Gramps and Gramma were lonely out on Tohatchi Flats while I was at Red Sands Residential Dormitory, thanks to our Arviso and Damon families.

A lot of that visiting one another left with the wind that whips across decades of ranch work and all its demand. These memories leave a smile and a tenderness in my heart strings. Uncle Charlie and Auntie Ann weren't at home when I visited that day. The notebook that would tell of their whereabouts was inside their locked home, so I guessed they most likely went to Gallup for supplies. Sigh.

I take the long bumpy dusty ride out to Tohatchi Flats inimes of despair, in times of reflection when city life gets too hectic. At times, I sit under the chaha'oh' trying to listen hard Sto hear the happy sounds of days gone by. Gramps retelling his grandchildren the Creation Story. Gramps telling Gramma what the reporter reported over the battery-operated transistor radio... Father Cormac giving his Sunday sermon.

Then again, if I listen too closely, all I heard was the sound of the lonely Tohatchi wind whistling its way through the broken windowpane, bringing me back to reality in every sense of the word. Deep breath, sigh..silence.

On cue, the Chuska Mountain breathes and the gentle wind whistled a special song as if to say; "That's what you think Grandchild"...Yes...that's what I think, Gramps...that's what I know... and just like that the wind whipped my hair slapping my face but mostly my mouth, as if to reply,..."No, that's what I think!!" It could've been Gramps making his point clear...or the Holy People. Probably Gramps... Chuckle!!

It took twice as long for me to climb the distance up the hill. The yellow mesa still bears the now fading markings of the names of my cousins and the date and years when they were carved in the distant past. SW, EH, CH, ML stood the test of time. I couldn't make out the date, but I think it was 1980. I looked across the vast desert floor, West, South, East and North, then down the dusty dirt road. Images of sheep grazing, cattle heading to the watering hole to the north were replaced with a vast network of sagebrush and tumbleweeds. Faded memories. I could see that very few had traveled down either road, as only the eastern road looked like it would be passable in inclement weather. I remembered sitting there, waiting for Uncle Leonard's square headlights, or Uncle Ed's rectangular ones, and the joy of reunions. I remembered gathering to listen to Cousin Chuckie's transistor radio at 9 P.M., when we could finally tune into X-Rock 80, Juarez, Mexico, while wondering how far the stars were, or where the lights that were traveling south or north on Hwy 666 were traveling to. It was a place to cool ourselves off from the summer heat. A place where we shared our lives and sometimes our secrets. The days when all of us religiously made our way come rain or shine every summer, every weekend had faded into the ages. It seems as if we all moved into a world of fast cars, color TV's, cell phones, personal computers, internet. Still no flying cars though – sigh..deep breath… "Grandchild…." The word floated past me and drifted eastward across touching all of Tohatchi Flats. I am reminded of how Uncle Andy spoke of how the city took his kids away from him… What took us away from Tohatchi Flats?

The only thing that was the same was Benny Jr. and Brayden tending to the ranch. Family gatherings only happened at funerals and the occasional wedding. The journey to Tohatchi Flats would never again be just because, or a weekend ritual. Gramps never told me this would be the future, although he probably knew and savored every minute with Gramma and his beloved family and grandchildren…all those years ago… Things will never be the same…sign deep breath…change is not fair.

The legacy that was theirs had been passed down to my generation and will be passed on to the next. I never thought I'd see the day when that would happen. Tohatchi Flats will always live in our minds as a place to rest, to visit, to find comfort. The wind whistled Gramps' words, and his favorite quote rushed across the desert and into the past…forever… "All that we send into the lives of others comes back into our own." The Stone

Castle took a deep breath and sounds of her age made cracking noises as I took a few pictures, before I headed back home. I took out my tádi'díín pouch, said a prayer, gave an offering and let the pollen scatter with the wind. I drove down the dusty worn road and began singing, "She'll be coming around the mountain when she comes. She'll be coming around the mountains, when she comes…" – one of Gramps' favorite songs to sing. Chuckle.. Deep breath, sigh. Silent tears.

Gramps and Gramma

Because I never believed
you would make the journey,
I lived my life on the fly –
chasing time,
as if it would wait
for you..

But even ageless vessels
grow weary.
Distance outpaced
our borrowed time.

Still,
In dreams,
you return-
Iridescent visitations
that softens the grief
I can't explain.

Because I never believed
you would truly go.

My Friend Time

Because I could not stop for Time -
Time kindly lingered near -
Seconds - minutes - hours -
And solitude

We watched the red sands whistle past
And I turned another page -
For posterity.

We passed nine years -
Where memories wait -
At dawn – in the gentle rain
We passed the sweet honeysuckle patch -
We passed the old Ranch House, nestled in the red hills
Or rather -
It passed on.

The silence whistled – danced - and echoed-
For ragged is my heart -
My childhood rusted -
Within the wind.

We paused before the Stone Castle-
Its windows tempered with age-
If life drowned-by utter silence-
Since then-and forever more.
Yesterday fades into black and white-
The graveyard of memories- silent
Dancing a song of dissonance-
Fighting times that slips away.

...deep breath, memories will never change..

Chapter 32 – The Gift of History

We established our home in the mountains of Sawmill, Arizona, nestled at the edge of the Defiance Plateau; the western winds naturally sound like the eerie, cold whistle of a broken windowpane as it makes it way towards Fuzzy Mountain in the East greeting the beautiful golden rays. Like clockwork, the sun rose on the left side of the Fuzzy Mountain in the wintertime, and slowly moved southwards, in the spring and summer months. The sun made his slow journey northward as the yellow leaves soon dotted the Chuska Mountain.

Although the roots of my life somewhat died in 1992 when Gramps stopped recognizing me, I did my best to carry on his wisdom to my sons. "Now here's another great story," as we opened book after book over the years. I thought they never saw the tear at the corner of my eye as I remember Gramps looking over his reading glasses with those hazel green eyes, while reading "The Last of the Mohicans".

I rescued the old brown leather couch with the saddle stitched in the middle of the back for our home library. I remember Gramps sat with his long legs crossed, while his grandchildren gathered around him…where I plucked his whiskers, telling him everything I had learned the year before and the books I read while passing the time at Red Sands Residential Dormitory.. The memory of his blue flannel shirt, jeans and mountain boots - that truck grease smell, those hands, the familiar, "Hello, Grandchild" flashed before my eyes with a smile as I took his spot on that same leather couch with my sons surrounding me. The blue transistor radio tuned to KGAK just in time for the evening news, and those times I needed their strength. My saviors Gramps and Gramma would often show up in a peyote song or an occasional yodel that somehow played on the radio at the right moment. Precious remnants of my beloved, Tohatchi Flats.

I learned with the help of Auntie Teri how to weave and found how difficult my Gramma's signature double stitch pattern really was. It was all about math…math! Gramma's loom lives in my living room as does the pedal sewing machine, I now use to create another one of my famous quilts. My twins, Kyle, or Todd, always ready to thread the needle when I couldn't…just as I did for Gramma – three lifetimes ago. Some things never leave us…

Black and white pictures lined the walls were all I had of Gramps, Gramma, Uncle Ed, Uncle Benny, Uncle Leonard, Uncle Andy, and Auntie Teresa. Of the ten children, three Aunties and my mother survived them.

Memories of days gone by and an era where demanding work, a good meal, and family were all we needed to survive. "Hmm…I mused as my mind went from picture frame to picture frame teaching my boys who they are and where they come from…. I never thought things would turn out like this when I was a child. I never thought Gramps would even die for he was so strong and wise, but he did. Death is a bitter reality. And yes, life does go on…."it's how you make use of it Grandchild," whispered Gramps in the back of my mind. Gramma's eyes silently agreeing… Sigh.

Honestly, I never thought Clarence would die, either. For a while, I was mad at the Pope and Jesus because the Holy People never let me down. Eventually, I quit going to the white man's church, preferring my Native American Church beliefs.

It was then that I retold the story Gramps had told me of the beginning – our Creation Story. "In the beginning, the world was Black….." As I retold the story, the little ones with big eyes listened, looking at each other with amazement…. Yes, time had come full circle, as it should be..as Gramps and Gramma would have wanted it to be.. sigh..smile..deep breath.. precious memories.

As a family, we took time to travel to the mountains to enjoy the lake, cookout, or do a little fishing. Each time, we would stop by to pay respect, leaving flowers or a nice rock I found along the way. My sons also learned about my love of rock collecting. As I drove the hour it took to get to Asaayi, Tommy requested the story of our family. My trusted Mustang, "Blue" heard this story told many times as she carried us here and there. Okay, where should I start? "Anywhere is good Mom," Tommy, Kyle, and Todd chiming in.

"I want to hear the Creation Story Momma," Nathan demanded.

"It's not wintertime yet Nate," Tommy reminded his little brother who sat in the back between Todd and Kyle.

That will be the first story I will tell when we have the first frost, Shí awéé', I assured. Ok, ready? "Yeah!" They always chimed in and quieted down.

Gramps always spoke of how to live and how to think about the life we live," so I'll start there. For the next hour there was silent reverence as the path of history unfolded.

The Navajo way of thinking is where people pampered themselves from the inside out through prayers, good thoughts, and songs passed down from generations. "A person without spirituality is penniless in a sea of stuff.."

The stories were told over and over and over again, with the promise that my own sons would carry them in their heart and pass them onto my grandchildren and great-grandchildren. Our visits to Tohatchi Flats were the hardest to take. The Stone Castle was slowly withering with the wind. Deep breath, cry…

Chapter 31 – Journey Back to Red Sands

It had been sixteen years since I left Red Sands Residential Dormitory for good, yet Clarice, Garnet, and I agreed it was time to return. As usual, Ruby resisted but said she would *try* to make it. It is not easy to raise four sons and work at the same time. By the time I reached thirty years old, I had resolved to understand why my mother made the decision to give up her parental responsibility for my safety. Even though she lived right next door to us, she was never home. Chuckle.. some things would be odd if they did change. Tsk, tsk.

My husband, Robert, the traditional Navajo he was, did not get involved with his in-law, and was my greatest support. There was never a dull moment in our home. The irony and the thought of was how my mother would say, "Turn that noise DOWN!" whenever I tried to enjoy Peter Frampton or Led Zeppelin too loud. Years ago, I vowed *never* to tell my children to do that because I *loved* music *every kind* of music…or so I thought. There came a time when I felt compelled to tell my eldest son Tommy, "Turn down that noise!" I caught myself at noi…s but it was too late, I had broken my vow… Ever since then I have tried to be reasonable about the choice and volume level of their music. Gramps and Gramma's patience ways were now mine… Reality comes full circle…like the journey I was about to make – Journey Back to Red Sands.

"Okay, I have to go see my friends for the day," hugging and kissing them as I tried to hide my anxiety about the trip. I assured them I would be back soon, made sure they had enough food and a few "dead Presidents," just in case. "Your dad will be home in an hour, and I'll be back after dark," I gave Tommy instructions.

"Yeah, yeah, Mom. I know how to take care of myself and my brothers! You don't have to worry."

"Be good, shí'yázhí. Dad will be home before you know it!" I tightly hugged my sons to take their love with me. Tommy helped me check the oil and fluids, while Nathan was bawling his eyes out… Kyle and Todd held onto his precious heart while I disappeared over five miles hill. Pulling out of the driveway of our adobe style home, I also wondered how everyone would look. It took me an hour and seven different outfits, before settling on the first choice, a red velvet top with a blue skirt – Wildcat colors I smiled. I wore Gramma's cherished turquoise necklace and earrings. The silver bracelet with the three turquoise stones my grandparents gave me for graduation always held a place on my left wrist. I didn't forget to add the necklace Clarice gifted me three lifetimes ago.

I took a deep breath, made my way down the Defiance Plateau and on to Window Rock – the capital of The Great Navajo Nation. I drove through Oak Springs and made my way to Lupton, which led to I-40. I took a right and eased my way onto Interstate 40 and drove west to Red Sands. I surfed through the different channels only to find music I didn't like. Honestly, I couldn't stand the noise played on the radio these days! Where is Harry Billy when I need a good ole' tune to get me ready for this reunion? I switched the channel and found the Oldies Channel that seemed to be fitting for this journey.

The drive to my childhood where I was left for my own good. A place where I was educated and learn to trust myself… Reality was coming full circle, and the memories were left to drift with the wind. across the desert that surrounded Red Sands, lost with time.

"Grandchild, Navajos are tough and can make something out of their lives, if they would just listen. Listen to the ancient Holy Winds. Listen to its lost wisdom that floats across an endless sea of dust once covered with precious sunflowers, ushering in spring and then summer." So many thoughts ran through my thirty-year old mind as I drove the three hours it took to get within Red Sands city limits.

The feeling I got in my gut as I pulled onto Interstate 40, remembering being, so young, sitting next to Gramps smelling that special smell, knowing Grandma secretly wept, swept my heart up in a moment as I tapped into that special time capsule...where wishes were pleaded under the stary nights... No one could take all the memories of living in two worlds: of my time in each world, of loving it and hating it, of sadness and joy. It was mine to keep forever locked up in the footlockers filled with notebooks of my life at Red Sand Residential Dormitory and the people who touched my life making me the person I became. I learned not to think of the past so much when I matriculated through college, got my first job, then marriage, and the birth of my four sons. I decided that living in the present would only help the story grow.

Besides, memories were just too much to handle, knowing that with time, people would leave for the Spirit World and that memories were all I would be left with. I pulled off the road to take time to weep. To weep for a childhood that was seemingly lost and then found through the writings of an innocent girl born in Clarksville, Tennessee, only to be locked up at Red Sands Residential Dormitory, Dorm A, in the name of Western education, and let's not forget, "for my own good." One more time to weep for the memories of separation and the jubilation of reunion. One more time to weep for the words of wisdom spoken at the right time and in the right way. One more time to weep for a life I thought I wanted and for the life I didn't appreciate. Right there at the entrance to I-40 was like a twilight zone where the past meets the present...where one life ended, and another one began.

By the time I arrived at Red Sands, the familiar wind blew over the red buttes, but everything was different. It was nearly 10:30 A.M. and I was desperate for coffee. Pulling off at Denny's, I grabbed my purse and walked to the door, when who should approach me? Terry! All windblown, scared face, dirty hair, unkempt and begging for a few dollars. I wasn't sure if he recognized me but those beat up pointy black Beatle shoes gave him away. As I dug through my purse, I thought, "Come in, I'll pay for your breakfast, anything you want. "*Tį'*, Let's go inside, it's time to eat," I said in Navajo and English. His eyes lit up and for a moment he seemed to recognize me. He followed me into the restaurant. Wash your hands, I instructed pointing towards the men's bathroom. "I'll take a large coffee with two creams and one sugar to go, and whatever the gentleman wants to eat, and I'd like to have his lunch order to go, when he's done with his breakfast." "Right away, Mam," the waiter finished writing my order and walked off to get my coffee. "Gosh, its reeel good to have a home cooked meal, even doe its Denny's," Terry, professed, rubbing his aged, sunburned hands and ragged nails. She's going to come and get your order. Make sure you order lunch, too, and I told them to wrap it to go," I offered seeing his young self through the worn feature and tired stature. "Gosh, that's too much!" No, you haven't eaten in a while, so you eat now and enjoy it." I bit my tongue and fought my tears knowing Terry, Delfred, and John were left to fend for themselves at Red Sands Residential Dormitory, Dorm C a lifetime ago. They, too, left their souls at Red Sands Residential Dormitory, and we never knew…

"You should go home and stop drinking. It's hard but there are people who can help you. Where you from?" "Oh, by the way, *Shí éí* Delfred Yazzie *yinishé, Tótsohnii nisłį, Tódích'ii'nii Báshíshchíín, Kinyaá áqnii dashicheii ado' Kinyaanii dashinalí.*" As I shook his hand, acknowledging his clans, while I recited mine. I was in shock as hints of memories of young Delfred peek through his weathered skin. I could only imagine what happened to Terry! I almost choked on the first sip of coffee pretending it was hot. The waiter came to take his order, while I sat next to him on the bar stool. I didn't quite know what to say. Should I tell him about Clarence? Should I ask about Terry? What good would that do at this point.

"Well, I hope you enjoy your meal. You take care and like I said, go home, your family misses you! *Hagoonee* As I told him goodbye, he said,

"Awww they don't care." His head bent down, and his shoulders collapsed in anguish. They lef me here at Red Sands Dorm B, anyways. This is my home..under da bridge," he pointed somewhere outside. He shook like a leaf, gobbling his food…"

~ 386 ~

Ahéhee', Shí dazhí', "Thank you my sister," he managed to say between gulps.

I paid and left a tip with the waiter because I knew that Delfred would keep it for himself and would probably use it for alcohol…the evil alcohol.. We paid with our innocence in that damned place..! I prayed, "Holy People – PLEASE Help Delfred!"

With an even heavier heart, I watched as he gobbled like he hadn't eaten in many days. Gone were the days of scheduled meals, a warm bed, and some semblance of *home* for him. I took a deep breath as I looked at him from my vehicle. His sad eyes peered out the window and he innocently waved at me. I backed out of Denny's parking lot, filled with even more tears in my eyes. Rambunctious Delfred had wound up like Clarence – another "drunken Indian. He ended up like my dad, too. Deeper breath….reality is reality…damn!! His soul will forever linger around Red Sands Residential Dormitory, even though he still lives.. sigh, deep breath…tears..

As I passed the Red Sands Fair Grounds, memories of Brownies, then Girls Scouts meetings where we experienced our first record player. Donny Osmond and Michael Jackson and The Jackson 5 were all the rage. Those good times kept me at the fairgrounds until near sunset, and I chose to walk by myself from the east side to the west side of Red Sands, while the other kids walked in groups. The familiar stained-glass windows of St. Francis stood in time, waiting for the ebb and flow of parishioners to listen to the word. I was sure Father Paul and Sister Marguerite had passed into the Spirit World, as others took their place of devotion. I drove down 3rd Street to see Mrs. Hamilton's house.

There stood the little old powder blue house dwarfed by the surrounding newer two-story homes, that her home looked like the Grandma House of the neighborhood. I was so excited that her home was one thing that didn't change. It was exactly how I remember it, with a fresh coat of paint. Thanks to the Holy People, for Mammy Hamilton. I got out to pick some honeysuckles, when a woman who looked to be my age stepped out.

"Can I help you?"

"Ahhh, Hi. I used to stop by here when I was growing up. I used to love picking Mrs. Hamilton's honeysuckles. How is she? I stammered.

"My grandmother died five years ago. I inherited her home, and she made me promise to keep it the same. Everyone who knew her, love to stop by."

I extended my hand and introduced myself. "I'm Florence. I don't know if your grandmother ever talked of me?" Her eyes lit up!

"I'm Sarah! I remember you!! Remember we used to sit on the porch and eat cherries?"

It was a happy surprise to see someone from my childhood, and that she remembered me. I didn't think anyone remembered me.

"Oh my gosh, Sarah Hamilton-Tate. You always made sure I called you by your full name".

"It's Sarah Hamilton-Tate-Babbitt now. I married Raymond Babbitt, remember him?"

"Oh, I don't remember a lot of people from here. Congratulations on your marriage! Thank you for keeping Mammy's promise…it means a lot."

"Yes."

Tears, deep breath.. I loved your grandmother. I always felt safe when I went down this road after Brownies or Girl Scouts or when I roamed around Red Sands on the weekends. They used to have club activities at the Fair Grounds, and I lived over near Eerie Street.

"Yeah, at that old government dormitory," Sarah's voice cracked. "Grandma never approved of that place. She made sure her voice was heard at the Red Sands City Council meetings. They concluded that all they could do was to watch and make sure the law was upheld. After all, they were the Bureau of Indian

Affairs of the almighty United States of America. I mean you know. It's hard to tell them anything!"

I agreed, realizing all those years ago, even the white folks thought like I did...Irony...

"The people of Red Sands had a lot to say about the Red Sands Residential Dormitory of your days, Florence."

"Why?"

Looking into the sky, Sarah claimed that the writings of a student led to the conviction of Superintendent Levin..or something like that... That was in 19...... 1976, 77... I think."

"Levinstein," I managed to say...thinking Frankenstein, but not speaking his true name out loud.

"Yes, that's it, Levinstein. He was a horrible man! He went to prison, you know."

My mouth dropped open, and my eyes widened at the news. I was stunned. Right then, I realized that memories could come back in a flash as if it was yesterday.

"Well, that some good news from the past was all I could manage to say." My thoughts went to the other evil person that hovered over our lives. I hoped that old starchy witch Becenti was put in the next jail cell! I had learned to keep my thoughts to myself, so I didn't bother to ask any questions. I took a good look at Mammy's porch, trying to imagine her lovely smile, waving at me while she rocked back-n-forth. Smile.

"I came to meet some friends for the day. I thought I'd stop by one of the few places I felt seen and cared for by a woman I barely knew. May I pick some honeysuckles for old time's sake?"

"Sure. It's good to see you, Florence Ann Arviso, that's your name, isn't it? Remember, you used to make me say your full name too?" Smile. "My grandmother always wondered what happened to you. It made her sad not to see you, but she figured you went back to the homeland you always talked about…Tohatchi Flats, right?" Chuckle, blush… Gramps would be smiling too…

Silly me. I told anyone who was willing to listen to me talk about home. Mammy was always good at lending an ear.

"I'm sorry I didn't stop by before I left in the summer of 1974. I still have the dried honeysuckles I picked so long ago, though. After I left, I went to high school in St. James, our archrival! It was the "Home of the Redskins", but I was the only "redskin" there. Chuckle. I graduated from the University of Arizona, and now I'm a middle school English teacher.

"St. James!" Sarah said, surprised. "That's in the middle of nowhere!"

"Yeah, it was hard, but I survived as you can see."

Looking at my watch, it was time to make the trek towards Eerie Street.

"You grew into a beautiful woman, Sarah. I mean, Sarah Hamilton-Tate-Babbitt. May I take a picture of you in front of the house? "Sure! She's buried at the community cemetery if you have time."

"Oh, ok. You take care of yourself! We gave each other a tight hug as if we knew each other for decades." I smiled as took one last look at Mammy's home and thought some things should never ever change!

"What a hoot seeing you after all these years! You take care of yourself and stop by when you're passing through. Florence Ann Arviso. It's been a pleasure seeing you after all these years. It is like looking into the past seein' you here picking flowers, and all. I'm just beside myself. Gramma would have loved to see you one more time before she took her last breath." Sigh.

I didn't know what to say. I loved Mammy Hamilton like a grandmother. I cherished her honeysuckles, her words, the sweet black cherries she shared, all those years ago, and most of all her generosity. When I left Red Sands Residential Dormitory, I knew that I would be leaving knowing that I would never see Mammy Hamilton again.

"I wrote a couple of poems about your grandmother and her garden. Maybe I'll send you a copy and you can put it next to her pictures."

"My Grandmother would have loved that. You'll never know, Florence. You'll never know. Come back when you have more time!"

Hugs, Sigh, Smile, Tears. You never know huh, you never know. I couldn't take any more heartache.

In all my childhood, I never even thought about how the whites viewed Red Sands Residential Dormitory or those of us held captive there. In my mind, we were invisible, unless we had money to spend at the beginning of any given month or patronize any one of the saloons established on every other street. Sixteen years later, I now knew that the white folks did care and voiced their concerns about how we lived in that dormitory. I wonder who that girl, Sarah, was talking about. I should celebrate that Levinstein finally got his just-dues! That was some good news from this trip, so far. I'll have to look up this crime later. Actually, thinking back, I don't know why my mother never informed me.

I made the one-mile drive down old Main Street to Jackson Avenue, saw that all the old houses were torn down and replaced with new houses and a couple of mobile homes parks (as they called them now). It wasn't the same as my memories, but in all this development, they forgot to fix the road though...some things should change...haha!! At the end of Jackson Avenue was a DEAD-END sign that led to Eerie Street and Red Sand Residential Dormitory compound looming in the distance. The familiar seven-foot fence still wrapped around the compound, only without the razor-sharp barbed wire at the top...the one that was meant to keep us captive.

Memories flashed before my eyes. By now, my nerves were frazzled from the drive, seeing Delfred, then Mammy's house, and of all the people, Sarah. I was somewhat of a shock to find out about Frankenstein!! Wow! My stomach turned with butterflies and the coffee didn't help. I made the ominous turn towards the compound revealing the familiar old buildings. The familiar thump, thump, bump drop in the pavement that in all his sweat, Mr. Yazzie was never able to fix. It was as if the pavement stubbornly rejected repairs. Nevertheless, it somehow welcomed me like an old friend, as if.

Familiar faces looked towards me with familiar smiles. I could still see the young faces of Clarice, Ruby, and Garnet as they talked outside their vehicles. They turned their attention to me as I made my way into the entrance of Red Sands Residential Dormitory. All but Ruby was dressed up. Tight hugs and a few tears shed and lots of smiles. After all these years, it was like we had left just yesterday.

Ruby stood with her hands on her hips. She wore Levi's and a button- down shirt with a red bandana tied around her neck. "Where have you been? We've been waiting for days," reported in her usual sarcastic way, as she gave me a side hug. I guess some things can't help but stay the same. Smiles, hugs… rough calloused hands. "Can you believe we're here! Shit this place still looks the same!" Ruby was still Ruby. By now, we didn't think twice about her attitude.

As we turned and looked around, taking a deep breath, remembering it as the shabby old building that remained just that, a shabby old building with a fresh coat of Nabaho White. It stood the test of time and remained standing because of Mr. Yazzie's handiwork, bless his heart. As we looked around our prison compound, memories quieted us into nostalgia. The past silently crossing our wide eyes. We peered into the clouded, dirty window that had been our home for nine long years. Our reflection stared at us, leaving an eerie feeling of knowing what we left behind.

What we saw left a sad sense of belonging to the things that stared back at us, as if asking where we had been. Clarice, Garnet, and I swallowed hard. We bit our lower lips, hands on window, and turned locking eyes. Inside, our well-worn mattresses were stacked up motionless. Those rigid mattresses that held our dried baby tears, guarded our teenage dreams of the future, and bearers of our nightmares for nine enduring years, now stacked – frozen in time…patiently waiting, for what? Hand over shoulders, our collective hearts tightened, deep breath, exhale…

"Who would've known they would close this place," Garnet cut the silence.

"Yeah, and they didn't dump our stuff at the landfill.," I added.

"All our tears, dreams, fears"… Clarice's voice drifted. She was always reading my mind.

In true Ruby fashion… "Our stuff? What do you mean? That stuff should've been burned! This place should be demolished!" She chose not to look inside, standing with a faraway sarcastic scowl on her face, instead.

Clarice looked at me and shrugged, not letting Ruby's usual behavior hinder our experience. We took another look inside, this time inspecting some of the details we might remember. Da Navabo white walls were still Navabo white with cobwebs strategically placed in the corners and on the steel metal bunkbeds. The only thing that was different were all those old Army bunk beds, Army mattresses, and all that Army stuff was stacked front to back in Dorm A, and the doors chained shut from the inside.

Hmmm, Dorm A seemed to say, "You can leave, but as long I stand, I'm gonna keep your memories, your tears, your dreams safe…" Just like the Stone House out at Tohatchi Flats. The memories of lonely cries, childish laughter, secrets told, secrets kept, echoed from the distant past came flooding through our nerves like acid, opening old wounds that never really healed. All of a sudden…

"Excuse me, excuse me. May I help you?" asked a man's voice.

"Hey, it's Ronald, Mr. Yazzie's son." Ruby interrupted our thoughts with her usual *let's get this show on the road* attitude.

"Maybe he'll let us in to take a look around," Clarice added.

"Yeah," Garnet and I agreed at the same time. "It's just like old times."

"Just like old times?" Ruby demanded, "Hey you gonna let us in to take a look around?" hands on her hips. Ruby being Ruby. Somethings *need* to change..oh well….eyes rolling..

I smiled with my hand extended, as we stepped away to greet Ronald Yazzie. I saw the familiar lines of his father's face and that smile was exactly the same. Ronald had taken over his dad's job whenever he wasn't strong enough to do it anymore.

"Well, some things never change." Ruby said with her familiar sarcastic downgrading tone of voice.

"Yeah, Ruby, some things never change, but they should, if you know what I mean…" Garnet retorted as she shook Ronald's hand.

"Yá'át'ééh! Is it okay if we look around in our old dorm? It's been many years since we've been in this building," Garnet, kindly, asked.

"I don't think that will be a good idea." Ronald responded with his glasses showing behind the brim of his L.A. Laker's hat. "Nobody is supposed to go in there because of asbestos and that hantavirus that's been going around. It's too dangerous." Ronald added.

"Well, what happened to this place anyway?" Clarice naturally instigated.

"The only thing that's open now is the girls' and boys' high school dorms, no more little kids here. Been like dat for long time." Ronald replied.

"How is your dad?" Garnet inquired.

"Dad went to the Spirit World ten years, five months and three days ago. He got sick, probably from asbestos. He couldn't breathe good at the end, and then he just gave up. Now they have rules about that stuff. Back then they didn't have any rules. Well, Dad said, don't throw those beds away. They been sleepin, dreaming, crying on dem over the years. Jus keep dem in der for the time being."

I stepped forward and told Ronald how thankful I was for his dad and how he tried to keep Red Sands Residential Dormitory a home for us, even though we didn't really like being there.

He looked at me and ask, "Umm, what is your name?" I'm Florence. "Oh, my dad talked about you, staying at the dorm most of the years. He promised your Cheii he would watch over you. He wondered where you went. Lot of kids just disappeared in his days. After 1974, a lot of kids left. Some went to other schools. Some live under the bridge today. Some, like my buddy, Clarence, ended at the end of a bottle." His eyes pierced me. My deep breath was his responses. Ronald shifted the sand with his boot, not knowing if he should tell them about his dad's former bosses, Mr. Levinstein or Mrs. Becenti and Mrs. Hagga. There was an awkward silence as the familiar Red Sands wind lifted a dust devil that twisted across the compound. Maybe it was the spirit of Mr. Yazzie. Maybe..

"Your dad was a welcomed guest whenever he worked to fix this or that I managed to survive the loneliness of Dorm A knowing he would be a familiar smile," I said with sincerity. Gramps always taking care of me…for my own good.

He shook hands one more time and told us he had to get back to work. Ronald's news was a shock for us. We stood there in silence as he backed away and headed for the building that looked like the warehouse. "Hágoshįį. Hagoonee'" (Ok, I have to go.)

"Thank you for the information." The girls nodded.

"Wow, asbestos." Clarice noted.

"Yeah, we must've high tailed it out of here just in time," I added.

We looked up to see if the football field was still there and in use, but the city built the Freeway right through the football field and our path to the old farmhouse.

"Asbestos? That shit will ruin your lungs! They didn't even try to contact us to see if we got sick! There were no rules for things that were bad, and plenty of rules for things that were good!" Ruby scowled!

"Shh, Ruby, settle down!" We took a familiar collective breath and changed the subject, like we did so many times before.

"Hey, remember the time we raced with the boys to see who would go with who to the end of the year dance?" I asked, looking up at the field wishing to relive those days.

"Yeah, remember when Clarence showed up with Julia? You were so mad, and it was all a set up!" Ruby just had to make it sound bad.

"Remember you practically had to beg to be taken to the dance?" Clarice chimed in, with a - "I'm joking, Ruby!"

Garnet, Clarice, and I kept our eyes on the imaginary football field as if to feel the moment before it faded back into a distant memory. The trek up to where the football field used to be took longer than it did when we were young. Sixteen years seemed like just yesterday. We got to what would've been the turnstile and stopped. We had to use our memory to envision what used to be and how we relished a little bit of freedom killing time there. Now, all we saw were railings and the paved road with vehicles passing at a high rate of speed.

Distant sounds of laughter and teenage angst made chills run up and down my spine, remembering everything we had experienced on that field. I almost told the girls about my encounter with Delfred, of Clarence's demise in Drunk Town USA. It would be just another story about two "drunken Indians" who were robbed by the demon at the bottom of every bottle, secondary to the loss of an innocent childhood – all in the name of education and the almighty United States dollar. I decided not to darken the mood even more than it was at that moment.

I almost told them about Levenstein going to prison, but I thought twice until I got more information. Besides that, I didn't want Ruby to go into her rage and relapse into disparity. By now, I understood her. I just couldn't believe I didn't hear about it! Deep breath, bite my lip, holding back the tears. Ruby's glaring eyes was a weight no one should carry. Our home chained and locked from the inside, made to wait in time. The bulldozed football field were reminders that our past closed its doors so we could not go back, as if any of us wanted to make that trek.

Sensing my emotions, Clarice wrapped her arm around my shoulder and reminded me of our early morning runs. "Remember how we risked a lot to hold true to our Dine' ways, Flo? I will always be grateful to you Flo. You showed me how to be brave when I am alone. You taught me how grandparents should treat their grandkids. I always kept your grandparents in my prayers because they helped you raise yourself."

"I did raise myself now that I think about it. You know when I started living with my mother, I didn't even know who she was. The worst part is that she didn't even know her only child. We were like strangers, living in a rectangle, in a strange town with two churches, that were attended by two different races. St. James was a trip. I'll tell you all about it someday...someday. Let's just say when I was released from this prison, I stepped into a whole different kind of prison and survived...the story of my life."

"We should see if there is a path to the Old Ranch House." Garnet interrupted our quiet conversation while gazing around, memories flashing across her eyes.

"Oh, that old house?" We didn't even notice Ronald had walked up and was busy painting the fence, giving it its 1,000[th] coat of Columbia Red. He stopped to inform us that some gang members graffitied the old ranch house- our sanctuary. It was mysteriously burned down a couple of years before they built that freeway. We silently realized nothing was the same, except for the experiences stored somewhere in our collective minds. In that moment of silence, the western wind picked up, and a red dust devil swirled from west to east, as if to rush us away, like the in-law winds telling them, "It's time to go home."

"That dude snuck up on us, like a real Indian!" Ruby crassness broke the silence…like she always did… "That dust devil is probably Miss Hagga's drunkass evil spirit trying to order us around one more time." Eyes roll. Silent exasperation.

"Well, at least no more **B**eans for **I**ndians **A**lways on the Menu!!" Laughter!!! Garnet, dear Garnet…always on point… I could see that little girl I spent so much time with a lifetime ago. She had a way of bringing us all back to Earth.

Ruby went on to ask what happened to Eugene, the Manual Labor Guy. "Oh, Eugene? He's our boss now. They don't give out manual labor anymore, though."

Collective snickers, chuckles. Ronald put his head down careful not to show, he joined in on our ridicule of his boss. His shoulders gave a fast up-and-down motion, were a dead giveaway.

We burst out laughing! "Are you here for da' Manual Labor?" I chimed in. More laughter. "Did you wanted me to pick up da rock?" More laughter. He shook his head, wiped his forehead, and said goodbyes. We watched as he laughed on his way to down the half-painted fence.

"What did you did?" Clarice chimed in! Manual Labor guy.

"His four-eyed goofy ass is probably 60 years old!" Garnet made us laugh even more!

"Let's go."

"Not before I say a prayer," Clarice demanded as she brought out her tá'di'díín pouch and began the prayers that bonded us together forever, all those years ago. Huddled together with heads bowed in reverent reflection we prayed…

As the Bluebird sings at dawn.
I breathe in the cool air to nourish my spirit.
As I sing words East to offer my Corn Pollen,
I ask Mother Earth and Father Sky to rejuvenate my spiritual,
physical, mental, and emotional health.
Through the blessing from the Holy People.

I shall Walk In Beauty of love and happiness.
The blessings shall always restore unity of my family and
\community.
Hózhó Nahasdlii'
Hózhó Nahasdlii'
Hózhó Nahasdlii'
Hózhó Nahasdlii'
It is finished in Beauty.

With gratitude we took a little, dabbed it on the tip of our tongue, and gave the rest eastward to the Holy People who continued to watch over us.

As I look back on my time at Red Sands Residential Dormitory, I understood so much from all that waiting, counting time, for what? It was for now. We had come full circle on that day. Deep breath, long exhale.

"Well, let's go down eat some Romo's Mexican food." Clarice suggested trying to keep from falling with her high heels. She must've forgotten the rocky path that led to Red Sands Residential Dormitory compound. "Yáadilá!" Good grief!

When we reached Dorm A, we took one last look in the dirty window, as if to relish one last good memory of our childhood home. I could sense the ghosts of Red Sands Residential Dormitory peering back at us, as if to say, take us with you! I heard my childhood spirit join in and whisper, "Turn around! Don't leave!! Don't leave me here!" running towards the fence. The echoes of Gramps' stock rack rattled into oblivion. I didn't realize how much I wished I could hear the stock rack knowing I would hear the words, "Hello, Grandchild. It's good to see you, Shísóók'é. Ayóó áníínishní" "My Grandchild, you are loved."

We had become the Ghosts of Red Sands Residential Dormitory, in so many ways, I had to admit.

We took a deep breath as Garnet started a group hug. The kind of hug we gave each other on the last day of our prison sentence. As we took one last look around, we knew we had seen enough and that was just fine. Together we turned, arm in arm, as the shivers of our past crept up our necks, raising the hairs in effigy. Silence…deep breath…sigh.. Taking one last look at the place and times, we all dreaded and loved at the same time. We took one last trip down the crumbled steps of Red Sands Residential Dormitory – Dorm A and quietly returned to our vehicles.

I was the last to leave. I stopped at the compound gate, taking one last look out the rear-view mirror/ I saw the small shadow of a little girl's figure looking out of the big window of Dorm A, hands pressed against the window, seemingly longing to go with me, begging me to turn around! Please turn around! The little girl's face and hands were pressed against the glass and then in a flash she was gone. Our childhoods were preserved in the halls of a locked-up dormitory. Time had rested in the seams of mattresses, waiting…waiting, locked from the inside, waiting for my return…waiting, like I did a lifetime ago, and just yesterday…. Thanks Mr. Yazzie. My childhood soul too was left at Red Sands Residential Dormitory – a ghost of a memory…

For the last time, I eased my vehicle over the thump, thump, bump out of Red Sands Residential Dormitory compound, and onto that same old street. I took one last look in my childhood home. I wondered how my grandparents and mother felt when they saw me standing at the window, face pressed against the glass, weeping, and wishing for them to turn around and take me home…all those years Gramps and Gramma had to leave me there, "For my own good." Reverent silence…a deep breath…nervous whistle to fight the tears Gramma's strong silence holding Gramps together, like Gramma knew how… Sigh. I decided that they too left a bit of their soul and there at Red Sands Residential Dormitory…trying to keep their grandchild safe in the Glittering World… Grandparents always know best. I understood this sacrifice after it was finally revealed to me why I was left at Red Sands Residential Dormitory. Hindsight 20-20, after all those years at Red Sands Residential Dormitory, it *was* "for my own good". In those years, after all my days locked up for my own good, I learned to accept my childhood the way it turned out. Period.

Tears welled up as I gathered them. I opened the window and splashed them to the ground…tears left there at the entrance of Red Sands Residential Dormitory. Tears that were eager to flow one last time, as I signaled left down old Route 66 to Romo's Mexican Restaurant.

Out of curiosity, I drove down Main Street passed where Babbitt's Meat Market used to be. The place where Harry Billy, our savior, announced the news from radio station 1270 AM KDJI. To my dismay, there stood a huge Wal-Mart, and no signs of the small market ever existed. Another door that was slammed shut by big box companies that sprung up to swallow small businesses.

Our dear Uncle Harry Billy died at the ripe old age of 93 of a heart attack…" Don't forget to visit the folks at the Pow-Wow Trading Post on your way back to the beautiful land of the Navajo…"…his voice echoed from the past…assuring smile saying, "Come back and visit me some time…Leaving on a Jet Plane girl.." Sigh…

The Allen Theatre was still there, although worn with years of the harsh Red Sands wind. A fresh coat of Navabo white kept it from burning down from the relentless desert sun.

Heap Thrift Shop still offered the best prices for the latest fashions, although Mrs. Heap no longer owned the place. I learned Mrs. Heap lived in a retirement home in Green Valley, spending her time sitting on the porch watching the beautiful Arizona sunrises and sunsets. She never returned to Red Sands once she left ten years ago. I vowed to check out thrift stores for some excellent prices for gently used clothing from then on. Mrs. Heap taught me that I don't that if I don't have brand new clothes, that was perfectly fine! Her thoughtfulness and kindness helped me shape my character as the protagonist in my life.

The light turned red so that the great Pacific Railroad could journey past Red Sands and onto Gallup, New Mexico. Hmmm…wonder what ever happened to Julia James… Smirk

If it weren't for Sarah, I would've never known that Julia James became a 4th grade teacher at Red Sands Elementary School. Her classroom was Mrs. Gardner's old classroom. She graduated from Red Sands High School and went on to Northern Arizona University, where she got a part-time job at a local pre-school. She found her niche in the classroom. Having saved so much money to move to California, Julia eventually took that fateful short trip to visit her mother. She quickly realized her mother had her own life and it didn't include Julia or her brothers. Instead of staying in California, she bought a home in Red Sands where she lives with her boyfriend, Clyde. These are things that Sarah Hamilton-Tate shared with me before I left her Grandmother Mammy's home, earlier that day. I was surprised Sarah knew Julie James, but it made sense because Sarah's older sister was Olivia. Olivia was a rebel and spent that fateful summer at school, paying penance for some unknown infraction. Flooded with realizations, I decided to let the past go when it came to Julia James.

I joined my sisters who were patiently waiting for me. "We ordered your favorite cheese enchiladas with extra lettuce, tomatoes, and a side of onions." Clarice smiled. Clarice knew me best. The meal was hard to swallow, as we took turns sharing our present lives with each other.

We came to the conclusion that the trials and tribulations of our childhood spent in the halls of Red Sands Residential Dormitory - Dorm A, were locked up - sealed for all time and eternity. Even though the occupants scattered to the wind, Red Sands Residential Dormitory life will remain an important part of our journey in the Glittering World. There was silent agreement, as usual.

Garnet was the first to admit, "If it weren't for Red Sands Residential Dormitory, I would be nothing. Now I'm a high-priced lawyer making the bucks! High five!"

"If it wasn't for Red Sands Residential Dormitory, I wouldn't have my own jewelry company because I never would have learned math without you, Flo. And, with all that money I saved, after we graduated from the University of Arizona, I went to

I.A.I.A., got my Master of Fine Arts, now I have my art showcased in museums across this great country! AND drum roll…I have a home that doesn't have wheels! Clarice squeezed my arm. We all cheered! High fives. Smiles.

Ruby chimed in "If it wasn't for Red Sands Residential Dormitory, my mom wouldn't have anywhere to dump me off, so she could live her busy life! *BUT* as it turned out, I wouldn't have met you three - my sisters from another mother! You gals helped me in so many ways, you will ever know. Her eyes locked mine in silence. "It was Tech School for me. I learned how to be a bad ass welder and pipe fitter, better than any of the men on my crew! Now I'm their boss!" High five! Ruby always had something sarcastic to say…little did they know why… Uneasy laughter, unspoken knowing. My eyes hugged the ground. Ruby kicked me from under the table. I gave her that I'm not saying nothing about nothing look…

"Okay, my turn. If it wasn't for Red Sands Residential Dormitory, I would never have met three wonderful sisters, whose presence I did not fully appreciate until after I left the halls of Dorm A. Besides, where would I get the material for my novel? It was a good day, right ladies?" High fives…

Finally, laughter…peace. It is what it is and will always be what it was…somewhere in time in Dorm A at Red Sands Residential Dormitory…the place where we left our childhood soul - all of us.. We were the Ghosts of Red Sands Residential Dormitory.

Of course, Ruby needed to make a complaint! "Girl, if my name is in our novel, I need royalties! Royalties!"

"Girl, why can't you be happy for my success? Royalties isss!"

Garnet shook her head and under her breath, said, "She doesn't have a case, Flo. Let it go."

I let her hear my dismay. "I mean, we're 30 years old! Ok! I'll change your name to something else", I suggested. "How about I name you Thomacita?"

Collective laughter.

Ruby was quick to say, "No, I'm ok." Ruby was just being Ruby, for Pete's sake, and after all these years of separation, there was a moment of unsettled silence. Then Clarice and Garnet looking at their watches announced they had to get on the road.

I felt that same dread of separation. I held their hands as if it would bring back the years, we were apart and bring back our childhood.

Clarice took out her *tá'didíin* pouch and we bowed our head, tightly holding hands. Her prayers began by thanking the Holy People for leading us to each other, and for bringing us back together. Her prayers were always strong and well-spoken. When she was finished everyone took a little bit of pollen, put some at the tip of our tongues and made another offering to properly finish our visit.

Hugs, giggles, laughter, joy….sisters forever…

"Red Sands Residential Dormitory will always be our time. But alas, it was time to part once again."

"Oh, I hate goodbyes to this day!" Clarice whined.

"We need to get together more often." Garnet suggested.

"Yeah, let's do that." Ruby and I found ourselves saying the same thing at once. "Jinks!" Hugs, tears, promises…sisters. "Let's take pictures before we go!" So much had happened in the sixteen years after our separation, but we survived a lifetime in nine of those years…and that had to be our legacy… Reality had to be what it was, reality.

The trip back to an old familiar place called I was forced to call home brought closure and a sense of healing. It was like that asbestos was secretly keeping our childhood alive…not thrown out…not relegated to the city dump or a Bureau of Indian Affairs junk yard…just silently waiting. "…you never know, huh Mom, you never know, my sons, Tommy, would say. Deep breath, Smile.

~ 404 ~

What I learned from my research was that Mrs. Gardner was very disturbed by a reference to a place called, "The Room," in my journal writing. I would never know that was the reason for her curled eyebrows, all those years ago. After our departure from Red Sands Residential Dormitory, Principal Burrows, the teachers, and many of the town people signed a petition and filed a complaint with the county courts who ordered a full-scale investigation of the goings on at Red Sands Residential Dormitory. It took several years to complete.

The summer the girls parted ways was not only a change in their lives, but in the way Red Sands Residential Dormitory operated. The investigation revealed the infamous dreaded Room. Mr. Levinstein's dirty deeds were also revealed as students stepped forward, some with babies that were a result of his evil deeds...explaining why some girls and boys were exiled to the Promised Land...and some weren't. Mr. Levenstein was convicted and sentenced to life in prison, and still sits in the Florence Correctional Facility to this day at the age of eighty-nine...his reality... The name of the prison is simply poetic justice! I had brought him down without even knowing it. There was victory in knowing the pen was more powerful than the sword!

As for Mrs. Becenti, she received a lighter sentence and was barred from ever working with children or for the U.S. Government. She was required to cut off her rats' nest hair bun into a pixie bowl cut when she entered Kingman Woman's Prison...Irony. There, her schedule included manual labor and attending church services every Sunday. She actually had read the Bible she professed knowing from front to back. Having had time to contemplate her actions in a prison cell for ten years, she finally succumbed to diabetes not long after her release at the age of eighty-eight. Her buddy, and partner in crime, Mrs. Hagga, died in 1983, finally drinking herself to death and was found asphyxiated in her tiny rundown shack of a house on the Mexican side of Red Sands. She hoarded junk, and empty boxes, empty cans were littered in every corner of her home like she didn't bother to clean her own home. Irony..

Beautiful Mrs. Montano, as old as she is, still works at Red Sands Residential Dormitory, no doubt still bringing the high school girls' popcorn. Only now, she didn't have to sneak in her popcorn maker to pop the corn, what with the invention of the microwave and all…

In my research, I did not find an article about the dormitory scandal. The investigation was not in the newspapers by order of the courts, and because it involved young children, the public didn't know. It seemed to be swept under the rug, while regulations were put in place and young children were not allowed to enroll. I decided I would ask Garnet to see if she could find anything else later.

As it turned out, while we did not return to Red Sands Residential Dormitory the following year, a lot of kids didn't return either. Who would blame us? It was a place where we had to face being alone in every sense of the word, and where we had grown to be family – even the guys were family. Many years after leaving Red Sands Residential Dormitory, from time to time, we shared a quiet contemplation, as if a death had occurred somewhere in our hearts. Perhaps that was the pain Clarence and Delfred aimlessly and recklessly sought to heal but never found a way to do…you never know, huh. I wondered about Terry and John, hoping they found a way to manage living in two worlds. Sigh. Deep breath…destiny.

The administration at Red Sands Residential Dormitory was ordered to stop admitting children under the age of fifteen in 1979, as with many border towns Bureau of Indian Affairs residential dormitories. High school students still go to Red Sands Public School, while staying in the new dormitory built in 1980. The government finally placed policies against just about everything and the people who would work at these facilities had to be reviewed on a regularly scheduled basis…like the government knows how… and no more military issues, and for God knows why, the Manual Labor Guy was now the maintenance boss…Irony… kidding. Chuckle…deep laughter!!

"Please God, send Delfred home." I prayed. Sigh.

As we followed each other past the city limits, it was like driving out of the past and into the present with a new perspective of our future. Each of us found a sense of closure for the first time in thirty years. Free at last. What we learned is that our lives at Red Sands Residential Dormitory taught us to live in both worlds from the inside out, just like Gramps and Gramma taught me. We had to be strong and tough, or we would not have survived.

And like magic, Carly Simon and James Taylor song, "You've Got a Friend" came on the Oldies Channel, and I just knew that my grandparents were with me all the while. I smiled, wiped my tears. Thanks, Gramps and Gramma. Then again, maybe it was Harry Billy saying thanks for remembering him after all those years. Besides, when it was popular, I was in his face requesting the song. I imagine he was happy that I wasn't requesting my other favorite song. His words lingered in my thoughts. "Don't tell me, leavin' on the jet plane"…mumbling something I couldn't understand as he harshly chopped up another perfect piece of meat. Smile. Harry Billy, Crazy Injun Number 9….hmm Smile.

"I'll come running to see you again…" I sang the rest of the song as I took a deep breath knowing that chapter of my life had finally ended.

Red Sands city limits slowly disappeared from my rearview mirror, and the familiar golden, orange gleaming sunset disappeared, as the familiar dark blue-purple night took over. The stars twinkled, ushering in the reverence needed to accept the chapters of my childhood, the people in it, and the experiences I encountered. I know the memories will live on in these pages, captured in my first novel. For sure, our time together shall remain the cornerstone of the lives of four Navajo girls for nine years a lifetime ago... Smile. Sigh. Okay deep breath, long drive home….

"Yes, it was for my own good, Gramma and Gramps. It was indeed…"

So, hug me and shine for me. ..tell me that you'll come back for me…

Yawn, sigh, deep breath.   Goodbye Red Sands Resident
Dormitory - Dorm A.

Free To Be Me

My childhood soul may linger in your halls,
but I no longer belong to you.
You tried to break my will,
but I did not fall—
I no longer belong to you.

The words and deeds that kept the oppressor strong
will not erase my rise.
What was meant to diminish
will return like a boomerang—
and I will stand,
free to be me.

We are still here....

Epilogue

Throughout the history of European Invasion, Indigenous People have had to adapt and survive - often at the expense of their precious ancient cultures and circular way of thinking. Yes, Native Americans of the past were fiercely determined, toughened by centuries of struggle, withstanding the shock and permanent deformation of a sacred way of life. Most of all, they have endured the theft of their homelands in the name of the cruel doctrine of Manifest Destiny.

The innocent spirits of countless generations of Indigenous children damaged from decades of denigration survived childhoods in Bureau of Indian Affairs residential dormitories – hidden crimes locked within the cold, cinder-block buildings, raised under the cruel motto of "Kill the Indian, Save the Man.".

Innocent children survived the brutality of the Bureau - and many did not. Years of being forced to learn the White Man's ways of enduring inhumane experience, left nations scarred wondering what happened to the children stolen, and never returned. In the end, they had to find moments of joy in the midst of despair, to survive heartbreak and separation. They endured the worst of times much like the Navajos subjugated at Fort Sumner in the 1860s, or the Cherokee forced to walk the Trail of Tears. The lists of Indigenous nations torn apart by family separation is long, and the pain endures.

For the Dine', it was the very prayers of the wrongfully imprisoned *Hwéeldi* Navajos that carried the Dine' People forward. Chief Manuelito and the Medicine People who hid on Navajo Mountain, used all their strength and cunning to confuse the government to secure the release the Dine' held captive for four long and miserable years. Survivors of the brutal 450+ mile walk were then forced to live in tents and underground dugouts in the blistering heat and ravaging winter storms in eastern New Mexico. So much has been lost - and what remains fiercely cherished and passed on to the next generation. The Keepers of the sacred prayers and ceremonies live on.

"Resilient" is defined as the ability to recover after stress or deformation, to return to an original shape. Anthropologists and ethnographers, in their infinite wisdom, label Indigenous People "resilient," as if centuries of oppression left no permanent mark. But the truth is, we are not resilient. We are survivors. We have learned to shift gears, to move forward – sometimes racing, sometime coasting through life in neutral. Societal normal pulled us away from ourselves. That is not resilience. That is survival.

It has taken many generations to feel the true deformation and compressed stress imposed when Europeans arrived on our sacred lands. Today, many Native Americans survive as second= or third- class citizens in the so-called United States. News reporters spend time talking about Third World countries when the Keepers of the Earth live in poverty and dependent on the United States government that barely honors its treaty obligations.

Understanding, adjusting, or recovering from inhumanity inflicted on Indigenous People in the name of education was not easy- and it never will be.

Even now, in 2025, Indigenous People are invisible in surveys and research, unless the topic is diabetes or alcohol-related accidents. Little is known – or cared – about our lives, our dreams, or our communities, unless there's an economic incentive or a tragedy to report. The dominant society has little concern for economic development in Indian Country, or whether we have access to clean water and electricity. Government officials rely on tribal infighting to block funding for essential programs. We watch water pass through our lands without being able to use it. We breathe polluted air and watch our children struggle with asthma. Our sacred places are desecrated with sewer water so white people can play on artificial snow. Mother Earth responds in her own way – with fires and floods, washing away the poisons left on once pristine mountains and shorelines.

In the dominant society, there is little sacred – only the relentless pursuit of Manifest Destiny and the power of the almighty dollar. Equality for Indigenous People remains out of reach. Border towns thrive on economic stratification, happily taking our hard-earned money while laughing their way to the bank. We carry the burden of racism and yes, we forgive and move forward – because to live from the inside out is the way of the Dine' - to live a long life in the Beauty Way, in the Glittering World.

We are in eternal culture shift. Many of us are in a language shift. Many have lost their native tongue. Few still speak Dine' exclusively or live a fully traditional life. We will never fully know how deformed or diluted our culture has become, for many of the ancient words given by the Holy People have faced into history. How can anthropologists expect us to "reshape" ourselves after 150 years of misalignment? Yet they stand proudly on their biased reports, mistaking their limited view for truth.

One of the deepest wounds of the Bureau of Indian Affairs boarding school system is how it severed the intergenerational transmission or parenting, culture, and language. Many of the boys and girls who grew up in those dormitories did not learn how to be parents. Too often, parents and grandparents came to rely on schools not only for education but for discipline – a Catch-22, a domino effect, that stratified and fractured the Navajo Nation. There is no resilience in that. Only survival.

Gramps was right. He worked hard his whole life, from sunrise to sunset…day in and day out…in sunshine, rain, or snowstorm – doing his best to keep his family and the cattle safe. With no electricity, no running water, always alongside his trusted horse and Gramma's silent strength and faith, he taught us to make the best of what the Holy People provided He often told us, "Grandchild, if you live from the outside in, it will trick your mind and your spirit. It might start to taste good, but it will poison your soul." That doesn't mean we should lay down and die. Living from the inside out takes courage – the kind of courage Gramps and Gramma lived every day.

And so, it is through the eyes of four young Navajo girls forced to live in an unnatural place, we remember the process of survival – learned, practiced, and perfected. They learned to make a difference in their own lives. They learned the White Man's way, and in the long run, they beat the Bureau of Indian Affairs system at its own game, back in the halls of Dorm A at Red Sands Residential Dormitory 0 Home of the Roadrunners, property of the Bureau of Indian Affairs.

Like Florence, Clarice, Garnet, Ruby, many Native Americans survived the brutality of the Indian experience in America and had no choice but to learn how to live in two worlds. Sadly, many were not as fortunate, succumbing to the social ills left in the wake of Manifest Destiny. Their story needed to be told- through the eyes of four little girls whose souls endured so much in the name of education. For this reason, "The Ghosts of Red Sands" was written. We are still here. We remember. We will never forget! We will forever live from the inside out, in the Glittering World!

As the Bluebird sings at dawn.

I breathe in the cool air to nourish my spirit.

As I sing words East to offer my Corn Pollen,

I ask Mother Earth and Father Sky to rejuvenate my spiritual, physical, mental, and emotional health.

Through the blessing from the Holy People.

I shall Walk In Beauty of love and happiness.

The blessings shall always restore unity of my family and community.

Hózhó Nahasdli,

Hózhó Nahasdlii,

Hózhó Nahasdli,

Hózhó Nahasdlii

It is finished with beauty.

About the Author

Connie Brown is a Diné mother, grandmother, and proud member of the Navajo Nation. Her maternal clan is Tsénjikiní (Honeycomb Cliff Dwellers), and her paternal clan is Tsén/ájiní (Black Streak Forest People). Her maternal grandfather's clan is Hashłshnii (Mud Clan), and her paternal grandfather's clan is Tachí/í/ Chishí/' (Red Forehead Apache Clan).

She holds a Bachelor of Arts in Elementary Education and a Master of Arts in Language, Reading, and Culture from the University of Arizona. Connie has spent over 30 years teaching in primary and middle school classrooms and has also taught courses at the community college level.

An accomplished artist, she has received numerous ribbons at the Navajo Nation and San Juan County Fairs for her beadwork, quilts, and photography.

The Ghosts of Red Sands is a lifelong endeavor, created to shine a light on the lasting effects the Bureau of Indian Affairs system has had on generations of Native children. Through poetry and narrative, Connie weaves hidden messages of oppression and triumph in a world where the spoken word could either shatter or uplift the spirit of a child.

www.ingramcontent.com/pod-product-compliance
Lightning Source LLC
Chambersburg PA
CBHW061510020726
47502CB00006B/2004